The Prince of Glencurragh

Other books by Nancy Blanton

Sharavogue
A Novel

Brand Yourself Royally in 8 Simple Steps:
Harness the Secrets of Kings and Queens
for a Personal Brand that Rules

The Curious Adventure of Roodle Jones

Heaven on the Half Shell:
The Story of the Northwest's Love Affair with the Oyster

The Prince of Glencurragh

A Novel of Ireland

Nancy Blanton

EDB

Ellys-Daughtrey Books
Fernandina Beach, Florida

Published by Ellys-Daughtrey Books
P.O. Box 15699, Fernandina Beach, FL 32035
http://ellys-daughtrey.blogspot.com

ISBN: 978-0-9967281-2-6 hard cover
ISBN: 978-0-9967281-3-3 paper cover
ISBN: 978-0-9967281-4-0 e-book

Library of Congress Control Number: 2016903938

Printed in the United States of America

Cover Design is a composite image featuring:
James Butler, 1st Duke of Ormonde by Sir Peter Lely, oil on canvas,
(circa 1665)- National Portrait Gallery: NPG 370; James Butler, 1st Duke of Ormonde,
William Wissing, (public domain); bigstockphoto.com images 78695654, 78814298,
88974959; Kingdome of Ireland map (public domain)

For Eddie and Teresa

Acknowledgements

I am grateful to the many individuals who have helped me during the research, writing and publication of The Prince of Glencurragh. This book has been years in the making and is truly a labor of love for me.

First and foremost, I thank my husband Karl Shaffer for supporting and encouraging me, giving me time and space when I needed it, and for making possible a lifestyle compatible with creative unpredictability. He even found a way to make light of my distant gaze by posting Facebook quips about his interactions with "the 17th century writer."

My sister Daphne has been beside me most of the way, always positive, always cheering me up when I'm slipping down, and always willing to help. She's my first reader, my book festival assistant, my audience persona, and my beloved friend.

Thank you to my dear friends Marilyn Paul Cook and Jean Gordon, for being there for more years than we really want to count, and for always being in my corner. I did not realize until I had finished the book how much these friendships enriched the relationship between Aengus and Faolán.

Scenes in this book would not have their authenticity without the help of Eddie and Teresa MacEoin, of Bandon, County Cork. Dear friends for many years, they shepherded me around to locations I longed to see but had no idea how to find down the long, winding and unmarked roads of West Cork. I thank them for their hospitality, encouragement and support, fact finding and good humor, and for sharing a bit of their wonderful family life with me.

They also introduced me to their knowledgeable friends. Many thanks to Pat Hogan, for his wealth of historical knowledge, for the tour of Barryscourt castle ruins, and for his insights into the geological changes of Ireland's southwest coastline. Thanks also to historian Gerald O'Brien for the background information about the castles of Skibbereen. And thanks to Tadgh Batt O'Sullivan for his information about sheep farming in Ireland.

For wise counsel and editorial reviews I thank Chuck Barrett, Barbara Bond, Emily Carmain, Terri Dean, Ed Mailey, Glatha Madden, Andrea Patten, Bonnie Rossa, Mick Shultz, Rob Walgren, and the YouWriteOn readers and writers network. For editing and proofreading I am indebted to the wise and hawkeyed Cheri Madison and Lynne Noble.

Additional thanks to my friends in the Florida Writers Association, Writers by the Sea of Amelia Island, and my own subgroup, Mastercrafters, for encouragement, experience, support, wisdom and fellowship. And, to Mr. Hugh Murphy, proprietor, and Mr. John Shovlin, the maitre'd of the Dunraven Arms Hotel, who looked after my father over many years when he visited, and for remembering and telling me stories of him when I visited myself. If there exists any place on earth where I could feel close to my father and to my own heritage, it is there.

Many of my neighbors, friends and readers have helped and encouraged me along the way with this book. For each of you, and for every kind word, I am grateful.

And one last comment on behalf of all authors, and especially independents: thank you to all the readers who are willing to look beyond the New York Times bestsellers to find good stories, who buy books instead of borrow, and who share their enjoyment in reviews, social media comments, and recommendations. Authors work years to create their books, usually with many sacrifices and out-of-pocket expenses. Your comments, recommendations and support help keep us going.

Glossary and Pronunciations

Aengus: Angus, male name using the Irish rather than Scottish spelling.

Ailbhe: Alva, a female Irish name meaning pure, white.

Avourneen: "Ah-vor-neen," from the Irish *a mhuirnín*, meaning my darling.

Bean sidhe: "ban-shee," referring to a keening or screaming woman, an apparition, omen of death.

Coddle: "Cah-dŭl," a slowly cooked stew, often including sausage and potatoes.

Curragh: "cur-ah," meaning small boat.

Dia ár sábháil: "DEE air SAH-wahl," meaning "God save us!"

Faolán: "FAL-lŏn" (i.e., Fallon). Irish male name from the word "faol" meaning wolf. The author recommends this pronunciation for simplicity's sake, begging forgiveness from the native Irish. "Fwāil + awn" is the official pronunciation but this is difficult for some readers to "say" in their heads.

Glencurragh: "Glen-cur-ah," meaning a place for small boats.

Ilen: "Eye-len," meaning island. The River Ilen runs through the village of Skebreen.

Imbolc: "IM + bowlk," meaning the time of milking, the celtic festival at the beginning of February that coincides with lambing season, and time to prepare for a new season of farming.

Lámha Mór: "lava + more," meaning big hands.

Lios Aird: "Liss Ard," meaning high fort.

Mairead: "mŭr + aid," Irish female name, the Irish form of Margaret.

Pike: a heavy spear with a long shaft used by infantry in Europe from the Middle Ages to the eighteenth century.

Poitin: "put-cheen," a traditional Irish beverage distilled in a small pot still from malted barley, grain, treacle (molasses), sugar or potatoes. The word comes from the Irish pota, meaning pot. Also spelled poteen.

Radha: "Row-ah," Irish female name meaning vision.

Samhain: "Sah-ween," the Gaelic festival celebrating the end of harvest season and the beginning of the coldest part of the year.

Sard: A medieval word from the Old English Bible referring to the sex act. Faolán uses it in place of the "f-word."

Sean: Shawn, Irish male name meaning God's gracious gift.

Sheelagh: Sheila, meaning pure and musical.

Skean: "skeen," a knife or dagger used in Ireland and in the Scottish Highlands.

Skebreen: "Skĕ-breen" from the Irish *An Sciobairín.* The modern-day name for this West Cork city is Skibbereen, a beautiful place unfortunately known for its devastation during the nineteenth century potato famine. Skebreen was the form used in the seventeenth century.

Sláinte mhaith: "Slawn-cha wah," an Irish toast to good health.

Tadhg: "Tie + gue" as in "vague," Irish male name meaning poet.

Teaghrán: "Tie + rawn" meaning string.

Tine chnámh: "chi-neh hrahv," from the Irish, the bone fire of the Celts, when the burned bones of the dead symbolized the release of spirits to the next world. Today, the "bon" fire of Samhain.

Uisce beatha: "ish-ke-ba-ha" (Irish whisky); the proper Irish spelling for whisky. An alternative spelling seen in a quotation is usquebagh. The word whisky (no e) is an anglicization of uisce beatha which means water of life in English.

Ireland

ULSTER

CONNACHT

Dublin

Galway

Portumna

LEINSTER

MUNSTER

Cashel

Carrick on Suir

Waterford

Mallow

Lismore

Cork

Bandon

Skebreen

Timoleague

Baltimore

Leap

Chapter One

January 1634
Bandon, County Cork, Ireland

Awake! Arise! my love, and fearless be,
For o'er the southern moors I have a home for thee.

~ John Keats, The Eve of St. Agnes

Of all the wily plans he'd invented, this was by far his most daring. I splashed the sticky pig's blood across his left shin where it glistened in the starlight, the same light that dusted his head in silver against the blue darkness. It may have been an omen of grace, but the January winds whipped around the stone wall and stung my cheeks like the slap of an icy palm. Yet, he had the stars in his eyes, did my friend Faolán Burke.

"Aengus?" he asked to check my readiness. My hands trembled, but I tightened my grip on the coiled hemp rope and nodded. How does one prepare for stealing an heiress from her bed in the dark of night?

Flanking us and pressed well out of sight against the damp walls, the brothers Sean and Thomas Barry completed our number. They nodded as well, poised for action. We all counted on Faolán, the clever one among us who'd thought it all through. The day, the time, the route we would take. Two horses rented, one borrowed from an uncle for Thomas, and one wholly owned—Faolán's trusted Dunerayl.

Our packs and supplies had been checked and rechecked. The new moon granted the benefit of darkness. It would be easy, and if we were quick we would suffer no consequences. Still, I gave silent thanks for the tall ash trees that shielded us from view should someone chance by on the road.

Faolán positioned himself before the rectory's threshold, touched the hilt of the sharp skean concealed in his boot, and flashed me a cocky grin and a wink. Our moment now had come. With a deep breath he banged his fist against the rectory door. The sound reverberated within the house, and my heart fluttered like a trapped bird. We were firmly committed now, be it a crime or no, for to stop would show the worst kind of cowardice among us, never to be overcome.

The wind rattled the fallen leaves in riotous warning. My chest tightened. If only in the next instant there would be no answer at the door, no one at home, the danger we faced would vanish. Faolán raised his palm for patience, and soon came the creak of a floorboard and a few plodding footsteps just beyond the door. It was Caleb Massy himself, for it could be no other.

Caleb had never shown a drop of passion or urgency his whole living life and would not hurry if a starving wolf were slobbering at his back. If not for his wife's cunning ways he would never have gained his post as pastor, for most of Bandon's townsfolk would sooner pay a fine than sit for hours through his meandering sermons.

The footsteps ceased, the iron door handle turned and the hinges groaned, then the door parted barely enough for an eye, a nose and the glow of a single candle. The scents of boiled onions, rye bread, and candle wax wafted out, as if I needed reminding we had missed our supper and were disturbing someone's private home.

"What is it now? Who's there?" Caleb called out.

"Tis myself, Caleb. Faolán Burke, come to ye for help. I have fallen from my horse and be in a bad way: me leg's bleedin' fierce. Can ye assist me, kind sir?"

At any other time Faolán and I would have laughed and teased him. Had we not all grown up together? And had we not known Caleb as a snotty boy whose pouty fox-face invited such sport? It is so, but there was no time for this rude pleasure: he was just a trifling obstacle to be removed from our path. Caleb scoffed but parted the door wide enough to poke his head out and look at Faolán's leg. I held my breath and pressed my back more firmly against the stones, and yet admired the lad for his caution. I'd have thrown the door wide for Faolán, who looked truly stricken, with his dark wiry hair and evincive forelock blasted by the wind, his doublet open to a dirt-streaked shirt, and breeches torn above his boot.

"Hmm. Mus' be able to walk, for I see ye made it here, didn't ye? Rise up and let me see how hurt ye are."

Faolán grunted with feigned discomfort. "It only makes the bleedin' worse, but I..." He pushed himself up several inches. Now he was positioned for a fine forward lunge, and as Caleb parted his door farther, we had our signal. Faolán leapt against the door, sending Caleb crashing to the planks at the foot of the stairs. The candle spun across the floor and lost its flame, plunging us into darkness but for the dim streams of starlight from the two front windows. Sean and Thomas burst through the opening brandishing pistols that were neither functioning nor loaded. I clambered in after them and shut the door behind me. Faolán had Caleb by the throat.

"I'm sorry to treat you so, Caleb. We've no time for pleasantries. We've come for Lord Cork's ward, the heiress, Lady FitzGerald. In which room does she sleep?"

Caleb gave a mighty twist to break Faolán's hold, but must have strained his own neck instead, for he cried out, then Sean stomped a muddy boot upon his thigh.

"We've not come to parry, Caleb. Now..."

A faint glow shined from above us. At the top of the stairs Caleb's wife, Margaret, held out her candle to see what the noise was about. When she saw Caleb on the floor she gripped the banister and screamed as keen as a seagull in chase. She touched the fine lace at her throat in so dramatic a pose she might have been in a painting, except that her face took a frightful grimace. She glared down on us with a fury to seize my spine. "You will all hang for this! And if the new Lord Deputy gets hold of you he'll use your innards for a garland!"

"Go back, Margaret!" Caleb shouted, still squirming, but Thomas leapt over Faolán and bolted up the stairs. Margaret dashed her candle toward his face, but it hit his shoulder and tumbled away. He chased her up a few steps and brought her back down, one hand squeezing that lace collar and the other shoving his pistol against her ribs. Thomas, the quiet one among us, lacked patience as well as vision, and liked to get things done. A chill at the back of my neck told me we'd now crossed the line from benign abductors to something far worse.

"Thomas!" Faolán shouted, and our man lowered his pistol. "Bring her down here and put her in a chair. We'll find the lass ourselves."

Thomas shoved the pistol in the waist of his breeches, and with a firm arm about her shoulders, steered Margaret to the parlor. She fired into his ear a string of curses too foul for a woman's lips, let alone a pastor's wife.

"Ye filthy stinkin' worm from a pig's backside, how dare ye ever touch me with yer dirty maggot fingers and yer thievin' ways, and may God bring his great mallet down upon yer empty skull to shatter it to splinters. Ye nasty, putrid, rat-arsed pit scum from the lowest depths of hell, may ye drown in weasel piss and the devil make a soup of ye. Let me go!"

Thomas chuckled but his grip was unrelenting. Faolán took my rope and tied Caleb's hands, then looped it tightly about his ankles so Caleb could not move except to squirm left or right. There was no one else to subdue, for the Massys had only one servant, who had gone home for the night. My rope was intended for the lass, though, and not Caleb. I feared we might face a bitter struggle when we took the heiress from her bed. Faolán read my thoughts.

"*Sard it.* We'll find something else for the lass." He turned to Sean. "Watch over our friends here, my lads. We'll make quick our business upstairs and be off. Follow me, Aengus."

Despite the darkness, Faolán bounded up the stairs two by two with me at his heels. The first door was open with a candle casting shadows on folded fabrics by the chair and a basket of yarns just beyond: Margaret's sewing room. Faolán peeked into the next room and closed the door again. Bedroom, empty.

The last door was on the north side of the house. Faolán turned the handle and then halted curiously, signaling me to stop. There was a sound, even and insistent, like the ocean's rhythmic roll. Our little heiress snored like a small dog dreaming. Faolán sighed heavily and whispered, "My lovely bride."

He pushed through. The hinges whined, and yet she did not wake. The room was fragrant with rose and lavender. A tiny votive candle still flickered on the chest of drawers. The bed was positioned below the window, the tiny diamond-shaped panes carving streams of ethereal light to define her slender form and the folds of white bed linens, gilding her bare shoulder and tinting the dark curls blue across her pillow. The vision was such perfection, in another time the extraordinary beauty of it might have swayed me, but I was of a different mind and had to keep Faolán's head in the moment. His breath caught in his throat and he hesitated. I shoved him forward.

"Right," he said, and went straight for the bed. "We'll wrap her in the bedclothes. Help me with her feet and we'll sit her up." Her head lolled backward but Faolán caught her nape and held her tumbled hair. Still she did not wake.

"Bring me that." Faolán pointed to a long woolen shawl draped across the back of a chair. He lifted her hands to her chest. "Hold this, my love," he whispered to her as he wrapped her hands with the shawl's fringe, and then wrapped the length of it twice around her shoulders. She murmured unintelligibly and Faolán's head suddenly lifted from her face.

"What is it?" I asked.

"Brandy, I think. A good bit, and quite sour at this stage. All right, let's heave her up, shall we?"

We wrapped the bedclothes about her as one might swaddle an infant. I lifted her bundled ankles and Faolán had her shoulders. "Wait, lad. I think it be troublesome, the two of us carrying her down those stairs in the dark. I'll shoulder her myself. Collect some of her belongings, will you, and then lead the way?"

I started. This, I realized, was a marked hole in our plan. We hadn't considered overmuch her need for clothing or other supplies. Food and shelter, yes, but we had not the means to transport the large wardrobe chest pressed against the wall, or the brushes and toiletries next to the dying votive light. I opened the chest to the perfume of lavender and lifted what appeared to be a neatly folded gown of some sort. If our lady would wake, she might tell us what she wished to bring, or else beat us off with the chair. But the brandy kept her securely in a slumberous state. I lifted the top two garments, scooped the hairbrushes into the skirts, and pressed them across the floor in a tight roll.

Sean shouted from below. "Faolán, make haste before Thomas goes off his head."

I hurried down the stairs with the belongings, Faolán following gingerly with his prize. Sean had opened the front door while Caleb remained motionless on the floor and Margaret wept.

"Stop, Faolán," Caleb said, "or I'll go straightaway to the sheriff. Leave her now, and all will be forgotten."

"Do not fuss with the sheriff, Caleb. He has likely dined with his betters and enjoyed their wine. He'll be difficult to raise at this hour," Faolán said. "Besides, he's no powers outside the town's walls, and your rectory is neatly beyond them."

It was so. That little detail was a primary reason we all believed Faolán's plan would succeed, and when he married the young heiress, he would rise to good standing with a considerable income. Sean, Thomas, and I would all join his household and be the better for it. Faolán was nothing if not a true believer, in himself and in his dreams. With confidence so great, none of us could refuse him. He fired his arrows straight and true, if sometimes beyond the mark.

"We will not fail, Caleb. We're already succeeding," he said. "And now we'll put as much distance between ourselves and Bandon as every moment will allow. You won't find us until we wish it so."

"We are ruined, don't you see?" Margaret cried at Caleb. "The earl will not forgive us for this: he will cast us out, with a great debt still to pay. Ruined!"

We burst through the open door and ran to the stone gate and the carriage road beyond it. At the bottom of the low hill, our horses waited in a copse of downy birch. Faolán had the worst of it, with the heiress awakening. She squirmed until Faolán nearly dropped her, but he held tight against the spitting and slurred cursing she unleashed to his face. He'd done well securing the shawl about her arms, but it wouldn't last. Bound as she was, it took Thomas, Sean, and I to hold her while Faolán mounted his horse, and then we lifted her to him. He pulled her close, held her waist with one hand and her jaw with the other, and pressed his lips to the back of her ear.

"Choose now, my lady. Come quietly with us to a sanctuary not far, where you can drink all you want and will not be harmed or molested, on my honor. Fight and scream, and you'll be dropped bound as you are into the cold Bandon River. That's it and we've no time to argue, so make your choice."

His voice was not gruff, but unyielding and dispassionate. She stopped, still as the dead for a few charged seconds. She spoke not a word, looked carefully at Faolán's face or what she could see of it in the starlight, then glanced quickly at each of us, somehow measuring her lot. Then it seemed as if a cloud shifted. A silver gleam touched the curve of her jaw and exposed a tender lip lifted to a peculiar smile. Her shoulders softened, and she settled more securely on Faolán's horse.

He released her jaw, slapped the reins against Dunerayl's hind, and we were off. We rode together in a tight band, following the icy river west until its northward bend. Then we turned sharply south across the rugged fields toward Timoleague, toward safety, and toward the next phase of Faolán's bold plan.

Chapter Two

Timoleague

On I went in sad dejection, careless where my footsteps bore,
Till a ruined church before me opened wide its ancient door

~ Seán Ó Coileáin

I tried to warn him. Beauty though she was, this woman would likely bring ill fortune. A red-haired lass was common enough in Ireland, but those tresses proved she carried the purest blood from ancient Celtic tribes, descending straight from the long-haired Merovingian kings of Gaul, who possessed great magical powers. She was touched by fire and prone to irascible tempers. Her flames were likely to blaze whenever adventure called him away. He'd fare much better with one of mouse-brown hair like mine: safe, calm, and ever loyal.

Sean and Thomas both had true black hair, also a good choice for a bride. The black Irish trace all the way to Brian Boru and the Vikings, so I could hardly call them safe, but these lads believed in honor, and men who so loved their mother could not be evil at heart. Both the brown and the black hair signified strength. A fair-haired lass was a little less suitable, touched by the wind and likely to attract the faeries. She'd be a weaker match to Faolán's bold temperament, but at least would bring no bad luck.

Best of all would be a rich mahogany mane like Faolán's, which would promise adventure but still be honorable. Faolán's hair had often turned the heads of the few maids in our village, being an uncommon style. I cut it myself just as he wanted it, short enough to curl slightly at his neck and about his ears but long in front to fall across his brow, a modified glibbe in the tradition of the great runners of Ireland, who existed long before the Normans invaded. Faolán's powerful legs and oversize hands served him well as a runner, delivering missives for noblemen until he earned enough coin to buy his own horse.

Like any good barber, along with haircutting I offered good counsel, and mine bore the wisdom of the O'Dalys in matters of omen and spirit, passed down for seven centuries. Tall and lean though I was, I couldn't heave a warrior's strength to a fight, but I had the blood of great prophets, poets, bards, and scholars. My ancestors survived the worst of disasters when other families were entirely destroyed or exiled. In the face of such resilience, others still choose blindly to discount our warnings and ridicule our beliefs, but not Faolán. Though he might ignore it, he always listened to my advice and respected it. On the matter of the lady, though, he heeded no warnings.

"I mean to court her, Aengus, and win her heart. If that means courting danger, so be it. I have loved her from the instant I saw her. If she were penniless I would love her still. That she isn't only means I have no other way to meet her, and must take a desperate chance." His mind was set, and so then was his fate. All I could do was help where I might, to save him from his worst.

The heiress being ensconced in a rectory outside the black slate walls of Bandon answered well to Faolán's strategy. Our greatest risk was not pursuit by the local authorities at all, but the response of Sir Richard Boyle, the Earl of Cork, whose influence covered the entire province of Munster. He'd purchased the Lady FitzGerald's wardship from King Charles and had hidden her away in Bandon while he negotiated with suitors for the most generous and profitable marriage arrangement. That he would be angry when he learned his plans were scuttled, we had no doubt. He could easily send hired mercenaries after us with orders that our remains would never be found. Our success depended on Lord Cork making the wisest choice, to accept that the lady was compromised as a virginal bride, and make a quick and quiet settlement with Faolán.

The earl owned most of the properties that formed Bandon, one of three English settlements—including Enniskeane and Castletown—that he'd proposed to King Charles as a line of defense against the wild western country. He built iron mines and timberworks, then used the profits to build castles, market houses, wells, and Protestant churches. He wished to win the king's favor, and then grow much more wealthy.

Beyond those settlements lay the natural boundary of Leap River, where Irish families still lived by the Catholic faith and the tenets of Brehon law. The English would say, "Beyond Leap, beyond the law," because the new English laws were not observed, and indeed in these times the region posed dangers even to the Irish. But we were outlaws now, and to us it meant safety. Beyond Leap was exactly where we were heading, though it would be many a day's journey.

The seven-mile ride to Timoleague Friary took nearly three hours. We had to walk the horses much of the way, picking through the dark, skirting washed-out and rocky pathways. The cold wind hounded us, but thanks be to God we had no rain. And when at last the centuries-old friary loomed before us, high and stoic on the sacred site of an ancient monastery, I was glad the Bishop of Ross had added the tall stone tower that guided us in. Thomas gave a whoop of gratitude, and we walked the horses through the tombs on the grassy hill until we could dismount within the long nave.

The church still showed signs of the sacking by the English nearly twenty years past. Under threat of a plundering by pirates, the few Franciscans who still lived within the ruins had removed themselves, at least temporarily, to Clogagh, several miles to the north. We had the old stone haven to ourselves. Sean tied the horses in the nave, where the walls would shield them from the wind, and saw to their food and water.

Thomas gathered sticks and dry grass for our fire, while Faolán and I moved the heiress and our baggage into the choir. A dramatic three-arch window opened up before us. The stained glass was gone, but the view overlooked the Argideen River, its black waters glittering. Flowing several miles in twists and turns from her source at Reenascreena to the Celtic Sea just a few miles away, the Argideen conjured pleasant memories for me, of days fishing with my father and finding salmon and trout so plentiful we could hardly carry them home. The friary overlooked the very point where the river found her passion, widened her boundaries, and quickened her rush away. Lady FitzGerald watched it in silence as we worked, still bound in her bedclothes and shawl.

"Are you well, my lady?" Faolán touched her shoulder and she turned to look at him. In the dim light her face seemed calm, but her jaw was set and defiant.

"Remarkably," she said. "It is January, you know, and cold. Quite. Aside from that, I'm thinking it's a pity. The sheriff will be coming for all of you."

Faolán nodded. "Likely he will, but we've broken no law."

"How can that be? It is acceptable in these parts to take a lady from her bed?"

"It is frowned upon, you might say."

"How nice for you."

"You needn't worry. If we were to deflower you, so to speak, well, then I suppose we'd have a heavy fine to pay, but that's not our plan."

"Your plan? Lord Cork will find you and do as he pleases."

"Not if we stay ahead of him. Aengus," he turned to me, "get her things, will you, and we'll let her dress."

Sean and Thomas returned and started building the fire, while I found the roll of clothing among my saddlebags. I unrolled it on a stone altar near her just as the flames gave us more light, revealing the copper highlights of her hair and the rich Lincolnshire green of her woolen shawl. She looked at the clothing, and her lips parted as if she might cry out.

"I am to be confined then?"

The shrillness of her voice alerted Faolán. "What is wrong?"

"He's brought two dressing gowns. It is very lovely if I'm to lounge in my closet and bedchamber or go as far as the breakfast room, but certainly not for the parlor or for travel. And why is there no shift? Nor any jacket?"

Faolán looked to me, and me right back at him. My stomach performed an unnatural twist. It had been dark, we were rushed, and how might I know a dressing gown from a travel gown when it is folded in a trunk? How was I to know about undergarments? Most women of my acquaintance had but one garment, and I was untrained in the proper attire for the parlor since none of us had one. People of our village felt fortunate to live all of their lives in one or two rooms only. We looked back at her, not a word to offer among us.

She shook her head as if to small children who had disappointed her somehow. "Bring them into the sacristy so I can change out of the wind. I have no cloak, so I'll wear them both. What shoes did you bring?"

I frowned, a twinge of shame chiding me for doing a poor job, but I shrugged.

Faolán smirked. "Not to concern yourself," he told her. "I will provide your shoes. For now, just dress. Aengus will put the bedding on the stones near the fire. Come and warm yourself when you're ready."

She released an exasperated sigh. "And now, where is the brandy you promised me?"

Without hesitation he pulled his flask from the inside of his doublet.

"Warmed by my own beating heart."

She scoffed, snatched the flask and headed for the sacristy where the walls were close and solid and the roof above was mostly intact, providing decent shelter. I turned my back to her as she dressed, and when she finished she handed me the bedding that had bound her. I carried the bundle out to the fire. Faolán ripped two strips from the bed-sheet, and then I folded the rest into a neat, soft cushion. She waddled toward it awkwardly in her double layer of gowns.

"You'll have to close it in the back. I cannot reach." The lady turned her back to me and waited. I fumbled a bit with the dangling ribbons, mostly from embarrassment. She sighed heavily.

"Just pull them together and tie them. It doesn't matter," she said. Impatience tinged her voice but she settled easily enough beside the fire. With the brushes I'd brought, she untangled the ends of her hair. At least I'd done that much right.

Chapter Three

Men of Good Intent

*Virtue is an extensive business, and in this agrees with the finest gold:
both of them will stretch as far as one would have them.*

*~ Sir Robert Southwell, Secretary to the
First Duke of Ormonde*

With the fabric strips, Faolán fashioned wrappings for her feet, fold-ing them this way and that until they resembled slippers, and then securing them inside leather soles and straps he had cut from one of his saddlebags. They looked to me like something I'd seen in a book once, a drawing of a Roman soldier's caligae, the thick-soled marching boots with straps across the instep and around the ankle. I was amazed. I knew Faolán to be resourceful, of course, but he had seldom shown the patience or ability for craftsmanship. The shoes were not beautiful and hardly the slippers of a lady, but would be quite functional for the journey ahead of us. On his knees he presented the shoes to her.

"These are not the finery to which you're accustomed, my lady, but they will keep your fair feet protected until we can get you into something suitable. May I?"

She stared at him for a long moment. I swallowed with some diffi-culty, awaiting her response, but Faolán returned her stare and held his ground. She shook her head in disgust but at last she waved a hand at him to proceed.

Her feet were narrow and well-formed. He lifted her right foot gently and pressed his hand around her toes. "So cold. This will help." He held her toes between his palms for a few seconds before slipping the boot on her foot and securing it, then did the same with the left foot. She sat stone-still, watching him, and he worked with a confidence I was not sure he fully possessed. When he finished he held both feet in his hands and looked into her eyes.

"I'll keep you safe and comfortable. We'll soon be well housed, and you have nothing to fear. It is my promise." He waited but she said nothing. He released her feet, took his place by the fire, and poked at it with a twig.

Our fire was small and provided little warmth unless we huddled around it, but to enlarge it would produce light and a billow of smoke that could signal our presence. Even so, just to look at the amber flames offered some measure of comfort. The heiress warmed her feet but otherwise kept her distance, watching us and occasionally tipping Faolán's flask to her lips. We talked little, and once we settled, the silence grew uncomfortable. We had completed our primary task: we had taken the heiress, and now here she was before us. What does one say to an heiress he has just abducted?

My embarrassment grew watching Faolán fiddle endlessly with his boot skean, cleaning the small blade, dropping it, cleaning it again, tucking it away, pulling it out again as if it were at once the most fascinating and irritating object. Coming to our rescue was Sean, but I might have known it would come at my own expense.

"Aengus," said he, "did ye feel a bit of a tingle up yer spine comin' through the graveyard just there? The broken headstones and the lids of old tombs all shifted about by the grave robbers? Some old spirits must have escaped and could be hoverin' about, so."

I shot him my most searing look, as if he could see it in such dim light. I knew the ways of the spirits better than most and took a care not to anger them, but Sean loved to make sport of it all, especially if he could see me on the sharp end of his barb. Faolán was our binding force, and I was Faolán's favorite as Sean would never be.

"We did what we had to and were quick about it, but it be not wise to walk amongst the graves," I warned him, "and more foolish still to amuse yourself with it. You risk serious misfortune."

"Bah! They're spirits because they had their misfortunes long ago and there's naught they can do about it now. This means nothing to me." He leaned closer to the fire so the light of the low flames flickered on his whiskered jowls. "But I'll tell you, there is a legend hereabouts of a young stone mason who worked on the walls of the friary many years ago.

"Here was he, a-poundin' away on the stones to shape them and form the outer walls whilst another lad worked on a scaffold high above him. This fellow above was tired, ye see, and raised his arms high in the air for a stretch, but of a sudden he lost his grip on his pickax. It fell from his hand, twirlin' through the sky and its weight pullin' it down so fast he'd no time to shout a warning, until it landed pick-first into the tender skull of the lad below."

My breath caught in my throat, and at the same time a gasp escaped the lips of the lady. She shot me a look of great alarm. In a tiny spark of recognition, I realized she knew the secrets of the spirit world and the dangers they presented. We shared something the others, out of their own fear, could not abide.

"The poor mason died where he stood," Sean continued, "and his mates were so afraid to disturb him they buried him right on the spot, with his hammer and trowel by his side. They covered him with a flagstone, and then built these walls right over the top of him."

The lady's fingers pressed against her lips, and I cast about to see the walls that surrounded us, dark with dread and several feet thick in some places. What horror to be forever sealed in such a place, even a holy place, if the spirit were not blessed and free. And if the spirit were angry, having been robbed of a life before his time, so much increased was our danger.

"Some say when the ghost of this man is aroused ye can hear his hammer poundin' the stone, and his wails of anguish will echo for miles and miles." Sean paused for effect and looked at each of us in turn. "And the legend is, he who finds the mason's remains will find the coin that was his pay still in his pocket. It bears the head of King Henry's son, Edward the sixth, who also died young. He who spends the coin will soon know his own doom." Sean reared back then, satisfied with his story and no doubt with the reactions he'd achieved on our lady's face and mine.

"You lie, Sean Barry. You've made the whole thing up just to scare us, so." I hissed at him, but I could not keep myself from glancing nervously about the walls, and I could not stay the telltale quiver in my voice. Sean and Thomas both chuckled, and Lady FitzGerald glared at them. Faolán clapped me on the shoulder.

"All right then," he said. "Haven't we enough concerns this night without adding ghost stories and such? That legend is from Bandon, Sean, not from Timoleague. You've mixed it up a bit and had your sport. It's enough now. We need to rest."

The lady dropped her gaze and pulled her skirts tightly about her knees. She seemed to accept her situation and gave no indication she might try to run away. We had at least a few hours to rest before moving on. If the sheriff at Bandon had roused at all from his drunkenness, he would need hours to collect his men and determine how best to pursue us. Faolán reckoned they would first head east, toward Barryscourt. It was logical to assume we might seek refuge there, being that Sean and Thomas were relations of Lord Barry and Faolán often worked for him.

Failing that, they might instead go to Faolán's great-aunt, Mary Bourke, who had properties near the earl's castle at Lismore. A third option was that they would ride straight through Clonakilty to Skebreen, knowing it was Faolán's home and mine. If they got a quick start, which we thought unlikely, they could arrive at Skeb ahead of us and cut us off from our intended path. In the worst-case option, if they rode to Timoleague, they'd need benefit of daylight to track us because of our unusual route, and we'd be gone well before they arrived.

Travel in winter could be treacherous with heavy rains, flash floods, and deep, swampy bogs. Sean and Thomas knew the roads and byways well, but Faolán knew them best of all, having created many of those byways himself. For every message he was hired to deliver, from gentleman to earl, from shopkeeper to merchant, from sheriff to constable, or from lady to lover, Faolán found his own paths and shortcuts that gave the added benefit of discretion. He had never disappointed a customer, for he could navigate without fail through the worst of conditions. And so I was convincing myself when the heiress decided to speak.

"Why did you take me?"

Her question was directed at Faolán, her voice calm and not unpleasant to the ear. She might have been asking if he thought it might rain. Faolán looked up, a half smile creasing his cheek and the firelight flickering in his eyes.

"Why, to marry you of course, my lady. If you will have me."

His voice was soft and kind, but she looked away. "I have grown accustomed to being carried about by men I don't know to places I've never heard of, on Lord Cork's whim," she said. "The earl has moved me many times, fearing something like this would happen. He sent me to Bandon to hide me away while he looked for the wealthiest suitor. How did you know I was there? Did the Massys send for you?"

At this the four of us burst into laughter. Caleb would first send for the Devil himself before any of us.

"No, not hardly, lass. I just…" Faolán ran a hand across the back of his neck, picked up his twig again, and stoked the embers. This was his way, to speak and then start doing something so he holds our attention, all watching his movements, while buying himself time to think. "I knew because I saw you. On the day you arrived in the town square."

"Aye," Sean joined. "The Earl of Cork does little without flourish, for he wants every soul in Munster to know of his great deeds, mayhap to help overshadow the selfish ones. Everyone knows he does nothing but for profit. So certain is he that his Bandon folk will do his bidding, he blatantly risks his own precious secret by delivering you there in his private coach. Did he really believe the mayor could hold his tongue?"

Two weeks prior, Faolán had ridden from Skebreen into Bandon to deliver a new hunting knife to the mayor. His reputation for delivering merchants' goods and gentlemen's letters swiftly and safely reached all across Munster, and he could converse at any social level for his great-aunt had provided him a tutor of good quality. He rarely lacked for something to do, and it's an answer to God's own curse, for the man could never sit still for long. He was chatting with Bandon's mayor at the moment Cork's coach arrived in the town square. The mayor himself, pleased at having privy information to impart, informed Faolán the lady was an heiress, worth more than £800 per year. "Her name is Vivienne FitzGerald, and she's as lovely as her mother before her, who married a son of the late Earl of Desmond," he'd said. "She'll make a fine catch for the proper nobleman or gentleman. I wonder where Lord Cork has been hiding her before now?"

"You were in a coach marked with the earl's coat of arms," Faolán continued, "and when it stopped by the inn, his liveried footmen fussed about, and the townspeople gathered near to take a look at the earl's pretty young ward. The coach door opened. Your shawl slipped from your shoulders as you stepped out, and it caught on the step. A footman quickly retrieved it and returned it to its most enviable resting place, across your shoulders and around your arms. I saw you smile."

And in fact he saw a good deal more than that. "Aengus," he told me when he'd returned to Skebreen, "when she accepted the shawl, she lifted her hair and it fell across her shoulder, silky as the tail of a copper bay mare. Her neck was long and white, beautiful with no need for adornment. Her gown was seafoam green with embroidered flowers of emerald and gold. And then her breast, Aengus, rising with a gentle breath until I could no longer breathe myself—I'll not forget the sight of it before I die.

When she looked up, her dark eyes sparkled with humor, her cheeks blushed, and her face was radiant with youth and life. Ah, she's fine, she is—*fine.*"

She jutted her chin at Faolán. "So it's my smile you're after, is it? Because you like my smile, you feel entitled to steal me from my bed? Well, here you are then." She flashed a bright smile that in the firelight looked more like the bared teeth of a she-wolf. It was enough to set Faolán back on his heels. He looked thoughtfully at each of us in turn, and gave me a solemn nod.

"Well now, gentlemen! Our lady is a bit cautious of her company as we can see, and who could blame her, aye? We are warriors, to be sure, but not woodkerns. We are men of honor and good intent. It is time we introduced ourselves. I am Faolán MacWilliam Burke, at your service."

He stood, sweeping one leg behind the other for a proper gentleman's bow, and his open palms out to the sides. He bent low, his hair looking all the more disheveled and his shirt falling open to expose the fine fur of his chest, and slowly lifted his gaze to meet hers. Then he stood tall.

"I hail from fair Skebreen, a good hamlet just four days hence, the most beautiful village ever to be seen along the banks of the River Ilen, where my father located his magnificent Glencurragh, a worthy castle that protects the fishing vessels and river commerce. My father was the greatest warrior in all of Munster, and my mother a beauty of fine noble blood."

"Aye, and we call him *Lámha Mór.* He has the big hands, among other things," Sean said, and he and Thomas broke into raucous laughter. Faolán's cheeks colored a bit but he ignored them and continued.

"We descend from Charlemagne—the greatest king ever known—and William de Burgh of Limerick, the great earl who fought at the side of Strongbow to reclaim Ireland from the Vikings, and who married the princess of Thomond. We descend further from Edmond of Clanwilliam and his sons Richard and Walter. I myself am a businessman in my own right, a fierce horseman and swordsman, and heir to the great heritage of Clan MacWilliam de Burgh."

At some point my palm had risen from my lap to cover my lips, for this was by the most generous terms an outrageous boast, if not an outright lie. The descendancy was basically true—we would have to rouse a long-dead monk from his moldy grave to prove otherwise—but Faolán would lead her to believe he was a man of position and fortune, and this most decidedly was false. It *might* have been true, had the English not come to

Ireland, had the plantations not been enforced since the time of Queen Elizabeth, had the rebellions of years past not failed, and had his father and mother not died leaving him no formal proofs of claim to his own lands and income.

I looked to Sean and Thomas to see which of them would break into laughter to reveal him, but Sean was stunned speechless, and Thomas had simply turned red-faced. Apparently the Lady FitzGerald inspired more embarrassment in them than swagger. She stared at Faolán, which he returned for a time, and something passed between them that I could not yet identify, sparking a sudden crispness of the air and a quickening of my own heart. Slowly she lifted her hand and offered it to him, which he then gently kissed. She smiled politely and repositioned her skirts. Then she seemed to take up the spirit of the game.

"Thank you, sir. It's an honor to make your acquaintance. Please be seated. And who shall be introduced next?"

Faolán stabbed a sharp elbow to my ribs, and I straightened my back. I'd no intention to marry her and no need to impress her, but she gazed at me in such sweet expectation. I wanted in that instance to be almost anyone other than who I was, to be handsome, to lean forward with broad muscular shoulders and strong jaw, to say something clever to make her smile. But I was just the sad-faced lad from the alehouse. I didn't even stand, for I hadn't the faintest idea how to produce a decent bow. A deep nod would have to do. "I, too, am at your service, my lady. I am Aengus O'Daly..."

"*Teaghrán*, the string bean!" Thomas quipped, and he and his brother laughed the harder. I frowned at them and turned away to face only Vivienne.

"Son of Fintan O'Daly, proprietor of the inn at Skebreen that quenches and nourishes the weary traveler. It is a useful trade to which I aspire one day to succeed him. I have many relations in the southern tip of the province, just away from the ruined village of Baltimore. Since my childhood I have been and remain a most loyal and trusted friend to each of these gentlemen seated before you."

Again she offered her hand, and a sweet, soft smile. I kissed her knuckles quickly.

"Delighted to meet you' Mister O'Daly. Nicknames are common among good friends. And you, sir?" She passed her attention to Sean.

Sean's laugh silenced as he was no doubt trying to form his thoughts.

The fire crackled until at last he bowed his head as I had done, which was a wise choice for I'm sure he'd have tottered like a bottle not set squarely on a shelf. He cleared his throat gruffly.

"I am Sean FitzStephen Barry, descendent of Phillip de Barry, who first built the great Castle of Barryscourt at Carrigtwohill. My brother Thomas and I are distant relatives to the Earl of Barrymore. Our family home is at Rathmore. I am quick of wit, strong of body, most faithful and honorable, and at your service."

"And quite the storyteller. Yes. Thank you sir." Sean kissed her hand, and then she turned to Thomas. "Your turn arrives at last, sir."

Even in the firelight his face looked puffed and embarrassed. "I am Thomas FitzStephen Barry of Rathmore, as my brother has said. It is my duty to protect you from harm during this journey, and that I will." He brushed her hand with his lips and looked away quickly.

Our lady tossed her hair behind her shoulders and folded her hands in her lap. "Gentlemen. It is good, don't you agree, for a woman to know her captors?" She offered a winsome smile.

"But my lady," Faolán said, "we are not complete until you have had your turn. Please introduce yourself."

"You knew who I was before you came for me."

"It is so, but...please."

She took a long drink from Faolán's flask, and I marveled that anything was left in it. She assembled her voluminous skirts and stood, but then tilted as if to fall and Faolán righted her. She thanked him and lowered into a quick bow, her long hair slipping from her back and down by her waist. Each of us was captivated. She took a deep breath, and then sighed in resignation.

"Gentlemen, I am Joan Vivienne O'Brien FitzGerald, descendent and namesake of the great Lady Joan FitzGerald and my grandfather, Gerald FitzGerald, the fifteenth Earl of Desmond. I am faithfully educated, but only in those skills that will make me a useful wife and bearer of children. I have been raised alone in country houses and abbeys where no one ever visited, and I had no society. My value is now being negotiated by the Earl of Cork with men whom I have never met, who would bed me, get me with child, and then put me back into some country house where I would raise the child alone and where no one ever would visit. My value now has, I am sure, plummeted." She shrugged and waved a dismissive hand. "I must admire your courageous endeavor. I do not expect you will survive it, but I must admit thus far you have provided the most exciting adventure I've yet experienced. You may call me Vivienne." She repeated her bow, this time with a little more stability.

Faolán laughed nervously, and we all joined in. I suspected Sean and Thomas were as disturbed as I by her remark on our survival. Faolán, if he heard it, was not likely to heed it. He took her hands and kissed them, and helped her back down to her seat. "Now that we're acquainted, we must celebrate your liberation," he said. "Sean, bring out the barley scones and cheese."

"Thomas, bring the food, will ye?" Sean pushed his brother's shoulder. Thomas left the fire to sort through the bags. As our lady settled and pulled her skirts tight about her legs, she turned to Faolán.

"And so, sir, I must ask again. If your heritage is what you say and your standing as such to be admired, your options must be many. Why did you take me?"

We were all silenced, awaiting Faolán's response. His grand boast failed, as of course it had to. She was a bright girl and evidently tired of being treated like a sack of corn without wits. Faolán hesitated far too long as he stared at her, choosing his words.

"Vivienne." He looked at his hands and took a long, silent breath. "What I have told you is true. The English and Protestant settlement has not altered who I am, only the circumstances by which my truths can unfold. The plantation of Munster has left me, and most young Irishmen, without opportunities to build a life and grow beyond the poverty to which we've been forced. A marriage between us has the power to restore what should have been."

"And so you are saying, win the bride, win the war? And me just another means to an end?"

Sean laughed a little, for she spoke the truth in its unveiled form, but Faolán did not flinch nor hesitate, fully committed as he was to his course.

"It is not the war to win, Vivienne, but far, far more. I believe in my soul we're meant to be joined, and together we'll make something perfect and lasting. We'll reclaim it all—the lands, the rank, the respect, and everything my father fought for and intended."

"Together?" she asked, an eyebrow raised.

"Yes, of course. You will have equal respect as you deserve, the respect Irish women have always known. And I'll see to it you have all the comforts and freedoms you desire. And the society. People will visit our castle because it lies at a great crossroad of travel and trade. We'll have music. Bards will visit from Aengus's own family. We'll have horses, cattle, and sheep in our pastures. We will not be as one or the other, but as partners on life's adventure.

"Vivienne, with me you will not be a possession. You will be loved and cherished, and I promise, you will know much laughter and you will not regret a moment of it."

She turned away, looking toward the arched window and the river beyond, her jaw clenched. Did she feel anger or was she struggling to hold back tears? Or, was it something much more complicated, akin to my own vulture's nest of tangled emotions, with twisted vines of self-scolding for leaping again into one of Faolán's schemes without thought for my own fate; with twining branches of love for Faolán that I wouldn't see him disappointed or unrequited; with white layers of sheep's wool binding the fear that our actions would bring unthinkable ends; and with green flecks of sodden moss, my envy for his pure, defenseless, expanding heart? I might never experience a love so brilliant as his. It melted every hard line on his face and illuminated his eyes with the glow of a hundred candles. Faolán reached toward Vivienne with a tenderness reserved for the most precious and fragile of things, but stopped when Thomas came back to the fire empty-handed.

"'Tis not there," said he.

"What d'ye mean, ''tis not there?' I packed it and strapped it on your horse myself," Sean said.

"Well it's gone then; must have fallen somewheres, I don't know."

Sean looked to Faolán, and the back of his neck stiffened, as did mine. Faolán's brow furrowed and his jaw hardened. "How far back d'you think, Thomas?"

"It was there when we left the rectory, for I put my hand on the bag then. It might have..."

Faolán held up his hand for silence. "No matter now. It won't take them long to discover where the horses were tied. If it fell there or by the river, it won't matter overmuch. If it fell on the southward turn, then we've given them a nice gift, haven't we?" He looked at each of us, and then settled his gaze on the fire. "Let us assume the bag was lost on the road to Timoleague. They will come straight to the friary, for it offers an outlaw the best shelter, as we've seen. I had hoped for a longer rest, but there's no time now.

We must put a few more hours between us and our pursuers."

Thomas and Sean needed no more prompting. They rose at once, collecting our packs and heading for the horses. Faolán helped Vivienne to stand as I gathered what was left and stomped out our fire.

"We'll ride at least to Clonakilty, Aengus, but we'll soon need rest and food. Mayhap we can hide in the wood, and before first light you can go into town to get us some bread and see if anything is amiss. You can be more invisible than the rest of us."

I shook my head. "I know someone who has a farm there. A cousin. She'll take us in."

Faolán smirked. "And is this not something you might have mentioned earlier, lad?"

I turned to face him and leveled my eyes at his. "I didn't know until just now, did I, that your plan might go awry?"

He laughed, and thanks be to God he could always keep a good humor to him, even in the worst of times, or I might have carried on. "It's a fair point, Aengus. Good, then. You can lead us there when we're close. For now, we shouldn't follow the river, and it is too dangerous to travel the coast road in darkness. I know another way, so everyone stay close behind me."

Vivienne sucked in her breath. Had the same thought occurred to her that had just clutched my own throat? To take an alternate route from a known coast road was yet another bad omen. I heard her whisper as we lifted her to Faolán's horse.

"There are troubles ahead. My palm tingles so with the warning. But there is goodness coming as well."

Chapter Four

A Woolen Cloak

I tasted of their milk, butter and cheese, and it was excellent good;
I never drunk so good buttermilk.

~ Sir William Brereton

My cousin Mairead married Hugh O'Donovan of Clonakilty when she was seventeen. I'd seen her last when I was ten years old and rode with the uncles in the hay wagon to deliver her to her new family. Within a few years, Hugh's father had died of the plague, and his mother survived but was old and frail. Hugh developed a fever and survived, but his strength was robbed, never to return. Mairead managed the farm, performed all the labor and made sure the rents were paid on time. She grew corn and peas, and made cheese and soap.

She was well-known for her buttermilk. The cow was milked in the morning and the churning done in the evening so that her buttermilk was sweeter and more wholesome than any to be found, and her butter rich and flavorful. For extra money she sometimes rented Hugh's horse to the English travelers who came looking for properties to buy.

To see us side by side, anyone would have difficulty recognizing our blood relationship, for she looked as opposite to me as a fish to a fencepost. Where my face was thin and angular, hers was round and full. Where my hair was dull and fine, hers was bright as a wheat field and wild as a thicket. Where my arms and legs were long and gangly, hers were compact, solid and muscular. From the back, her shape was womanly, but her shoulders were broad as a man's. From the front, Mairead had the kind eyes of an angel and ample bosoms straining at her bodice. Though we had only the dim light of early morning, when she realized it was me tapping on her door she threw it wide to welcome each of us with strong arms and a cherub smile.

"Ye look like the same lad ye were when ye brought me here, Aengus! 'Cept much taller, and now ye can gaze at the top o' my head. Have ye been eatin' the sea kelp to make ye so long and lean? And why did ye not write ye were comin'? It's nearly daybreak, and me nothing to offer!"

I hugged her again, glad Faolán had stayed behind in the wood while Sean, Thomas, and I approached the house. We had not wanted Mairead to see Vivienne, both to prevent her from having knowledge if she were to be questioned by the sheriff, and to prevent her from gossiping with the townsfolk if that was her nature. But we must have looked as poorly as we felt. The journey across rugged fields and through wooded glens was slow and tiresome, yet we had to keep sharp to avoid encounters with outlaws worse than ourselves who might give us grief on our way. She dropped her pleasantries straightaway.

"Look at the three of you, as if ye've been dragged through the mud by yer ears. I've no beds in the house what with Hugh and his mum, but ye can wash in the trough just there, and take yer rest in the stable. My horse Bridget is there, but Hugh's horse is rented so there's plenty of space. It may not smell like a garden, but it's been cleaned. I'll see what I can bring ye from the pantry."

The barn was still dark and smelled of horsehair, leather, manure, and musty old wood mingling with hay. We walked the horses to the empty stall, a cold wind gusting through the wooden slats. She returned after a few minutes with bits of bread and cheese, a jug of beer, and a large, well-used canvas for us to sit on, and then left us alone while she started her daily chores. Before the sun could peek over the horizon, Faolán slipped from behind the barn and walked Dunerayl through the doors with Vivienne clinging to his mane. She was shivering mightily. Faolán lay beside her to warm her. I offered a piece of cheese, but she refused it. The rest of us gathered for warmth while we ate.

"Your cousin is a fine woman," Thomas said, wiping a spot of beer from his chin.

"Aye, she is." I smiled and offered him another piece of cheese.

"And a good hard worker," Sean added. "It's a pity she's married, eh, Thomas?"

Thomas grinned. For all of his brawn and his brusque manners, they only masked what a bashful boy he truly was. He longed for a girlfriend or a wife, but he never knew quite what to say to a woman and stood apart from them at gatherings with a surly look on his face. The girls were put off, but it was only a reflection of his self-loathing and the fear that he'd be rejected. What boy in our village had not experienced that? It was the lads who could cast their feelings aside, throw on a hearty smile and dance them across the floor anyway who always charmed the lassies. One day, I was sure, Thomas would find the girl who could see the man inside. And despite his frequent teasing, Sean knew it as well.

"Ah, ye'll find yer proper bride one day, Thomas. And if not, ye can just go out and grab one like our Faolán here has done, right?" Sean and Thomas both laughed and I could not help but snicker a bit, for it was true even though Faolán could've had his pick of the girls of Munster. Faolán was not amused. He would not be the butt of jokes in front of his lady, at least not before they were securely wed. He gave us all his most hateful expression. Had his arms not been wrapped about Vivienne, he might well have thrown a warning punch to Sean's jaw. Our mirth soon died away, and we grew quiet. After a few moments Vivienne pushed Faolán away and sat upright, as if someone had jerked her up by the back of her neck.

"Someone is coming," she whispered, and in her eyes an uneasy foreboding replaced the benign resignation she'd shown us before. A prickling cold climbed the back of my neck and into my scalp. Sean peered out of the barn door and across the farmyard.

"Mairead is heading this way from the house," he said.

Vivienne grasped her elbows. "No, not a woman. Someone else. Someone is coming for me."

My mouth went dry. There was no use trying to hide Faolán and Vivienne from my cousin now. There was no place for them to go, and she was too close. I would have to explain our predicament to her somehow. But if it was the sheriff Vivienne was sensing, we were as good as trapped hares and would have to surrender, or fight our way out. Faolán rose from the canvas and moved uneasily about the barn. He shot me a troubled look, his jaw clenched.

The old hinges creaked as Mairead opened the barn door and stepped inside, looking angelic in the pearly light of dawn. She led a sturdy white goat behind her and tied its rope firmly to a wooden post. "There ye go then Mona; take ye a little nap with our friends here." Then she turned to us, and her eyes fixed on Vivienne.

"So there's more of ye, I see. Aengus, is this it, then? No one else?"

I shook my head. "I'm sorry, Mairead; they were following us. I should have told you about them from the beginning."

Mairead wagged an index finger at my nose, but then Faolán came to my defense.

"I'm Aengus's friend Faolán, Mairead. Aengus thought you might not mind if we rested here for a while. We're on our way to Skebreen. We'll not trouble you for long."

She nodded. "I remember you, boy. Ye weren't but a wee drab of a thing the last I saw you, but bringing Aengus into mischief even then, so. What have we here?" She peered at Vivienne, and what a sight she must have presented with her disheveled hair, two dressing gowns, and oddly contrived shoes.

"The lady and I are to be married. We must get to Rathmore to receive Lord Barry's blessing, and then to Skebreen. We're overdue and have a long journey ahead of us."

Mairead lifted her chin and looked into Faolán's eyes as a mother to an errant child, seeking the signs of a lie. To his mind, Faolán's words were true, and she would find no shadows lurking and no flinch of shame to betray him. If she saw anything untoward, she didn't show it. She nodded and looked to Vivienne.

"And this is so, miss? Ye've agreed to marry this shaggy fellow here?"

"We have an agreement," Vivienne answered, but offered nothing more. My heart leaped in my chest, and Faolán's must have near exploded. She had agreed to nothing yet, but something in Faolán's promise must have touched her enough that she would stay with us and not betray us, at least for now. Mayhap an agreement needs to be tested before it becomes a full commitment, or a journey with us was preferable to joining the goats on a family farm.

"The lady is frightfully cold. I'll see do I have some blankets then. And those shoes? *Dia ár sábháil!* God save us!" She turned to go back to the house, but then stopped, looking back at Vivienne. She stepped closer and spoke to Faolán and me. "She's the one he's looking for."

The back of my neck stiffened and stung as if a thousand tiny spikes pierced the skin. "Who? Who is looking?"

"The fellow who rented Hugh's horse, whilst his own horse rests in the pasture. He seeks a red-haired lady who got lost on her way to visit relatives. She'd no business traveling alone in these parts, and so I told him, but now I see she does not. She's the one he's after, all right, and don't try to tell me different. I can feel it. She's someone special."

"She is special," Faolán said. "What is this fellow's name?"

"Said his name was Eames. Geoffrey Eames from Dungarvan. Said her family was quite worried, and he would see the girl home again. But he's got a hawk's look in his eyes, that one, and I don't believe he's out for kindness' sake. There must be a purse offered for her." Mairead frowned, but Vivienne squeezed Faolán's wrist, her face pleading. She was fierce frightened.

Faolán's chest broadened, his back stiff. "The man Eames is an imposter. I believe he means to abduct her and inflict great harm."

Mairead took a step back and looked us over carefully. "Ye must leave here then and not rest any longer in case he's to return. I am sorry, but I cannot abide danger; I am barely keeping the farm as it is. I canna give anyone a reason to take it from me." Mairead turned to go but then stopped, looking thoughtfully at Vivienne. "Wait just a moment before ye go; I've something for you."

Vivienne cried—whether from weariness, hunger, cold, anxiety, or all these things combined, I didn't know. Faolán held her shoulders and in that moment he probably would have done anything to return her to her warm safe bed rather than put her in danger, but there was no going back. We had to keep moving, and there would be no comfort or safety yet for days.

Mairead returned with arms loaded. To me she offered a sack of food, and for sure I would not be passing it along to the Barrys for safekeeping. To Vivienne she offered a pair of old boots and a folded gray blanket. "The boots were my mother-in-law's; she hasn't used them in I don't remember when. They might be a bit big for you but better by far than what ye're wearing."

Then she touched a finger to Vivienne's chin and gestured to the blanket. "Open it out, girl. It is a hooded cloak to warm ye and to conceal ye. Given me by my mum so many years ago, it is precious to me. Return it to me unharmed, do ye hear?"

Vivienne nodded, weeping all the harder, and unfolded the cloak.

Faolán pressed a few coins into Mairead's palm. "You're kind beyond words, and understanding beyond all knowing. There will be more when we return, to thank you properly."

Mairead's eyes glistened. "Just go. I'm afeared for you all." She hugged me quickly and whispered into my ear, "Aengus, ye'll know him by the thin dark beard that comes to a point at his chin, and the parted lobe of his ear, as if a jewel had been ripped from it." She pushed me away and then ran out of the barn. Mona watched her go and released a small, plaintive bleat, then turned to stare at us scornfully.

"What now, Faolán?" Sean asked, watching Vivienne slip on the boots and cinch the cloak about her waist. Faolán picked up the shoes he had fashioned for her, buying himself a moment as he stuffed them into his saddlebag. I was glad of it, for the shoes would be a bad thing for this Eames fellow to find.

"This changes nothing," Faolán answered at last. "We knew we would be pursued, and will be until we reach Rathmore. Let's get to the coast road now, then travel alongside it toward Knockdrum. Thomas can ride before us and give a signal if someone approaches."

Thomas nodded, and the brothers set about preparing the horses. Faolán helped Vivienne onto Dunerayl, who pawed the ground and nuzzled Faolán's shoulder.

"I know, I know, lad. It won't be much longer now, and you can get a full meal." Faolán stroked the horse's forelock and looked up at Vivienne. "It was a fine thing you did just there, your answer to Mairead, and I'll see that you don't regret it. We do have an agreement, you and I, and all will be made clear when we get to Rathmore. Do you trust me for that?"

She looked down on him, no longer crying, but her visage hardened. "You said we were going to Skebreen," she said.

"And so we are, but first Rathmore. Lord Barry is there, the Earl of Cork's son-in-law and a relation to Sean and Thomas. We'll find comfort, food, and rest there, and protection. He understands our case and will speak for us to the earl. From there we'll go to Skebreen."

"What about the brandy? Give me more of that and see us safely to Rathmore. Then we'll see what can be said about trust."

Faolán smirked. "You're a hard one, lass. But I'd feel the same were I in your new boots. At least now you'll be warm for the ride."

Thomas rode out first, and we followed after a few minutes. The roads and pathways heading south were deserted, and we hoped to reach the coast road within an hour's ride. From Clonakilty heading west, there was really no road at all, but a worn trail for deer, sheep, and horses. Tinker and hay wagons were better off using the Cork road, and thus we expected swifter passage without obstruction.

The morning sun was short-lived. Clouds moved in low, thick waves, delivering a cold damp mist that settled on our hair and our faces, chilling our hands and wetting the tops of our clothing. When at last the surf roared before us, Faolán turned our group to the west along a rising bluff. We had just gone beyond it when he signaled us to stop. I rode up beside him until I could see what concerned him. Just where the westward road turned south again, a body lay half-covered by the tall grasses along the right side of the road—a body looking much like our Thomas.

Chapter Five

Rathbarry

The Irish houses are the poorest cabins I have seen,
erected in the middle of the fields and grounds,
which they farm and rent.

~ Sir William Brereton

Sean was the first off his mount to where Thomas lay on his back, his legs splayed out, one arm at his side the other stretched above his head as if he reached for something. Sean touched Thomas's face, then rolled him slightly towards him. "He breathes, but he does not rouse. His body seems well but his head is bloodied. We must get him back to Mairead!"

I was beside them in seconds. A bloody gash above Thomas's right eye was bleeding and was starting to swell. A few feet away, a round gray stone the size of a man's fist was bloodied on one side. I pressed my hand on Thomas's chest.

"His heart is strong, Faolán. Can you see his horse about?"

Faolán rose up in his stirrups to scan the nearby fields and horizon. Vivienne remained before him, her eyes closed, lips moving as if in prayer. "No sign of him from here, but we must find him. Mayhap he's been stolen. Can you lift Thomas?"

Sean and I looked at each other. Thomas was the larger and heavier of the brothers, and Sean larger and stronger than I. The two of us could probably lift Thomas, but we'd need a third to get him to horse, and I was not certain Sean's horse could bear the weight of two large men for long. Faolán dismounted, leaving Vivienne on Dunerayl.

"We've come too far now to return to Mairead's, Sean, and a long ride will do him no good. There is an old healer nearby, if he still lives. We'll have shelter and can find someone to revive Thomas."

"The quickest thing then," Sean muttered to Thomas, patting his cheeks to try and awaken him but Thomas made no change.

"You must bandage his head to stop the bleeding," Vivienne said. "And he cannot ride on his belly, or the bleeding will worsen. He must be upright."

Sean scratched his head. "I'll have to lash him to the mane then, and walk alongside."

I ripped more material from Vivienne's bedroll to use for the bandage. Who might have known those bedclothes would become so valuable? Sean used the reins to bind poor Thomas to Sean's horse. The terror of what had happened set us quickly into motion, the better to act than to think or feel. Except for Faolán, whose gaze was now lost to the distance. He said nothing, but we all knew what this meant. We were delayed by at least a day, and without Thomas's horse, our progress would be slow. A visit to the healer was a serious diversion from our intended course, and that Eames fellow could be about.

Something about that name Eames was starting to bother me, and I wanted no part of him. If he was near and had any talent as a tracker, he could easily follow us, for there was only one way to pass in these parts and little cover. We would be trapped. The best I could do for Faolán was keep him confident and swift of mind. Delay was truly our greatest enemy.

"It's just a woodkern wanting the horse, Faolán," I assured him. "He won't have gone far and we'll find him soon enough. With any luck Bram will shake the brute off and come running back to us." Faolán turned to help Sean, and a strange look played across Vivienne's face. She was alone on Dunerayl, the reins across her thigh. She moved her hand over them and curled her fingers around.

"Vivienne," I said, startling her. Her lips parted, and she stared into my eyes as if measuring her chances. "Are you well? Do you need some water?" I stood next to Thomas, pleading with her as well as I could make my eyes do. I might not be able to stop the horse if she gave him one good kick. I could only call upon her mercy not to run, or at least upon her fear. "Ye must keep your strength," I warned, "for clearly there are bandits about."

Faolán caught my meaning, and turned slowly as if to catch a fawn that had wandered into our midst. "Ye needn't worry, my lady," he said softly, "for our Dunerayl is a highly trained professional. Should thieves come for us, he'll be shut of them in minutes, but he'll always find his way back to me. We're a team, he and I."

She glared at him for a long instant, and though no more words passed there was a conversation between them as if they argued face to face. Her eyes brightened and her face flushed, while Faolán's eyes grew dark and serious, his jaw clenched. When she dropped her gaze, I knew she'd made her decision. She let go the reins, and both Faolán and I released a sigh of relief.

"I'm blistering hot wearing two ridiculous dressing gowns beneath this heavy cloak, and I've a tremendous thirst. My head thunders as well. Is there any more brandy or wine?"

"We'll have to wait just a bit longer for that, but soon you'll have it. You wouldn't want us leaving poor Thomas this way, would you?"

She turned her face away. "No."

Faolán helped her down and she pushed away, casting off the cloak, then yanking and struggling to remove the top layer dressing gown. Once free of it, she cast it into the dirt. "May I never see the filthy thing again!" She tossed the green shawl roughly about her neck and slipped back into the cloak. Faolán picked up the discarded garment and rolled it into one of his saddlebags.

"How far must we go for this healer, and when will we see Lord Barry?" she asked.

Faolán responded as if to a petulant child, "The healer's house is just around the bend a ways, but not far. We'll be there soon enough. And Rathmore is three days ride if we push through."

Vivienne sighed. Her hair was quite undone at this point, and the cloak was a bit too large, looking even more so now that she'd removed the dressing gown. Her face showed all of her discomfort and weariness, and yet a spark of defiance burned in her eyes. All this, and still she looked lovelier than an angel in a painting. Faolán turned to me and could not suppress the tiny grin that creased his cheek.

I cleaned the gash on Thomas's head as best I could and then wrapped it with a strip from the bedsheet. Suddenly he jerked and let out a rough cough, then heaved up to vomit violently what little he had in his stomach. He fell back, and I caught his head to keep him from hitting it again. He looked at me, but his eyes seemed unfocused and his lips sagged.

"Thomas? What has happened?" I asked him. Sean was beside us again, patting his brother's chest.

"Thomas! Stay with us," he urged, but Thomas groaned with pain.

"He's roused," I shouted. "He'll recover, but he's in a bad way. There's no time to waste."

Faolán and I helped Sean get him mounted, his bandaged head cradled against the horse's neck, and then we pushed on through the gray morning light as quickly as Sean could keep up. We crossed undulating ground at once low, sandy, and sparse, and then high and dense with scrub. The high ground gave expansive views of the lands behind us and I searched for signs of other travelers, and especially for Thomas's horse, but the fields and hills were strangely barren. I was glad for the cry of a lone seagull to remind me we were not alone on the earth. Through the clearing fog, the outlines of a crenellated tower appeared high on a hill just ahead.

"That is Rathbarry before us," Faolán said. "Can you see it, Sean? Do you know it?"

"Aye, it was a Barry stronghold once, but lost to the English long before I was born. I've never been there. Some English officer owns it now. Dirty bastard. The only thing left to our clan in these parts is Barryscourt, just east of Cork City. If not for the Earl of Cork, we'd not have Rathmore either. There was a fearsome stone tower there once. Cork bought it and returned it to us as part of the dowry when Lord Barry married his daughter. Lord Barry has been renovating it. Lady FitzGerald will be pleased when she sees the fine manor house he's built from the rubble."

Faolán nodded as we approached a castle gate that towered above our heads. They were columns of piled slate with pointed tops punctuated by large stone spheres. The castle wall seemed to stretch left and right to infinity. "It's near this gate that I met the healer. His name is Pol-Liam, or at least I think it is. On this very path some years ago, I fell asleep in my saddle and tumbled to the ground. I must have fallen on my wrist, for its pain was fierce and I couldn't move it.

"This fellow happened along, looking more fragile than a faerie, bowlegged and hunched over, his pate bald but for a crescent of white fuzz that fringed his nape. Face was craggy as a mountainside, and he cursed and mumbled, arguing to himself so intently he nearly stumbled over my legs before realizing I was sitting in his path.

"He took one look and spat out a curse in some language all his own, but patted my hand and gestured me to follow. Took me to an old shack close to the shore outside the castle wall. Later I learned he'd been a caretaker at the castle until the Englishman grew tired of his odd speech and cast him out. He gave me a drink of bark brew, then took my hand and gave it a good yank. Worst pain I've known my whole life, like he'd stabbed a knife through it.

"Then he says something like, '*Baw heppey day froo! Baw heppey day froo!*' Like some kind of druid chant, and he kept repeating it over and over. For a while I thought it was a devil's language and we'd slip into hell at any moment, but later I realized he just had a speech problem. He was speaking English as best he could, and while he wrapped a poultice around my wrist, I listened carefully until I understood bits of it. I fell asleep, and when I woke my wrist was much better. Then I realized what he'd been chanting. It was 'God helps the fool!'"

Sean snorted. "Well, he was right in your case. Let's hope his theory still holds, for there's no bigger fool than Thomas."

"Go and yank yerself, Sean," Thomas said.

We found the old man's house just as Faolán said, little more than a lean-to fashioned from stones and scavenged wood planks wedged between two trees. It was well hidden in a dense copse between the castle wall and the bluffs. I inhaled the scents of rich, damp earth, the freshening juniper, the salt of the ocean, and smoke from castle fires.

From his doorstep, the castle tower was visible through the trees on one side, and on the other side, there was a path to the roiling sea. No visitors would be surprising this fellow, crackling and rustling through the copse as we were. Faolán tapped on the door, and it swung open before we could even catch our breath.

"*Baw blammy, wot be!*" The old man's voice was creaky but still strong, though his bowed legs seemed to tremble. "*Wot be!*" he shouted again.

"Pol-Liam, kind sir, you helped me once, and I fear I need your help again. I am Faolán, of Skebreen. You healed my wrist for me."

The man reared his head so far I feared he would break his brittle neck bones. "*BAW BLAMMY!*" he hollered, and then grasped Faolán's hand. He leaned forward to look us over. He gave Faolán's chest a dismissive slap, and looked at me with pure contempt. When he pushed Vivienne's hood back, his eyes popped wide and his mouth fell open, revealing few teeth. "*Baw blammy, wot be fe!*"

He ignored Sean entirely, as if he wasn't even standing there, and his eyes fixed on Thomas, still strapped to Sean's horse. "*Baw blammy*," he muttered over and over, touching Thomas's shoulder, his hands, his bandage, and then looking at his eyes. "*Blammy baw blammy!*"

"What is he saying?" I whispered.

Faolán smirked. "I'd not place a wager on it, but I'd guess it is his own version of 'God damn it.'"

Chapter Six

The Red Strand

These wild Irish never set any candles upon tables.
What do I speak of tables? since, indeed, they have no tables...

~ Fynes Moryson

Pol-Liam gestured impatiently for us to carry Thomas into his house and lay him on the floor. We had barely enough room to get Thomas's feet inside, and then Pol-Liam tugged my arm and brought me to Thomas's head to hold him steady. He gestured for Faolán to come beside me, and pulled Vivienne to his side. There was no room left, so Sean kept watch outside the door. Pol-Liam slowly unwrapped the strip of bedsheet to inspect Thomas's wound.

Even in the dim light it looked purpled, bloody, and still oozing. Pol-Liam shook his head and muttered, then gestured angrily for me to hand him something. Behind and on either side of me were all sorts of bottles and jars, seaweed and moss hanging from nails in the boards, small boxes, and felt sacks. When I touched a box about the size of my shoe near his bed pallet, he grunted. He opened it to reveal several instruments, and selected a small curved knife.

"*Peed ter awd mane, awd mane, rel, baw blammy. Imo.*"

I looked to Faolán for translation, but he just shook his head. Pol-Liam grabbed a corked bottle behind Vivienne and opened it, then splashed the liquid over Thomas's forehead. Thomas flinched, and then I smelled the wine. The old man pressed the wound with two fingers, and inserted the edge of the knife right into the middle. Thomas jerked and cried out, and Faolán pressed his shoulders down firmly while I stilled his head. Then

Pol-Liam pushed his pinky finger into the wound, turning this way and that as if searching for something, while Thomas kicked and pounded his feet. Suddenly Pol-Liam popped his finger out and sat back on his heels, apparently satisfied. "Na berken. Ina mash."

"Wha'd he say, Faolán?" I asked.

"I think he means the skull's not fractured. Good news."

Pol-Liam poured more wine into the wound, then blotted it with a scrap of linen cloth pulled from another box. He shook Vivienne's shoulder, gave her a wooden bowl and pestle, and started her mixing a plaster of some kind, with ingredients from various jars including some kind of jelly-like substance and a clump of rabbit fur. When this was ready, he applied it directly to the wound. Then he started her on a second mixture, this time with clay, herbs, and crushed rose petals. When this was ready he fashioned a collar encircling Thomas's neck, about four fingers wide. When he finished he patted Vivienne's hand and gave her a wink. "Bud. Nammy beed appa de hod."

"I'm guessing, but I think he might be saying this will stop the bleeding," Vivienne said.

Thomas was fully alert now, and the old fellow gave him a sip of the wine from the bottle. Thomas grimaced, but then we settled him back down for a rest. The old man waved us out of his cabin.

We dared not light a fire to attract attention, so we fashioned a semi-circular camp beside the little house, sitting close for warmth and waiting for word on Thomas's condition. The old man muttered constantly, sometimes softer, then louder. I imagined Thomas was getting an earful, but I rather liked the odd little fellow. Here we were, strangers with little to offer, but without hesitation he applied his skills to help our poor injured friend. And what a character he was, with his funny looks and mysterious language. Funnier still that Faolán and Vivienne could so quickly understand him. After several long minutes, Pol-Liam opened his door. He had a small pail in his hand, and gestured toward the dunes.

"Imo. Rebby sam don de be. Rebby sam heppe heeb."

Faolán nodded, and the old man tottered off toward the dunes, his pail swaying.

"What say he now, Faolán?" Sean asked.

"He needs the red sand from the strand. Or it's something about red anyways."

Sean shook his head, and I looked in on Thomas. The bleeding had stopped. Now I had respect for the old man, and confidence that Thomas would be well again soon. Thomas's eyes focused on me but he did not speak or move his head. I pressed a finger to his lips. "Rest now, Thomas. We are just outside. All is well."

I crouched beside him for a few more minutes, remembering a tale from several years back about a reddish sand believed to have magical qualities. Colored by the crushed shells of ancient sea creatures, this sand was legendary for healing the worst wounds and ailments, and could even promote fertility. Some farmers sprinkled it upon their soil in hopes to improve the yield of their crops and would travel miles to obtain it. But the red sand could be found in only one place, on a hidden strand but a half mile wide. I realized with some excitement the famous strand lay footsteps away from me, just beyond the cliffs. I wanted to see it, but dared not leave our group while we all waited so anxiously for Thomas's recovery.

We waited outside for the old man to return, each in our own silence and discomfort, each in our own uneasiness for what lay ahead. A quarter hour passed and then another and another. It was near an hour gone when Thomas snored to break the silence. I looked up, and Vivienne watched me with a frightened stare.

"Something is wrong." She swallowed and nodded toward the sea.

Sean jumped up to check on Thomas, but he lay sleeping, undisturbed. Faolán looked from Vivienne to me and back to Vivienne. Already we had learned to heed her premonitions. "What is it, Vivienne?" Faolán asked softly.

"I think it is Pol-Liam."

Faolán was on his feet in an instant.

"Wait, I'll go with you. You may need help," I said, rising beside him. And, I shamefully must admit, I wished to see that red strand for myself before we moved away from it—a terrible, selfish thought at such a moment.

"Come then. Sean, stay with Vivienne and Thomas. We'll return straightaway."

We ran toward the path the old man had walked. The way was narrow at first and thick with grasses and sea holly, then it widened like a great V until the strand opened up before us, looking more pink than red in the gray light of the day. The waves crashed against it and I welcomed the cool mist on my face and the roar of its motion in my ears. At first the strand seemed deserted, with wide vacant stretches spotted only by scattered clumps of dark seaweed, some red and some black, and stones of all shapes and sizes and shades of gray, pink and green. Then I noticed something dark and angular several yards away. "Faolán, look."

He ran toward it, the upturned pail the old man had been carrying. He must have dropped it, but up and down the shoreline there was no one. "Could a strong wave have carried him away, Faolán?"

He looked toward the foaming tide and shook his head. "The old man knows the sea. He's lived his life here. Something is badly amiss."

He walked back toward the cliffs on either side of the pass. A few tangled clumps of tall sea grass swayed in the wind. Dark chunks of the cliff had split from the edge and fallen to the beach, looking like little islands with the layer of black mud and green moss still growing on the crest. We split apart, searching every spot where the man might have fallen or stopped to rest. Faolán called Pol-Liam's name while I peered about the larger collections of seaweed.

I bent low and scooped a handful of the red sand. Within its coarseness lay the tiny pieces of shell from the ancient creatures that resembled a snake, possibly driven into the sea by Saint Patrick himself if the story be true. It smelled of salt and of rich sea life, but a constriction at my throat and a twinge in my belly warned me of its power. It might have held the power to enrich life, but it held death within it as well. I cast it down to be free of it, but then I reconsidered. We might be wise to have a bit of healing magic with us for the journey that lay ahead, and what magic does not leave a person uneasy? I scooped it into Pol-Liam's pail.

After only a few minutes Faolán called out, his sound urgent. From across the strand he waved and I ran to him. A dark cliff jutted skyward, showing layer upon layer of dirt, rock and the passage of time. Faolán had found our man beneath it, facedown in the jagged crevice between the cliff and its fallen edge, his tattered clothes wet with clinging sand. We turned him over. Pol-Liam's face was set in a painful grimace, his eyes popped wide. His left ear was bloodied, the lobe slashed away. His bony hands clawed uselessly against the blood-splattered white scarf cinched around his throat that had cut off his last breath.

"Help me lift him, Aengus. We must get him back to his house," Faolán said, his voice strained and low.

To lift and carry a body raised the bumps on my skin and the hair at my nape. I had done it only to help Faolán with Sir William's body, and feared it nonetheless. But I would not give in to my fear and risk Faolán's respect, which I cherished greatly. I cast it off as if it belonged to someone else and shoved my hands beneath Pol-Liam's ankles. His body was heavier than I expected, without the spirit that lifts the flesh, and we stumbled a bit through the soft sand. When we climbed above the bluff I was grateful to see the crumbling old shack, but for an instant Faolán froze like a statue. Sean stood outside the door with his arms around Vivienne.

When he saw us, Sean dropped his arms and Vivienne pushed away from him. Sean came to help us. "My God, what has happened?"

"He's been strangled," I said. Sean gasped, but Faolán said nothing. He shot Sean a fierce glare and held him in it.

"I was only keeping her warm, ye see," Sean said, backing away.

Faolán's cheeks were dark as the peat, his eyes reddened and glassy. "I see, Sean. I see exactly."

Chapter Seven

Faults of Memory

Four angels to my bed, four angels to my head,
One to watch, one to pray, and two to bear my soul away.

~ Thomas Ady

Vivienne touched Pol-Liam's hand as we brought him in, and I could not expel the ants that crawled in my belly. We found no trace of the one who'd attacked Pol-Liam. No unusual horse tracks near the house, no footprints on the strand, all signs either washed or brushed away so that we could not even see a direction from which the attacker had come. An eerie tingling crept up the back of my neck. A professional, shrewd, and deadly predator now stalked us and had sent his clear message. He would pick us apart slowly, and we'd never know from which direction he'd come.

Thomas did not rouse when we entered. He slept, and yet seemed fitful and groaned when touched, his forehead and scalp sweaty. What would Pol-Liam have done for him? How would he have used the red sand? A poultice? I scraped it from the pail into a bowl. It stuck thickly to my fingers when I mixed it with an herbal oil found among Pol-Liam's things. I spread the mixture on a rag and pressed it gently to Thomas's wound. The sand was cool. If nothing else, it would draw the heat from his head and allow him to heal.

We sat silently together looking upon Pol-Liam's body, each of us in our own thoughts. With a young woman to protect, a wounded man, and a dead body, Faolán's plan was a few steps off track. And yet we needed speed, to escape this killer and reach the safety of Rathmore. After only a few moments, Thomas roused, touched the poultice gingerly, and flinched at the sight of the old man's body. The horror that spread across his face expressed what all of us were feeling. The old man had helped us, and we had brought a murderer upon him.

"I'll go no farther, Faolán." Thomas stared at the ground as if his eyes were fixed to it. "I'll not leave Pol-Liam as he lay after what he's done for me. I'll have a care for his body and his burial."

He still had no memory of what had happened on the road when he was wounded. He had seen no one, heard no sound that suggested trouble before he was hit. There was nothing he could offer to help us understand what might have happened to him or to Pol-Liam, or to prepare for whatever danger might yet await us.

"This old fellow mebbe saved my life, and now he's come to a bad end because we came here," Thomas continued. "He needs my help, as you no longer do. I'm sure to be myself again in a few days. I will see to his body and burial, and then search for my horse."

Vivienne had found a jug of spirits that Pol-Liam had tucked into the straw of his bed, and was sipping it. God himself only knows what vile elixir was in that jug, but she swallowed without a wince, wiped her lips with the back of her hand like an old sailor, and passed the jug to Thomas.

Sean pleaded with him. "Thomas, someone has tried ta kill ye, and now we've a murderer about. Yer askin' us to leave ye alone here, no horse, no weapon, no food. What's to happen to ye? And how are we ta go without worryin'?"

"It is true, Thomas," Faolán added. "We're safer as a group. I should not have sent you ahead. If we'd been together, it may not have happened, or at least one of us would have seen the scoundrel and mayhap could have caught him."

"Mebbe so, but ye've wasted enough time already, and you must go on without me. Much longer and Lord Barry will return to Barryscourt and ye'll have no audience with him."

"There's truth to that, Faolán." I had to say it, knowing how hard it would be for Faolán to leave Thomas or any of us behind, but his plan for Vivienne depended upon the support of Lord Barry, and this was not a man to keep waiting.

"That knock on the head has cast the sense out your ear, Thomas," Sean said. Faolán cast a sharp glance at Sean, who seemed to have lost some sense as well.

Thomas raised his palm to silence his brother. "I'll allow ye this. When the old fella is laid to rest and my horse is again beneath me, I'll make my way back to Mairead's. I can stay hidden there, rest a bit, and mebbe give her a little help on the farm. Ye can come for me there when this venture is done."

Sean and Faolán looked at each other as Thomas returned the jug of spirits to Vivienne, who seemed not to care one way or another what happened next.

"All right then, Thomas. *Sard it.* Ye'll stay," Faolán said. "God be with you. Mayhap one day you'll find yourself traipsin' through the valley with sweet Mairead while her husband lay dyin' in his bed." His cheeks darkened again. His eyes turned fierce and his tone harsh. "But here's how it will go, lad. A terrible murder has been committed, so. Someone in the village will realize old Pol-Liam hasn't come 'round beggin' as he had, and then someone comes looking for him. Here you are with a fresh hole in the ground where the old man is buried, and a wound on your head. The old man must've hit you while trying to defend himself, he'll say. Someone goes for the constable, who now wants to ask a lot of questions. Next thing, the townsfolk rise up. Suddenly they realize they all loved old Pol-Liam, and they don't know you from the dirt you stand upon. They need a hanging to make things right again, and hanging you is easier than running after some phantom you say did the killing.

"Next, you've got a thick scratchy rope around your neck, and you're staring down at the townsfolk who've brought their young ones and old ones and a basket of sweetmeats to eat while they watch you die. Two months later, we come for you; nobody remembers a thing, and we cannot even bring your bones back home to your ma. Or worse, the folk will decide we are all accomplices and hang us as well. Is that your plan, Thomas? *Is it?*"

Thomas's face had gone white as marble. Vivienne clutched the jug to her chest, her lips pressed into a firm line, her eyes wide and dark. Sean stared at his feet. All went quiet, without the call of a bird nor a crashing ocean wave, just a high, shrill ringing in my ears. And then Faolán released a long sigh.

"You mean to hunt down this killer by way of finding your horse. The risk is too high, Thomas. We'll help lay the man to rest. He was a good man: he deserves the care, and you are right in that. But we bury him here, 'neath the floor of his own house, and not outside where we might draw attention. Say the words you want over the sad grave. Sean and Aengus can prepare the horses on the south side of the house where they won't be seen from the village. At dusk we mount up, and then we are gone from here as fast as we might. We'll ride all night. No one's to go ten feet beyond this house until then. And if I am right, this killer will need no hunting, for it is he who hunts us, and we will get him. For Pol-Liam, for Vivienne, and for our own sakes, we *will* get him."

A hard moment followed, as the truth did alight in our heads and come to roost in our bellies. Our lark of an abduction had become a life-or-death quest, with someone picking away at our flanks. No one moved nor even breathed as the moment passed, and not a word was spoken until Thomas broke the silence with a painful grunt, rose up, and tended the old man's body. We dug at the ground with sticks, an old drinking cup, a gourd, whatever we could find inside the house. In somber moods we kept to ourselves as we worked. The grave would be shallow and narrow, but perhaps old Pol-Liam would like his final resting place.

I breathed in the scent of the dirt. How strange it is when something so ordinary comes to stir the memory, the way roasting meat can remind you of your family home or the curve of a flower petal conjures the memory of a kind act. A spoken word, the rustle of a passing skirt, a cold wind, the sweet taste of honey from a little clay jar, bringing up a word or an image suppressed either because it was so long ago, or so painful, or just unimportant at the time and never expected to be.

There'd been a conversation in my father's alehouse about the men, women, and children of Baltimore, just a few miles from our destination of Rathmore, who were abducted from their homes in the night by merciless Algerian pirates. More than one hundred were taken, common folk who had no way to pay their ransoms and would live and die as slaves, "their remains never again to touch the soil of home," one of the customers said.

Then a story was told of one young fellow headed for Kinsale, a passenger aboard an English merchant ship attacked by such pirates. All souls were taken, the cargo ransacked, the ship scuttled. The young man was whipped and tortured and saw the rape of every woman captive. Yet he was one of the fortunate. His family paid a high ransom for his return, and the fellow would have to work like the devil the rest of his life to repay his enormous debt. Rumor had it that the money was borrowed from none other than Lord Cork, and the young man would do anything, *anything*, to settle it. I was confident now that the full memory had returned: the young fellow's name was Eames.

The hairs on the back of my neck and on my forearms stood to attention. I had nothing to go on but a certainty in my veins that this was the man who stalked us. I had to tell Faolán, but to speak of this now would alarm everyone, and once the work was done we would have but a few hours to rest before nightfall. It was best not to fuel the fears that already churned. My belly tightened into knots as I wondered whether the man was somewhere outside the little house, watching for a propitious moment to kill us all. Nevertheless, I kept my silence until we were well down the road and stopped to allow Vivienne to relieve herself, when I could get Faolán alone. We stood close together with Dunerayl between us, the Barry lads on one side, a patch of wood and shrub shielding Vivienne on the other.

"And when were you going to tell me this!" Faolán nearly shouted before I could finish talking, but I grabbed his wrist to stop him.

"It only just came to me, Faolán! It was not important until now. Do you think it is he who stalks us?"

"Of course it is. No one else would even know what we're about. And what could make a man more devious and desperate than the weight of tremendous debt? He is either being paid by Cork to hunt us, or he seeks a reward for Vivienne. Is there anything else you can tell me?"

"There isn't. I am sorry. What do you think we must do?"

Faolán watched as Vivienne emerged from the shrubs behind us, pulling her cloak tightly around her body. The ends of her hair were damp, hanging in dark ringlets over her shoulders. In the fading light of evening, her skin glowed like alabaster against the dark gray of her hood. On another face, such a glow would have made a ghostly impression, but the light made her visage like an angel in a painting. Their eyes met, and the beginnings of a sweet smile formed on her lips. A swell in my chest grew to a knot within my throat. She lifted her chin, but then pulled the hood low over her eyes and walked on to stroke Dunerayl's forelock. I swallowed with difficulty. What was happening to me? Was this what Faolán felt when he saw her, each time he saw her? He lifted her to the saddle as if she were weightless, his hand lingering lightly on her knee, and then he turned to me.

"He may be watching us even now. It *must not* continue another day. We must set a trap for him, Aengus."

"Aye, a fine thought, but we have little cover for that."

"It is so, but Eames has no cover either, and we can assume he travels alone with two horses. I have a plan. We'll move off the coast road to where there are hills and woods enough to cover us, then set up camp and we'll wait for him." He turned to the Barrys. "Sean, Thomas, stay close and keep a wary ear for trouble. We'll go as far as Lios Aird.

"Faolán, shall I take a turn with Sean to walk beside Thomas?" I asked.

"Why? Let Sean walk, and keep his mind on his brother and not on things that don't concern him."

"Aye." I kept my place behind Faolán and Vivienne. I suspected Sean would not get close to Vivienne for the remainder of our journey, and rightly so. My mind turned to the task ahead, and my unspoken question. After we waited for Eames, what would we do when he arrived?

Chapter Eight

Lios Aird, the High Fort

The world wants to be deceived.

~ Franck Sebastian

Lios Aird was an ancient circular fort on high ground, built from flat rock stacked one upon the other until the walls were chest high on a man, and as thick as he was tall. The ruins were no longer visible except for a single ring of great stones where the druids might have called down their gods. To see them was thrilling, but I'd never dared to enter the ring. To be aware of the spirits within those spaces was to feel their presence from a quarter mile's distance, with a heightening of the pulse, a cool sweat on the brow and an urge to cry out without words or reason.

The fort was eight miles distant, a quick trip for a game horse, but with one of us always on foot, we would take hours. The way was troublesome in places and risky, through dense thickets with moss-covered trees and long, ropey vines to entrap us, leafy depressions where horses could step into holes, and deep crevices that were hard to avoid in the darkness.

Faolán led us between the hills and beside the lake of great beauty, long and narrow with a curve and widening at one end, the shape of a whale with his tail flipped up behind him. Thanks be to God Faolán knew every square mile of the province, for we'd have been lost a hundred times over. We allowed the horses to drink before hobbling them in a low copse of hazel. While the rest of us made camp, Faolán unpacked a saddlebag.

We'd used two pistols to abduct our mistress, Vivienne. Buried for years in the mud of an abandoned battlefield, they were corroded and of little use except as souvenirs or as mild deterrents in a dark stairway. In broad daylight they would frighten only a gunsmith asked to repair them. But Faolán owned another gun, a wheel-lock pistol for which he had paid dearly, as added protection along with his sword against attack during his travels. He pulled it gently from the bag to clean and check its parts.

He worked carefully with his brow deeply furrowed, reminding me of his dislike for guns. They were clumsy, loud, and inaccurate except at close range, when a sword or dagger would work as well or better, and by the time one could reload for a second shot he might be overtaken. I despised them for their use of the Devil's substances—sulphur, saltpeter and charcoal. Even the most experienced warriors called them diabolical, and yet they said guns were the way of the future and soon the archers, pikemen and swordsmen would disappear. When that time came, I would cast aside my hatred and learn to use a firearm. I'd no wish to be defenseless in such a violent world.

As we worked at our tasks, Vivienne stood in the center of activity, her gaze passing from one to the other until settling on Faolán. She marched forward and stood before him. "You are going to kill someone now? Is that your plan? Because if it is, I will not be a part of it."

Faolán looked up quickly. "You would allow him to kill us then? One at a time? And we're to offer no defense?"

"Of course not, but I don't care for being the bait in a murder trap. Why can't we just ride on? We could move faster and leave him far behind us. You promised I'd be as your equal, and so far I feel like nothing more than some prize for men to fight over. I might as well return to Lord Cork. I might as well be a *horse*."

Faolán smirked. "I promised we'd be equals once we were married, Vivienne. Are you saying you're ready to marry?"

Could I have seen her cheeks in the darkness, sure they would have been a deep crimson just then.

"Let us move on!" she complained. "Let us get to Rathmore and make our decisions from there. I tire of the darkness, the stops and starts, the damp cold that seeps into my bones. If not for Mairead's cloak, I would have frozen to death by now. I am weary of all of this, and especially of sharing your horse, when I am a better rider and should have my own."

Faolán released a long sigh. "A better rider? I cannot wait to see it.

I will get you the finest horse you've ever seen, Vivienne. But for now, we are moving as fast as we can. I know you are frightened and weary. We all are. One of us is injured. We've lost a horse. One of us must walk. And one man is dead. I don't think we can continue in this manner, do you?"

She turned away from him, her arms folded across her waist. "May we at least have a fire?"

"At your service, my dear. Aengus, will you build a warm fire for the lady, please? Not too large just yet, but gather the wood that we can make the flames tall as soon as we are ready."

"Ready for what?" she asked.

"There is no time to explain, Vivienne, but watch and you'll see. Everything will be well. And Aengus, we'll need our blankets from the packs. At least two."

Faolán sent Sean and Thomas to conceal the horses in a thicket farther away, and then to find hiding places from which they could watch the camp. He went about cutting and gathering scrub from the surrounding woods. Even I was not sure what he was up to, but would know soon enough.

When camp was set and the fire glowing, with Vivienne seated beside it, I joined her there to stoke the fire. "Thank you, Aengus," she said. "So we must wait now. We are like rabbits in a snare. How do we even know this man is about?"

"We don't, but so far he has been, and if what we are thinking is true, he cannot afford to pass us by."

Vivienne looked up at me, and as the glow of the flames grew stronger, her eyes widened with fear.

"If he comes...He is cruel, Aengus. I know it. He will make me..." She wrapped her arms around her shoulders. "He is a vulture."

Her anxiety penetrated my heart. How I wished I had some way to comfort her. I simply clenched my teeth, knowing it was not my place to do so. I wanted as she did, to be done with these troubles and move on.

"He will never lay eyes on you, my love." Faolán's arms were loaded with the scrub. He dropped it at his feet and arranged it in two large heaps on the opposite side of the fire. Then he covered each heap with a blanket and tugged and poked at them until they looked like two sleeping lads covered up against the cold night. I should have thought of it myself. It was true artistry.

"Make the left one a bit larger. Our Thomas has gained some weight."

Faolán smirked at me. "Aye, well, I've cut his rations for tonight." Dusting the dirt and debris from his hands, he leaned down to help Vivienne stand. "Follow me, will you please, my lady?"

He led her to the trunk of an old yew tree, massive and strong with thick, waxy needles on ropy branches nearly touching the ground, and a low crook where a fellow might get a foothold and lift himself into its highest reaches.

"Just for a little while, Vivienne, in that fat branch just above, you can find a comfortable place to hide. I have tested it myself, and it is good. Even if you sleep you should not fall. Stay silent and as still as you can until we have captured this beast. Will you help me this way?"

"I will, I promise," she replied simply.

"Thank you, lass. First, we must make an exchange. I give you my doublet for warmth, for the loan of your cloak."

"But why would..."

"Just for now: you'll have it back safe and sound in no time at all. Trust me?"

She looked at her boots and slowly shrugged off the cloak. In turn he removed his doublet and draped it over her shoulders, then cast the gray cloak over his back and pulled the hood over his head. "See? Am I not charming?"

She shook her head. "You are something. I do not think charm comes to mind."

"Ah, well, there's a puzzle to work on while you wait." He helped her into the crook of the tree and watched until she settled herself safely, then joined me beside the campfire.

"Aengus, it asks much of you, but will you wear this cloak while we sit here? I'm afraid I might split the shoulder seams. You, on the other hand, would cut a fine figure and make our Mister Eames swoon."

"Bastard," I said, and gave him a smile. I donned the cloak and covered my head with the hood. It did in fact fit me better, and in such warmth, I knew why Vivienne loathed giving it up.

Faolán and I lay near the fire, setting the scene of a sleeping camp that might easily be attacked by our stalker. The flames crackled softly, sending gray smoke spiraling through an opening in the canopy of branches above. Just a few steps distant, the lake rippled. Water lapped the shore, leaves rattled as the night wind played in the boughs, and a wood owl offered a contemplative hoot. An idyllic setting, and yet my breathing was shallow, my ribs constricting about my lungs. An ache in my back spanned toward my shoulders—my body bracing itself against something unseen and malevolent. A branch snapped; a pistol hammer clicked. *The killer was upon us.* But it was only Faolán's boot upon a broken twig, his hand readying the pistol.

He leaned on an elbow to poke the fire with the twig. My God, he could not be near a fire without worrying it, and sure he poked at life the same way, always trying to bring forth the brighter light, the higher flame, and the greater warmth. At times this constant urging annoyed me, but mostly I admired him for it. Just his physical presence brought forth something greater in me that alone I couldn't attain. We were just ten years old when first I knew this.

"Do you remember that night..."

"Don't say it, Aengus." Faolan shook his head. "You are always bringing it up at the strangest times. Do you really think tonight we should remember my father's death?"

"It's a night such as this that brings it roaring back to me."

He grunted and lowered his head, tilting it just as his father had done. Faolán was so like Sir William. Fierce and loyal, defending the good land against any threats to his properties or his clan. Sir William was especially wary of the new English gentry, who imagined the Irish as barbarians, and our lands as emeralds to be plucked away. Such men convinced themselves they were improving the land by taking it, disguising their greed as a service. Many of them were second sons who had no inheritance in England and saw Ireland as their grand opportunity. They found any means of taking acceptable, whether by swindling and fraud or by outright murder and confiscation. Some men hired brigands to terrorize Irish farmers from their homes.

And in Dublin Castle, the very symbol of order and justice, an entire team of lawyers toiled on one assignment: to search out weak land claims and contestable deeds and then seize those properties for the crown. Irish sons like Faolán, inheriting from fathers but without the English deeds, had no laws protecting them and no judge who wouldn't sooner take the English bribe than defend a young man's heritage.

On that fateful night of which Faolán would not speak, the mournful dove's cry came just before dusk, and a burning seized my stomach and fingertips. Faolán was a runner for the earl and brought the message himself. Near Adare, bands of raiders were burning out the Earl of

Clanricarde's Irish tenants to steal away their cattle.

Sir William mounted his horse at once and rode out with his soldiers. Though he was sternly warned to stay away, Faolán followed his father, so I followed as well. We always expected Sir William to be the victor, but this night the skirmish was swift and exceedingly violent. When we arrived on the field, a trail of bodies marked the site and soaked the grasses with blood. The brave and honorable William Burke, ever alert and skillful on the battlefield, must have turned the wrong direction at a crucial moment. His body lay motionless on the trampled ground, his breath stilled, his neck broken and skull cracked by the mighty swing of an ax.

Faolán cried out, a sound more terrible to my ears than the shriek of the banshee. He fell upon his father's body, his face smeared with dirt and tears. He struggled to lift Sir William's shoulders and drag him away from the others, but one of the raiders approached with a bloody sword, dispatching any enemies left breathing. He raised his sword and came at us. Faolán's eyes blazed with the ferocity of a cornered wolf. He sprung at the man and seized him by the neck, set to rip the man's throat open with his teeth. The raider screamed and twisted to free himself, but I grabbed a bloodied pike from the ground and ran the man through from his belly to his chest until a fountain of blood spouted from his lips. I released the pike as if it were molten.

The raider dropped his sword, quivered wildly, and fell, Faolán tumbling away from him and landing in a sprawl at my feet. My arms burned and trembled, my back suddenly ached, but I stood my ground. For a long time, Faolán didn't stir but simply stared at the fallen man as he died, and then at me. He could not have been more surprised than I to find such an act within me.

We were changed after that. We'd been children, and now we'd progressed to the front line in the long march of generations. We'd been boys and now we were warriors, bearing the heavy weight of heritage, vengeance, mourning and remembrance. Faolán's charmed life as a prince became far more serious, his mind focused on his legacy and all that was lost with his father's passing. And I became a man, if not in my own father's eyes, more than I'd ever believed I could be.

Faolán sighed, as did I, releasing to the wind the frustration of waiting. We were forever linked, both ready to do whatever was necessary, without hesitation, to protect each other and those we loved. And as he forged his life's mission, I'd be a part of it. *Always.*

"Do not worry, Faolán."

"I'm not worried. I am angry that we are hindered and hounded in this way. I mean for us to end it once and for all." He squeezed my shoulder as he stood. "Stay put, Aengus, and look fetching. I need a piss."

He headed toward the nearby reeds to relieve himself. I picked up the twig he had dropped and poked a darkening ember. He had only been gone a few moments when a faint whisper came from somewhere close behind me: *"Vivienne! Vivienne!"*

I lifted my head sharply, still covered by the hood. My back stiffened. Had I imagined it? Was it real? And if real, which way should I turn to exploit what might come next?

"Come to me. The earl sends me. I will take you home."

The whisper was stronger this time, coming from the brush at the edge of the lake, but Faolán was nowhere to be seen. I turned slowly toward the sound, my skean now in hand.

"Vivienne, hurry to me, before he returns. I will take you home!"

I rose to my feet, hoping my movement might draw him near so that I could see him. I turned, careful not to reveal my face. A shadow edged closer. If I lunged for him, how far was he, and what weapon might he hold? Then came a vicious howl and a terrible cry: the hedges behind me burst into a mad rustle of branches and leaves until two tangled bodies fell into view, tossed and rolled and came to a stop near the fire. On top a stranger lay on his back, his face drawn into a grotesque and bloodied snarl. Beneath him was Faolán, his skean pressed firmly against the stranger's throat, his other hand twisting the man's arm behind him in an unnatural angle. The man shrieked in pain.

"Quickly! Take a look, Aengus!" Faolán's voice was strained.

I knelt beside the man and jerked the wool cap from his head. Light brown hair fell to his shoulders, his gaze darting about like a trapped rat. His dark beard came to a sharp point beneath his chin. I pushed his chin to one side and pinched his ear so I could get a good look at it. The lobe was split just as Mairead had said, where once a fine earring had been ripped away.

"'Tis he, Faolán."

I released a sound like a hoot owl from deep in my throat, a call long known between us lads that would bring Sean and Thomas to us in an instant. Then I searched the man's pockets for weapons and tossed his blade and a pistol closer to the fire. Faolán had full control of him and dragged him by the neck to the fireside. Coming out of the darkness, Sean slammed into the man's side and pressed a blade to his throat where Faolán's had been, giving Faolán relief while Thomas pressed his boot on the man's groin to hold him down.

Faolán, regaining his breath and balance, stepped closer to the captive. "We know who you are, Mister Eames. We know a lot about you. Who sends you to follow us?" His voice was harsh, but I knew he was trying to calm it. To show anger or fear would only give this fellow greater confidence.

"The Earl of Cork sends me." He coughed and groaned against Thomas's pressure. "And the High Sheriff as well. I come for the Lady FitzGerald. You're a doomed man, Faolán Burke."

Faolán leaned in. "You are the doomed one, sir. You are outnumbered in spite of your efforts to reduce us, and you'll never get near the lady, I promise you that. You've done enough damage. It's time to return to England, or whatever den of hell you've come from, and leave us to our journey. Follow us no more."

Eames recovered his breath and spoke with some difficulty. "It won't be so easy. I must return the lady to their custody. And if not me, others will come. The earl means to have her back, and if she has been…compromised…you'll hang."

Faolán stared at the man and then laughed, strong and genuine. "I am amazed, sir! This is the warning that comes from one who creased the skull of a traveler on the road and then stole his horse? The envoy from Satan who strangled a poor, fragile old man with a silk scarf, and then left his cold body on the strand for the crabs? I hardly think you should be warning *us* about the hangman's noose."

Eames twisted and struggled, but Sean held him tighter, drawing a drop of blood with his skean. "What is this you say?" Eames protested. "I've done nothing of the sort. You conjure tales for your own amusement and have no proof for anything."

"Proof? Why under the heavens would I need proof? There are four men before you who will swear you are a murderer. Four who had to prepare an old man's body and then bury the poor suffering soul. Four witnesses to your cruelty and treachery who would gladly deliver you to the sheriff, or better still to an angry mob of villagers who would tear you apart. You threaten us with blades of grass. Enough of you. Now tell me, where are the horses?"

"I have no horses. I followed you on foot, your trail as clear to see as if it were torchlit."

"And who said we were trying to conceal our trail? You are the one who must hide, sir. Where have you left the horses? We know you've stolen at least one."

Eames turned his face away, and Sean jerked his grip even tighter. Thomas increased the pressure of his boot until Eames grunted in pain, yet the man said nothing. Thomas turned toward the path from which we'd come to set up camp.

"Bram!" he shouted, and whistled sharply. At first there was only the rustling wind. "BRAM!" he shouted again. Then came a baritone whinny from somewhere nearby.

"It's not far to where he's left them. I'll get them," Thomas said, and then ran toward the path and the sound.

"I have stolen nothing." Eames spat his words, and my contempt for him doubled.

"It is well then," Faolán said. "You won't mind as we return the mounts to their rightful owners. If we had the time, we would happily deliver you to the hangman today, but we have more pressing business."

"If it is business you want, then let us speak of it," Eames said.

Faolán turned. "My God, you have neither conscience nor loyalties. What are you after now?"

"I give you a good offer. I can get you out of this trouble you've got yourself into, and clear you with the earl."

"I see. A moment ago you wished to kill me, and now you would save me. Please continue."

"Release me and give me the lady. I will tell Cork I never saw you, nor any of you, but found her alone and confused in the wood. I'll take the lady home safely, the earl can arrange his profitable marriage for her, and you and your lads will go free."

Faolán took a step back. "As if nothing ever happened. How interesting, the way you think. You would do all this for us? And what profit for yourself?"

"My liberty, first. And the earl would compensate me for my time, nothing more."

"Ah, I see. And who might be the lucky gentleman to marry the fine heiress? You, mayhap? To satisfy your aunt's debt?"

"What do you know of this?" Eames shouted and struggled against the holds.

Faolán smiled. "Margaret Massy said she was ruined when we took away the Lady FitzGerald. And then you arrive amid rumors of a debt to clear. It was a bit of a leap, but now you've proved the assumption correct. Margaret and Caleb borrowed from the earl to pay your ransom to the Algerian pirates. Then she volunteered to house the heiress with an eye to your wedding and the lady's fortune. Is that about right?"

"The earl's interest in you will disappear when he is forced to negotiate with my family for her dowry and inheritance," Eames said. "What difference does it make to you who she marries? You and your men are free to go and abduct someone else as you please. Her situation will be restored, and the earl's pride is satisfied."

"Are there others who track us?"

"The earl knows I'm quite capable."

"I suppose there is a reward offered."

"Only to be posted if I come back empty-handed, so to speak. Let me take her. It's money you're after. Once it is all settled, I'll offer you a portion. Say, ten percent of what the earl pays me. And I will see her safely home."

Faolán grinned and scratched behind his ear. Of course he would never negotiate any sort of deal with Eames, not if it meant giving up Vivienne. And it is unlikely the earl would be satisfied if he did. Still, we might learn more about what the earl was planning if Faolán asked a few more questions. He never got the chance.

"Liar! You will not take me home. I have no home, and I'll never be safe with you!" Vivienne shouted from the tree.

Faolán's mouth popped open, and mine as well. If only we could reel back in the words she'd just blurted. What game was she playing? Wasn't it clear Faolán did not want Eames to know where she was hidden? If she had been drinking, it might have been understandable, but the lady was as sober as I, with far more to lose by exposing her location this way. Eames's face had been contorted in anger and frustration as he tried to break free of us, but now he stopped struggling, looked up into the tree and grinned a kind of satisfied, sly way as if he had just gained a measure of power over us.

"Ah!" He shouted into the boughs with a greased and mocking voice, "There you are, Lady FitzGerald! Won't you go back to your safe warm room, your silken dresses and satin slippers? The soft bed and hot meals? You are sorely missed. Your mother asks after you, my lady."

"Liar. She does not!" Vivienne cried out.

Faolán leapt forward and kicked Eames in the ribs. Eames heaved with a loud groan, but Sean still held him fast.

"Quiet! Who gave you permission to speak to the lady? Speak to her again and we'll cut out your tongue."

Eames silenced, but the smug look remained.

"There will never be business between us, Eames. Forget that. We will leave you here, and I want never to lay eyes on your face again. Sean, Aengus, tie him fast to that tree near the water's edge, facing away from us that he should not watch our departure. And if he is able to free himself before the constable finds him, we will be long gone from him. Mister Eames, if I ever do see your face again, I will kill you. If I suspect you are continuing to stalk us, I will go to the nearest constable and report your vicious murder of Pol-Liam, which I intend to do anyway when we are arrived at our destination."

Within a few moments Thomas came into the camp with the two horses, his own Bram and the horse rented from Mairead. I stood watch over our prisoner while the others struck camp. Faolán brought Dunerayl to the tree where Vivienne was waiting and lifted her to him. Her feet never touched the ground, and Eames never saw her. I returned her cloak. Faolán fastened his doublet, then took the reins of Mairead's horse. Without a word he mounted and waved us forward. We climbed up out of the valley that surrounded the lake, able to move more swiftly now that each of us was well mounted. I urged my horse forward next to Faolán, leaving Vivienne between the Barry brothers and me.

"Do you think Eames will stop now, Faolán?"

"No. He needs money and would not return to the earl having failed." His voice was terse and his words clipped. He cleared his throat and repositioned himself in the saddle. "He will come, Aengus. But we can put time and distance between us, and Lord Barry will have the Earl of Cork call off his dogs as soon as he sees we have done as we pledged to him. We can have no fear of that." He pulled up on the reins and fell back beside Vivienne, who had spoken not a word since we left the lake.

"Why did you do it, Vivienne?"

"Because you were negotiating with him. For my life, sir, you were negotiating."

"I was not! I was trying to learn what Cork was up to. Hadn't you just promised to stay silent in the tree?"

"Yes, I had."

"Then why? What came over you?"

Vivienne hesitated and released a heavy, defeated sigh that reached me though I was more than a horse's length in front of her.

"Have you ever sat still in a tree while others bargained for *your* life? It is quite difficult. And the worst of it is this: you were smiling."

"I smiled because I knew I had control of the situation."

"You had control. *I* had none."

Faolán huffed loudly. I glanced back but could not see his face, though I was sure he was near to exploding.

"My throat ached until I could not bear it. He is a killer," she said, "and he is cruel. And your bargaining was quite convincing. I was frightened, and I lost my head. I spoke, and I wish I hadn't."

"Well, you're right. He *is* a killer. Did you truly think I might allow him anywhere near you? I told you he would never even see you."

"Yes…"

Faolán stayed beside her, waiting for more, but she remained silent, while I wondered. Had the druid stones affected her as they sometimes affected me? Did the spirits squeeze her throat until she blurted out her words? Or was this volatile nature the very reason Lord Cork had kept her hidden?

"You put yourself in greater danger," Faolán said, "and each of us as well. And you broke your word to me. How am I to trust you now?"

Before she could answer, he left her side and rode past me, well into the lead. I looked back to Vivienne. She sat defiantly tall, but kept her gaze on the horse's withers. She did not look up but allowed the horse to simply follow. How quickly turn the tables, of Faolán striving to build her trust, and now Vivienne left to wonder whether she could regain his.

We melted into the darkness and surrounding woods in darkness except for the horse hooves stirring the dead leaves. We rode until dawn, putting the lake and Eames far behind us, and stopped only briefly to rest. We rode on through the gray winter day. We would journey two days more until I would see the gables of Rathmore Castle through the early morning fog. I breathed a sigh of relief that the earl's flag still beckoned from above the stone walls and I whispered a plea to the heavens that he would see us, and most importantly that he would do as he had promised.

Chapter Nine

Rathmore Castle

*My Lord Barry, tho' it was Sunday, upon an untimely falling out
at dice, wounded Malperos, the usher of my hall,
very dangerously with the firefork.*

~ Richard Boyle, Earl of Cork

As the sun burned through the fog, the tile roof of Rathmore Castle glinted
and steamed. The sight of it warmed and somewhat alarmed me. Was it an
omen of sorts, or was I being oversensitive now after so many difficulties
we had faced on the way to this place? I turned to Vivienne to see if she
had seen the same sight, for we could communicate nonverbally on these
things and I needed only to see her eyes. But Vivienne still brooded from
her words with Faolán. They had barely spoken since the event. Her gaze
shifted from Dunerayl's mane to Faolán's back and again to Dunerayl as if
I wasn't there at all.

I studied the castle, truly more of a fortified country house, being
smaller in stature than a tower house and smaller by far in ground cov-
erage than the sprawling castles being built by most of the English gentry.
Rathmore was older and had been in Lord Barry's family since his grandfather's time. It had fallen into decay in recent decades, but now that he
was the Earl of Barrymore, Lord Barry had done much to restore it. Facing
southeast, it stood three stories high, the rectangular castle at the center
with wings on each side, and another wing facing west, so that it had eight
gables. The large mullioned windows offered dramatic views of the sea in
almost every direction.

From the coast road, a sand path led up the rise to a walled enclosure of pinkish stone and an entrance arch. The stones of the house also appeared pinkish, colored by the fading dawn. We approached the main door, the ocean gasping forward upon the strand behind us and then sighing away in persistent waking rhythm. I breathed deeply of the freshened salt air. Faolán was first to dismount, and asked a passing servant where we might store the horses. He pointed toward a stable to the rear of the house, but did not offer to take them. We were stiff and sore from the journey, and our mounts more tired than we. Thomas and Sean volunteered to get them fed and watered while we alerted Lord Barry of our arrival. A steward in Barrymore livery opened the door to Faolán's knock.

"Good morn, sir. I am Faolán Burke, this is the lady Vivienne FitzGerald, and Mister Aengus O'Daly. We've just arrived from Bandon to see Lord Barry. We are traveling with my lord's kinsmen, Sean and Thomas Barry. Lord Barry will be expecting us."

The steward nodded solemnly but held his place. "The earl is resting today, not to be disturbed before four of the clock. If you would see him, you may wait in the gardens."

Faolán started to protest, but Vivienne grasped Faolán's wrist and stepped boldly in front of him. "Sir, we will do no such thing. I am Lady Vivienne FitzGerald, ward of the Earl of Cork, and these fine gentlemen are my escorts. We will not be treated as commoners, tenants, or beggars off the street. We have been on a long journey, and Lord Barry awaits us. I will have a bath, and some warmed wine while it is being prepared. And then I expect a fresh gown to wear. These gentlemen shall have similar attentions at once, and as soon as we are done, we will greet the earl. Now step aside and we will wait in the hall, or rather in my lord's library, while you see to our needs."

She did not wait for his response but pushed past him through the doors, with Faolán and me following. In the entry she shrugged Mairead's cloak from her shoulders and allowed it to fall to the floor. "Please have this cleaned and brushed." She pushed through the first set of double doors and found the library. "You may have the wine brought here, sir, and make haste: we are parched from our journey."

"My lady," the fellow muttered and bowed, then hurried away. I hoped he would not return with an armed guard to usher us back outside. Vivienne collapsed in a green velvet chair near the window, but Faolán remained standing, the lopsided grin brightening his face.

"Very clever, my love." He reached for her hand and kissed her fingers.

Her lips lifted into a half smile.

"We are here, at long last, Faolán. I cannot countenance a longer wait in these clothes," she said. "One thing I've had plenty of training in is how to address servants. Being that Lord Barry should not even have had his breakfast yet, it is odd that he must be *resting* the greater part of the day. I am sure once we are refreshed he will see us. Have I redeemed myself a little bit?"

"You have." Faolán gave her a courtly nod.

The steward brought the wine and three glasses. He poured one for Vivienne, and then backed out of the room with a scowl.

"Insolence." Vivienne filled the other glasses, and we drank together in silence. The wine worked immediately to lower my stiff shoulders. The sweet scent of it mingled pleasantly with the old wood and mustiness, furniture oil, and candle wax. Soft early light streamed through the window directly before me, illuminating the spines of books that filled the dark cedar shelving. Some were bound in leather, some in linen, and some sewn together with heavy thread. My reading was perfunctory, hardly as strong as Faolán's, but now in my heart I committed to improving it, for clearly the world of knowledge could be accessed within these bindings. The thought of it stirred my blood.

To my right, a round table's surface was painted with a map of the seas and continents. A cedar desk was stacked with more books, and a leather-backed chair with claw-feet awaited its occupant. To the left, more books and a movable stair to reach them, as well as a green and white striped lounge where one could read and nap. Were I lord of the house, I would never leave this room but have my meals brought to me, and I would begin at one end and read every volume until either I ran out of them or died of old age.

At the far end of the room, a narrow door was partially open, exposing a dark winding stair behind. I glanced quickly at Faolán. Was the door intended for servants, or a private access for Lord Barry? Was it left open accidentally, or intentionally? Where would this stair lead? Faolán was thinking ahead of me, for a small muscle in his jaw twitched. He started for it, but then the double doors creaked open and the steward entered and cleared his gravelly throat.

"My lady, your bath. The maid will escort you upstairs and attend to you there." He stepped aside for her to pass, and looked back at Faolán and me as if we were a pair of dead rats left on the doorstep by the barn cat.

He closed the door. Faolán gave me a wink, and we were on our way up the narrow stair.

At the top, another door was open just a crack. Faolán pulled it inward until we could step through, and then we found ourselves in a large chamber. French doors at one end were open to the earl's bedchamber. We were in his antechamber then, a private room with a writing desk near a black marble fireplace. A fire burned low in the grate. Lord Barry, awake and fully dressed, leaned against an enormous ebony cabinet, one hand holding a steaming cup of wine. In his black frock coat, he stood out like a rook against the dark yellow damask walls.

Compared to the last time we had seen him, he looked pale and distracted, a garnet jerkin buttoned too tightly across his belly and a white ruff about his neck that had lost its starch and lay flat upon his shoulders. He looked childlike with the fine light curls above his brow. A wisp of light fuzz stood for his mustache, but his spade-shaped beard was a full blond patch extending from the corners of his lips to a point beneath his rounded chin. He twisted a large ring on his right index finger and nodded toward the narrow door.

"You have discovered my subtle invitation. I observed your arrival from my bedchamber but was not quite prepared to receive you. Do sit down, Faolán. And remind me, your companion's name?"

"Lord Barry, how good it is to see you. My friend here is Aengus O'Daly, sir. A relation to the many O'Dalys that live in these parts." At the earl's invitation Faolán sat in a carved walnut chair near the cabinet, and I sat on a stool near the far wall, more than a little conscious of my soiled clothing and unwashed face.

"Please forgive us our appearance, sir," Faolán offered. "We have been traveling a long distance and have not yet been able to..."

"Yes, yes. It is better that we meet this way, of course."

"You mean, privately?"

"Privately. Unofficially. Privately, yes."

"I...we...have brought the heiress, Lady FitzGerald, sir."

The earl brushed the back of his hand against his brow and his lips parted as if to speak, but then he stopped and took a quick breath. "Indeed, I saw a young woman on your horse. A beautiful woman even in such strange costume."

"Sir. Yes, she is. And of fiery character."

The earl moved toward the window and paced in front of a red velvet window seat. "Has she…" he swallowed hard and turned to face Faolán squarely. "Have you…"

"We are not yet wed, if that is what you ask. She is untouched. We came to you first, and if you will help us as we discussed, I am confident she'll agree to the marriage."

Lord Barry sat down on the edge of the window seat, exhaled slowly, and looked out. "Good. Good. You understand I could not receive you, I could not…"

A clamor developed in the narrow stairway and the door jerked open, producing Sean with Thomas right behind him. They'd washed the grime from their face, ears, and hands, probably using the rain trough outside the kitchen, and had brushed the dust from their clothing, but looked only slightly better than Faolán and me. They seemed quite jovial until realizing they were in the presence of the earl.

"My lord," Thomas said first, bowing low. Sean did the same.

"Good morn, lads," Lord Barry replied. He did not invite them to sit, so they stood where they were and quieted themselves.

Faolán shifted his chair around to face the earl more directly. "You were saying, Lord Barry, that you could not receive us?"

"It is unfortunate. Yes. I am sorry. But you must realize, in spite of your honorable intentions, a serious crime has been committed. Even though she has not, as you say, well…the perception and all that…I could not…I couldn't, ah, you must understand I am indebted to the Earl of Cork in many ways, not just financially. I did not…"

"But you knew we were coming, sir. We told you our plans before we even began, back at Barryscourt. It is all as we arranged." Faolán scratched a red streak from his chin to his collarbone. "You do remember you promised to support us, to speak for us to the Earl of Cork."

Lord Barry's eyes darkened. "It was some weeks past. I believe we were having a little fun, just a harmless little game. But only talk, and boasting. Yes. Boasting. That is all. I did not believe you were quite serious to do such a thing."

He turned toward the window. Thomas grunted, and Sean burst out, "But, good sir! We…we acted on trust that…as our kinsman you would…"

Faolán stood. "We did as we promised. We acted on trust that you would stand with us, see that the marriage was handled swiftly and legally, and help me negotiate with the earl thereafter. You will not?"

Lord Barry stood and took a few steps toward the fireplace, brushing his palm across the smooth marble mantel. "I...I can have no such intentions. Of course I thought it perfectly obvious to you. I owe my life to Sir Richard Boyle. He is my father-in-law, and he has covered...well, there was a rather significant gaming debt that he settled for me. These are enormous truths to begin with, but are the least of my reasons. He bought, you know, my wardship when I was just a boy, and saw that I was educated. And only a few years ago he...you understand, he secured my earldom with the king. The *king*. I cannot stand against him, and most certainly not in such a public way, or I could risk losing everything. You see that, don't you? I have received a letter, and Lord Cork is infuriated. To lose this heiress not only embarrasses him but will cost him dearly."

"And so you never..." Faolán's throat caught: he swallowed and started again. "You never intended to stand with us. You were just...just having us on for a merry little fantasy then."

Lord Barry sighed, and his shoulders dropped. "Good, good, you do understand. A debt such as this to Lord Cork is a terrible weight to bear. It is a merry fantasy indeed to think him tripped up this way. I did enjoy the idea of it, just as a borrower enjoys the demise of the lender. But I never thought to, well you see, to actually, ah. It simply cannot be. My wife, my children...I cannot be associated in any way."

Faolán fell back in his chair. "*Sard*. We are lost then."

Sean had turned an odd shade of green, and I was certain he would vomit, but he simply stood, staring at his relative. Thomas looked from Sean to Faolán and back to Lord Barry in disbelief. I realized my own hands had turned clammy and my mouth dry. The awkwardness and realization descended around us as a miasma we dared not breathe. Then came the knock on the chamber door.

"My lord Barry," the steward called. "The lady Vivienne FitzGerald to see you."

The doors opened and Vivienne stood before us, her skin glowing bright and pink as a healthy infant, her hair still damp on the ends and hanging in long copper ringlets to her waist. She wore a simple skirt of dark green fustian that seemed to fit well enough, and a jacket was trimmed in the same green and embroidered with black wool. It was a bit too broad for the shoulders but comely just the same. She smiled proudly as if dressed in the finest silk, her eyes sparkling like the Irish Sea in summer. She extended her hand in greeting, a soft and precious dove. "My lord, Earl Barrymore."

The earl stared at her, not breathing. The legs of Faolán's chair scraped the floor as he stood, while the rest of us offered our embarrassed bows. Faolán stood taller than ever, his jaw set, his eyes narrowed, his fists clenched. The earl regained his composure and kissed her hand.

"How delightful to meet you, my lady. The rumors of your beauty fall terribly short of your true loveliness. Please come in and sit down. You must rest yourself after such a journey." He gestured for Sean to bring a cushioned chair. "Steward! Bring us wine."

Vivienne looked to Faolán, offering a coy smile. She must have expected his admiration for her beauty now that she was scrubbed and groomed, her hair gleaming, but she saw his eyes and her smile faltered. Her lips parted as she recognized the tension in the room, and rested a hand on the chair back. "What is it? What is wrong here?"

The earl took a step backward and said nothing. Only Faolán found the words to speak.

"My lady, I am afraid I have misled you. Unintentionally, for certain, but it is so. Lord Barry has just explained he is unable to stand for us against the Earl of Cork. He has his reasons, but without his stature to defend us, we are but criminals in Lord Cork's eyes. I have troubled you deeply and put you through great hardship. I must find a way to return you home."

"No!" Vivienne blurted, her cheeks suddenly shot crimson, her eyes flashing. Faolán steadied her chair, but she refused to sit, and then suddenly she grabbed the arm of it and plopped into the seat in a huff. "I am not going home. I have no home, and you will not return me to that rectory. Not ever."

Faolán knelt on one knee before her. "Vivienne, it is my only wish to marry you, to be your husband, for the two of us to create a life together. But, without Lord Barry to arrange it for us..."

"A marriage may pose some difficulty. It cannot be performed here in my chapel," Lord Barry said, "and even if it could, the banns must be read. It would take weeks."

"If we are married legally, my love, Lord Cork will have no alternative but to acknowledge the union and provide you your inheritance," Faolán said.

"You would have to avoid capture all that time," Lord Barry continued. "He likely wants you hanged quite hastily, Faolán. He is writing letters. You'll be seen as an outlaw. The inheritance is attractive enough, as is the woman, such that even if it seems she has been damaged—if you will pardon my words, my lady—he still might try to negotiate a better match."

This time it was Faolán's face turning crimson with anger. He kept his eyes on Vivienne. "Marry me, and we will take our chances."

Vivienne faced Faolán fully, her eyes wide and glistening, but she did not answer.

"I cannot let you stay here, Faolán, not even for a night," Lord Barry said. "The servants will gossip and I will be seen as aiding your cause. I can't allow my name to be brought into this, nor any of my kin. That means Sean and Thomas cannot continue with you either. They are my clan: they bear my name."

At this, Sean and Thomas stood as if ready to fight. Thomas paced. Sean could not hold his tongue and shouted, "You agreed to this plan!"

Faolán did not even look at Lord Barry, but I could not help but glare at him. The man had sat with us by the fireside in Barryscourt Castle only weeks before, listened with pleasure to Faolán's ideas and plan of action, schemed with the four of us, and laughed at how angry Lord Cork would be. He had even suggested the friary at Timoleague as a good resting place after the abduction, and that he would wait for us at Rathmore. And now, now we were left flailing at the air.

"Will you go with me?" Faolán placed his hand over Vivienne's, and the room hummed with passions, or else it was my imagination, my ears ringing and my heart pounding. Their eyes were locked on each other, and I wondered why she hesitated, as if she dreamed she might yet escape each of these alternatives and somehow be alone and free. But for a woman, and this woman especially, the next phase of life depended on a marriage as surely as the ocean wave must crest before it surges to the strand. I gazed at her with hope that she would seize the moment, accept the risk that now beckoned her, grasp the adventure, and learn to love all the things about Faolán that I already knew but she had yet to discover.

"And yet, there may be another option I had not thought of before," Lord Barry said; his eyes widened with the surprise of his own idea. He sat again on the window seat, his back erect and his face more animated than before. "The Burkes are your kinsmen, correct?"

Of course Lord Barry knew the answer. Faolán did not respond but kept his focus on Vivienne's eyes.

"Ulick Burke is the son of Richard, the Earl of Clanricarde." Lord Barry scratched his beard thoughtfully. "The earl is an aged and sickly man, but he owns more land in Ireland than anyone else. He has great power in the government and is well-liked by King Charles. Thomas Wentworth is the king's new Lord Deputy in Dublin. He has been ravenous, picking away at old Richard's landholdings, looking for a means to either take the land for himself or secure it for the crown. It is driving the poor old earl to his bed."

Sean and Thomas stared at Lord Barry blankly, and Faolán did not waver, his gaze locked on Vivienne.

"The point is, Ulick represents his father's interests as the Clanricarde," Lord Barry continued, "and he hates no man better than Thomas Wentworth. Now, listen carefully. Because Lord Cork acquired Vivienne's wardship from the king and Wentworth must oversee her marriage on the king's behalf, it reflects quite poorly on both of them if she is not well settled."

He paused, apparently waiting for some response, but there was only silence.

"Do you not see?" Lord Barry said. "If, as your kinsman, he supports *your* side in this matter, Clanricarde can use it as a certain leverage, a sharp thorn he can lodge deeply in *Wentworth's* side—and then viciously twist. Should the king learn of Lord Cork's *mistakes*, shall we say, in allowing the lady to be abducted, and Lord Wentworth's poor oversight in managing the interests of this young lady, he would be quite angry and likely take Ulick's part. Ulick enjoys the king's favor far above Lord Cork and even Wentworth. Ulick very well may be your perfect ally to support the marriage and demand the settlement."

"Lord Barry, where might we find the Lord Ulick?" I asked, seeing that Faolán's attentions were detained. "Is he in Limerick?"

"Normally he is. The family seat is at Portumna," Lord Barry said, "but I have heard these days he is collecting on a gambling debt owed him by Sir John Jephson. Jephson owns the most desirable estate and castle at Mallow. Years ago, Queen Elizabeth gifted the castle with a herd of white fallow deer from Persia. Magnificent animals they are. Lord Clanricarde is hunting the finest specimens for his trophy room. I am sure this arrangement irks old Jephson endlessly." He smiled.

"Mallow," I repeated. "It must be several days' ride from here."

"It is a long journey, but only half as far as Limerick. A gamble of your own, mayhap, but well worth it, if he accepts the challenge."

"Mallow, Faolán." I put a bit of urgency into my voice, hoping to nudge his attention to what could be a grand solution. "The Earl of Clanricarde could arrange your wedding there and take up the case with

Lord Cork."

"It is your decision, Vivienne. I know marriage will change your life forever, and I only want you to do it willingly. You will be loved. Always. And I am asking you. Will you go to Mallow? And will you marry me there?" Faolán spoke softly, almost a whisper, and Vivienne's cheeks blushed until even my own began to heat. Her lips parted. We waited, all of us barely breathing.

"I will." She cupped his face in her hands. "And, Faolán, I *will* keep this promise."

Shouts rose to the ceiling: *Maith thú! Moh hoo! Moh hoo! Good for you! Well-done!*

It was a joy long awaited and gratefully received, even if it was to be short-lived.

Chapter Ten

Across the River Ilen

It is a wise father that knows his own child.

~ William Shakespeare

Though we were weary of travel and disturbed by the change of plans, Vivienne's decision made all things seem possible again, and therefore less of a blow when Lord Barry refused to house us even for a night. Instead, he sent us off with a parcel of bread and cheese, a bladder of wine, and a wish that we would not return. The sad irony tarnishing everything was, through no effort of his own, Mister Jeffrey Eames had now got his way. Thomas and Sean were headed to their mother's house a few miles west of Rathmore, reducing our traveling party by two.

Our destination now was Mallow Castle, but the route would lead directly through our home village, just a few hours ride away. It was still risky to go there, but we were tired, it was home, and Faolán was eager for Vivienne to see it. *An Sciobairín*, or Skebreen as we called it. How I would welcome the sight.

As small as it was, no finer village ever hugged the banks of a river. The McCarthys had always known that, for they owned most of the lands around this part of the province and leased out a few choice spots to the crofters and drovers, it being fertile and fairly flat for easy farming. For the fishermen, the sea was just a few miles away by curragh. The bridge over the Ilen had once connected three great castles that guarded the lands and commerce in the region. But the castles had fallen in battles long forgotten, and the old bridge timbers had been replaced and supported with stone masonry in some places to support the hay wagons, sheep flocks, and wayfarers who crossed it. The result was a village of lively conversation, storytelling and gossip.

After the pirate attack on Baltimore in 1631, a few survivors abandoned that seaside village and increased Skebreen's population, but mostly it remained a closely knit and unchartered hamlet. Which is not to say we were quiet. The McCarthys had always welcomed the O'Dalys for the quality of our spirits, both the drinking and the ancestral kind, and they liked their cups at the inn where both were appreciated.

On the south bank of the Ilen, my father's inn thrived with business when there were market days at Macroom or Bandon, especially on the return trip if sellers had sold their goods for a worthy price. Faolán's home was northeast of the bridge. Here Sir William had been granted a vast parcel of land, on which he set the foundation for his castle and called it Glencurragh—meaning a place for small boats. The castle tower would have looked upon the river and the fishing boats heading out to sea, but Sir William never lived to see it. He was barely in his grave before the scavengers carted away most of the foundation stones.

Faolán built his own small cottage against what remained of one of the bailey walls. Of stone, daub, and wattle, it had a good thatch roof and a single window, a sturdy hearth, and a clever vent to funnel smoke out behind the house instead of through the doorway. He'd fashioned a fine door of solid wood to help keep out the cold. I myself had planted the faery thorn just outside that door to ward off evil, and it had developed into a healthy shrub that would one day be a graceful and lovely tree.

Faolán and I were proud of our village, but I worried the lady Vivienne might find nothing to impress her in either the inn or the cottage. I prayed she could be enchanted first by our river, that it would soften her heart for the rest. She would sense the ancient spirits about it, for I sensed them myself every time I gazed on the sparkling waters: spirits of abundance and fertility, urging the tiniest head of fern or milkweed to rise up to the sun. Spirits of war, surging forth with great strength, bombarding the rocks and pounding the river bottom until it released its captive souls, sometimes swelling the river to such a fury she roared forth in a thunderous gush and swept away all that lay between Skebreen and the sea. But in truth, these spirits only turned darker when threatened, as is so with all wild creatures.

After the spirits, the many sounds of the river would seduce her. The gentle stroking of the shore, the clear tinkling of little bells rippling about when a soft breeze blew, or the rushing in spring like the blood in your veins when passions or excitements ignite your soul. And the birds—always singing their songs about the Ilen, and chirping their praises and thanks for her bounty. Surely the first time Vivienne walked to the river from the cottage door, she would delight in these sounds, and with her bare feet feel the soft green moss and the cool amber waters. She would lose her heart to it, our Ilen.

When the church steeple at the village square could be seen above the trees, the midday bells announced prayer time. The alehouse was our first stop, but we approached cautiously lest there be a sheriff's emissary coming to find us there. Seeing no unfamiliar horses or carriage outside, it was possible they were in the byre, so we took the precaution of tying our horses in the back. Inside, my father was serving a meal and a jar of ale to Mister FitzGibbon, the village elder. He glanced up, one eye opening wide, his thin white hair a shambles about his head and his old brown cardigan smeared with grease.

"Father," I said, nodding respectfully. But he simply grunted, inspected Faolán and Vivienne with a frown, and glared back at me.

"Father, may I introduce the lady Vivienne FitzGerald."

He nodded to her, grunted again, and gestured to a table by the door where we might sit. He shuffled slowly to his worktable and returned with ale and bread, then turned away.

"Father, can ye talk with us?"

He faced me, the one eye wide, sharp, and fierce, the other nearly closed by a sagging brow. "Well now, some of us have work to do."

"I know. I've been away but a few days, Father. I'll be back to help you soon."

"So then, yer not back yet. Where ha' ye been?"

"We were to collect the lady Vivienne for Faolán, sir. As I told you."

Faolán took Vivienne's hand. "Mister O'Daly, Vivienne and I mean to be wed."

I glanced at Mister FitzGibbon who was slowly eating his peas and drinking his ale, but I had no doubt he took in every word. Mister Fitz-Gibbon knew everything that happened in Skebreen, and a good distance beyond. He wrote letters and received them, and was considered the wisest among us. Father paid him no heed. He scanned each of our faces as he scratched the back of his head, his whiskered jaw shifting from side to side. "Let me see now. I believe there was a fella, days back, askin' particular for our Faolán here, and lookin' fer a lady. Can't recall the feller's name."

"Did he wear a broad felt hat, this fella?" Faolán asked.

My father looked him up and down, and then turned his scornful eye back to me.

"A broad hat. I believe he did, so. Said a crime ha' been done, with a hangin' ta follow, is what he said."

Mister FitzGibbon's gaze lifted from his supper to Vivienne and Faolán, and back down again. He was paying sharp attention, was he.

"Am I ta unnerstand, Aengus, ye been out on some holiday, have ye? Runnin' wild? An' me here wi' work ta be done and no help but fer yer sister comin' in when she pleases to wash a few tankards and be off again dilly-dallyin'. Now here ye are an' there's trouble. Did I not warn ye time and again, son?"

"Father!" I knew I sounded anxious, and a bit embarrassed in front of Vivienne. Faolán had witnessed such talk many times before, but now there was a more serious nature to it, being that my pale father's cheeks were red with fury. "We've been gone but a few days, as I told you before we left."

"Nigh onto two weeks now! Ye told me ye were off wi' Faolán on some business, not out running with yer friends and pickin' up wee lassies who got no business wi' the likes o' you folk!"

"We've been to see Lord Barry at Rathmore. He promised he would stand with us, and there's no crime done if he…"

"A waste a time, that, an' I could ha' told ye so. He sent ye away, I can see it plain. Did ye not know already he would not risk a penny for ye? Not with the Earl of Cork as a father-in-law. Fools, all of ye. So, when are ye comin' back ta work?"

"Soon, but not yet. We must go to Mallow to see Lord Ulick Burke of Clanricarde, Faolán's kin."

"Hopin' mebbe for a different answer than ye got from Lord Barry. Well then. A fool's journey never ends."

I looked down at the table. I did not have a smart answer for him, fearing as he did that Lord Burke might cast us off as well. Getting no response from me, Father turned on Faolán.

"An' you, Faolán Burke, with yer fine horse and grand ideas. Yer father and mother. What would they be sayin' to ye now? Sir William spent years buildin' a reputation on honor, fightin' skills, and hard work, not freebootin' like ye done. Ye've disgraced them, haven't ye? And drawn Aengus to ruination besides."

Faolán's face turned dark as ash. "Sir, our goal was to lift everyone up, not pull us down. I am in love with Vivienne, I mean to be honorable by her, and we've done nothing to dishonor..."

"Bah!" Father cast his hand out over us as if to shoo away a swarm of flies. "Love, in this day an' age." He looked back at me. "I s'pose now I'll be needin' Sheelagh ta come take over the inn: can't depend on me only son who'll be swingin' from a tree or a scaffold soon enough."

"Sheelagh! She could not possibly...what has she said to you?" I blurted, my face no doubt turning green. I loved my sister but she missed no opportunity to tarnish me in Father's eyes to make herself look the brighter, and yet she could no more manage the alehouse properly than grow her own cock.

"What matter, Aengus? God rest yer mother that she cannot see the terrible place we've come. Take the bread and go. I canna have criminals here a-frightenin' off the good townsfolk. My son can come back to me when he's prepared to be a proper man, and not before."

A proper man. We'd had this discussion before as well. A fellow my age should be looking to earn his living and marry, he'd say. Should be having children, and they to produce the grandchildren he could look upon as his lasting legacy before he dies. Should be tending my home, our crops, learning the secrets of the trade to brew the spirits that are the blood of our livelihood. I should be an anchor of our community, lusty, strong, and wise, so the villagers would come to my father and compliment him on his fine upstanding son. I should have been more than the slump-shouldered quiet boy I was. I should have been more of everything. I should have been born a different person.

I glanced at Vivienne, who had been silent through all of this, sipping her ale and watching our faces. I feared she would hate us now, all of our shortcomings held up for her to see, but she lifted her hand to my father.

"Mister O'Daly. I thank you for the food and drink: it is truly a kindness. I must thank your fine son for bringing me here. It has been my pleasure to meet you. I bid you good health, and promise we will meet again."

My father, still steaming with his anger, appeared stunned. He looked at her hand, then her face, then her hand again. At last, saving us all from even greater embarrassment, he straightened his shoulders and took her fingers in his. Though he did not kiss her hand, he bowed his head to her.

"I bid you well, m' lady." He turned and walked away.

We stood to leave, collecting what remained of the bread for our journey. Mister FitzGibbon waved us over to his table. Wiping a bit of ale from his lower lip, he looked to Faolán.

"Ye've a difficult road ahead, lad, wi' Lord Barry the least of yer troubles. Yer headin' into a crossfire not of yer makin'. I advise ye to heed the wind at yer heels and ride it through. Lord Burke is testy but wise, and not likely to turn his back on a good fellow." He stood up from his bench with some difficulty, coughed, cleared his throat, and made an awkward bow to Vivienne. "A safe journey to you, my lady. Your feet will bring you to where your heart is."

Chapter Eleven

Knowing

In this wood I observed and tasted of the dew
which fell upon the oak leaves, which glistened
and shined and tasted like honey.

~ Sir William Brereton

We crossed the bridge amid sounds of the dark water washing gently against the piers, the horses' hooves clomping, and the wind rustling through the trees along the mossy banks. The wind lifted my hat and chilled my scalp. Faolán was in the lead, moving more slowly than before, his shoulders sagging, his head tilted. Behind him even Dunerayl's head was low as he carried Vivienne toward his home. He might have been glad for the familiar place and a signal that his journey was done, but instead he plodded like a tired old plow horse.

I had longed to see the sights of home, but now I cared little for any of it, bruised in the heart, shamed before Faolán and Vivienne. Who was I to think I might do something more in life than spend all my days serving ale under my father's stern eye? Who was I to imagine we were clever or gallant? We were not. And I had fallen for Faolán's dreams when I should have known from the start I was not meant for something better. I was a village idiot, a pretender, and a poor son, and here it all was for everyone to see. Surely I deserved a hanging if it come to that, for I had nothing of value to contribute to the world and would be missed by no one after I was gone. As we reached the bridge, a crow on the ground watched us pass, cocking his head to and fro as if we were a funeral procession and he wondered who had died.

"No one of consequence," I told him, and spat upon the ground.

"What did you say, Aengus?" Vivienne asked.

"Nothing, my lady. Just nudging my horse."

Faolán turned in his saddle to call to us. "It's just a bit farther. At the curve before the main road and just over the rise. I'll be glad to see it. We're all in need of a rest."

Faolán's eyes were dark, his face ruddy, his voice almost apologetic. I was wrapped so much in myself I'd not considered what he might be thinking. How could my father, who had known Faolán his whole life, cast so piercing a dart into the lad's breast, comparing his actions to Sir William's lifelong accomplishments? And in the presence of Vivienne, to bring him so low as an errant boy, with him yet to have the lady's hand in marriage? She had said yes, but there were many miles to go during which she could easily change her mind. Where was he to go? How was he to win her from this sad and sunken place?

We approached the house through a thin, lingering mist, the horses clopping over the exposed stones in the yard. The thatch on the roof had turned from brown to ashen gray, but the sturdy door was a welcome sight. Water drained in a rivulet that skirted the right side of the house, crossed between the flagstones leading to the door and continued on a downhill path in front of the faerie thorn. I reminded myself to warn Vivienne that the faerie thorn guarded the house, but it was unlucky and dangerous to touch. Grown men had lost entire limbs if not their lives for disturbing such a tree.

Faolán dismounted first and lifted Vivienne from Dunerayl. "I'll take him," I offered, reaching for the bridle and giving the two of them a private moment as he brought her into his home. A crude shelter to the west of the house would be a bit crowded with three horses for the night, but it surpassed what they'd had in nights before this. They'd be back on the road tomorrow and would need their rest. I took my time getting them unsaddled, watered, and fed. From the time we had collected Vivienne I did not know of any time she and Faolán had been truly alone. If he could find a way to redeem himself in her eyes, now was the time, before we found Lord Clanricarde.

I hoped to find them in each other's arms, but it was wishful thinking at best. The two were silent, Vivienne sitting in Faolán's only chair, Faolán crouched next to a bench lighting a fire in the hearth. Gray light from the window cast shadows across the small table and cabinet. Rushes on the floor were old and musty. His bed was in disarray. He'd left his home on a glorious mission, expecting to be well housed at Lord Barry's until he was wed. There should have been time and money later to prepare the home for his love. As it was, it can only have compounded his shame before her.

"Is there food or drink, Faolán?"

"Sorry, Aengus. Only what we brought from your da's place. I'll fetch some water once the fire's going."

"I'll go."

"May I join you, Aengus? I'd like to wash a little," Vivienne asked.

"Of course. You'll love the river."

"Keep a wary eye, Aengus," Faolán warned, and continued stoking the fire.

Vivienne followed me down the path so crossed with brown vines it would be difficult to distinguish if one did not already know the way. Soon enough we could hear the river rippling against its banks and the constant flow like an exhale that never ends. We ducked beneath low branches and down to the gray pebble slope, where Faolán sometimes stored a small curragh for crossing the river. Across from there a tiny mud and stone island supported three or four spindly birch trees and a thick blanket of green moss.

"Faolán and I spent many an hour tossing pebbles across to that island," I told her. "There should have been enough to build our own bridge by now."

Vivienne picked up a pebble and cast it toward the island. It plunked into the water just short of the exposed fern roots at its edge. Then she knelt to wash her delicate hands and wrists with such grace I longed to reach down and touch them. They were wrong, these thoughts, but I could not keep them from coming.

"Aengus, do you believe your father loves you?"

My breath caught in my throat suddenly. I hadn't expected such a question. Though I was angry and hurt by him, the answer was immediate and plain.

"I do."

"I am glad. I believe so as well. He fears for you, and worries he might lose you. He doesn't know how to say it: that's the reason he's so coarse. It must be fortunate to have such a parent, even after the quarrel you've had."

"I must say, at the moment I do not feel so fortunate."

"I know, but you are. You have the position of honor as his son. You will always be the one who carries his hopes and dreams. I see it plainly and it will never change."

"I am a disappointment."

She reached into the water and allowed it to play through her open fingers back to its source. "All that will pass, Aengus. It will be all right again, I'm sure of it."

"What makes you so? Have you seen something?"

"No, it's but a knowing, a strong one. It's difficult to explain, but in my head I just know. The bond between you is strained, but not weakened. You've probably had such a feeling before."

"I have, yes."

"Do you know, then, whether Faolán truly loves me?"

"Oh, Vivienne." I looked into her sad, doe eyes. "He's loved you from the moment he saw you. He has been unable to sleep since and has talked of you night and day. There is nothing he has wanted more in his life than you. It may have been your beauty and your inheritance that first drew him to you, but by the blood of my father, I swear it. Faolán is truly in love."

She broke from my gaze and focused on the water. "He has barely spoken to me since we left Lord Barry's house. I know he is troubled, but I've begun to wonder if he may be regretting his choices."

"Why would he do that?"

"Because he is ashamed of what he has done, and now feels trapped by it."

"Trapped is not the word. More likely he fears he will not succeed. Vivienne, do you love him?"

She sighed. "I believe we are meant to be together, but I have never known much about love. I only know that my skin tingles when he touches me, and when he doesn't speak I'm afraid." She backed a step away from the river and dried her hands on her skirt.

"But do you *love* him? I am hardly one to advise on matters of love, but I know if you don't love him, you must tell him straightaway. And if you think you might, go to him. Look into his eyes for your answer. Talk to him as we're talking now. If, after this, his feelings aren't clear, then you'll have your own choices to make. But I'm sure you'll have your knowing."

I filled a gourd with water and we returned to the house. Faolán had a fire blazing on the hearth and had straightened his bed and the rest of the house; the mustiness was gone and the sweet scent of a pine bough in its place. Vivienne marched up to him, touched his face and laid her hand on his shoulder. She looked into his eyes just as I had suggested.

"Faolán, are you well?"

His lips parted and his shoulders stiffened as if he would push her away from him. But then he exhaled slowly and settled his hands about her waist as a fallen petal settles to the earth. She moved closer.

Chapter Twelve

Dreams Remembered

*Into her dream he melted, as the rose
blendeth its odour with the violet.*

~ John Keats

We ate our bread by firelight. I rubbed my brow, feigning greater fatigue than I truly felt. "My eyes seem to be closing by their own weight. I'll lay my bedroll just there by the kitchen," I told them. Their eyes seemed bright, and I wished I could at once leave them their privacy and stay near to know what would happen between them. I closed my eyes and managed to produce a soft snore that they might forget my presence, yet I lay awake with my ears perked. It was a foul invasion on my part, but I could not help myself. Faolán was first to speak.

"I have set your bed for you Vivienne. It should be quite comfortable after the long day we have had. I'll lay on the floor beside you."

"I am sorry to take your bed," she said softly.

"Do not concern yourself, love. Tonight I could lie on a bed of spikes and would hardly know the difference. I shall sleep. And in the dawn, I will take you wherever you want to go."

"Wherever I want to go? I thought our plan was to find Lord Clanricarde at Mallow."

Faolán did not respond, and a silence settled between them except for the scrapings and clunking sound as the kindling crumbled—Faolán poking ineffectively at the fire. How many times had he made me wait for an answer in exactly this way?

"Faolán? Are we not?"

Faolán heaved a sigh. "Why do you stay with me?"

"I believe you abducted me."

"Yes, I did. But I have not held you prisoner. You could have run away many times. You could have stayed with Lord Barry if you had wanted. He'd love to have been the hero who returned you to Lord Cork. By now the truth is clear. I have little to offer a beautiful heiress who is accustomed to finery. I have this little plot of land, a pittance from what my father once owned. This tiny, dark cottage. A decent horse. An empty larder. Ambitious dreams without promise. That is all. It is nothing. You are free to do as you please, and I will no longer try to convince you to stay with me. Just say where it is you want to go, and I will take you there."

For a few moments, only the crackle of the burning turf broke the silence. Then Vivienne spoke.

"I thought you had a few things more when we met. Honor, for one. You've never harmed me but always protected me, and I've been at your mercy."

"I haven't violated you, if that's what you mean. But I did steal you from your bed."

"And then I would say kindness. Remember those horrid shoes you made for me?"

Faolán huffed. "And you would call that a kindness?"

"Things might have been worse. And then I would add bravery. You protected me from that Eames fellow."

"I should have killed him when I had the chance."

"But you're not a murderer."

"No."

"There is another thing you had when we began."

"Aye, and what is that?"

"Hope."

"Hmm. I see. There's something useful."

"Critical, I would say. For any successful man."

"I suppose I left that back at Rathmore with Lord Barry, along with my pride."

"Ah, that sounds more like self-pity, then. Are you a man so easily defeated?"

There was silence, and then a deep inhale. Faolán's voice was strained.

"Vivienne, I care for you, but you deserve much more than I seem destined for. I wanted to create for you what my father had intended for my mother. A sparkling palace with warmth, plentiful food, all the comforts of royalty, a strong and loyal clan, and prosperity for everyone. He had such a wondrous vision, and the power to build it. Mister O'Daly made it quite clear today: I can never be the warrior my father was. The world is different now. The best I can do for you and for myself is to return you to your right and true life. I cannot drag you down into mine."

They fell silent again but for some rustling of clothes and the rushes on the floor.

"Faolán," Vivienne said, "do you truly want to know why I have stayed with you?"

"I do, though I suppose it doesn't matter now."

"The night you came for me. Do you remember what night it was?"

"It was a Friday. I do not recall the exact date, no."

"Friday, January twentieth. There was a new moon. It was the Eve of St. Agnes. What do the lassies all over the land do on that day?"

Dear God, I wanted to jump up and shout, for I knew where she was headed, but I held my tongue. I gave a light snort and continued my pretended sleep.

"I don't know," Faolán said. The dolt.

"I am wrong then. I thought you had intentionally planned it. If a young lady wishes to know the man she will marry, she must perform certain rituals on the Eve of St. Agnes. She must go without her supper. Just before midnight she must light a candle and say a prayer to St. Agnes, asking her to kindly reveal the future. Then she must remove every shred of clothing until she is completely naked, lie in bed on her back with her hands beneath her pillow, and look up into the heavens. If she does everything just right, she will dream of her true husband. She will see his face."

Faolán must have been looking at her with confusion, because she still had to explain.

"Faolán, how did you find me that night? Was there a candle burning? Was I unclothed? Did I slumber beneath the window? St. Agnes sent me a dream, and I saw *you* that night, exactly as you are right now, the fire lighting your eyes, the wonder on your face, the strength in your hands. I saw *you*. And if I had not recognized your face from the first moment when you sat me on your horse, you can be sure you'd have had a nightmare on your hands. But why should I fight my true destiny when he holds me in his arms?"

"But you did try, that once with Dunerayl, after we left Timoleague."

"It's true. I did. There have been many times I have wanted to mount a horse and gallop away, never to stop. Of the demands and expectations heaved upon a woman, and the limitations, you would have no idea. I've often felt no better than a slave. That day there was a moment when my heart saw an opening. I would not have been running away from you, but running toward another life."

"Yet you stayed."

"You made it clear I would not get far, and without money or escort I could easily find myself in far worse conditions. And so, I put my trust in St. Agnes."

Faolán sighed. "And did St. Agnes happen to mention a life of terrible squalor?"

"Hush, Faolán. You will rise up from where you are today. You're a resourceful man. Besides, I'm interested in what Lord Clanricarde has to say. You asked me where I want to go? Mallow, that's where. But for now, I am cold. Come and lay down beside me and warm me until we fall asleep."

"Are you not concerned that my passion will overtake me?"

"Oh, I am still safe, at least until Mallow. And I have three very good reasons to believe so. First of all, we are not exactly alone. Aengus is listening to every word we say; he is terrible at feigning sleep."

I popped my eyes open in surprise, and Vivienne laughed.

"There, you see? And second, if we are to be married, a certain degree of closeness is acceptable. Especially on a cold night such as this. And third, the plain fact is that it doesn't matter now, Faolán, because I know this is my destiny. I am meant to be with you, and I will never leave you."

Without hesitation, Faolán whisked her into his arms and carried her to the bed. He cast me a wink. I closed my eyes and listened to the crackle of settling coals. It was time truly to sleep, for what happened between them after that I did not need to know.

Chapter Thirteen

Mallow Castle

*The land of Ireland is uneven, mountainous, soft, watery, woody,
and open to winds and floods of rain, and so fenny as it hath
bogs on the very tops of mountains, not bearing
man or beast, but dangerous to pass...*

~ Fynes Moryson

The way from Skebreen to Mallow was more troublesome than any parts of our journey thus far. The first leg of it, heading northeast to Macroom, was fairly swift. Macroom had been a meeting place for the druids centuries ago, but now the road was well worn by farmers taking grain and corn to be milled and by merchants taking goods to the market center. Between Macroom and Mallow lay the Boggeragh Mountains, with pathways far less traveled and entirely, it seemed to me, uphill.

Faolán led us, carefully picking through steep and rocky switchbacks. Strange voices and the scent of fresh manure warned me that we approached a rebel camp. They might not harm Faolán and me, but would surely relieve us of our money and horses. Vivienne, on the other hand, faced a serious danger. Faolán held his pistol ready, but when we turned the bend we laughed, for it was only a group of cows grumbling to each other, their numbers well hidden in a natural rock enclosure. Several of them looking up at us through the sopping ferns and gorse.

We continued on, and all the while it rained until we were drenched to the skin, until the bright green trees and tangled vines seemed to close in about us, streaming and dripping as if continuously washed by God's watercolors. And then the way before us lost all definition, fading to white within the thick wet mists.

Beyond the mountains at last, the land opened up to puddled bogs and expansive, heathered moors. At Lombardstown we turned due east, and then Mallow was just a few miles distant. Faolán's steady inner compass guided us for two and a half days until we approached the castle, its three dark towers cutting a black outline from the dim gray sky. The closer we drew, the more magnificent the structure. On all sides were dramatic Tudor windows with small square panes, but the FitzGeralds of Desmond had held the grounds of Mallow long before the Tudors, since the thirteenth century. Their lives were of cautionary legend now, and Vivienne a living vestige. She slowed her horse to walk beside me.

"Something happened here, Aengus. Something stirs of fear and desperation, even through the peace of the meadows. There is hate here. And a terrible sorrow."

Faolán reined his horse, stopping in front of us. "Vivienne, Lord Cork has withheld from you your own history. Mallow Castle once belonged to the FitzGeralds. Sir John lived here. It was he, the Earl of Desmond's brother, who led the men into battle during the great rebellion."

"What became of him?" Vivienne asked.

"He was cruelly betrayed," he said. "The FitzGeralds fought the English for control of their own clansmen and lands, and John was known for uniting the clans against them. One day he set out on this very road, but he and his men were surprised by a band of English horsemen. They tried to escape, but one man among the English—once Sir John's own servant—recognized Sir John and shot him in the throat. He died as they carried his body back to Cork, and they chained it to the city gate."

Vivienne turned pale, her lips parted. "And what of the earl?"

Faolán jutted his chin at me. "Tell her, Aengus."

"He was betrayed as well. A local farmer took a thousand silver pieces in exchange for the earl's location in the mountains near Tralee. When the English soldiers found him, crippled and broken in the corner of an old cabin, they murdered him and sent his head to London as a trophy for the queen."

"Aye, and that's not the end of it, Aengus," Faolán said.

I nodded. "On a dark November night in the glen where he was killed, you'll see a company of horsemen and the great earl, wearing his silver brocade and riding a white horse. And if a lad asks to shoe his horse, the earl will toss him a purse with a thousand silver pieces."

Vivienne sat stiffly, looking toward Mallow. "Now I'm afraid to enter this castle."

Faolán shook his head. "On the contrary, love. You are a FitzGerald. The Desmond spirits will rise up and rejoice when you set foot on the stones. It is just."

She took a deep breath. "I had not thought of it that way. My stomach flutters. I will think of it as excitement, rather than fear. It is redemption."

Faolán smiled. "Not fully, not yet, but it is a step toward it. We'll be honored to stand beside you."

And so we crossed the stout bridge over the River Blackwater. The great stone walls were increasingly imposing as we approached, the three towers on the west side rising like giant fists that might come pounding down on our heads, and on the north, a great clock tower heralded the passage of time and questioned our worthiness. We entered through a stone gate where others passed in and out freely, and were halted by a guard.

"State your business," the man shouted.

"We are sent by the Earl of Barrymore with news for Ulick Burke, of Clanricarde," Faolán said.

"Sir John Jephson lives here. He is not in residence. Go away and return another time."

"We do not seek Sir Jephson. Lord Clanricarde is hunting here. It is *his* presence we seek. Our message is urgent."

The guard scowled but allowed entry. We passed through and found ourselves in a large barbican. On our right was a muddied yard and stable. Faolán repeated to the porter our business with Clanricarde, and our mounts were taken to the stable yard. A huge wooden door on the right opened into a smaller court and the castle house, with vaulted cellars on the ground and stairs leading up to the great hall.

We waited at the foot of the stairs while the porter informed a steward of our presence. All the while the work of the castle bustled and churned around us. Men pushed carts full of goods or refuse amid the constant creak and clang of provisions being delivered to the kitchen. Women with baskets sought the laundry or hurried across the yard for the kitchen garden. Chickens clucked and squawked; dogs gamboled about and roamed freely, sniffing for any discarded crumb. Heavy smoke billowed from chimneys and mixed with the acrid odors of human and horse excrement, and yet I could catch a passing scent of rich broth from the boiling-house, and of baking bread.

Across the trampled yard, the stable master argued with the saltpeter men collecting horse droppings as an ingredient for the king's gunpowder. Children of the servants tossed sticks and kicked balls, tumbling into the mud puddles and bouncing back up again to chase their playmates with screams, threats, and laughter. We waited nearly an hour until the steward found us.

"We wish to see Sir Ulick of Clanricarde. We bring important news from the Earl of Barrymore," Faolán said.

The steward regarded us suspiciously. We were Irish of course, rugged and tired, but Faolán had experience aplenty bringing messages to the English gentry. He stood tall and glared at the young servant.

The servant blinked. "Give me your letter. I will deliver it."

"That is not possible," Faolán said, leaning forward.

Vivienne, waiting on a bench beside the stairs, rose to her feet making rather a big fuss of fluttering and arranging her skirts. She pushed back her hood to reveal her splendid hair, and her open cloak showed the fine garment beneath.

"I beg your pardon." She spoke directly to the steward. "There is no letter, and I am the message in my person. I am Lady Vivienne FitzGerald, to see Lord Clanricarde. He will have heard of me, and he will be most displeased to learn you have kept us waiting all this time. Have a care, sir, when deciding whom you'll disrespect. Our memory is long."

The steward appraised her from her visage to her muddied boots, and took such a swallow his Adam's apple traveled the full length of his neck and bobbed back to the middle. "Follow me, my lady." Faolán and I followed the swish of Vivienne's skirt across the stone floor of the great hall. A hearth fire burned brightly and maids bustled about cleaning and polishing furniture, sweeping out the corners and replenishing wood for the fire. We stepped into a smaller room with gleaming wood planks, tapestries on the walls, and a great chandelier hanging low from the beams. A fire burned in a grate on the far wall. Benches lined the sidewalls and chairs with embroidered cushions positioned oddly in twos and threes, as if groups of people had arranged them for conversation.

"Please wait and I will collect you when my lord is ready to receive you. There is wine on the sideboard, and one may refresh himself behind the partition. What shall I say is the purpose of your visit?"

She sighed heavily and looked to us and then back to the steward. She spoke very slowly as if to a dullard. "Tell him it is the Lady Vivienne Fitz-Gerald. That is all."

We'd arrived in midafternoon, timed so that the men had finished their midday meal, followed by some mead or French wine. "Best they be well-fed and somewhat bored, and with any luck feeling a bit generous after the drink," Faolán said. "We have a second chance here, and it'll be our last one. We *must* bring him to our cause."

The rains had stopped but for occasional showers and sprays carried on the wind. Gray light filtered through droplets on the windows and dappled the floor with soft, fanciful shapes. I was dazed and too comfortable in the warm room. Fatigue and drowsiness overtook me. I floated for a time between sublime reverie and a disturbing flutter of my heart. Faolán shook my shoulder until I roused, and I followed him into the next chamber.

We entered through a side door into a room small by comparison to those we had seen thus far. To our left was a three-arch window overlooking the privy garden, and to our right an alcove with gilt carvings around its frame and a single armchair. Here sat himself, Sir Ulick of Clanricarde. The steward gestured for us to bow, while Vivienne dipped low with her hand outstretched. The steward announced Vivienne—and her escorts.

Clanricarde nodded for us to stand, for there were no other chairs in the room. At first he seemed an enormous person, broad of pockmarked cheek and muscled shoulder, but it was an illusion. A sunbreak angled through the window, falling brightly upon his oversize upholstered chair, positioned several inches above the floor on a dais inside the alcove. He was dressed entirely in black but for the white collar that overlay his doublet, the wide brown belt at his waist and the fine leather hunting boots. An embroidered gray cloak swept back from his shoulders made him seem larger, like the wings of a hawk coming to roost. His gray beard was large and bushy, trimmed to a long rectangle from his lower lip to midchest. His nose was hawklike as well, pointed and narrow, but above the cheeks his dark eyes declared him a proud Burke and without question Faolán's kinsman.

Vivienne stood slightly in front of us. Lord Clanricarde's eyes focused on her and I was glad for it, not quite prepared to withstand his penetrating stare. We dared not speak until asked, and with clasped hands we waited the long moments while he considered us.

"And so," he said at last, "you are the young lady heiress who has confounded the Earl of Cork. Is that so?"

Vivienne nodded. "May I speak, my lord?"

"Please."

"I am Vivienne FitzGerald, and yes, I am the ward of Lord Cork. Beside me are Faolán Burke, your kinsman, and Aengus O'Daly of Skebreen. We are sent by Lord Barry to seek your assistance. Faolán and I wish to be married."

"Sir," Faolán said, bowing again. He was ignored.

"I am told you were abducted from your bed, my lady. Is this true?"

"I must confess it is so, sir, but I am well cared for and I stand before you by choice. I believe it is God's intention that I marry Mister Burke, though it may be against Lord Cork's wishes. Lord Barry had promised to speak for us, but he feared to offend his father-in-law, and so he has recommended us to you."

"Well, then, has he now? The scoundrel. And why should I be involved in your plight? I see no obvious reason. Why should I not just deliver you as you are to Lord Cork?"

"If I may, sir?" Faolán asked.

"You may."

"Lord Cork purchased Vivienne's wardship from King Charles. In Ireland, Cork's marriage arrangement for her must be overseen by the king's deputy, Thomas Wentworth. Lord Barry believed this might be of interest to you."

A man laughed, though it was not Clanricarde and no one else was in the room. Faolán looked disconcerted but continued.

"As a proud man of Burke blood, I beg your personal consideration of my marriage suit, for without your support it will be suicide to go up against them."

Clanricarde huffed. "Most decidedly it would," he said. "Tell me, my lady, why do you want to marry this lad?"

"It may sound strange, but it is because I saw him in a dream, sir."

Again a laugh, and Clanricarde raised his brows at someone inside the alcove, and smiled.

"In a dream. Is that all?"

Vivienne's face reddened, but her voice remained steady. "I believe in my heart he is my destiny. I have come to know something of his person and his honor in these past weeks. He has cared for me and protected me, and I believe he will treat me well."

"His *honor*? An abductor? Even if he is a kinsman I cannot condone any act of..."

The man in the alcove reached out and touched Clanricarde's shoulder. "Might I..." he asked.

"I s'pose you might, my friend, for you surely cannot keep your silence," Clanricarde said.

Chapter Fourteen

The Earl's Design

*Faithfulness and truth are the most sacred excellences
and endowments of the human mind.*

~ Cicero

"Eavesdropping is no enjoyment if one wants to ask questions and cannot," said the man who emerged from the alcove's shadows.

He looked to be in his midtwenties, close in age to Faolán and me. It may have been the sunlight from the windows or the tension of the moment, but something about him was different. He was perhaps the most remarkable man I'd ever seen. His brown hunting breeches and a dark damask frock coat were of obvious quality. His blond hair tumbled in waved locks past his shoulders. Fair brows, his nose well sculpted, and then a strong jaw and chin to bond these features in a visage both sensitive and robust. But more remarkable than his appearance alone was the certainty in his presence. His stance was not arrogant, but approachable. His gaze not distant, but searching, as if he looked through the surface of things where most men wouldn't bother. He sought truths. This was a man of honor who championed the rightness of things above profit.

Clanricarde gestured, as if casting a playing card at our feet. "Gentlemen and lady, I introduce to you my great friend, my lord James Butler, who has ascended to the earldom of Ormonde, and joins me here from his castle along the River Suir."

I knew a little something of Ormonde. His father had drowned when he was a child, and so the title came to him directly upon the death of his elderly grandfather, Walter Butler, about a year ago. While

Clanricarde owned most of the territories from Limerick to Galway and well to the north, the Ormonde lands stretched from Wexford to Kildare and then fanned out across a vast area that shared a border with Clanricarde at the great lake, Lough Derg. It was said Ormonde owned more than thirty manors and houses, and half as many abbeys. Both of these men had descended from nobility spanning at least two centuries. I was awed to be in such a presence. What would it be like to have the power and wealth of these men, the confidence of their decisions, the ability to move others to action on a word? Ormonde smiled softly at Vivienne, and then turned his attention to Faolán.

"Mister Burke, you say you are a kinsman of Lord Clanricarde. What is your lineage?"

"My Lord, you may know of my great aunt, Mary Bourke, whose properties lie along the River Blackwater near your home. I am the only son of Sir William Burke, who served the Earl of Clanricarde faithfully until his death fourteen years ago. As such I am an heir of Clan MacWilliam de Burgo."

"I knew Sir William. And where is your home?"

"Most of our lands were awarded to an English army officer after my father was killed, but I live on the grounds that remain to us, along the River Ilen and near the village of Skebreen. Should ever I find it within my power, I will restore those lands to Clan MacWilliam, where they belong. May you pardon my boldness, sir."

Ormonde's eyebrows lifted and then furrowed as he studied Faolán's face and stance, then he turned to Clanricarde. "Are you aware of these lands, Ulick?"

Clanricarde's lips were parted, his eyes shone, and his ears had flushed the color of a cardinal's robe. "Indeed I am aware, sir." He leaned forward in his chair and glared at Faolán. "What I say now shall never leave these walls on pain of death, but it is something you must know. My father the earl loved Sir William. After he was killed, my father did everything within his power to retain those lands. They should have reverted to Clanricarde holdings, but through trickery and whatever means they could devise, the lawyers refuted all claims.

"It was only the beginning of an incessant march of greedy pretenders who believe they have a right to my father's lands simply because they wish it so. It is a painful struggle worsened tenfold by the arrival of Lord Deputy Thomas Wentworth and his assistants, and a severe detriment to my father's health. It troubled his heart that he could not secure the estate bestowed upon your father, causing him to pay dearly for the forged documents protecting the castle grounds upon which you now live. Do you hear? Yes, you are a kinsman, and you are indebted. You owe your gratitude and fealty to my father, the Earl of Clanricarde, not Clanwilliam. Never forget it."

Faolán appeared stunned. "My lord." He repeated the bow he had made upon introduction, and kept it. "I never knew."

Ormonde swept back the tails of his hunting coat and stepped closer to Clanricarde. "Ulick, for some time you have been interested in an… opportunity, shall we say…to nick Wentworth's tough hide. I wonder if there might be something of value here? It seems harmless enough. To be sure, this young couple is in love, and the lady sees her destiny. Who are we to stand in the way of love and destiny? As well, this lad seems to have the fire in his belly. A useful fire if well-channeled. It should be quite troubling, I think, if it comes to the king's attention that two of his exalted officers, Lord Wentworth and Lord Cork, did not perform their duties and see to this lady's proper welfare. It is they who should be punished, and not our young lad who fell in love and simply took advantage of an opportunity at his feet. A kinsman of the groom might be deeply offended."

The color drained from Clanricarde's ears and stained his cheeks, then his lips stretched into a half-grin. "Goodness, Ormonde. You do have a streak of deviousness to you, I am delighted to know. Mayhap Lord Barry was right in sending these petitioners to us. I should send him a cask of wine, or a hindquarter off our next kill. You've set me alight, and I am already forming an amusing little plan." He turned his attention to Faolán. "You may rise, Burke. I think we may be able to do something for your cause."

Faolán stood tall again, and I breathed more easily, encouraged by the turn of conversation. Vivienne remained silent, waiting.

"Mistress Jephson has been bored of late, with Sir John so long at court. She may accept a wedding as a most engaging activity," Clanricarde said. "We shall see will she allow it and what she can do for it. With any luck you could be married in two days time. Once the nuptials are performed, we'll arrange a meeting with Lord Wentworth and Lord Cork.

"Until then, there is an unoccupied cottage just outside the oak grove. You will stay there and do nothing to upset or alter our plans. I will take care of the rest. But remember, Burke. You are indebted to my father, and now you will be indebted to me. I require of you to accomplish what you have set out to do. From the day you are wed, you will pay me five percent of this lady's annual inheritance, whether or not you receive it, every year until you have restored to Burke ownership all of the lands that once belonged to Sir William, your father. That done, I will see the castle raised as well. I care not how it is done—that is your challenge—but that must be the cost of my support."

"My lord," Faolán said, the relief clear in his voice, "challenge accepted. I am your faithful servant."

Vivienne bowed graciously, and Ormonde nodded. "You shall be a most lovely bride, my lady."

A dull ache seized the pit of my stomach. What kind of debt had Faolán so willingly accepted with his lofty dreams in charge of his head? To restore lands that to my estimation reached one hundred and twenty acres, and then to build a grand castle, with as yet little to no income, and a high fee to pay whether or not he is able to generate any? Little wonder the lords of the land remain the lords, with the aspiring ones ever crushed beneath the heels of their boots.

"And now, what of you, Mister O'Daly, the silent one. What is your stake in this romantic drama?" Ormonde asked.

Startled, I straightened my back. I had not expected to be spoken to, accustomed as I was in the alehouse to listen but not be observed, and I'd expected no notice at all by the Earl of Ormonde. "My lord, I..." I cleared my throat quickly. "I have been a friend to Faolán Burke all of our lives. I stand by him, sir, to be as he needs me in any circumstance."

"Ah, and everyone needs such a trusted friend," Ormonde said. "Good man to be so loyal and risk one's self in a dangerous venture to secure another's happiness. Mister Burke, it's a rare thing you have here. Cicero once said of friendship, nothing in the world is so hard to find as a thing entirely and completely perfect of its kind. Cherish and protect this friend and treat him with equal affection."

"I do, sir," Faolán said.

Ormonde turned. "You would do the same for me, dear Ulick?"

Clanricarde smirked. "Is there profit in it?" Both gentlemen laughed, and when the mirth died away, he grasped the arms of his great chair and nodded to us. "See yourselves out now, but don't stray too far. I have a special entertainment planned for this evening, and you may be needed."

Faolán escorted Vivienne through the door we had entered, but

I wanted one last look at Ormonde. His majestic profile was tinted a golden ivory by the afternoon light. What gave a man such presence and confidence? Was it money? Title? A combination of both? Or was it truly something in the noble blood that allowed him to simply be, and yet emanate fortitude and dignity? He turned suddenly and smiled back at me. I was transfixed until embarrassment flushed my cheeks. Faolán grasped my sleeve and jerked me back into the gallery. The grate fire still flickered there, but the long hall beyond seemed cavernous and cold.

I followed Faolán and Vivienne through the grove outside the castle wall and to the far edge of it where a small cottage waited just as Clanricarde had described. The walls were splattered with mud, the thatch caving in on the roof, the door rotted and stinking. Inside the rats scurried, disturbed by our arrival, and filthy moth-eaten woolens strewn across the floor made it appear that the last inhabitant had simply shrugged them from his shoulders and departed. A chill crept up my spine. Vivienne refused to even peer beyond the door.

"Someone died of the plague here, and recently. It may have been an entire family. Do not go inside, Aengus," Vivienne said.

Faolán scowled, turned away from the door and cast his gaze about the adjacent grounds. "Clanricarde is testing us. He means to know of our resolve and whether I carry my father's formidable nature. Had I known of his resentfulness over my father's lands, I might have handled the situation differently. We must prove to him we are worthy of his trust and support. Beware, we may all be tested, with this just the beginning. Pray the tests may not be too severe."

"He will not be disappointed," Vivienne said.

Faolán kissed her hand. "We'll make a camp in the grove, but within view of the cottage. We'll see them or hear them if they come for us."

I clapped Faolán on the back as Sean might have done. "I heard a raven's cry as Lord Clanricarde said the word 'entertainment'—you may be a fatted pig on their platter. Better rest up now, brother."

I only meant to chide him, but those words so foolish, I should never have spoken them. There was no rest to be had.

Chapter Fifteen

Heart of a Wolf

...woods on two sides and plains on the other; these are moors and mountains, whereon they say there are wolves.

~ Sir William Brereton

We had hardly begun to site our camp when the thunder of hooves reached our ears and the churlish castle steward galloped toward us on a white mare, dismounting so quickly he nearly lost his footing.

"My lady," he said, gasping for breath, "Mrs. Jephson begs your forgiveness for not greeting you upon your arrival. Lord Clanricarde did not alert her until just a little while ago, and she wishes your presence in the castle, where she will see you to your rooms and arrange for your comforts. She has asked me to provide this horse for your immediate transportation."

Vivienne inspected the horse's face and patted her mane. "How very kind and thoughtful of Mrs. Jephson. I am grateful." The steward handed her the leather reins, then bowed quickly, offering his hand to assist her into the saddle.

Faolán stepped in front of him and offered Vivienne his hand. She accepted and he lifted her gently until she was well seated.

"Thank you, sir." She nodded to Faolán. "And now, steward, what of my companions here? This cottage is quite uninhabitable."

The steward cleared his throat. "The gentlemen are to come with me. They are wanted at the hunting lodge, in the park just beyond the castle. There is to be a wolf hunt, sirs. Lord Clanricarde requests your attendance."

Vivienne straightened her back. "A hunt? I would enjoy such an entertainment. It has been some time since I've been allowed to hunt.

I will go with them to join the hunting party, and then see Mrs. Jephson when we return. Please give her my apologies."

"Muh...My lady, the hunt is likely to be very dangerous. There are no other ladies participating. A large gray wolf has been roaming the castle properties. It is Imbolc, you see. The time of milking. The lambing season. A lamb was taken just a week ago, and before that a two-year-old child was taken and then dropped at the edge of the wood, saved only by the scarf about his neck too thick for the wolf to penetrate. The earls mean to kill this wolf before it can cause greater harm, and the hunt may be a bloody one. Surely your companions would want to know you are safe within the castle."

"Steward, are you suggesting I am not fit for a vigorous hunt?"

"No, never, my lady."

"That is good, because I am quite accomplished. Are you telling me I am not welcome at the hunt?"

"Not at all, my lady."

"That is well, for I would hate to learn that Lord Clanricarde or Lord Ormonde would refuse me. I can see no reason that I should not attend, and it is to my liking. Please direct us to the hunting lodge, and alert Mrs. Jephson as to my whereabouts. I will be grateful to meet her when we return."

Faolán touched her ankle at the stirrup. "Vivienne, are you sure? Are you not tired and wanting to rest after our journey? You could..."

"I don't care how tired I may be; I wish to see the hunt, Faolán. I do not want you to go without me."

There was no use arguing. She was in her element now, accustomed to directing servants, to being served. We had, for a while, possessed her as our captive. Or had we? I looked to Faolán. His expression was odd, and I understood why. In less than a moment Vivienne was gone from us on someone else's horse. She was free, and we were to follow this steward on foot to an unknown place, an unfamiliar situation, to join a hunt we had never tried on lands of which we knew nothing. She was fluent in the realm where he and I were like Philistines on strange, foreign ground. Faolán masked expression, held his head high. We had no choice but to assume all was well until we knew otherwise. One thing was certain: we could not show weakness or fear.

"Lead on, man," Faolán said.

We walked for some distance until we came upon a smaller gate in the castle wall. Beyond it, a stone and thatch lodge bustled with activity from the adjacent stable and kennel. Hounds barked and whined, horses whinnied their excitement, and men shouted orders to each other while terriers played at their heels. Horses outfitted for a hunt were tethered to a rail beside the stable and all about were the smells of leather, hay, and dung. The steward led Vivienne beside the other horses, and Faolán and I were mostly ignored until a stableboy brought hunt coats bearing the Clanricarde coat of arms. We put them on, seeing clearly we were meant to act as servants to Clanricarde, even though our own horses were idle in the stable near the main gate.

I tried not to stare as Clanricarde and Lord Ormonde arrived a few moments later, coming on foot from the castle wearing the hunting garments we had seen earlier in the day. They moved with such ease and grace, perfectly certain that all would be prepared for them. Clanricarde walked with determination, while Lord Ormonde's countenance revealed a more agreeable nature. There was determination in his eyes as well, and in the set of his jaw, but not in the form of aggression. It was more like benevolent purpose. They joined Vivienne with the horses. Faolán and I approached.

"Ah, you are ready. And I see your lady is quite brave, Burke."

"Aye, brave and skilled, Lord Clanricarde. I trust she will be a fine addition to the hunt party. May I ask how Aengus and I may best serve you today?"

"Of course. Sir Jephson's hunt master has spent days scouting the probable location of our troublesome wolf. We think we have his lair. We'll surround the area with the hounds and close in. I'd like you to stay with the hunt team, and when our prey is cornered, dispatch him with the dagger. Short work, I suppose."

He waved to a man in the doorway of the lodge, who brought Faolán a long dagger in a leather scabbard. Faolán slipped off the scabbard and tested the blade against his thumb. He maintained his confident mask, but I knew of no hunts of this sort that he'd attended before, and never a wolf hunt, or the Barrys and I would have heard the story countless times over a campfire. This would be a new experience for both of us. Did Clanricarde hope he would fail in front of Vivienne so that she might change her mind about the wedding? Did he want to test Faolán's prowess for his own amusement? Or was he betting on the wolf to remove Faolán altogether?

Clanricarde nodded in my direction. "Mister O'Daly may join the spearmen to keep the wolf at bay. We'll have the carcass brought here for skinning. Ormonde may need a new fur collar."

Lord Ormonde laughed. "No collar needed here, but Vivienne may need it as part of her bridal chest. My lady, if the hunt grows violent, do stay close to me."

"My lord." She smiled. "Who has brought the port?"

"There is what I like in a lady. Forthright. Mindful." Clanricarde gestured toward the lodge again, and a servant brought a silver tray with three glasses of dark liquid. "Ah, good man." He took a glass. "You might bring two more as well for our hunting guests." He indicated Faolán and me.

"None needed here," Faolán said. "We'll want our wits sharp, should we encounter the beast. But afterward, it would be most welcome."

"As you please."

In the yard behind us, the hunt team assembled. The hunt master at the lead dispatched a pack of bloodhounds to seek out the wolf's fresh trail. Behind him the kennel masters led two sets of wolfhounds—not the ratcatchers or the foxhounds to which we were accustomed, but leggy animals the size of foals, with long, wiry fir, broad head and snout so high and pointed he might poke you in the chest. Added to these was one set of dogues—the large, muscular mastiffs that could overpower even the most aggressive wolf. Ormonde and Clanricarde followed on horseback, with Vivienne between them. Faolán and I walked with the remaining crew bringing up the rear: the spearmen, cudgelers, butchers and skinners, pages and grooms, and the physician.

We crossed stony hills, barren cornfields, and dense forest. The scents of earth and oak enveloped us and I prayed they would give us strength. Dusk was falling and yet the sun cast its last splinters of light into the darkening canopy, here to light a sapling's dead leaves, there to illuminate the bare white antler rub on a tree trunk, and above to turn a leafy bough into a bronze chandelier. In the distance, a hound bellowed. One of the bloodhounds alerted. The hunt master silenced him, signaled for everyone to stop, and then directed the dog handlers with their teams to the left and right, to surround our prey within the wood. Talking ceased. Movements became slow and deliberate. I followed Faolán forward.

The hunt master chose his moment, bowed slightly, and swept his arms forward like the horns of a great stag, sending us ahead of him into the wood with the spearmen and riders behind. Faolán began a steady trot, plowing through the thick brush clawing at our knees. He came to a rise, started to the left, and hesitated. There was a movement above. We'd startled a raven from its perch on a limb. Faolán saw it, and some kind of instinct locked in. He charged to the right into a dense patch of elder and hazel.

The hounds gave voice only yards away and closed in. Faolán crouched low, peering through the brush. He crept into a cave-like opening in the hedge, and there came face-to-face with his namesake, a half-starved and terrorized wolf, alone and aged, black as coal but for the light gray fringe about his face and across his ribs. His eyes blazed, his muzzle rippled and bared his teeth, but he made no sound or movement. For a second he and Faolán seemed frozen in silent engagement. Carefully I lifted my spear, for if the wolf attacked, he'd leap for Faolán's exposed throat.

With hounds crying and calling among the bushes, the great wolf reared his shoulders and snapped his jaws. Two hounds leapt in, and then two more from the opposite side. A mastiff barreled into the opening with an agonizing wail. The earls with their swords hacked through the undergrowth, exposing the wolf and all of his assailants. I poked with my spear to keep the frothing jaws from Faolán. The wolf lunged, then yelped when another spearman stabbed his ribs. He snapped and foamed, and then a harsh order came, the hunt master withdrawing the hounds. The mastiff retreated, but the wolfhounds still circled, whining and growling, refusing to abandon their prey.

Faolán found a position, the dagger in hand and glinting. The wolf leapt forward; Faolán flung up his wrist in defense, but the jaws closed around it. I stabbed with my spear to no avail, and Faolán rolled with the monster, the hounds nipping at the wolf's legs until the two rolled over and Faolán was on top. His left hand freed from the jaws, he gripped the wolf by the neck. With his right he stabbed the long dagger quickly and soundly between the wolf's shoulder blades, deep into its heart. The two collapsed to the ground. The wolf sprawled across Faolán's thighs, its hind legs kicking until at last it heaved a final groan, twitched, and lay still.

For a mere second, all came to a halt, as if the hounds, the birds and even the wind paused to acknowledge the great wolf's death. Vivienne leapt from her horse and came to Faolán's side, while Clanricarde shouted orders and Ormonde cleared a path. Two of the spearmen lifted the wolf from Faolán while Vivienne and I pulled him to safety. His forearm and the edge of his hand dripped blood. His face beaded with sweat. The hunt master arrived with lanterns, and the physician came to tend Faolán's wounds. Clanricarde dismounted and inspected the dead wolf, and with a quick flash of a blade tore into its chest and cut out its damaged heart. He held it up before Faolán's face, oozing onto the breast of his hunt coat.

"You must eat of it. Your first wolf kill," Clanricarde said. "To eat the heart of a wolf gives you its courage in battle."

Vivienne turned away. Clanricarde's lips were parted as if he was eager to see the response to this crude gesture. With his injured hand Faolán grabbed the heart and took a savage bite, then tossed the organ at Clanricarde's feet.

"And so, Mister Burke, it appears you have some bloodlust in you after all. Excellent. Well-done. When the physician has done with you, we must get you cleaned up. You'll all dine tonight at the castle. Yes, yes, well-done. And here is something truly deserved." He handed Faolán a silver flask. Faolán accepted it, sniffed the wine he had refused before, and passed it first to me. I took a quick swallow and returned it. He wiped his bloodied mouth on his sleeve and took a long draught, then gave the blood-smeared flask back to the Clanricarde. The man nodded. Without another word he mounted his horse and turned back toward the lodge.

The rains began again, softly at first but with sounds of distant thunder building. Instead of returning to our sodden campsite, the steward led us to a small room on the uppermost floor of one of the towers. Warmed by a good fire, we also had clean shirts and doublets to wear. And yet, Faolán brooded. Vivienne had been taken to her own room, and we had not seen her since. He would not talk of her when I asked, nor about the hunt, nor Clanricarde. Faolán had experienced more than I in the games gentlemen play, but now we were engaged in a very big game indeed, with players who knew the rules and could change them on their whim. We were moving deeper into a maze with no torch to light our way. But down in the great hall, the roaring hearth fire was friendly and welcoming, and my concerns evaporated as we moved toward the scents of hot baked bread and roasted meat.

"Burke!" Clanricarde called out. "You must join me here." He waved Faolán to a bench at the far end of a long trestle table. Vivienne was seated already at the center of the table, several feet away from him. Next to

Vivienne was a lady I believed to be Mrs. Jephson, though we were not introduced. Her brown hair showed at her forehead but was mostly covered by an embroidered coif. She was thin and fine-boned, her face long, plain, and pale.

Vivienne, however, was glowing like an angel. She must have bloodied her clothes when she attended to Faolán at the hunt, for she'd been given a new gown, pink as the dawn, with red and yellow flower buds embroidered along the neckline and sleeves. She wore a small white cap, but her hair had been brushed to a brilliant shine and hung in a single silky rope over one shoulder. She glanced in our direction and nodded as if she were a princess and we just distant acquaintances, and then continued her happy chatter with the other women around her. What a temptress she was. In the corner near the hearth, a young man plucked a sultry melody on a lute.

"Burke, you must be starved after your adventure, but you're not eating. Don't hold back: reach for what you want. Here, try some of this." Clanricarde stabbed at one of the platters with his dagger and dropped half a grouse onto Faolán's trencher. "Fine quality."

"Mayhap a bite of the wolf's heart has satisfied my hunger."

Clanricarde elbowed Lord Ormonde, who was at his left, and the two men laughed out loud.

"Like it or not, it is tradition, Mister Burke. We do love our traditions, don't we?" Ormonde lifted his cup and drained it of wine. Every finger of his hand bore a gold ring, and the sleeve at his wrist was satin bound with ribbons. Caught up as I was in the wine, the gentle music, the warmth of the room and the clatter of voices, I began to drift, barely tasting the meat on my own plate. I was too pleasantly tired to care about noblemen and their schemes.

"Eat well, lads," Clanricarde continued. "Tomorrow my friend Ormonde must leave us, but we will practice archery in the morning, if the weather will allow. Tonight we enjoy the hospitality of Mrs. Jephson and her husband who is away in service of the king."

"*Sláinte mhaith*," Ormonde shouted. "To good health!" And the table erupted in a roar of shouts, table pounding and laughter.

"Oh yes, and I have something for you, Burke. A talisman." Clanricarde placed something on the table next to Faolán's trencher. Faolán lifted the thin leather thong, at the end of which hung a silver clasp holding a thick lock of hair.

"It is a trophy from your wolf, lad. A lock of fur from a wolf's tail will protect you from evil." He turned and grinned at Ormonde. "But it may also have the power to charm the love of your heart."

The two men laughed again. Faolán smiled with little humor and hung the talisman around his neck. "I thank you, fine sirs. It is a worthy gift, for clearly I am in dire need of both."

Chapter Sixteen

An Abha Mór

*But men pass through terror unto courage.
The quarry at bay forgets fear, and fights for dear life.*

~ J.F. Taylor

I awoke early, grateful to have slept like a child in a warm, fine bed. I had once visited Barryscourt Castle to see the Earl of Barrymore and had slept in good beds at the homes of my wealthier relations, but this was the first time I had spent a night inside a castle chamber.

I hurried down the winding stair in hopes of being in the great hall to see Lord Ormonde before he left. I was curious about him. Was he as confident and assured every part of the day? Or would he be sluggish and short-tempered in the early hours? But I was to be disappointed. A kitchen maid told me he rode out before dawn, and so I satisfied myself with the fresh milk that was offered, the dark bread, the pale yellow cheese and the sweet flavors of dried fruits. By the time Faolán came down, I was drowsy again and nearly drifting to sleep beside the fire. Clanricarde arrived with such a clamor I was shaken to readiness.

"You have broken your fast, I see. Good. You are ready then, for the business of the day?" Clanricarde tugged on heavy gloves and smoothed the wine-colored sash across his chest. Faolán seemed not to notice, looking about the hall to the left and to the right, searching the alcoves. "The women are still dressing, Burke," Clanricarde said. "We'll leave them to their own entertainments."

He led us to a garden along one side of the castle, where servants had set up the archery targets. The night's rain had passed, the white light of the early sun setting everything aglow, but dark clouds moved with haste to spoil the day. I wished I could escape to the stables or back to the hall. I had learned to handle a spear or a pike well enough, but I lacked the controlled skill of a good archer.

Clanricarde shot first, cursing with frustration at his form but missing not a single target, though some arrows flew a bit wide of center. Faolán deferred to me, and I had to step up second. My arrows fell short, and only once did I land a respectable hit. Clanricarde either smirked at me or looked bored.

Faolán, with his large strong hands, could have bested us both with solid hits on most counts, but he turned his head at every sound, glancing hopefully at the doors and windows of the castle until a passing magpie distracted his vision, causing his last arrow to veer wide.

The steward approached at a trot, red-faced and short of breath. "My lord," he said to Clanricarde. "There is word from one of the groundskeepers. The night's rain has damaged the eastern wall."

"Blast it all," Clanricarde said, scowling. "I feared as much. I will see that it is inspected for Mistress Jephson. Send for our mounts."

"Yes, at once sir." A gust of wind caught the tail of his livery jacket, making him look like a winged grasshopper skipping away.

Clanricarde scratched beneath his beard and looked about thoughtfully. The clouds were darker still, and moving closer. The first droplets touched my cheeks. "The walls enclosing the hunting park protect those famous white deer. Though it would be a hanging offense if anyone dared kill one without the permission of Sir Jephson," he said, looking us over thoughtfully, "we wouldn't have one drown in the river either. I think your help in this could be most illuminating."

Oddly, he called no servants to attend us on this errand, when so many had been in the hunt party. But men had to mind the castle operations, I supposed, while women had chores of their own. Once mounted, Clanricarde led the way, and when he rode ahead of us, Faolán finally spoke.

"He is watching us, Aengus. Keeping us distracted. And he is keeping Vivienne well away. She should have been at the archery field this morning, but she never appeared. I fear he has sealed her in the castle, and has sent Lord Ormonde to Lismore to see the Earl of Cork. Cork will come back here to arrest us."

I was stunned. The thought had not occurred to me. I am far too trusting, I suppose, but Faolán seemed quite suspicious. "Faolán, if you believe that, we are not restrained. We are astride our own horses. We could ride away from this place right now."

He shook his head. "I cannot leave Vivienne. Returned to a place like this, I wonder does she question her decision to stay with me, and will she prefer instead this pampered life she's always known? Even if that's true, I must first hear it from her own lips. Until then, I cannot turn away. At the same time, it won't matter what we feel for each other if Clanricarde has his own scheme. He was quick to accept our case when Ormonde suggested it, and I fear he may have regrets. There may be workings afoot that we cannot know. There is a history, my friend."

"Well, now is a fine time to mention it, eh? What kind of history?"

"Aye, a few things you and I might ha' talked through a bit further. Many years ago the Burke clan was forever torn, and we do not forget. William de Burgo was a well-loved chieftain, but when he died, three men claimed his place. The clash turned into war, which ended with a three-way split of the clan. One part took the north. The second part was led by Ulick Burke, a predecessor of the Ulick we know. This man emerged as *the Clanricarde*— the son of Richard and a powerful leader—who reigned over vast lands across the middle west."

"Galway?" I asked.

"Yes, to the north and east of the bay. The third part of the de Burgo clan was my own, Clanwilliam, which moved into Munster. Ever since, there has been friction over the borders with the Clanricarde side.

"My father served both Clanricarde and Clanwilliam—we were all Burkes in his mind—and his service helped to mend the rift. I think this fellow before us still seeks to reunite the three sects, to be king of all the Burkes. It would make him the most powerful noble in the land. He'd hold more properties than any other man in Ireland. He could be wealthier and have a greater army even than the king of England.

"He is scheming, and the hair on my neck rises. Is he better served to help me, or to deliver me as a prisoner? What comes next may make facing down a vicious wolf seem easy. The only thing of which I'm certain is this, Aengus: you needn't risk it. You're a free man, not entangled in any clan war. Go home to your father and Skebreen."

I shook my head. "I am sworn to stand beside you. My father would expect me to do exactly that. Why would you think I would leave? You know I never could, and never ask me to." I did not say that I would no more leave

Vivienne than he.

Faolán exhaled in relief. "Thank you, my friend. Then we stay. Truly if you were to leave me I would lose half my strength. I do not trust Clanricarde. I can't read his eyes, and he purposely separates me from Vivienne. I don't like it, Aengus. I've grown fond of having her near me. Something has changed in me, and I no longer feel myself when she's not here. But you are right Aengus. Always you are right. We'll stay our course and face whatever comes. Let's see how he tests us today."

The castle overlooked the Blackwater River, with three towers defending the western side. Blackwater was the English name, but to the Irish she was *An Abha Mór*, the Big River, known for an abundance of salmon and for rapid, deadly floods. From the mountains along the Kerry border, she cuts a jagged path through Mallow, winds past the Earl of Cork's Castle at Lismore, and then turns south to spill into the sea. The rains we suffered on our way had pressed the river's limit. And the rain fell heavier as we followed Clanricarde along the outer castle wall. He pulled a cloak about his shoulders, but we had no cloaks and only our hats to protect our heads.

Our clothes were quickly soaked. Raindrops splashed the river's surface as if thousands of heavy pebbles fell from the sky. When we neared the river's edge, the wall dipped sharply toward the bank where the water swelled and trembled, ready to burst. The wall had been in good repair until we reached this point, but several black stones had dislodged where the ground beneath had saturated and washed away.

Clanricarde stopped his horse and pointed to a section of the wall where the stones jutted like an arrow's point toward the river before turning southeast. Threatened by the unstable ground beneath it, the wall was further compromised by a large oak tree from the inside growing stubbornly against it, reaching broad arms across the top that cascaded down toward the tall grass. One could only imagine a root system below pressing upward and outward with equal vigor.

"It's here that grieves me most, Burke. I think it may be breached, but I need more detail of the damage to report back to Mistress Jephson. You, being stronger and more agile than I, could you take a closer look and tell me what you see?"

Faolán hesitated a few seconds, looking about. Dunerayl had alerted on something, ears forward. Raindrops kept tapping on leaves and breaking the water's surface, and the wind shuddered the boughs above us.

Faolán dismounted, and I jumped down to help. Why would Clanricarde not have a servant do this, or a builder who knew about structures? But Faolán waved me off.

"There's little choice at this point. I'll just take a look." He walked toward the wall through wet clumps of earth and grasses that slapped at his thighs, and bent low to examine the washed-out area.

"Some stones are missing, sure enough," he called out, "but the wall is thick and remains solid just a hand's width beyond the opening, sir."

"Promising news. Thank you, Faolán. Now, about the other side?"

Faolán glanced at me, and then stepped gingerly along the wall. The mud was thick and slippery where the point jutted outward, and the water swelled just inches from his boots. He swung around to the other side, his fingertips the last to disappear behind the wall. Something tussled violently and then came a *whoomph,* and then the splash and churn of rushing water. Faolán cried out.

"Faolán!" I shouted and ran toward the wall, but there was no response. I gave the owl call we always used, but still there was no response. I glanced back at Clanricarde. His face was pale, his eyes flat and alert, but he was not moving. I hurled myself around the edge.

Had I not firmly gripped the tree branch above, I would have plunged into the river as Faolán had, for the ground opposite had given way entirely, stones with it dashed into the water, nothing but slick black silt sluicing away and the hole growing larger. The placid swell of the water against the bank disguised a ripping beast of current beneath. The tree limb creaked with my weight and could snap at any moment. I swung myself to the edge of a rock on a firmer patch of earth. From there I found solid ground and peered down the river. There was no sign of Faolán, and the water rushed past me. Faolán had been sucked away.

I hooted the call again and leapt to a ridge, where I might run along the river's edge. The water slapped and roiled, hiding its secrets beneath a silver-white glare. I ran along it until at last there was something against a fallen tree, just a dark mass where the water pooled and eddied. Faolán lifted his head slightly, pulling himself higher, but something was wrong. A broken tree limb had snagged his doublet, probably saving him from drowning, but it had pierced his shoulder just under the collarbone. He was bleeding badly. I had to free him somehow. I edged out onto the downed tree.

"Don't try it, Aengus," Faolán tried to shout, but pain and too much water mangled his voice.

I kept going, down on my belly, hoping to stabilize the tree while I cut his doublet free of the limb; then I gripped the doublet to pull Faolán with me as I backed off the tree toward the riverbank. Faolán shivered and coughed, and vomited water as soon as he had his knees under him. I waited beside him until he could breathe steadily. When he was able to stand, it took a moment until his legs stopped shaking. A few minutes more, and the cold water alone would have killed him.

Suddenly he turned and glared, his face the image of vicious hate, his eyes blazing, jaw clenched, cheeks and ears infused with a purple fury. He jerked the doublet into place, pressed a hand against my chest and pushed me aside. He marched straight back to where the ground had given way, grabbing fallen branches as he went. When he reached the wall he jammed the branches into the breach, just enough to allow us to cross. Once on the other side, he marched to Dunerayl and ripped his pistol from the side of his saddle. His hands trembled but he hoisted it and aimed at Clanricarde's chest. Then his arm became rock steady.

"I'm surprised you even waited, Sir Ulick. Is it well enough for you?" Faolán asked, his voice harsh and strained.

"What is this, Burke? What has happened?"

"You know exactly. You knew the ground and the danger, and sent me out in hopes I would drown. Is it enough? You have tested me three times. Have I met your requirement? Do I stand *well enough* for you to back me, or are you set on seeing me dead first?"

Clanricarde said nothing, his eyes wide and lips parted as if waiting for words to come. Faolán held his aim and took a step forward. River water streamed down the side of his face, staining his shirt with the drips from his blood-smeared jaw.

"I am no fool, sir. I am my father's son. If it's a death you seek, then yours will come swiftly."

Chapter Seventeen

For a Year and a Day

Grace was in all her steps, Heav'n in her Eye,
In every gesture dignity and love.

~ John Milton

Clanricarde stared at the pistol, his face turning pale. "Faolán, please lower your pistol." He spoke slowly, his voice softened. "You are right. Forgive me. I have tested your mettle a bit too far." Yet, Faolán's aim did not waver. "I never wished to see you dead," the earl continued, "but these are dangerous times, and the years ahead are likely to worsen. I needed to know your strength and your resolve before I risked my father's standing on your behalf. He spent his life building influence with the king and his deputies here in Ireland, so to protect all that belongs to us. It dwindles even now under the constant pricking of the Lord Deputy Wentworth. You have proved yourself beyond my expectations."

"As if I care a whit about your problems or your expectations." Faolán took another step closer, lifting the pistol even higher toward Clanricarde's face. "Tell me, sir, why should I trust you now?"

Clanricarde drew a deep breath. "I was of mixed minds. I needed to know God's will. If he allowed the river to take you, then I had my answer. But he has returned you instead, and now I see that I was the one being tested after all. God means for me to help you. I remain a man of opportunity, and you represent a solid avenue by which I may confront the Lord Deputy. That is still my goal. I will do nothing to shame or disappoint my father while he lives. I can be certain now this is what he would want me to do as well. And to prove my good intentions, I swear to this: you will be married tomorrow."

Faolán shook his head. "No. We will return to the castle. Your physician will tend to my wound. Vivienne and I will be married *tonight*."

Clanricarde nodded. "If that is your wish, I shall see to it."

Faolán lowered the pistol slightly, then raised it back up. "And, sir, I have asked for and expect your support as my kinsman. Should there be even one more *game* of this sort to either hinder the marriage or wreck my case with Cork and Wentworth, I will come for you, and you'll find no haven."

"Rest assured, Faolán. Things were set into motion on the day we first met. I had already written to Lord Wentworth to request the meeting before I decided to test you. On my honor and that of my father, we will proceed, and I will speak for you."

In the castle hall, Faolán still seethed. We sat by the fire while Clanricarde's physician addressed Faolán's wound. The gash was deep and painful, but once the bleeding was stopped it was not life-threatening. The physician chattered, cleaning the open wound with wine, praising the surgeons of Padua and Bologna for their new techniques that dismissed the use of plasters and ointments on open wounds. Pus was pus, he said. There was no such thing as good pus or bad. Best be free of it, he said. Faolán clenched his teeth as the man carefully closed the wound with small stitches, then bandaged the shoulder with linen, chattering all the while.

Faolán drank more wine to ease his pain. Slowly the anger drained away as well, especially with the physician gone and the lady of the castle, Mistress Jephson, approaching. She wore a dark gown with high white collar. Looking as pale as before, a timid smile suggested a brighter mood. A sparkle of pleasure marked her eyes as she looked upon Faolán's bare shoulders.

"I have learned we are to have a wedding this night, Mister Burke." She addressed Faolán but nodded to me to include me in her conversation.

"I am eager to wed my sweet love, Mistress Jephson, if the lady is in agreement. Is she?"

"She is. And what a merry time we'll make of it." Mistress Jephson smiled broadly, and I noted one tooth missing from the upper left.

"May I see her, mistress?" Faolán asked.

"Oh dear, no, I'm sorry, Mister Burke. Lady FitzGerald is dressing, and you mustn't look upon her before she is ready. She'll have supper in her room and you will meet her in the chapel at midnight."

"Midnight. So very late, my lady?"

"Ah, you are an impatient boy, I know. But a wedding is quite important, don't you agree? The preparations were well underway for tomorrow, but now we must rush ahead. Men are always impatient to be done with these things. But there are requirements, and there is great value in ceremony. Surely you will allow us these few hours, Mister Burke."

"As you are so kind, I could not refuse you."

"Thank you, sir. I'm sure you'll be pleased. In the meantime, you must have your own supper and enjoy your wine. My steward will come for you when it is time for you to dress."

"To dress."

"Yes, of course. If you'll pardon my saying it, your clothing is soiled and damaged, understandably so considering the traveling and activities you have been doing of late and your troublesome injury today. You would not think to wed the Lady FitzGerald in such a state, would you? You honor your bride when you look your best. A suit of clothes is being prepared for you, and for Mister O'Daly as well so that he may stand as your witness."

"That is thoughtful and deeply appreciated, my lady," Faolán said.

"Yes," I added. "Very kind, ma'am."

"And one more thing, Mister Burke. The servants are all aflutter. This is the most exciting thing to happen at Mallow in some time. Mayhap you would not be offended if they participated in the celebration after the nuptials are taken?"

"Not at all, Mistress Jephson. I am honored, and they are most welcome as long as my lady agrees."

Mistress Jephson smiled demurely and took her leave.

By the time the steward came for us, we were quite drunk but not fully drunk, which is to say we were still able to stand. In an upstairs room by a warm fireplace we were led toward a steaming tub of water. Faolán balked, I bumped into him and we both laughed.

"You first, Faolán."

"But I canna; I'm wounded!"

"Sirs," the steward said, "Mistress Jephson insists we're not to dress you in these clothes without first seeing to your bath. The water is ready. In ye go."

The servants stripped Faolán down and led him to the tub, taking care not to disturb his bandaged shoulder. Even his hair was washed and then he was toweled and set naked by the fire to dry while it was my turn to wash. The water was still warm and my toes thawed as the soap and brush scraped across my back.

"How long, Faolán, since we've been this clean?"

"Shite, Aengus, you don't even look the same man without a smear of manure across your mug."

We drank more wine and they groomed our hair, then we stood like scarecrows in the wind while two servants dressed us under the steward's supervision. Faolán slipped into a white linen shirt and a gold-colored doublet, then the steward attached a white lace collar and cuffs. My doublet was darker with shorter tabs that came to a point beneath the long row of covered buttons. Our breeches were loose and dark, our hose white, and instead of boots we were given men's slippers whichcould be forgiven if the fit was not exact.

We stood side by side before a luxurious glass mirror imported from France. How long since we had actually seen ourselves in a mirror, let alone in such splendor? The change was astonishing, and Faolán's visage glowed with pride, if perhaps also the wine.

"You are a gentleman at last," I whispered. "Your father and mother are smiling down on you, *Lámha mór.*"

"And look at you. Likely to catch the eye of a few someones tonight, *Teaghrán.*"

"I pray you are right."

We followed a wide stairway of fine wood with a balustrade of carved weapons and shields, and atop the newel posts were baskets of flowers carved from the same wood. At the bottom stair, double doors opened to the wood-paneled chapel. Lord Clanricarde sat in the front left pew, with Mistress Jephson beside him and the ladies who served her sitting just behind. The physician and several men of the household sat on the right. The chapel smelled of rose and lavender, and glowed amber with the light of a hundred flickering candles. At our feet the black and white marble shone. The altar was draped in crimson damask, On its surface, two bright candles flanked a magnificent gold basin.

Faolán stepped toward the altar, I to his right. If I could not hear his heart fluttering in his breast, I truly felt its panic. The long-awaited moment was now before us. It was well and good to dream of a finer life, to fantasize about your love, to imagine the day when at last you would come together as husband and wife. But to actually stand before the altar and know within a few moments your freedom as a single man would be a thing of your past, exchanged for the responsibilities of a husband and potential father, and all at your own insistence—well now, that was monumental.

It was as if I too would take the vows, so intertwined were our lives. I knew the world would not be the same once the words were spoken. The solid ground beneath us would slip, casting us into a tempest over which we would have little control. We'd achieved the next phase of Faolán's plan. As a married man he would soon face the most powerful men in Ireland. Faolán shifted on his feet as the music started, a sweet melody plucked from a lute. Only one thing could stop him from bolting for the door: the sweet rustling sound of a fine silk skirt. We turned.

Her hair was the first thing I noticed. Brushed to such a fine, shimmering silk, it fell in thick, coppery spirals to her waist. Next her eyes: big, brown and shining brightly. Her lips were tinged the color of ripe strawberries, her long neck was bare and white, and the tops of her shoulders were tucked just beneath the wide neckline of a sky-blue satin gown, the traditional blue of purity. The fabric was so fine every fold and drape captured the candlelight and teased the eye so I could not look away. She carried a nosegay of white-petaled flowers tied with blue satin ribbons. When she moved, a soft breeze played through the leaves of a willow.

I glanced to Mistress Jephson. How had she managed to produce such finery in so little time? Had the gown once been hers? She beamed, but I had no more time to ruminate, for Faolán had stopped breathing. I poked him with my elbow, and he drew a quick breath. Vivienne took her place beside him, smiled up at him, and took his hand. A bead of sweat trickled down the side of his cheek and into his collar.

The cleric had entered before her, dressed in black robes, but Vivienne was so magnificent we hardly noticed him. He stood at the altar, positioned the two before him, and quietly lifted his book. When Clanricarde gave approval, he turned a stern gaze across each person in the small chapel, securing their silent attention. The scents of melting candles, fragrant flowers, and human bodies thickened and weighted the air, and yet the cleric lingered so long over his pages I could barely breathe. I could not stifle my sigh of relief when at last he began.

"Dearly beloved friends, we are gathered together here in the sight of

God, to join together this man and this woman in holy matrimony, which is an honorable state, instituted of God in Paradise, in the time of man's innocence..."

And on and on he spoke, or so it seemed until Clanricarde cleared his throat loudly, which spurred the fellow forward. He reached for Faolán's hand and joined it with Vivienne's. Then he continued the traditional vows so softly that only the voices of the groom and bride could be heard.

Vivienne," Faolán said, his surety made clear, "I take you to be my wife and my spouse, and I pledge to you the faith of my body, that I will be faithful to you and loyal with my body and my goods and that I will keep you in sickness and in health and in whatever condition it will please the Lord to place you, and that I shall not exchange you for better or worse until the end."

Vivienne repeated the same words to Faolán, speaking very slowly, the rims of her eyes glistening in the candlelight.

When the cleric called for the rings, it was my turn to contribute, and I produced what Faolán had entrusted to me since before our journey began: the wedding rings that had belonged to Sir William and Faolán's mother.

"With this ring," Faolán said, and his voice cracked. He started again. "With this ring I wed you." He slipped his mother's ring onto her finger, and she slipped his father's ring onto his. He lifted her hand to his lips. "With my body I honor you, and I endow you with all that I have and all that I am as the son of William Burke."

This was the place in the ceremony where a reference to dowry might be included, but these things were yet to be negotiated. Instead, Vivienne spoke her own vows in place of the traditional bridal vow to honor and obey.

"I endow you with all that I have, all that I am, and I promise to stand beside you in this life and forever."

The cleric's eyes widened, but Faolán did not delay. He reached for Vivienne's left hand, and they faced each other, then he took one of the ribbons from Vivienne's nosegay and bound their left wrists together in the ancient Irish custom from Brehon law.

"For a year and a day, Vivienne," he promised. "if at the end of that time you wish your freedom, it will be yours. You will never be bound against your heart or your will."

Together they spoke the vow:

You are blood of my blood, and bone of my bone.
I give you my body, that we two might be one.
I give you my spirit, 'til our life shall be done.
You cannot possess me for I belong to myself
But while we both wish it, I give you that which is mine to give.
You cannot command me, for I am a free person,
But I shall serve you in those ways you require,
And the honeycomb will taste sweeter coming from my hand.

They held each other's gaze until Vivienne's tears spilled, and they came together in a tender embrace. Faolán lifted her chin and kissed her lips, a kiss so sweet and so imbued with emotion it caused a warmth within me to bloom like a rose and expand to my every extremity. That is what joy feels like.

And so it was done. I was exhilarated, the good cheer surging through my veins. We left the chapel and were greeted by a servant with a tray offering drams of mead. "To the bride and groom," Clanricarde offered, and all glasses were raised. In the great hall, the hearth fire blazed, torches were lit, and flickering candles ran the length of the trestle table, where trenchers were heaped with a midnight meal of fruits, breads, cheeses and sweetmeats. The musician played a lively tune and a young woman started to sing.

"Burke," Clanricarde called out before we could join the celebration. He stepped closer, grasping Faolán's arm. "You understand, we will need proof that the marriage has been consummated when we meet with Cork and Wentworth."

"I understand, and Vivienne understands, sir. We will have what is needed, if it is needed."

"It is well," Clanricarde said. "And one more thing. I received a message this afternoon that the Lord Deputy Wentworth has accepted our request for a meeting. You see, Burke? You needn't have worried. The meeting will be in six days, in the abbey at Cashel. Lord Cork will attend also, and apparently he is most eager to make your acquaintance. I suggest you ask Mistress Jephson if you might borrow that suit or something of similar quality. It is best to make a strong impression. And be sure he notices your father's ring. There is only one thing Cork loves better than money, and that is bloodline. He seeks any drop of noble blood to strengthen his family's position. But most urgently, we must get a message to my lord Ormonde to meet us at Cashel. We will need a swift rider."

"Aengus could go," Faolán offered. I was astonished at first, but I'd had enough wine that it quickly turned to excitement. To carry a message and deliver it personally to the Earl of Ormonde? To report to him, face-to-face? To see the grand and legendary castle, Carrick on Suir? Yes, of course I could go.

"You can take Dunerayl," Faolán said. "He is quick and sure and will see you there safely. It is two and a half days ride if you have no delays. I'll mark out the best route for you."

"I accept," I said.

Clanricarde nodded. "I'll prepare the message. You should start out at first light."

And then we danced. Faolán led Vivienne to the stone floor, holding her waist tightly against his and sweeping her across the room, her hair flowing like streamers of red and gold at Bealtane. They faced each other, cheeks flushed and bright with the firelight. Faolán kissed the palms of her hands and bowed to her. Then it was Clanricarde who danced her gently and sedately through a song. She smiled at him as if he were a father. To my delight, he passed her then to me as he reached for Mistress Jephson.

I must say I am by far superior on the dance floor than on the archery field. I pulled Vivienne near with a kiss on her cheek, and then led her in bold steps to the center of the floor. There I spun her until those voluminous blue skirts twirled like a dervish and she giggled like a little girl.

She waved a sweet good-bye to me as Faolán led her up the stair, and a great cheer arose from the revelers. The solemn ritual was accomplished; the merriment was done. An emptiness gaped within me as they disappeared from sight. What would it be like, that first night together as man and wife? I held at bay the spill of envy that threatened to stain the scene, and hoped the new couple would enjoy a blissful night, for we all knew the highest hurdle still lay ahead.

Chapter Eighteen

Carrick on Suir

*Here is my Lord of Ormond's house, daintily seated on the
river bank, which flows even to the walls of his house...*

~ Sir William Brereton

I had never traveled such a distance alone before. I was both excited for the
independence and a bit frightened of it. Faolán's instructions were clear,
and Clanricarde had given me coins for bed and board. My fascination with
Ormonde won out over the fears and made me push the harder to close
the distance. I aimed for speed, riding as long and as fast as Dunerayl could
withstand. He was a hearty beast, and truth be told, it was I who could not
bear another hour on the road long before he.

When I passed the mill at Glanworth Castle, I stayed north of the
mountains and followed the River Suir. Late on the third morning the old
Plantagenet towers of Ormonde's Carrick appeared above the trees. Then
the pointed gables of the attached Tudor mansion came into view. I marveled at the mullioned windows and the small square lights that reflect-
ed sunlight like hundreds of bright eyes blinking. At one point the light
gleamed through an upper-floor window right through from windows on
the opposite side of the castle. What a place of illumination it must be. How
eager I was to see within those walls.

The earl's standard waved above the gate, where I was welcomed
at the mere mention of Clanricarde's name. A servant led me through
the arch and into the courtyard, where I waited while he announced
me to the earl. I swelled with importance, climbing a grand stone stairway and into a gallery. A large bust of Queen Elizabeth stared down at

me, and then life-size portraits of the royal family, courtiers and Butler ancestors. Between the portraits, enormous tapestries in brilliant colors depicted famous Bible scenes or ancient mythology, until my swell of importance utterly dissolved. At the far end of the gallery near a crackling fire, the earl sat in a high-backed red velvet chair, perusing papers on a huge desk ornately carved with the powerful legs of a lion.

"Mister O'Daly," Ormonde called. "Please come near; there is a chair by the fire for you, and a goblet of wine."

I moved toward him as quietly as possible, careful to touch nothing. I sat on the edge of the silk brocade seat, fearful of soiling something I could never afford to replace. And yet my heart pounded to be so near to the Earl of Ormonde, to look upon his gentle and astounding visage, to be in a cavernous room dripping with wealth. My father had never done such a thing. What might he say of it? It was incorrect for a man of my stature to look directly at him, and so I became fascinated by his jacket of fawn-colored velvet with covered buttons, so fine I wished I could reach out and touch it, and mayhap I admired it too long.

"You have a missive for me from Sir Ulick?" His voice was kind, as I remembered it.

"Yes, my lord." I pulled the letter from my doublet and handed it to him. I looked away, not to intrude upon his reading or his thoughts. I pretended to examine the tapestry behind him, the love story of Echo and Narcissus in brilliant blues, greens and ruby reds, with hunting dogs sniffing about. In fact, I could not hold a clear thought in my head, waiting for him to speak. How silly to be so awestruck by nobility. He was just a man, wasn't he? My hand trembled when I lifted the goblet.

"Ah! So there has been a wedding. Excellent. It would have been wrong for the two lovers to be parted. I believe they are well matched. Cork would never have agreed, so I am pleased the deed has been done before the meeting. Faolán and Vivienne are both orphans of a sort, though Vivienne's mother still lives. I understand their circumstances and how it must feel to have found each other. I lost my own father to a shipwreck when I was just a child."

"I am sorry, my lord, I had heard about your father."

"It was long ago. I used to play in this room, behind this very chair while my grandfather was working. He prophesied that one day I would lead the family to prosperity. I must hope his prophecy was correct."

"It was, my lord," I said emphatically. I know not the source of my certainty, but I could not help but say it. He smiled.

"I suppose after the wedding there was celebrating."

"Yes, my lord. With mead, and dancing."

He traced my gaze to the tapestry and then looked back at me. "Do you like the tapestry, Mister O'Daly?"

"It is beautiful," I said, "but sad."

"Yes, I suppose it is a sad story. Unrequited and useless love. It was my grandfather's purchase. He became sentimental as he grew old. I prefer the scenes of battles won and happy endings." He looked at me thoughtfully. "Have you ever been in love, Mister O'Daly?"

I swallowed, my throat dry in spite of the wine. "I have not, my lord."

"Well, you are young," he said, which seemed strange since we were quite nearly the same age. And yet, I knew he had wisdom and experience greater than mine. "Love will come and it will be a wonder for you. As Plato said, 'Love is the joy of the good, the wonder of the wise, the amazement of the gods.'"

"Thank you, my lord." I said. "I do not feel so very...wise."

Ormonde laughed. "Some days I do not feel wise either, Mr. O'Daly. He who thinks himself wise is often proved incorrect." He glanced again at the tapestry. "In some ways I envy Faolán and Vivienne in their passion, although I have been fortunate in love. My marriage was a design to end a long-running feud between our families. It has been successful, and over time I've found my wife to be a clever woman with a faithful heart. She is a help to me, and a lovely companion. Fidelity, it is said, is among the most sacred endowments of the human mind."

He sipped his wine and looked at his goblet, turning it this way and that with the sun glinting through the pale rose color. "We lost our first son. Elizabeth struggled mightily. She nearly died herself, and in the end she was heartsick and devastated. Life was difficult for a long time, but now we've been blessed with another child to be born in just a few months. During our troubles I learned a valuable lesson from Elizabeth—that life is seldom fair, but what is right is what is most important and worth fighting for, even if it risks a heavy cost."

I hoped the heat of my face did not betray my deep admiration. To hear someone of such high rank and power have a care for the rightness of things was truly unheard of in these times. What an honor that he should speak to me this way.

"Forgive me for boring you with my chatter," Ormonde said.

"Not at all, sir. I wish you a healthy child and great happiness."

"Yes, thank you." He stood at the desk and faced the window. "Travel is in order first thing on the morrow. I expect it will require two days. I will begin preparations. You will ride with my party, of course. You may wish to spend the afternoon seeing to your horse. The steward will call you for supper and arrange your bed for the night. We will leave for Cashel before dawn."

"Thank you, my lord. I will be ready."

I took supper in the castle kitchen with the other servants, and was led to a cot in the servants' quarters for the night. There upon the blanket was a fine linen shirt and the earl's velvet jacket, brushed and neatly folded.

"My lord wishes you to have these, to wear at the meeting at Cashel," the steward told me. "Ye mus' make a good impression, he said."

I touched a finger to the jacket. The velvet was even softer than I had imagined. "I am honored. Please tell him so."

He turned and was gone.

It was still dark when we departed. Despite a good roadway and an aggressive pace it was exactly two days to Cashel. Approaching from the south in late afternoon, the cathedral fortress seemed to rise from its high limestone seat and come smashing down before us like the staff of a god, as if to say *you will halt here and go no farther*. The ages swarmed, from Cormac's twelfth-century round tower and the ancient Gothic chapel, around St. Patrick's cross and along the well-worn pathways of ten thousand priests. The faint voices of singing men who filled the choirs for centuries whispered through windblown grasses. And slow, intense vibrations surged through the bones of my legs and spiraled up the core of my spine, the spirits of the Tara kings converging.

Chapter Nineteen

The Lord Deputy's Call

A most cursed man to all Ireland and to me in particular.

~ Richard Boyle, Earl of Cork
regarding Lord Deputy Thomas Wentworth

The half-moon was still visible over Cashel when I rose that Monday. Ormonde's camp was just beginning to stir and Clanricarde's had not yet arrived. I was certain they would come, for Sir Ulick had called the meeting, but among Ormonde's men I was like a distant cousin, politely accepted but oddly disconnected. How soon would I see Faolán and Vivienne again? Ormonde slept in guest quarters within the cathedral. Among the four nobles invited to the meeting, he was first to arrive at Cashel. He would be first to arrive anywhere, for he was serious and prompt, always embarking before dawn, and kept his entourage small: his steward, his horseman, his secretary, and four guards. He wore a breastplate and cape when he traveled. He moved fast and made few rest stops.

Lord Cork arrived soon after we did, in quite a different style. He had the shortest distance to travel and brought the largest group. Along with his ornate coach and six horses came two coachmen, four farriers, eight guards, two pages, his secretary and two lawyers, a steward, and a few others whose occupation I did not know. Last in the procession was a wagon creaking along beneath the weight of wardrobe chests and other baggage. Except for Cork and those with him inside the coach, all were dressed in fine livery, and all had to be housed for the night at an inn nearby. I wished it could have been my father's inn, for in a single night we would have exceeded our income for a year.

Clanricarde arrived about midmorning, allowing barely enough time for everyone to get settled and refreshed before the meeting, and for Sir Ulick to confer with Ormonde. Tending to be more frugal and less organized, his group included two guards, a secretary, one stable boy, his impertinent steward, and a dog, one of his favorite wolfhounds.

My excitement peaked when Mairead's gray cloak appeared at the end of the procession. Faolán and Vivienne rode close together, legs touching and their faces bright. I waved wildly from my perch at the cathedral steps, but so engrossed were they in each other they did not see me until they were within a stone's throw. We hugged when we came together, but spoke little. All was eerily quiet near the cathedral considering the numbers gathering, and the mood as gray as the incoming clouds. We were about to enter a room with the most powerful men in all of Ireland, where the course of our lives would be decided and we had no control over the outcome.

The Lord Deputy Wentworth arrived less than an hour before the meeting was to start. I anticipated a great entourage, for the rumors of his arrival in Ireland the previous summer had him with thirty coaches and six, an arrival fit for a king and causing quite a bitter stir. But he seemed to be a man who favored unpredictability. A tall and imposing figure, he set a frightful tone with his black horse, black breastplate, broad black hat with a large black plume. About him were his secretary Philip Mainwaring, a lawyer, a steward, and four guards, all of them dressed in black. Wentworth dismounted, his face stern, eyes dark and severe. He seemed to take in everything as a criminal, who scans his surroundings in fear of apprehension.

Instead of heading for the cathedral's south transept where the others were assembling, he turned first toward the vicar's private rooms to confer with the Dean of Cashel, William Chappell. The dean emerged a few moments later looking shaken, and hurried into the cathedral.

He soon returned with my lord Ormonde. Dressed in buff-colored hose and a jacket of dark wine with lengths of lace at his neck, wrists, and knees, he looked refined and formidable, the powerful nobleman secure in his purpose and position. He followed Dean Chappell back to his rooms. At least ten minutes passed before he returned, his face looking gray and rather dispirited. Halfway up the steps, he paused. "Come along, Mister O'Daly. You should hear my announcement."

I was almost comfortable being near him in that I wore his velvet jacket and could have been mistaken for an elevated member of his household.

"Gentlemen, I bring word," he said when we had reached the south transept. The men gathered around a refectory table silenced their talk and turned to him. "My Lord Deputy has arrived. He requests that we attend him in the dormitory dining room adjacent to the vicar's kitchen. It is just across the yard. Dean Chappell is now arranging the room for us."

"But we are here," Clanricarde argued, his ears reddening. "This was what we agreed. We can accommodate everyone much better in the larger space."

Ormonde shook his head. "The Lord Deputy calls for the meeting at the appointed time in the dining room. The cook has fresh bread baking, and there will be beer after the meeting."

This seemed to soften the blow, and a few men moved toward the hall though it was still twenty minutes before the appointed time. With one swift move, Wentworth had effectively taken control of the meeting. Ormonde turned and walked out with Clanricarde, and I followed.

Vivienne and Faolán had changed from their traveling clothes and waited outside in the courtyard. Vivienne wore the becoming green gown given her by Lord Barry. Her hair was bound in a chignon in the back, with copper ringlets at the sides of her face. She looked happy and hopeful, as if she were on a spring picnic and prayed it would not rain. Faolán wore a linen shirt with lace collar, a buff leather jerkin with tawny ribbons at the waist, and peat-colored breeches with his hose. The clothing transformed him into a gentleman, especially now that his hair grew long. He seemed to stand a little taller as well.

In the dining room, a fire blazed in the hearth against the far wall, and at the head of the room, a long trestle table nearly filled the space. A large and colorful tapestry on the wall behind depicted King Solomon as the Queen of Sheba knelt before him. The Lord Deputy's hand rested on the back of the chair beneath King Solomon, while he spoke in whispers to Mainwaring.

Mullioned double windows on each side of the room shed a gloomy gray light on the open floor. The dean had his assistants placing as many chairs as could be found to accommodate what had become a large number of people. A window seat put me near enough to hear the discussion and aside from those who attended the earls, but the backs of other men quickly blocked my view. I took the narrow stair in the hall to a gallery above the kitchen, and from there I could see everything and everyone.

Indeed, the scent of baking bread was especially strong in the gallery. I inhaled deeply until my mouth watered, and examined the masterful carpentry that adorned the ceiling. Decorative underpurlins with carved flowers connected the ceiling timbers to the walls, and carved wooden angels anchored the bottoms of the rafters. The one nearest me had red wings and yellow hair. She held a white shield bearing crossed swords, and wore a sweet smile. Sure it was a good omen for the day's proceedings. But then the next one, with wings of green, a blue shield, and a decidedly bitter frown, contradicted me. They were no help to me as the rest of the participants arrived. I squeezed my hands together. How would the winds blow for Faolán in such a convergence? If only Sir William was beside him.

Lord Cork leaned his head in the door before entering, his bald pate fringed with graying fuzz and his lace ruff thick and stiff about his neck. He stepped back, using his cane to hold the door for a lady and child. Dressed in a dark blue gown parted in front to show an ivory lace underskirt, I knew at once she was Vivienne's mother. She was the image of Vivienne, except her fuller lips formed a permanent pout and her blue eyes were at once sad and defiant. She led a companion child by the hand, a native most likely brought from the Americas. He wore only short breeches and a saffron vest, the patterned markings visible across his face, pate, and neck, and along both of his bare arms. She helped him onto one of the window seats and stood against the wall beside him, refusing a chair. Beginning to fume and mutter, Lord Cork left her there and took the end chair on the far right of the table, directly opposite from Ormonde.

Clanricarde guided Vivienne and Faolán to chairs facing the Lord Deputy Wentworth, and sat down beside them. The room grew quiet.

"My Lord Cork, where is your hat?" the Lord Deputy chided him.

Cork grunted, offered a half smile, and waved him off. "It is too warm in Munster; we enjoy such a pleasurable climate," he replied, though we all knew the winter had been uncommonly cold.

"Ah yes, I remember now. It was lost, wasn't it? In a bit of gaming? Pity. I must get you a new one or you'll catch your death. A fine beaver would be just the style for you. They are quite favored in London as of late."

"Hmmph," Cork replied.

"Gentlemen," Ormonde said, "shall we to business?

"Of course, Lord Ormonde. Proceed with good haste." The Lord Deputy nodded.

"My Lord of Clanricarde brings forth a situation on his father the earl's behalf." When Ormonde spoke my admiration grew. He was the most neutral and forthright of men, respected by all others. His voice was soothing and kindly, but also authoritative, as a father to a young son. He gestured for Clanricarde to begin, though Cork still scowled.

Clanricarde stood slowly, making a show of it and pushing his chair back noisily. He cleared his throat, straightened his doublet, and smoothed his beard. "My Lord Deputy, Lord Cork, Lord Ormonde, and to all who are gathered here. I bring forth the case of my dear and noble kinsman, Faolán MacWilliam Burke, son of the famed knight Sir William Burke of Skebreen, from the far west of Munster. He is newly wed to the loveliest bride Vivienne, of late FitzGerald, who has been a ward under the *protection* of Lord Cork. Their union is indeed a love match and favorable under God..."

Lord Cork made a loud and guttural sound and turned his face away, but Clanricarde did not hesitate.

"...and though they had not permission to marry from her guardian, theirs was an unstoppable passion. We present them now, and beseech you to recognize theirs as a loving and appropriate union. We seek your forgiveness and understanding of their departure from the customary path, for they came together on the Eve of St. Agnes, surrendering to a far more ancient and potent spell of legend that unites young lovers. We ask as well for the right and proper settlement of Vivienne's inheritance to maintain this new and industrious family, who will improve the lands and welfare of Ireland and will ever be faithful servants to the crown."

Wentworth looked appraisingly at Faolán and then at Vivienne, but Cork could not hold his peace. He banged the top of his cane on the table for attention.

"See here, Clanricarde. This was no proper courtship. My young and tender ward, entrusted to me by the king in all his authority, was abducted. *Abducted.* From her warm bed in my vicar's house. It was a most heinous and unlawful act by a ruffian far beneath her station. He must be hanged at once."

Wentworth's eyes widened. "Is this so, Lord Clanricarde?"

"My Lord Deputy," Clanricarde said, "my kinsman admits that he did collect her from the vicar's rectory in Bandon. However, as you see before you, she is a willing companion, they are in love, and the marriage has been consummated."

Lord Cork growled and spat on the floor. "We should not even be here today. The lady Vivienne must be returned to me, this foul criminal arrested, and his execution determined and handled by the assizes."

"If I may," Ormonde said, placing a palm gently but firmly on the table's surface, "no crime can be committed if no law is written and in place to be broken. While society may frown on the taking of a young woman for marriage..."

"Abduction!" Cork shouted.

"...there is no such law confirmed in Ireland. Mister Burke is not arrested, no trial is warranted, and no execution can be decided."

"No law against the abduction of an heiress?"

"My Lord Deputy, my research has discovered no such law. A kidnapping of sorts would be unlawful within the walls of Bandon, but the law does not reach beyond the township's walls, where the rectory lies. To understand what has happened, one must consider the customs in Ireland and the changes being wrought by English plantation. There had never been need for such a law before, because marriages and inheritances were handled differently under Brehon law. Sometimes things are slow to change in the regions beyond the pale. But as you can see, the marriage is consensual between two individuals of age. It would be difficult to establish a crime."

"By God, if there is no law now, there will be one." Wentworth stabbed an index finger onto Mainwaring's writing papers. Mainwaring blanched.

Ormonde continued, "I have language I might offer for your lawyers to consider, for this and several others I would propose to you, Lord Deputy. And as your advisor, I could further illuminate these intricacies, and smooth your way." Law and order, then, and a seat on the Lord Deputy's council—such was Ormonde's agenda for the meeting.

"Mayhap you will attend me in the summer, then. I have permission from his majesty King Charles to open the Irish Parliament in July. There is much to be done in preparation."

"Indeed there is, sir. Truly, it will be an honor," Ormonde said.

Cork sputtered. "Good God, gentlemen, what are we talking of here? If there be no law to call into force, let there be common sense! This man cannot be allowed to remove a poor, defenseless young woman from her bed. What of the precedence? What of the crude treatment of the vicar and his wife?

"Were the vicar and his wife physically harmed, Lord Cork?" the Lord Deputy asked.

"Well, no, sir, but their home was breached, and they were frightened; they were...well, I, don't...ah...but what of this man's accomplices? There were three of them, Lord Deputy. Should they all be allowed to walk free among us after such a dreadful act?"

A shiver ran down my spine. I had not considered that even if Faolán was not prosecuted they might want to charge the Barrys and me for assisting him. Cork must not have known Sean and Thomas were involved, or he would not have risked his own son-in-law's embarrassment. But my worry was short-lived.

"Lord Deputy," Ormonde said, "I believe we are straying from the central issue, which is the maintenance of this young couple seated before us. Now that they are wed, there is little point in looking backward; we must address what is at hand."

Wentworth looked at Ormonde for a long moment, then glanced at Clanricarde, and finally turned a steady gaze on Cork. For an instant it seemed as if Faolán and Vivienne were not even there, so little of consequence were they to what was occurring at the table. Faolán's head turned this way and that as if watching a match sport from the sidelines. At last, Wentworth tilted his head backward slightly and seemed to have made a decision. The look in his eyes changed. He leaned forward, facing Cork.

"I must say I am touched, Lord Cork, by your concern for the vicar and his wife, and for an heiress entrusted to your care. But I must ask: Was it not you who placed her in the vicar's unguarded house, far from your oversight, with no one but himself to defend her? How many miles is it from Lismore to Bandon? Fifty or sixty?"

"Fifty-five, sir," Mainwaring said.

"You had to pay a fee to the king for her guardianship, correct? And until you arrange a proper marriage for her, you have complete control of her income. How much is it?"

Cork glared at the Lord Deputy but remained silent.

"About £800 annually, Lord Deputy," Mainwaring said.

"Eight hundred." Wentworth stroked his pointed beard thoughtfully. "Was her income entrusted to the vicar as well, my lord, or did you keep that under your careful watch at Lismore?"

"My Lord Deputy, I..." Cork raised his palm.

"You should have protected her, and you didn't; I'm glad she got away," Vivienne's mother cried—an outburst reminding me instantly of Vivienne calling out from her tree.

"Deirdre, please go outside," Cork said.

"I would not be ordered about like a child," she said. "Vivienne is my daughter. May she not suffer the same fate as I."

"Who is this woman?" Wentworth asked.

"She is Deirdre FitzGerald, sir," Mainwaring answered, referring to his notes. "It is true; she is the lady Vivienne's mother."

"And the child?"

"A gift," Cork said before Mainwaring could respond. "I purchased him for her while in London last, from a merchant back from the Americas. A companion, I thought, to cheer her out of her melancholy."

"All right, then. Tell me this: why is the lady Vivienne in wardship under your care, Lord Cork, when her mother is alive to care for her?"

"Sadly, she is driven to fits, Lord Deputy. The physicians say the poor dear is unstable."

Deirdre wept, and the companion child stood and hugged her about the waist. Vivienne's shoulders and back stiffened.

"I suppose you are managing her finances as well."

Cork sighed audibly and leaned toward Mainwaring and the Lord Deputy as if to impart something confidential, yet all the room could hear him.

"Lord Deputy, our poor Deirdre lost her husband, a son of the late Gerald FitzGerald, Earl of Desmond. He was a prosperous trader, but was lost at sea years ago, just after young Vivienne was born. My wife and I opened our arms and our home to her in her grief. She became a joy to our household, and we have looked after her as if she were a daughter. Surely you can see she could not care for an infant, and arrangements had to be made at my considerable expense," Cork said, pressing a hand to his chest.

"We have always wanted only the best for poor Deirdre and her child, which is why I was willing to pay a tremendous fee for Vivienne's wardship, you see." He pressed forward in his chair as if to speak even more intimately, softening his voice. "Surely you will understand, Lord Deputy. It was my duty to arrange the most suitable and profitable marriage for the young lady, and would not have her troubled by a parade of young men at Lismore before we had found the most beneficial match. I made what I thought a reasonable decision. Bandon belongs to me. I built it. I have populated it. I felt certain the townspeople would protect her for me."

"Yet you placed no guards to protect her?"

"I believed the guards would only call attention, when her placement was meant to be secretive, my lord."

Wentworth seemed amazed by Lord Cork's story, and stared at him with interest for a moment or two before he scoffed and shook his head. "It was not enough that you, as Lord Treasurer, have all the wealth of Ireland under your management. And need I mention the misuse of tithe monies from the churches where your relatives have been placed? My Lord Clanricarde has paid restitution for his mistakes with church properties, but I have yet to see any activity toward recompense from you. And what of the charitable income from the college at Youghal? You understand we are investigating this thoroughly. Thorough and through, as you have often heard me say. And I will get to the bottom of it, I assure you."

Cork was silent, his face darkened. Wentworth continued.

"And so, with all of this, am I to understand you have had management of the lady Deirdre's inheritance for these twenty years? And young Vivienne's? Lord Treasurer, I am left to wonder. Who has perpetrated the greater crime against this lady? The young man who swears his love for her, or the old man who clutches her inheritance as if it were his own?"

"My Lord Deputy!" Cork said as his eyes popped wide, his face flushed. Wentworth's face was impenetrable.

Wentworth seemed bent on Lord Cork's humiliation, and the tension smoldered between them. Gossip reached all the way to Skebreen that Wentworth had planted his boot upon Lord Cork's back. His first act upon arrival in Ireland was to force Cork to remove his wife's tomb from the high altar at St. Patrick's Cathedral. It was an inappropriate place for it according to most, but Wentworth's attack was personal, causing Cork great distress. Wentworth turned to Faolán.

"Young man, I will hear from you now. What is your circumstance in Skebreen? Are you prepared to care for your bride properly?"

Clanricarde tapped his shoulder, and Faolán stood tall.

"My Lord Deputy, I am born of proud tradition. My ancestor fought the Vikings at the side of Strongbow. As son of Sir William Burke, my household is at Glencurragh, along the banks of the River Ilen.

"Construction of my father's castle was halted with his untimely death, but together Vivienne and I will complete it. It stands on fertile land, and we will raise our family there. We will provide work for many, and support the good education and industry of our township. I have proved myself a faithful servant to the Burke clan, to my lord Clanricarde, and to the Earl of Ormonde."

"And will be faithful to them second only to the King of England and myself," Wentworth said sternly.

"Without question, Lord Deputy." Faolán bowed.

"You have the deeds to this land you claim? I understood that region to be McCarthy territory."

Clanricarde said, "It is Burke land, sir. My father the earl holds the deed, and it is proper, and it is legal. The adjacent lands as well belong to Burke. Through some kind of legal trickery, they were taken unlawfully, without compensation, and bestowed to an army officer. My father suffers to have all of these ancestral lands returned."

He leaned closer. "Such takings must stop, Lord Deputy. They are the reason our woods and mountains are infested with angry, desperate men, and why we must all travel with guards. And yet the trouble grows. It is a shameful circumstance for Ireland, and an unwanted consequence of the plantation that must be amended."

Wentworth frowned, and his eyes narrowed. "Here now, Clanricarde. Are you not enjoying the hospitality of Mallow Castle, which is owned by an army officer, Sir John Jephson, as a result of plantation?"

"It is true, sir, but the circumstance differs. Mallow was confiscated legally after the execution of the war chief in the Desmond Rebellion. It displaced no clan or family in a line of heritage, for the land was abandoned after that. Sir Jephson married into the ownership of Mallow, and the hospitality you speak of is simply because of a debt he owes from a failed night at the gaming table. I am compensated for the debt by a hunt in his castle park.

"By way of comparison, the Burke lands and others like them are handed down through the generations of loyal subjects. These lands are not compromised by any rebellion, and are populated by husbands and wives, uncles and cousins, and the young men and women who keep the land productive and pay their rents and fees. Takings on the basis of a legal loophole displace all of them, with nowhere for them to go, and thereby ignite the very rebellious nature you wish to suppress."

Wentworth fumed silently for a few tense moments, his eyes focused on the table's surface, while Mainwaring furiously scribbled notes. A troubling situation, indeed, because many of the lawyers in the room were Wentworth's, the very ones tasked with finding and perhaps creating the loopholes through which to claim ancestral lands from Irish owners. It was to the greater benefit, Wentworth was known to say, because the English knew how to farm the land to higher productivity than the Irish, and could thereby increase prosperity for all. In truth, the prosperity went to the king's coffers. Wentworth seemed not to notice the Irish families left homeless and starving.

"Mayhap I will see Sir William's castle one day at Glencurragh. As for the rest of it, be that a discussion for another day, Clanricarde."

My lord Clanricarde nodded. He'd had his say. Some of the lawyers grumbled and shuffled their feet on the cold stone floor.

"Again we stray, Lord Deputy," Cork said. "But of the marriage, there is no proof of consummation, and I say it must be dissolved today, and the lady returned to me for a marriage arrangement. I have already found her a far more agreeable match."

"Is there proof of consummation?"

"There is proof, Lord Deputy," Faolán said.

"I would see it," Cork said.

"Good sir," Vivienne spoke out boldly, "please do not embarrass me before all of these gentlemen. Trust that the evidence is true. Please, from the lips of a consenting bride, hear that we are properly and fully wed. The marriage may *not* be dissolved."

Silence stilled the room. The men at the table stared at Vivienne but she held her back straight, her head high. She did not apologize for her outburst, but looked back at each man in turn. Wentworth exhaled audibly and clasped his hands on the table.

"Lord Cork," Wentworth said, "you will determine an appropriate dowry for the lady Vivienne, and arrange for her income to be redistributed to herself and her husband. I would hear news of how this has been done in one month's time. And in the interim, I would ask you to provide a letter detailing exactly what I should tell King Charles of the result of your wardship."

Cork stopped breathing and clutched the silver head of his cane until his knuckles turned white. It was clear Wentworth had made up his mind; no use in arguing now. Cork exhaled until he coughed, and forced a tight smile. "Of course, Lord Deputy. As you wish."

"Now then, gentlemen, the day grows long and my throat is parched. Is there other business to discuss, or may we adjourn to enjoy the fruits of Dean Chappell's kitchen?"

"That concludes the business of today, Lord Deputy," Ormonde said.

I was elated. I wanted to shout congratulations to Faolán and pour buckets of cold water upon the lawyers on the floor below me. Faolán and Vivienne would be free, would be able to return to Skebreen with an income, and we would all work together until the great Castle Glencurragh rose so high and strong it nearly blotted out the sky. I wanted to hug them both and twirl Vivienne across the floor as I had on her wedding day.

But the room remained quiet. The men stood, and slowly the onlookers scraped back their chairs and moved out into the courtyard. Mainwaring remained at the table studying his papers. Ormonde and Clanricarde chatted quietly with Wentworth. Lord Cork remained in his chair, seething. He spoke to no one, but gestured for his secretary to bring him his drink.

We waited in the courtyard until Faolán could thank both Clanricarde and Ormonde, and Vivienne kissed their cheeks.

"A productive day, in which a marriage is confirmed and seeds are well planted," Ormonde said. "And Cork is appropriately perturbed." He and Clanricarde looked at each other and chuckled.

"Well worth the journey just for that, my good friend," Clanricarde said. He turned to Faolán and clapped him on the shoulder. "You have done well. I wish you both a long and happy marriage, with many children. And do not forget your obligations to me, will you Faolán?"

"My lord." Faolán bowed gallantly.

To Lord Ormonde I offered my thanks for his kindness and hospitality. "The jacket suits you. It is yours, Mister O'Daly. Care for it well," he said. "And do look after this young couple. They make me long for my wife and home. I bid you safe journey." His face was wistful and kind. The afternoon sun on his hair gave the impression of a halo, or mayhap my eyes just played with me. That is how I would remember him, for I knew not when or if ever I might see him again.

Across the yard, Deirdre FitzGerald waited by Lord Cork's coach as the drivers prepared for their departure. She watched us while her companion boy slept at her feet.

"We must speak to her, Vivienne," Faolán said.

"Why must we? She does not love me."

"Surely she does. She is here. She spoke for you. She *cried* for you."

"She cries for everything. She has not cared for me a day in her life. She let them take me from her when I was an infant, and never tried to take me back. She says I should not be trapped as she was, and yet leads me into it herself and stands by while Lord Cork directs my life."

"Is she troubled, as they said?" I asked.

"What would I know of her troubles?" Vivienne turned away and walked toward the horses. Faolán looked back at Deirdre.

"Come along, Aengus. We must speak to her. It would be hurtful otherwise."

She watched us approach, and her eyes slowly rimmed with tears. She wiped them away as they spilled. She was thin and frail, with faint lines about her eyes. Those eyes still held a spark of untouchable youth marked with resentment and distrust. And yet she was a remarkable beauty, of fine features and silky, rust-colored hair.

"Mistress FitzGerald, I am Faolán Burke, and this is Aengus O'Daly, at your service."

"Thank you," she said. "Of course I know who you are." At the sound of her voice the boy stirred, sat up, and watched us curiously.

"We must thank you for speaking for Vivienne today."

"But she does not come."

"She is weary, ma'am, she is..."

"No. I understand. She should not. Tell her I...No. Tell her nothing. We must go soon, to return to Lismore. Lord Cork holds February 16 dear, and commands all his household to observe fasting and prayer. It is how we must mourn his poor wife, Katherine, dead these past four years. Go now, before he comes, and be happy. Do not let them take anything from you, not ever. These earls are demons, constructing traps to torment good, honest folk." A spark of anger flared, but then it failed her, and she wept again. The boy stroked her hand.

Cork walked toward the coach, crushing the gravel beneath his boots, his secretary and lawyers just behind. He pressed against the cane with each step, scowling from what I assumed to be pain in his hip or leg, but his scowl became more of a snarl when he saw Faolán speaking to Deirdre.

"Burke," he said angrily, "you need nothing more from us here. Be off now and let us be. I will send for you in one month's time, and not before."

"Lord Cork." Faolán bowed and we moved away from the coach. We had made an enemy, and a ruthless one at that.

Ormonde and Clanricarde paid Dean Chappell well for use of his rooms, and so the dean was generous in offering Faolán and Vivienne a hamper of bread, cheese, wine, and honey as a wedding gift for the journey home. The truth be told, I know not how we would have managed without it. We had weeks to wait before we would learn the settlement from Cork and likely even longer before the money would be forthcoming. We were down to our last few coins.

We accompanied Clanricarde as far as Mitchelstown, and then turned south from there to shorten our distance to Skebreen. We had traveled far by the second morning, still with four days of hard riding ahead of us. We would cover some of the same ways we had traveled when we first took Vivienne. Now that she and Faolán were wed, and the settlement commanded, we could travel without urgency. This time we need not worry about being pursued.

The night was cold with a strong wind. An inn at Rathcormac offered shelter from the weather, and Faolán negotiated a lower rate for the newlyweds. I slept on a pallet and twitched like a dog in deep, fitful dreams. When we awoke in the morning, Vivienne was gone.

Chapter Twenty

Trail of Ribbons

A desperate disease requires a dangerous remedy.

~ Guy Fawkes

We had been so very tired the night before. We slept heavily. Faolán walked about sleepily at first, thinking she had just gone to the kitchen or outside for some air. Her horse was where we had left it, in the paddock with the others. We waited for a few moments, looking about. Faolán asked the innkeeper and his children, had they seen her. In the carriageway, and in the wood behind, he called out for her. He was quickly rising to a panic.

"Has she has left me, Aengus?"

"How can you ask such a thing after what you've just been through? She made her choice clear to everyone. She would not leave. She is near."

"But where?"

He sat on the flagstone at the door of the inn, looking about and trying, I supposed, to decide what next to do, until his eyes settled on something. He pointed toward a hill we had crossed the night before. A crooked tree at the side of the road had an outstretched limb reaching to the north. And on the tip of the farthest branch something flickered, like a piece of ribbon held by a bony finger and fluttering in the wind.

"Do you see it, Aengus?"

A sudden twist squeezed my gut. "She's been taken."

We ran for the horses, leaving Vivienne's with the innkeeper until we could return. The ribbon was green, from Vivienne's dress. Tracks in the carriageway and on the ground confirmed what we suspected, leading back toward Fermoy, the last town we'd passed through before stopping at the inn. We galloped for nearly two miles until Faolán saw something and stopped. Clearly visible in the wheel ruts beside the tall grasses, another piece of green ribbon.

"Either she is leaving these for us, or her captor signals us to follow. Have your skean ready, Aengus."

We rode two miles farther, punishing the horses for greater speed, Faolán looking frantically for another piece of ribbon or any sign at all. Dark images coursed through my mind of terrible things that could happen to her at the hands of cruel men. A fierce pain clawed into the pit of my gut and the blood stormed through my veins. And then, at the moment I thought I might explode in anger, I knew.

"Faolán!" I called to him. "Stop! I know where she is."

We were close to Mitchelstown. Just before us, a tumble of large rocks leaned against each other like coffins stacked upright. Amidst the piled rock, a dark, jagged hole marked the surface, like an inkblot on parchment. There was no ribbon, but fresh tracks led directly into the ancient cave.

"Eames," Faolán said.

"Eames."

Caves could be found in many places at the foot of mountains or along coastal cliffs, but I never wished to enter one. They were naught but mysterious caverns where no sun shone, open gates reaching deep into hell to release the worst kinds of evil. Men entered caves and never came out again, swallowed up in the Devil's throat of stone.

Faolán dismounted quickly and checked his weaponry: a skean in his boot, his pistol in the waist of his breeches, a dagger in his sleeve. "Take everything you have that might help, Aengus. Bring the rope. We don't know what we'll find in there. Bring that skin of wine; she will surely need that. He left a trail for us. He has set his trap."

"Faolán, we've no light. How can we..."

"We'll tether the horses in those trees. Be as quiet as you can. He'll be waiting, but anything we can do to catch him off guard will be in our favor."

We entered the cave slowly. Sand and pebbles crunched beneath our boots though we tried to step lightly. The opening chamber was large enough for a horse to enter, and we found one hobbled inside. In the dim light it peered over its shoulder at us, curious but indifferent. The muscles seized about my ribs. Beyond where we stood, the daylight faded. Vivienne was somewhere within these black depths in the hands of a monster, and we must descend into the darkness to free her.

The width of the ground narrowed as we stepped. Cool air smelled of metal and sulphur and grew colder as we moved into the next chamber. The sounds of dripping water were all about us, as if we walked in a wood after a rain shower. But it was no wood. It was dark as night, and the only thing guiding us forward was a faint glow of amber light reflecting on a wall, where bright specks glinted at us as if to tease and beckon. Whispers echoed in all directions, and I knew not whether they were from Eames and Vivienne or from spirits trapped among the slimy rocks. Thin outlines of large rock cones reached up toward the ceiling, and smaller ones above them, some sharp as daggers, dripped and dripped down.

We felt our way forward by hand and foot, stepping carefully, knowing not where we had solid ground. The cave floor took a turn around a large boulder. Beyond it a new chamber opened, and the lantern light grew full. At the far end of the chamber Vivienne was on the ground against the stone cave wall, hands tied behind her, naked to the waist. Eames knelt before her, passing a lit candle stub back and forth beneath her nipples until she cried out.

"At long last." He turned and grinned at us, the light glinting off a new pearl earring that dangled from his undamaged ear, a bauble probably purchased with Cork's money. "We grew bored with all the waiting. You took a very long time to arrive. Didn't they, Vivienne? We're just having a little bit of entertainment to relieve our dreariness."

Her face was swollen red and streaked with tears. He pressed the stub against her breast to snuff the flame. She screamed and Faolán bolted, but Eames raised a pistol and grabbed a fistful of Vivienne's hair.

"Back off, you stinking bastard!" His lips curled to a snarl. He stood up slowly from his knees, pulling Vivienne up with him. Her eyes streamed, but she firmed her jaw and focused on Faolán.

"It took me hours to free myself from that tree back at the lake. It was quite frustrating, and I'll not forget. You should have just released her to me then. Your entire effort has been futile," Eames said.

"Get your *sarding* hands off her. Let her go. She's of no use to you now. She is wed to me. The Earl of Cork is ordered to settle with us. Your pursuit is over." Faolán's voice was surprisingly calm.

"Of course she'll be let go. Eventually. She is just a plaything now, Burke. She is no longer my target."

"Then release her."

"Eventually, I said. She is useful to me presently. Lord Cork grows tired of you meddling in his affairs. You are nothing, and he has much at stake. So, you must die, and he is willing to pay well for it. And I suppose your friend must die, too. So, then, welcome to your tomb. You will fall down the depths of the cavern, not to be found until you are nothing but bones. I am not sure what to do with her yet, but it doesn't matter— no one cares."

Eames jerked Vivienne closer and slowly drew his tongue up the side of her cheek, all the while his eyes focused on Faolán and his pistol aimed at his face. "She is quite tasty, is she not?"

Suddenly he shoved her to the ground and she shrieked. His pistol hand not wavering, he pressed his knee on her thigh. "Ah. This will be my prize as soon as you are dead." He thrust his free hand up her skirt. She screamed again and squirmed and bucked against him but could not break free. She managed to kick his chest just as Faolán leapt forward. I threw myself at him to push him away, knowing Eames would fire his shot. The explosion rang out and echoed around the chamber, repeating in my ears, hollow and heavy, a furious roar that filled the gaping maw of the cavern, and surrounded us as I fell. Then time suddenly slowed, and each of their faces loomed in turn before my eyes: Eames in surprise, Vivienne in horror, and Faolán in absolute rage. I hit the ground, but Faolán leapt past me. Both he and Vivienne threw themselves at Eames until I could no longer see him. Faolán pounded the man's face and chest as Vivienne used her weight against him, until Faolán had him by the throat, and then slammed Eames's skull against the stone; and then came a cracking sound and the unmistakable snap of Eames's neck. And at last, the whump of his body to the ground as Faolán released him and grasped Vivienne to his chest.

The echoes receded until only breathing remained, mingled with a loud rushing sound like the tiny ocean within a spiraled seashell. I was numb at first, except my body did not seem to move. And then as a wave washes into the shore, a searing pain pierced my side and surged through my body until it reached my scalp and my toes. Then it settled to one side of my body and bored into my ribs.

My face burned. My scalp sweated. I must have drifted away, for when I looked up again, Faolán and Vivienne were beside me. There was pressure on my side where Faolán had shoved his shirt, and Mairead's woolen cloak lay across me.

"We can't take Aengus to the castle," Faolán said. "It would mean trouble for all of us. We must find a healer nearby, who won't ask questions."

"Faolán, we've killed a man. We had to: it is justified. But we can't just leave him here."

"It's what he would have done with us. If we carry Eames into the village, what will we say? We will be called murderers, and we will not survive it. He is Cork's man, Cork will demand hanging for us all, and he owns all the judges. We have come too far, Vivienne. And we have to worry about Aengus. He is bleeding badly. If we do not see to it, I fear for him."

"You are right. We must find a healer straightaway. We'll say there was an accident."

"I've no coin left to pay, but we'll find something."

"Eames must have money."

"I'll take nothing from him," Faolán said. "Except..." Faolán went to Eames's body and plucked off the pearl earring. "This. I think he owes us this. I'll drag his body outside. It will look as if he fell from the stones and broke his neck. We'll release his horse, and someone will find him. Bring the lantern, will you? We must first get Aengus outside."

I must have slipped away again, and when I woke, I was held tightly in Faolán's arms, on a horse slowly crossing a field beneath a gloomy gray sky. Vivienne rode beside me, her hair in tangles, her face red and streaked. She'd wrapped her green shawl about her torn bodice for warmth, for I still had her cloak about me.

"Vivienne," I said. But nothing came out. I tried again, but it seemed my lips did not want to move. I forced them. "Viv."

She looked at me. "Oh, Aengus, please stay with us; we'll find help very soon. You will be well. You will."

"How..."

She shook her head. "I woke from my sleep and couldn't swallow, nor could I find the wine without waking you, so I went to the kitchen for water and found him waiting on the stair. I could not escape or make a sound, and I am so sorry." Her eyes filled with tears.

"I..." I wanted to tell her I was sorry she had been hurt, and now I was hurt, too, and sorry we were not on our happy journey home as we should have been, that she was not coming into the sunlit glen of her new home with the perfume of spring flowers all around her. I wanted to tell her things would be all right, and she was free, and I would see her dancing again soon, but I could not speak; it hurt to breathe, and though Faolán held me securely, with each step of his horse I was slipping closer and closer to the ground.

"I have you, *Teaghrán*," Faolán said, reading my mind once again.

Chapter Twenty-One

Glencurragh

*Tempt not the stars, young man, thou
canst not play with the severity of fate.*

~ John Ford

They'd cleansed my wound with the last of our wine. The healer in Fermoy said it had been wise to do so. The ball passed through the fleshy part between my ribs, but damage had been done that would take time to heal. He closed the wound, packed my bandage with herbs, and gladly took the earring, worth many times what he normally would have received as payment. And though I was no stronger, the bleeding had been stopped.

We collected Vivienne's horse from the inn and headed for Skebreen, but our pace was hindered by my soreness, and our moods weighed heavily with dread and uncertainty. Eames would have killed us and it was good that he was dead, but we had left him. Something about that seemed cruel and unclean. Faolán was right; we had no choice if we were to survive. Now it was up to each of us to forget, to make peace in our own souls, and to forgive ourselves for our part in what had happened.

When we arrived at Skebreen, Faolán took me to my father and claimed an accident with his pistol had been his fault. Knowing Faolán's prowess with weapons, my father was skeptical, but accepted the story quietly and took care of me. He grumbled and complained of my uselessness until time spent in bed was intolerable. Any morning I could not rise meant a day closer to death. I willed myself to sit instead of lay, and to read instead of sleep. I pushed myself until I was strong again. When I could walk steadily, I walked every day. And when I could cross the river and walk the hill to

Glencurragh, Faolán and Vivienne welcomed me joyfully.

Faolán showed me where he had cleared away the vines and rubble to define the ground for the new castle walls adjoining the remains of the old ones. Vivienne had revived the kitchen garden and found double rows of peas. People from the village had brought bread, corn, eggs, cheese, and beer to welcome Faolán's new bride. And the little thatched cottage was cleaner and brighter than ever I had seen it. The landscape seemed to take notice, for the bluebells were blooming early among the trees nearby, and even the faerie thorn by the front door showed tender green sprouts.

"I had to barter some good hard labor for it, but we'll have meat in our stew this evening, Aengus." Faolán slipped an arm around Vivienne's waist and pulled her close. He looked lean, strong, and confident, the swaggering warrior he'd been when we were teenagers learning our books and our weapons. Vivienne looked calm, her smile bright and cheerful, and the angry and doubtful cast behind her eyes had been replaced with something both complex and serene. Maybe it was what love looked like, and belief in a new life.

The wind changed direction, coming out of the northwest and bringing a colder air that swept along the riverbanks and heaved the tree branches toward the sea. We moved indoors to escape it. Faolán stoked the hearth fire to a crackle of orange flames while we allowed the stew to simmer.

"We are managing, my friend," Faolán told me. "Our physical wounds have healed, but we've yet to cast off the shadows of that day. It will take more time. And we have each other and our projects to tend. Work has been harder to find. I have visited some who use me as their messenger, but I'm told they have no work for me. Even Lord Condon, who has typically kept me most busy, claims he has nothing to offer. It is a curious thing."

"Aye, it is queer," I answered. "And what of Lord Cork?"

"We'll hear from him soon, I reckon. And in the meantime, I've a lovely bride to feed, and Dunerayl as well, who has the appetite of three stallions." He smiled. "We'll be all right for a while yet."

"Look, Aengus," Vivienne said. "Faolán has taught me how to make camp bread." She proudly lifted the ash-dusted lid from an iron pot to reveal a rounded loaf within, slowly baked from top and bottom by the smoldering coals of the hearth fire. Her loaf was slightly charred on the top, but it smelled fine enough to set my mouth watering.

I stayed the night, for it was well past dark after we enjoyed the hearty stew. In the morning Vivienne filled me with more bread and honey before I started home again. There was much to be done at my father's inn, but I was bothered by what Faolán had said about Lord Condon. Here was a man of letters, always at his desk penning messages of some sort, whether they be advice or complaints to the local constable, business with his agent in Dublin, or news to his relations at Castletownroche and Midleton. He signed them all with a flourish and sealed them with wax. Being that his legs were a bit palsied, it was his way of socializing in the world. I decided I must see him myself.

Lord Condon's stone house faced east on a hill just west of the village, with great windows overlooking the River Ilen. It was still a challenge for me to climb a steep rise, but I was determined to gain all of my strength back and curiosity was a strong driver. The plain oak door to his house had been painted a dark forest green since I'd visited last. Nara, his maid for many years, admitted me. And though to Lord Condon I was just a lowborn village boy, he welcomed me graciously from his wingback chair facing the window, a book in his hand, his long white hair a shambles about his face and his wiry eyebrows a mad ruckus.

"And there you are," he said. "Faolán Burke was here not a week ago. Used to be, you boys never went annawheres the one without the other."

"Lord Condon, I came to see if you are well. I am happy to find that you are. Faolán said you had no letters to send, and I couldn't recall a week to pass without at least one to be delivered from your fiery pen."

"Still the smart one o' you two rambunctious boys. I hear Faolán has got himself wed, and to a ginger-haired lass."

"She's a beauty, sir, and nearly as fiery as you. They mean to build up Sir William's castle."

"There's a chore for any man. Little to build from, I'd say. He's set himself a steep mountain to climb. Are you to help him with it?"

"It is my plan, yes, once things get started. For now I owe my father a good bit of time and labor."

Lord Condon laughed. "And so you will until the day the old fella passes from the earth. Say, I'm glad you've come, because as a matter of fact, I did have a thought or two and wrote a couple of letters, just for in the village, you see." Lord Condon patted his coat pockets and ran his fingers beside the cushion of his chair. "I'll find them in just…"

"'Tis no hurry, Lord Condon. I'll tell Faolán to stop by."

Lord Condon frowned, and his face turned pale. "I'd rather you just take them yourself now, if you would. It's no need to bother for Faolán and his fast horse."

"I could hardly take his work from him, Lord Condon." He blinked his small blue eyes at me, and my breath caught in my throat. "It's Lord Cork, isn't it?"

Lord Condon looked away from me and sighed. "The smart one, as I said." He gazed out the window.

"Has he written to you? Has he warned the gentlemen of Munster not to hire Faolán Burke?"

He was silent for a moment, then rubbed his jaw and faced me.

"A man must pay careful attention, Aengus, to events and relationships that weigh upon one's own livelihood. A decision, however beneficial in the moment, may have much broader consequences not apparent forthwith. It takes experience, hard lessons, and some wise ancestors a-whisperin' in your ear to help you navigate each day, protecting and maintaining what belongs to you. Risk is for the young.

"Faolán? Now, that boy has an enviable passion for life, the imagination and belief he can make things happen, and he is driven by a long ago promise that his father never imposed on him. He is a man of heart, but foolhardy. He takes risks. He rushes in when caution be the rule of the day. You were always the boy with his eyes open and his feet upon the ground. 'Tis your loyalty that trips you."

A little uneasiness stirred the pit of my stomach. "Thank you for the compliment, Lord Condon. But I am concerned for my friend. Faolán only does what he does because we have no choices here to make a good living. He reaches higher, for all of us. But he has a new wife now, and debts to pay. They'll likely have a family coming. Is this something he'll be able to overcome?"

Lord Condon laughed, not a hearty laugh, but a kind one. "My boy, everything can change on a whim. You are certainly old enough to have discovered that. But you're the O'Daly. What do the omens tell you? I have no vision to the future. I can only say be careful, the both of you. Now, let me see."

Lord Condon fumbled around and finally produced a letter, folded to palm size and sealed with his signature wax. "Here, lad, 'tis nothing but a note for the constable in Skebreen. McTeige thinks he's got a lamb missing. Probably a wolf prowling around at night, or mebbe he just miscounted. But the constable ought be aware."

I took the letter in my hand, though it did burn me to do so.

Chapter Twenty-Two

Letters

No beauty doth she miss, when all her robes are on,
but beauty's self she is, when all her robes are gone

~ Madrigal, 1602

On the last day of February, the letter arrived from Lord Cork. I was first to know, for Cork's messenger left it at the inn rather than crossing the Ilen to find Faolán's home. I carried it there early the next morning. He stood outside his door, his hair a bushy tangle, his eyes still puffy with sleep, and read it carefully. Relief washed over his face.

"He's set a meeting in five days, Aengus, at Lismore Castle. We'll need to leave early tomorrow. You'll be coming, won't you?"

"Of course," I said quickly, though I could already feel Da cuffing the top of my head at the mere mention of it.

"Vivienne!" he shouted, "We've good news and Aengus is here for breakfast!"

She came outside, and he scooped her up by the waist and twirled her in circles around the faerie thorn tree. She laughed and squealed like a child.

The day was sunny and warmer than it had been for several weeks. When we'd finished packing for the journey, Faolán built a campfire by the river, and we gathered around it, talking excitedly about the journey. Vivienne refused to wear the green gown again after the experience in Fermoy, but she was skilled in needlework and had repurposed some of its parts into a new dress that would work well for the meeting with the earl. Faolán focused on the route we would take, from the Dunmanway townland straight through Cork City and then back to Rathcormac.

"From there it's a day's ride to Lismore. You won't believe the size of Cork's castle, Aengus. I've been through there just once, but cannot forget it."

"When we return home, we'll start on our own castle right away," Vivienne said.

"Aye, we've already started, love. We have our plans, and the ways are cleared. We've been busy, have we not?"

"We have." She smiled. "I want to have a balcony, so that when we wake in the morning we can throw the doors wide, step out into the sunshine, and look out across the meadow to the river."

"You shall have it, my beauty."

"And in the great room, a wide stair with spiraling newels."

"It shall be the envy of all. And you will glide down the steps in gowns of silk and satin, and everyone will cast roses at your feet."

Vivienne laughed as he kissed her fingers.

Faolán nodded. "And so it shall be. But for now I must practice my swordsmanship, to protect my lovely queen from dangers on our long journey."

Vivienne and I sat comfortably on the grasses and stoked our small fire while Faolán retrieved his sword from its place inside the cottage, beneath the rushes against the wall by the door. It was a long and mighty broadsword, but in his hands it looked as light as a rapier. He found a flat portion of ground several yards away where he'd have plenty of room to work. We watched him maneuver, thrusting forward, skipping back, widening his stance, and swinging a killing blow from the left and then from the right.

"He is good with a sword, isn't he?" Vivienne asked.

"He is. He was well trained and practices his skills when most men have cast off their swords to take up the plow."

"He is different, though. He knows he has a higher destiny."

"I suppose he is lucky in that, Vivienne. It drives him, and he does not sadly accept whatever is placed at his feet. He fights for what he wants."

"Tell me of his mother, please, Aengus? Faolán won't speak of her, nor even mention her name."

"Always that will be a sore spot for him, I s'pose. She died when he was ten years old."

"Isn't that when his father died?"

"Aye, within a few weeks. After Sir William died, she locked herself in her bedchamber and would not come out for food or water. They had to break the door down, but by the time they reached her, she was burning with a fever that would not break. People say she willed herself to die, her heart broken."

"She didn't love her son enough to live for him?"

"I think she loved him very much, but mebbe her soul died along with Sir William and she had nothing left to give. It's the only way I can make any sense of it."

"How terribly sad. I see now why he wants so much to rebuild what they had. Their dream became his dream, and it is how he keeps them alive. Without it he would have nothing left at all."

"And now he has you. But what about your own mother?"

"Och!" she scoffed. "I am as Faolán in that I don't care to speak of her, but for you, Aengus, I shall. My mother, darling Deirdre, married Alfred, a son of the fifteenth Earl of Desmond. He had a manor house near Dungarvan. He would not ascend to the earldom, but was considered a good match because he was of noble blood, and quite a successful merchant. That is, until he was lost at sea to a storm on the Atlantic when I was just a baby. She lost her mind then. She had such poor behavior as a mother some of the townspeople asked Lord Cork to step in.

"And so he did, and brought us into his household happily, because my mother was quite beautiful and he could take complete control of all her finances. He was never kind to me, but moved me about from monastery to foster homes until I was of marriageable age. In all those years she has shown nothing but weakness, bowing to his every decision. She lives under his *protection*, but to my eyes she's nothing more than his housemaid."

"I am sorry, Vivienne."

She sighed and then shrugged as if casting it all from her shoulders.

"Begging your pardon," Faolán called from the grasses, "but I am doing magnificent work out here, and have heard not a single whistle for my splendid abilities. Of what on earth do you speak?"

"Your father!" Vivienne called to him. "Come here and tell us your stories."

"Ah! That I can do." Faolán placed the sword flat in front of him and sat on the ground between us. "I was just thinking of one of my father's tales. To handle the sword always brings the memories. Aengus, can you bear it yet again? Well, no matter anyhow, I must tell it." He interlaced his fingers and turned his palms inside out for a great crack.

"Now then. My father had a cousin of his own age named Barra. As boys they trained together to fight and wield a sword, and had kissed their first lassies beneath the same August moon. But when my father went to serve the Earl of Clanricarde, Barra joined Redmond Burke's famous band of rebels. Redmond's was the path of hopelessness, but his ranks swelled with Irishmen as angry as he, who'd been displaced from their homes.

"Redmond swore to destroy everything in sight before letting the English have it. One day, with bad intent, Redmond marched his men toward the villages and castles of Clanricarde.

"Sir William knew he'd be in for a fight, but couldn't bear the idea of having to kill his cousin. Barra felt the same for William. So, they made a pact. In a light skirmish, each would make a great show of outfighting the other, Barra to look fierce in front of his mates as William escaped, and then vice versa, for William to appear to best his cousin. Both would look formidable, and both would survive." Faolán stood with his sword so he could act out the next part. He waved a palm toward the horizon.

"When the time came and the skirmish was at hand, a vast storm formed over the mountaintops as if to herald the great fight. The two cousins stood face-to-face, but the terrain had forced the men of both sides into close contact. Both sides were watching the parry. For either William or Barra to back away would show cowardice. And so they circled, they growled, and they swung their swords." Faolán swung his broadsword in a great arc over his head.

"As they made their show, each wondering what the other would do, a great thunderclap split the clouds." Faolán dropped his sword and clapped his hands together. "A bright bolt of lightning burst from the heavens and struck a nearby tree, exploding it to splinters and dashing the two warriors apart.

"The men on both sides ran to the woods for safety. But William and Barra tarried just long enough to exchange a wink and a smile. Neither could be labeled the coward, for God made his intentions clear: both were to live in peace. And never again would the two cousins meet."

He raised his hands before him. "It is truth, I swear it." He looked at us as if expecting high praise or applause. I smirked, having heard the story at least a thousand times. It was an ancient Irish legend, but it had little to do with Sir William. Vivienne tilted her head and pursed her lips as if deep in thought.

"Aengus, will you look at those hands? Truly, they are large enough for two men. I believe, had we a boat, they could be our oars."

"Aye, 'tis true, and didn't we warn you about them the night you met? Should you need a shovel for your garden, you'd need to look no further."

"It is so. And I don't know why I bother carrying a jug down to the river for water. In his bare hands he can scoop up more than I can carry." Faolán stared at us, his face reddening, and then he caught the humor and grinned.

Vivienne stood next to Faolán, plucked up his hand, and inspected the palm. "Quite honestly, a fellow with such hands ought to do something useful with them."

"Useful, is it?" Faolán said. "Usefulness is what you're looking for? Because I can show you"—he flipped his hand around and caught her by the wrist—"something wicked useful."

She wrenched her arm away and ran into the bluebells with him right after her, the two of them laughing all the way. Vivienne was swift and light, but Faolán was a trained runner and much faster. He brought her down with ease among the flowers. I watched them frolic until Vivienne's heels kicked into the air. I should have turned away, I know, but I am human after all, and it was much more amusing and interesting than gazing at the fire. Eventually I lost sight of them amidst the thrashing and blending of green grasses, blue petals, and warm, dappled sunlight.

When Faolán returned to the campfire, we were alone. We sat together silently for a few moments while he poked the coals with a stick, and I knew I had to tell him. There would never be a good time.

"Faolán, I've been to see Lord Condon."

His face brightened. "Well, have you now? And is he well?"

"He is himself, as always. Nara looks after him. I'm to take a letter to the constable."

"A letter? But he did not give it to me?"

"He had just written, it Faolán. I didn't want to take it but he insisted. He wanted to tell the constable that MacTiege has a lamb missing."

"Does he? Terribly bad, then."

"Faolán, please tell me you've not gone to stealin' lamb to keep the meat in your pot."

Faolán stared blankly into my eyes. "Aengus, is that what you're thinking? You should have asked me straightaway. I told you I'd worked hard for a bit of meat, and so I had; I'd not steal it. You must trust me better than that."

"I do, but you've not had a beautiful wife to feed before now."

Faolán grinned. "Well, she doesn't eat much, lad. If I was stealing somethin' for her, it would be spirits from your father's inn!"

We laughed. Thanks be to God my fears had been wrong. But still I had to tell him the rest.

"There is more, Faolán. I'm afraid your lack of income could worsen. Lord Condon admitted he'd had a letter from Lord Cork, warning him not to use you as his runner anymore."

Faolán's cheeks flushed dark. "Is it so? Well now, that would be a cruel bit of business."

He was silent for a few moments, staring into the fire. Then he shrugged it off. "Well, sard it. No matter. We're not reliant on that work alone, Aengus. Vivienne and I have made plans. We'll buy a few head of cattle, and when we get a bit more money, we'll buy horses. We plan to breed them, train them and sell them. We'll be known throughout Munster as the finest of horse breeders, and it'll make a legacy for our children. And more than that, when Clanricarde negotiates the return of the lands north of here, I know a place where there's ore to be found. We'll have a smelter."

I gave out a big sigh. Faolán and his plans, always changing, always growing. "I'm glad, Faolán." I said it, and I was glad. But I was starting to despair for the great Glencurragh. The age of castles already had passed, though we refused to know it.

Chapter Twenty-Three

The Settlement

The blood-thirsty tyrant in one man's eyes,
is but a strong-minded prince in those of another.

~ George Bennett, Esq.

The next morning we broke our fast with bread and broth, and then I helped Faolán gather the blanket rolls and the saddlebags packed with essentials, while Vivienne packed food and water. I borrowed my uncle's horse again and carried most of the packs. Vivienne rode with Faolán on Dunerayl.

In the brief time the three of us had been together, so many memories had been created on the pathways we followed, from the first trip to see Lord Barry, to the return trip from Cashel and the trouble in Mitchelstown. At least now we were able to keep to the main coast road, no longer seeking cover as outlaws.

In three days we reached Rathcormac. From there to Lismore, the way was dense with brush and a few forested hills. We forded the River Bride near a southward bend where the early March wind was unimpeded. It whipped around our faces and chilled our hands. We descended into a valley and when we came around a low hill the tall corner bastions of Lismore Castle came into view. We crossed the stone bridge on its west wall, and approached the ancient stone gate. Above it the Earl of Cork's arms were chiseled, and his motto: *God's providence is our inheritance.*

We entered there, passing two sentries, and lodged our horses in the arched openings of the enormous carriage house just inside. Even more than at Mallow, people hurried about to accomplish their daily tasks,

scurrying in and out of the archways and picking through the mud puddles, running across the manure-scented courtyard, scattering chickens
and sloshing water pails. A wagon creaked as a young man relieved it of
a load of hay. We walked along a vast, shaded avenue with stone walls on
each side, our pace slowed by the lumbering steps of a portly maid, who
herded her cackling flock of geese with a broom and a spotted dog.

At last the castle entrance loomed before us, framed by large white columns with Greek scrolls, as if Cork thought he had descended from Mount
Olympus. We looked at one another without speaking, already knowing,
anxious of entering a lion's den. Why hadn't we asked Ormonde or Clanricarde to attend with us? Even in the best of circumstances, we were at a
disadvantage.

Cork's steward led us through a shadowy wood-paneled hallway
across marble floors and into the great room where Lord Cork would
receive us. Here the floor was dark polished wood, reflecting the bright
glare from many tall windows. Near the blazing fireplace there were
stag hides on the floor, and antlers hung on either side of a large Dutch
tapestry. Cork watched us from behind his desk, situated on a dais
inside an alcove of seven windows.

The light was nearly blinding to anyone who faced him from the chairs,
making it difficult at times to read or even see Cork's eyes. A lawyer in a
black coat stood to his left, reading from some papers, and to his right Deirdre sat in a high-backed chair, her dark blue skirts almost obscuring her
exotic boy-companion. Two more lawyers talked quietly in chairs against
the wall, and two liveried servants flanked the great doors.

"Come in, gentlemen and Vivienne, and sit down," Cork said, waving us forward. There were three high-backed chairs arranged for us
in front of his desk. They were hard and uncomfortable, especially
after our long ride, and we had to look up and into the light to see Lord
Cork's unsmiling face. He called to the steward.

"Our guests must be parched after their journey. Please bring us
some wine."

He spoke no pleasantries while we waited, but scratched his pen across
the page of a journal while the lawyer stood by. Deirdre remained silent,
but her eyes flicked back and forth between Cork, the lawyer and Vivienne, while the boy occasionally sighed and stroked the hem of her skirt.
Vivienne sat stiff and straight-backed, staring toward the windows behind
Cork. Faolán's face was firm and impassive. He held Vivienne's hand, and

glanced at me only once, as if to reassure me or himself that all would be well.

At last the steward returned with a large silver platter, followed by a servant carrying a second platter. The steward served a light-colored wine to Cork, Deirdre, and his lawyers, who vulgarly smacked their lips. From the second platter the servant offered us short glasses half-filled with an amber wine. Everyone took a glass except for the boy, as there was nothing offered to him. I sipped. The taste was sour and the wine probably quite old, but I didn't reveal my displeasure. Cork had deliberately served us an inferior drink, the spiteful old man. We waited in silence until he set down his pen and folded his hands upon the desktop.

"Gentlemen and ladies," he said, "as you know, we are here today to conclude the settlement of the Lady Vivienne's inheritance for her new household, in compliance with the request of our Lord Deputy, Thomas Wentworth. I thank you, Mister Burke, Mister O'Daly, and Mistress Vivienne for making the long journey.

"My secretary is on an important assignment for me today and could not join us. Standing in for him are Thomson here, and my lawyers Bentall and Witham. It is of grave importance that they assist me in this process. We must be certain for all parties involved that we are detailed and diligent, that our actions are beyond question or reproach by any future proceeding. Are we agreed?"

I looked to Faolán, but he did not turn, his face as stiff and proud as a wood owl. He nodded, and then Vivienne nodded.

"Fine then. Let's to our business. The lady Vivienne's expected inheritance prior to her marriage was approximately £800 annually. This money comes in part through a small allowance from the Earl of Desmond estate, and the larger balance from the estate of his second son, Alfred. We are charged with ensuring this money is properly distributed to bona fide recipients."

I did not know what Cork was getting at, using words like "bona fide." The recipients were very clear and seated before him. I tried not to appear impatient, but I noticed the fingers of Faolán's right hand had coiled to a fist.

"To do this," Cork continued, "my lawyers have combed through the records to document the lineage of both Vivienne and her husband, Faolán Burke. Let us begin with Mister Burke."

Thomson straightened his back, took a breath, and read from his papers in grandiloquent language I could not understand or repeat.

"And so," he concluded at the end of his gibberish, "it appears all in order: you are who you claim, son of Sir William of Skebreen and Elisabeth of Thurles, and claimed as kinsman by Sir Ulick Burke, son of the Earl of Clanricarde."

"Thank you, Thomson," Faolán said, an edge in his voice. "These things are already established."

"And now they are recorded," Cork said sternly.

"I beg your pardon, sir," Thomson said, looking up from his papers, "if you should find yourself bored by your own heritage. I wonder will you be better entertained by the lineage of your new bride."

Cork grinned and then tried unsuccessfully to stifle it. "Proceed, Mister Thomson."

"Thank you, my lord." Thomson returned to his papers and turned a page. "Now then, in our discovery of the lineage of Vivienne FitzGerald, we must go back further in time based on claims that her mother, the Lady Deirdre, is descended directly from the great Lady Joan FitzGerald on the maternal side. Our diligent search has turned up no such record. In fact, we find no birth record at all for her that can be traced back to Joan." He paused, looking at each of us to measure the effect of his information. The hairs on the back of my neck began to rise. It was not clear where he was heading, but for certain it was not where we would have intended.

"There is a record, however," he continued, "written in the priest's own hand, dating back to 1550. At this time, the Lady Joan was married to Sir Francis Bryan. Sir Francis was, as we all know, the famed courtier and diplomat who had served our King Henry VIII."

"Sir," Faolán interrupted the lawyer, "please excuse me, but you are addressing a time more than eighty years past. I cannot imagine any bearing it may have on the inheritance bestowed on our lady Vivienne by her father."

Cork said nothing, his face like stone, but the lawyer fumed. "You must allow me to finish. My research is excellent and of tremendous importance. It is recorded that a daughter was born in that year to one Dorothy Leach, with Sir Francis's name written next to it. That daughter was Sir Francis's bastard, because he was, of course, married. As we follow the line of Dorothy Leach, we find that in 1594, her granddaughter Mary gave birth to a baby girl, given the name of Deirdre."

Deirdre wept, and Vivienne stared at her. Faolán rose from his chair.

"Now wait just a moment, Thomson. What are you trying to do here?" Faolán asked, a clear warning in his voice. Thomson took a small step back, but Lord Cork sat still as a hawk, only his gaze shifting, focused sharply on the movements of his prey.

"I am simply reporting the facts, Mister Burke. Sir Francis Bryan was well-known for his extramarital activities. He was admired at court, but also was known as a rake. By this time he had earned the nickname 'the vicar from hell.' It is not surprising that he would have fathered bastard children."

"I don't believe I have questioned Sir Francis's character. Study any courtier from King Henry's time and you will find dalliance. It is ancient history and has no bearing *here*," Faolán said.

"Our concern is only with Sir Francis and the Lady Joan as a means of confirming noble blood. Joan was widely known to be of kind heart. She bore her husband seven sons and would not have turned away a bastard child in need of a nurturing home," Thomson continued.

Deirdre sobbed and wailed, and the boy at her feet wailed along with her. Vivienne turned away from them, rose to her feet beside Faolán, and spoke. "This was all so long ago. What does any of it have to do with..."

"We are suggesting," Thomson interrupted her, "or rather postulating, that Lady Joan must have kindheartedly taken in Dorothy Leach's illegitimate child, perhaps as a favor before Sir Bryan died. Once he had passed away and Joan was wed to her *third* and much younger husband, Gerald FitzGerald," Thomson said, his lips turning into a sneer, "then, well, it is not exactly clear what happened, but our research strongly indicates that Deirdre descends not from Joan, but from Dorothy Leach. And out of sheer kindness in her later years, Lady Joan saw Deirdre matched to Alfred FitzGerald, Gerald's second son, thereby keeping her within the same noble family."

"You *suggest* this to be true?" Faolán raised his voice. "You don't *know* what happened, but we are to take *your word* on this absurd meandering of lineage you have concocted to discredit my wife?" Foalán's fists were clenched, his jaw throbbing. "It is nothing but imaginings and despicable lies."

Cork raised his hands. "Gentlemen, please! Let's settle down. Faolán and Vivienne, sit down. Let me explain what I will do."

Faolán's cheeks had turned a dark crimson, while Vivienne's were completely drained of color and her eyes had turned dark as tar.

"Please," Vivienne said, "do tell us exactly what is to be done with *my* inheritance."

Lord Cork smiled benevolently, as a priest to a sinner. "My dear, that is my intention. As you know, Deirdre has been a part of my household for many years now, and my family has come to treasure her and rely on her. It is within my power and within my heart that, though she is not a true descendent of Joan, she shall remain here with us, and we will treat her exactly the same. She is not diminished in our eyes. You will not have to concern yourselves for her maintenance; I will take very good care of her for all of her life."

At this, Deirdre rose up from her chair and ran from the room, the boy running after her.

"You see?" Cork said. "She is relieved and overcome, and I am grateful to God that I may be of such standing to do this for her. Now let us turn to other matters."

"We are waiting," Faolán said.

"As you know, we must adhere strictly to the exact wording of a last will and testament and any defined trust or inheritance. A nobleman's legacy is at stake. I cannot in good conscience release funds from the estate of a nobleman into the hands of an illegitimate offspring without clear direction thereto."

"I am not illegitimate," Vivienne said flatly. "I am born of my father, who was legally wed to my mother, and he was a true FitzGerald, son of the earl. The blood of my mother does not change that."

"It does, my dear, if he was misled, if he wed Deirdre under false representation, assuming she was of pure and noble blood when in fact we have no clear knowledge of her bloodline after Sir Francis. Surely you can understand our predicament. It is not of our choosing, but we must protect the bloodline and legacy, as well as the assets of this great historic family."

"And what of the daughter?" Vivienne asked. "Do you think this is what my father would have wanted for me? Is my blood not of his?"

"The daughter bears a stain on her descendancy. We cannot know what the father truly would have wished because he was unaware of this at the time of his death, and so propriety must be our guide. The daughter must count herself fortunate to have wed a healthy young man who can work hard to support her. We must all work hard for our gains in life, my dear."

"I am asking you for what is rightfully mine, Lord Cork. Your assignment from the Lord Deputy was to prepare my settlement." Her voice was strong, but her eyes had begun to fill. "You had no concerns about my lineage when you were negotiating with other suitors."

"The rightfulness has only now been questioned, Vivienne. We must be diligent. You are not a bastard child yourself, that is true, but you are not a true and pure descendent of nobility according to the law. Your blood is tainted on your mother's side, and therefore you are not eligible for the inheritance you seek."

Faolán jumped to his feet and swung across the desk, but I caught his arm or he would have bloodied Lord Cork's nose, and then we'd all be accused of assaulting the earl. All three lawyers leapt to their feet to protect him.

"You will not get away with this. If my father was alive he would have your head for it." Vivienne said. "May he and the Lady Joan haunt you for all the days remaining in your cruel and wretched life, *sir*."

Cork appeared unshaken, but I do believe his cheeks flushed. He stood, and Thomson pulled the chair back behind him. "Haunt? *I* should be haunted?" Cork said, lifting his chin. "What an interesting choice of words, Vivienne. I think it may rather be you and your husband to be haunted. Our business is done and decided. Now you will excuse me; I must go. I have an important meeting to attend. Bentall, please fetch my hat, will you, the one gifted to me by the Lord Deputy."

The lawyer fetched the earl's hat from the sideboard, a tall beaver skin with a wide brim. Cork stared at Faolán as he placed the hat firmly on his head and arranged it so the brim turned up over his right ear. A jewel was pinned there to decorate the smooth black fur—the pearl earring that had belonged to Geoffrey Eames.

Chapter Twenty-Four

Insult and Injury

Doubt thou the stars are fire; Doubt that the sun doth move;
Doubt truth to be a liar; But never doubt I love

~ William Shakespeare

Having been escorted from the castle, there was nothing we could do but return to Skebreen and try to determine our next course of action. Vivienne fumed in icy silence as Faolán and I tried to decipher what had happened.

"It was Eames's pearl, I am sure of it. The healer must have sold it," Faolán said.

"How would Cork know? How would he have found such a thing?"

"You know Cork has spies everywhere. Something like that pearl is easy to remember. If the healer tried to sell it, he probably raised some gossip. Someone remembered it to one of Cork's men, that's all. I never should have taken it."

"But what became of Eames?"

"How would I know? I am sure someone found his body, as we'd expected. We had no choice in what we did. You were injured and might have died, *Teaghrán*. There's no point in rethinking it all now. But the message from Cork is clear, isn't it?"

"He can't accuse us of murder. No one even knows we were there. And besides that, Cork is the one who sent Eames to murder *us*."

"So he did, and he would do it again. If we make trouble, he'll make more."

"Cork made a point of telling us his secretary was on a special assignment. I think I know where that was."

"Aye, Aengus, and what does your insight tell you now? Mine is screaming loudly in my ears that he rides like the wind to Dublin to present this *settlement* to the Lord Deputy and get it approved and signed before we have time to refute it. What lawyers shall we hire, using our vast fortune, to dig up new evidence and show we are of sufficient pedigree to receive what is already ours?"

Vivienne pressed against Faolán. "Stop and let me down, please."

Faolán reined Dunerayl to stop, dismounted, and lifted Vivienne to the ground.

"Thank you," she said. "Now go."

Faolán looked at her. "Vivi, do you need to relieve yourself?"

She scoffed. "Go! Please. I am of no use to you now. Leave me here. I will do what I must do, and it means going back to Lismore. That money belongs to me, and I won't let him keep it because he wears a pearl on his hat."

"Vivienne, it is more than that. You understand we..."

"I understand that everything we've been through together, everything since you swept me from my bed in Bandon, has been for nothing without my inheritance. All the dreams we talked about in Skebreen were just useless prattle without it." She turned and walked away from him in the direction from which we'd come.

"But where are you going?" Faolán asked, sounding confused and strained.

"I am just baggage on your horse, Faolán. I cannot accept this. I can't live with it. All my life, my inheritance was the one thing that was going to set me free, to make me worthy of respect, and to give me some control over my own life. Now Cork has stolen it from me. I have to go back. I'll beg him, even be a maid in his house like my mother, whatever it requires. I will *make* him pay, even if I have to steal it back day-by-day. At least I'll have food, clean clothes, and a solid roof over my head while I do it."

Faolán looked stricken. His voice softened. "Viv, I will give you all those things. I will give you more."

Vivienne shook her head. "What more? You have been squeezed by Cork as much as I, and you've just said you have no way even to fight back."

"Have we not been happy together? I will give you love, and you know you'll never find it at Lismore. I will give you freedom; you will not be imprisoned as your mother has been. And I am a warrior. Look at me. I am strong, and I am fierce. I will fight for you in ways you've not yet seen."

She looked away, as if she could not pass the spot on which she stood or she'd be forever changed, as if to move in either direction would tear her heart.

"Please, Vivienne, you must trust me. Or if you can't, remember and trust St. Agnes. And then think of our vows. A year and a day, wasn't it? Give me that much, at least, to prove to you that we'll have everything we've dreamed."

The tension melted from her face and her gaze was locked on Faolán's, yet she stood her ground. I waited, watching, barely able to breathe as they studied each other, the stillness pooling and bracing like water before cascading over a fall. Then Faolán reached out his hand to her.

"I can't do anything without you, Viv. Not anymore." His eyes glistened. Vivienne lost her resolve then, and she ran to him.

They held each other for a long time, until the scents of the air grew smoky and the fresh March wind swirled around us, until Dunerayl shifted impatiently and released a heavy sigh, and until the cold sprinkle of rain wet my scalp and the backs of my hands. Without a word they mounted Dunerayl, and we continued our journey. Vivienne pulled the hood over her hair, and Faolán held her closely. I couldn't see her face, but I knew she was weeping.

When we came to Skebreen, it was night under heavy clouds, only the tip of a half-moon showing like the head of a broad arrow, and our way was brooding and dark. There was no one in the village, and even my father was sleeping, not a single candle shining through the windows of the inn. They left me there, just as eager as I to be home.

I unsaddled and watered my uncle's horse and left him resting in the byre, then crept silently along the passageway through the door into the inn. How I would have loved to see a big fire burning in the hearth, but it was securely banked for the night. Before me was pure darkness. I felt my way along every support beam, every table and every bench, the shelf against the wall where we prepared the food, the stands for the hogsheads of ale from the brewhouse out back. I swelled with joy from the smell of it. To my right, the creaky little staircase would lead me to my own lumpy bed for a sleep. To my left a thin moonbeam pierced the clouds to light the floor and give me a start, illuminating the hem of a skirt and a pair of muddy boots.

"And where have *you* been?" Sheelagh's voice was sharp and accusing. With one small phrase my sister ripped from beneath me all the joy of homecoming.

"Sheelagh, you startled me. Could you not have had a candle end lit or something? I have been with Faolán and Vivienne up to Lismore. We are just returned. What are you doing here?"

"I've been helpin' our father, ye selfish brute. Ye think he's a young man and can handle on his own all there's to do here? He's gone sick, he has, groanin' in his bed. It's his back mostly. He can't sleep for the pain of it and won't eat at all."

"And so you've left him alone upstairs in the cold and dark, not even a fire to warm his bones?"

"I'm here, ain't I? He refused it!"

"Bah! He'd refuse a stack of gold coins if it was handed to him, complainin' it's too heavy. I'll light it myself and pay no heed to his complaints. Raise a cook fire, would you, and we'll get some broth into him?"

"All right then, but I've got me own home and family to get back to now yer here."

"Aye, but just a bit longer, sis."

I bounded up the stairs, not caring for the noise I made. In his cold, dark room, I could barely make out the shape of my father, lying stiffly on his side. I touched his brow.

"What on earth has happened, Da?"

"Had ye been where ye were supposed to...well, I, I fell, tippin' a hogshead to its bottom...couldna rise up again. FitzGibbon brung me up, sent for Sheelagh. Can find no comfort, boy. No way to sit, stand or lay without pain. 'Tis the end o' me when a man can't do his work."

"Shush, Da! You need a remedy is all, to give you ease. A chickweed poultice and some boiled-nettle brew, then you'll heal just fine. I'll take care of everything until we get you right again."

I hollered down the stair. "Sheelagh, I'll bring him by the hearth to warm his bones. He needs a boiled nettle—can you fetch it?"

"The whole world's asleep: are ye daft?"

"Try Sheelagh, please. They'll wake for it, to help Da. 'Tis the last I'll ask of you."

She grumbled angrily but went out as I knew she would, and I settled

Da on a pallet near the crackling fire. He groaned until the tears slipped from the corners of his eyes. Never in my life had I seen the man weep, and I wept just as surely, helpless to make it better for him. He drank his brew when Sheelagh brought it, and a dram of spirits as well, and seemed to find a tolerable position after a while.

"Where be Sheelagh?" he asked.

"Gone home now, Da. I've got you."

He released a long sigh. "I am dying, boy."

"You are not. You've just hurt your back, and it will get better in time."

"The Devil has rammed a pike into my spine, torturin' me for all my worldly sins."

"What sins, Da? You never leave the inn to commit anathin' but a blaspheme now and then. The Devil gets nothing out of that."

"I should not ha' married your ma. She was too young, and she didna love me. If she had, she would never ha' drowned herself."

"It's not so. She didn't drown herself. The spirits entranced her. They lured her out in the night and she slipped into the horsepond. It was not your fault. And even if it were so, it would mean she did not love me nor Sheelagh, the same. D'you think that's so? D'you think she never loved her babies?"

"No. She did love the two o' ye."

"Then stop your carping. She loved us all. Something got into her, that's all. No one could have done anything. And she must have known you'd take good care of us, as you have."

"I am old, Aengus. Listen to me now. Sheelagh, she's a smart girl, and the customers love her. But she's got her family and she doesn't belong here, ye see?"

"Well, she pokes her nose in anaways, doesn't she?"

"Ye love yer friend Faolán, so, an' he's like a son to me as well. He's got his bride now and a full life ahead o' him. 'Tis long past time for you to..."

"Da! I'm far from finding a bride of my own. Don't say it."

"Needs sayin'. Need ye here, boy. When I'm gone I need ta know it's you a-carryin' on wi' things. Otherwise, what have I been livin' fer? What's the bother been all these years? Let Faolán do what he might an' stop yer gallivantin'."

I shook my head. "You're not dying, Da. That's the first thing. And second is I'm here, always have been, and only leave when he needs me. You know it. And isn't that the kind of man you raised me to be? I'll always be here to look after everything. I promise. So drink your damned broth and get well, for chrissakes. Start yelling at me again, and I'll know you're back to yourself."

He closed his eyes and smiled. "Bleedin' hogshead."

Chapter Twenty-Five

Work of a Spiteful Man

...this Irish usquebagh as it is prepared and qualified,
it will help to digest all raw humours, expel wind
and keep his inward parts warm all day after,
without any offence to his stomack.

~ Richard Boyle, Earl of Cork

I kept Da as comfortable as I could over the next several days, especially with the uisce beatha, the water of life. The way we spoke it, the words sounded to the English like wish-ke-ba-ha, and soon they had shortened it to "whisky." Da much preferred it to boiled nettle. Soon his pain seemed to ease and he could sit up. Village folk kept coming in for ale, and would give him a nod and ask after him, then settle at a table to drink.

Supplies were low and I had yet to clean up the broken hogshead in the storeroom where Da had fallen, and then see to the brew of the ale. We were fortunate to have the sweet waters of the Ilen, the secret to the smooth flavor of our ale. Malted barley and rye were easy to come by from local folk. Sheelagh's in-laws kept the bees to provide the finest clover honey. The hops were imported from England, and we had to wait for deliveries from Dublin or Kinsale. I had enough to start a good batch, but soon I'd need to write an order for more supplies.

The next week I started the soak of the malt in Da's big mash tub, and sat on the rough wooden bench beneath the limbs of an old yew. The afternoon was warm for mid-March, the sun having pressed its way through the clouds to open the buds and encourage the sprouts of early spring. Far across the river I could see Faolán and Vivienne. They had probably come down to fill their water jugs. They moved beneath the trees, where rays of sun spread like a fan upon the riverbank.

Faolán led Dunerayl along a path with Vivienne riding, her hair blowing free, her shawl around her shoulders, but her feet and legs bare, her skirt tucked up around her knees. They seemed to glide along the path, weightless and ethereal. Faolán picked a flower and gave it to her, then kissed the hand that held it.

Something was different about them now that the journeying was over, and though the outcome was not as planned, the urgency was set aside. They smiled serenely and sometimes kissed, and it was as if they dwelled in a secret world, a gold-dusted Eden where no one could penetrate unless invited, and none could shatter the fragile peace that was theirs and theirs alone.

They had it all then, didn't they, with their companionship and their dreams, when before me was only the work of the alehouse and the loneliness my father had to bear. He had suffered it, and mine likely would be worse with no wife to laugh with or children who wanted my care. But envy was a bad thing, an ugly demon capable of driving a sharp wedge between two friends until the thing that was most cherished between them was forever lost. I would not let it happen. Without Faolán I'd have no true friends at all, and no adventures for he was always the one to conjure them. I would be left with only the sorrow and self-loathing for causing it by my own sour and disloyal heart.

When he visited us two weeks later, I was so grateful to see his face I completely forgot my envy. He brought bread from Vivienne, again blackened but still welcome, and a sack of dried peas. Da was still confined to the chair, for it pained him to walk. Faolán grasped Da's shoulder.

"So, you've finally found the solution for makin' Aengus put in a full day's work, have you?"

Da smiled. "Seems to serve me so far, lad. But I've not yet found the secret for working you."

"Ah, there ye go again, sir. I have a wife to try and figure me out now, so you can stop your struggling."

"So ye have."

I handed Faolán a full jar of ale. "Why does Vivienne not ride with you today?"

"She's not quite herself, Aengus, my friend. Can't keep her breakfast down." He winked. "We believe she might be with child, you see."

"Faolán, my boy!" Da shouted. "'Tis God's great miracle."

I clapped Faolán on the back. "Congratulations! So fast? You have been a busy man."

"Ah, none of that now, none of that," and he laughed. "It's fortunate, we are. I'm hoping for a baby girl as gorgeous as her mother; then I'll have the two of 'em to tease and spoil. I'm off to fetch her a remedy from Mistress Barry." Thomas and Sean's mother lived just a short distance away near Rathmore, and was widely known for her skills as midwife. "I'm also to see Lord Condon on the way. I must ask him to write the petition to the Lord Deputy, to reconsider Vivienne's settlement. He can be quite persuasive with his pen if he has a mind to be. She is beyond distress over Lord Cork's decision, and we must remind the Lord Deputy of her right and noble birth. Lord Condon may not wish to get involved, but it's for the child now. He's a kind man and will see reason in it. And if he's in good humor, mayhap I can convince him to do business with me again. I'll need the coin more than ever now."

"Sure, sure, he'll be reasonable," I said. "I'll have a letter for the agent in Kinsale next time you go." I walked outside with him as he prepared to continue his journey, leaving Da mumbling to himself by the hearth fire. "Faolán, are you sure you can leave Vivienne alone like this?"

"It's not my pleasure, *Teaghrán,* but I've little choice. It won't be for long. I'll be home again tonight."

"She can stay here if..."

"Thank you, friend. We'll be fine; no need to worry."

He rode off in a friendly clop of Dunerayl's hooves toward Lord Condon's hill house, and I made a silent prayer, both to ask that Lord Condon be generous at least for the baby's sake and to ask forgiveness for my foolish heart that now wanted only health and happiness for Faolán and Vivienne. They were near; they were my family just as much as my own blood, and I would never be lonely.

As the dusk settled, Faolán returned and my joy faded beneath the dark gloom on his face. He came in for a quick rest before returning home to Vivienne. Two men from the village were talking with Da by the hearth and slowly sipping their ale. We led Dunerayl into the byre to give him water and to talk without being overheard.

"Lord Condon has no work for you?" I asked.

"It is far worse, brother. Before, his message from Lord Cork was that I should not be welcomed at any gate or door east of Skebreen. The message now has changed. Lord Cork's letters say I am a criminal, not to be trusted, a suspected rebel, and as such most dangerous. Lord Condon says he cannot write the petition, and in fact he cannot help me at all."

The strangest heaviness settled upon my chest and pressed in at my sides. My face grew hot and my fingertips cold. We tried to stay on the side of peace. To survive within the confines of what was left to the Irish as the king's plantation system crept across the lands. We abandoned religion as much as possible, seeing it could be fatal depending upon the direction of the political winds. We tried to be smart. We tried to be of service. And now came an accusation based solely on malice. "He cannot do this."

"He has."

"But why? It wasn't enough to steal Vivienne's inheritance?"

"He is a spiteful man, Aengus. I'd no idea how great the extent. He wants to ruin me completely. It is not about the money, not this time. He was furious at the Lord Deputy's order to settle with us, and disgruntled that he could not make his deal for Vivienne's marriage. Then Eames failed to remove us from his world. I suppose now he will see that we are starved to death."

"But if he knew there was a child…"

"He must not know, Aengus. I fear he would only turn his hate on the babe in some way, and I cannot let my unborn child be made so vulnerable because of the things I have done."

"Yes. You are right. But what will you do now?"

"I must travel, Aengus. I must go to my customers, remind them of my honorable service and ask them to trust me. I must get to them before their minds are turned. And if I am too late, my last hope is Lord Clanricarde. I'm not confident he'll assist me if it means going head-to-head against Cork, and he will surely say I owe him money. But if all others are against me, he is the only one with the power and stature to truly restore my honor. We are clan, after all. In good conscience, he will have to help me."

"That is true."

"The trouble is, I could be gone for weeks. I don't want to leave Vivienne alone at Glencurragh at such a time. Our position grows desperate; she cannot go and I cannot stay. I need your help to look after her while I am gone."

"Of course, Faolán."

"I'll bring Vivienne in the morning, then."

"I will have her room ready, and all will be fine."

"Well," Faolán said, scratching his chin, "she will be unhappy, but she will understand."

Chapter Twenty-Six

Swept Clean

Sweet are the uses of adversity which, like the toad, ugly and venomous, wears yet a precious jewel in his head.

~ William Shakespeare

Vivienne sat on a stool beside my father for hours, telling him stories, making him laugh, and I'm sure it was the best medicine for an ailing man. By the end of the first day he was on his feet and walking slowly about the kitchen garden with her at his arm. He tired quickly, but she made sure he ate well and then helped him back to bed with a good measure of the whisky to ease him to sleep. She filled it twice, took the second one herself in one swallow, and then glared at me with contempt. Yes, she was unhappy, and no, she did not understand.

"I could have gone with him, you know. I'm feeling better now, and it will be winter before the baby comes. I should be with him."

"I am glad you didn't go, Vivienne. Look what you have done for my father, and how you've relieved me of worry. Faolán can ride much faster alone on Dunerayl, and speed is important to him now."

"*Pffft,*" she scoffed. "Cork will have reached all of them by now, I am certain. To ask any of the gentry to go against Lord Cork is wasted breath. I think he is better to go straight to Lord Clanricarde. He could not refuse a kinsman. He brings shame on his own clan to do so. He is our best hope, and can help us apply to the Lord Deputy to restore my money."

"Do you believe there's still a chance?"

"I believe we must try, at least for our child's sake."

"And if it doesn't work?"

"Oh, Aengus." Tears rimmed her eyes, but she held back. "It must. Something must."

"I'm sorry, Vivienne, I did not mean to…"

"Please tell me it will work, because I do not know what else to do. He is a miserable farmer. He hates it. He is of great humor, a clever thinker, and a born leader. He is made to run, to ride, to hunt, to win battles with his sword. But he is not meant for the labor of the field, just as I am not meant for the laundry tub."

"Aye, it is so. His mind is in the clouds most of the time. But you know, 'tis a fertile mind. He'll come up with something. Especially with the young one coming." I touched her shoulder. She sniffed a little and it gave me a sudden inspiration. "As long as you're here, Vivienne, could you help me? This inn has been here since before I was born, and Da has never done much by way of improvements. He never saw the need, this being the only inn for miles. There's not much money for anything big, but might there be some little things we could do to cheer the place up a bit?"

She looked up, her eyes brightening with interest. She looked this way and that as if gathering her thoughts. "I just might have some ideas for you, Aengus. Has anyone ever thought of washing the windows?"

I laughed. "Let's take a walk outside."

The inn was built like a conical whale's tooth tipped on its side. The tip pointed east, and at that end a triangular-shaped room with two windows was the byre for the animals. It was separated from the drinking establishment by a narrow aisle. In the middle of the aisle a door opened to the hearth on the right and the tables and stools on the left. Always smelling of stale brew and onion, this was where everyone met and all the gossip of the village was shared. At the opposite end of the room another aisle led to the brewing house and storage. Against the far wall on the right were the jugs and barrels and a wooden trestle table for serving.

Behind the serving area, the narrow, creaky stair led up to the second floor, a cramped hallway dividing three small rooms on the left, and a dormitory on the right that could sleep eight people. Travelers could pay extra for their own private room, or just rent a pallet. When we were children, my father would move us to the dormitory to rent our rooms. No matter the weather or the time of year, the rooms always smelled of mildew, urine, and sweat.

If the inside was not bad enough, the outside was worse. The white-washed walls had faded to a dull gray, with mud splatters from many heavy rains. The ridge on the thatch roof had begun to slip and had been in urgent need of repair for at least three years. At the entry, the scents of animal urine and manure welcomed our guests because the same aisle served the horse byre. At the rear door, dead weeds crowded the opening to a yard cluttered with brewing trash, old broomstraw and ash cleaned from the hearth.

I led Vivienne around, truly noticing for myself the poor conditions, embarrassed I hadn't done more to clean it up for my da. But I'd sparked an instinct deep within her that now came roaring to the forefront: the desire to create the perfect nest for the baby to be born. Vivienne unleashed a fierce need to clean and organize every inch of the inn.

With broom in hand she attacked the cobwebs, then swept and scrubbed every crack and corner of the floor, and every table, bench and stool as well. Next the windows, with me scrubbing outside as she scrubbed inside. Years of mud and grime came away, letting in more light than I could ever remember. Mugs, glasses, pewter plate and crockery we thoroughly washed and arranged, doorways swept clean and flowering shrubs dug up from the roadside and replanted by the stoop. She cut fragrant boughs and placed them near the hearth.

Even Da decided to join in—not to work, mind you, but to issue orders from his chair by the fire. Scrub down the hearthstones, chop more wood, muck out the byre, "and fetch me the uisce beatha while you're at it." He finally called a halt to it when she stuffed glassware with bluebells to decorate the tables. "What kind o' lad wants to savor his brew with the bluebells a-ticklin' 'is nose? Bah!"

It took a few days, but when we finished, the inn was clean from top to bottom and smelled of wood and soap. I swelled like a toadfish. "I do not believe the inn has been so fine, not even when Ma still lived," I said.

"Thatch still needs fixin', boy."

"Yes, it does, Da."

After several more days had passed, the clop of Dunerayl's hooves alerted us to Faolán's return. It was late afternoon. Vivienne ran to the upstairs window to confirm it was Faolán, and then burst from the doorway and down the road to greet him. He swept her from the ground as if she were light as a faerie. She smothered him with kisses. The envy nibbled at my ears.

"I've brought gifts," Faolán said as he came into the inn. He dropped his saddlebags, gave me a mighty bear hug, clasped hands with Da, and then breathed in, a bright smile crossing his lips. "What on earth has happened here, Aengus? I hardly recognize the place. I believe a tempest has passed through, and her name was Vivienne."

"You'd be wise not to shed a speck of mud from your boots." I passed him a drink.

Vivienne pressed against his side as he dug into his bags. "I was fortunate. A customer owed me a debt and paid in goods instead of money. A bottle of good wine for Mister O'Daly. A book for Aengus. Scented water for Vivienne." She kissed him firmly. "And still strapped on Dunerayl, a sack of hops for you, Aengus, just a wee bit to see you through. And some good linen for Vivienne."

I looked at the small book, *The Purple Island*.

"It's poetry, *Teaghrán*. About rivers that are really the veins in the body, and the mountains are meant to be the bones. It starts out with two young shepherd boys playing by the river. I thought you might like that."

We dined on hearty barley broth and Vivienne's bread, and when my father drifted off to sleep, we moved to a table at the back of the room.

"What happened, Faolán?" Vivienne asked. We were both eager to hear.

His happy and generous face now melted into a somber visage with downcast eyes. "I'd pay the Devil not to have to say it, Vivienne, but you will know soon enough. I have visited every household and manor I have ever served within a day's ride of here. Some would not even receive me, and others were kind enough to tell me they had received Lord Cork's warning and could not hire me until the stain of suspicion has been cleared. Cork has been most thorough."

"And Clanricarde?" I asked.

"I rode swiftly to Mallow when I realized what I was facing. His is the worst injury of all. He refused even to see me. He was packing to return to his family home near Galway, and sent word by his steward that he wouldn't admit me unless I paid the debt of £40, the percentage of Vivienne's inheritance I'd promised whether or not we received it. I was a fool to agree to such a thing, but we needed his help and it seemed a small enough sum for the size of the income. I cannot count on him to help me now, kinsman or no."

"But that's a fortune, Faolán. You could not produce that much in a short time."

"No. Without a miracle I could not produce that in a year."

"Are there others about?" Vivienne asked. "Men who remember your father and…"

"I am sorry, love. There are those who once would have been happy to lift us up, but now are without means themselves." He squeezed her hand. "Not to fret. It will pass soon enough, and I am not without options. I will keep us warm and fed, and will find a way to turn it all around. I'll find Cork's vulnerabilities. He has them just as any man, and no right to drive anyone to ruin."

Vivienne's hand fell to her belly though the swelling there was barely visible. She gazed out the window for a few seconds, then turned back to Faolán looking cheerful. A tiny falter in her smile betrayed her confidence. I was sure Faolán would rather die than disappoint her. They rode home in the deepening twilight, and I gave thanks they were safely reunited.

Though Faolán had told Vivienne he still had options, as far as I knew he'd exhausted all of them. But the next morning two riders passed by the inn and headed straight for the bridge across the Ilen. They didn't stop at the inn for a visit, our Sean and Thomas Barry.

Chapter Twenty-Seven

The Book

Thus ran the rash Tolmetes, never viewing
the fearful fiends that duly him attended.

~ Phineas Fletcher

On the last night of April, the eve of the Bealtaine marks the end of spring, the time to drive cattle to their summer pastures. The villagers celebrated with a lusty bonfire, but the dawn charged in on a cold wind. I huddled by the hearth, grateful to be indoors with a full box of turf to keep us warm, and to have my brewing supplies that arrived days before. Da was much improved physically, but the weather aggravated his pains and piqued his attitude. He scowled at nothing, groaned regularly, and everything I did should be improved to better suit him.

By late morning the wind had eased. Mister McSherry had caught a fat rabbit in his snare, skinned it, and brought us half for a stew. He refused to join us for the meal but did not mind a complimentary dram or two to warm his bones.

"Didja hear the news, lads?"

"And what is that?" Da responded.

Mister McSherry loved to be the first to deliver information. He pulled up a stool and settled between Da and myself to begin the telling.

"I had word from me cousin Odhran, ye see," McSherry said, "up at Drinagh. Fine lad he is, married a lass from up Ballingeary way, on the River Lee. She's wide as an ox but a fine lass, and she…"

"Bloody hell, McSherry! The news?" Da said.

"Yes, well then." He sat back and crossed his legs, clearly disappointed he would not be allowed to prattle, but Da's patience had grown finer than a dragonfly's wing. "Odhran heard tell an Englishman by name o' William Smith in the next parish had his house raided. Irish, he said, come in, turned him out o' the house, went in an' took everthin' o' value, and then disappeared into the bog. Was three or four o' them, he said."

"Zat so?" Da frowned.

"'Twas the only English-owned farm in the parish. There ha' been some takin's farther to the east, east o' Cork town I mean ta say, but 'tis first I heard o' sometin' so far west, an' so close ta home, ye see."

"Bound to happen, isn't it?" I said. "More English coming, more lands being taken. Rebel bands moving west to escape the English regiments?"

"Aye, I s'pose," McSherry said, "but the English got no problem at all ridin' roughshod over Munster. No problem at all. An' now they'll be havin' a fine excuse ta do it."

"They will, so," Da grumbled.

"You mean..." I tried to get a word in between the two of them but McSherry wouldn't have it.

"I mean, the soldiers don't need much encouragement for ridin' in here makin' troubles worse. They'll be conjuring stories, sayin' we're all in on it, protectin' our clan or whatever. They're no lookin' for truth; it's more like recreation to 'em. If they catch the fellas straightaway, we'll likely be all right. They won't ride out here lookin' fer 'em. But woe be to the lads who done it. The English'll put 'em to sword without a regret or even a passin' thought."

A chill crept up my spine, and I didn't even want to think why, but then my traitor eyes turned to the table by the hearth where I'd left the book Faolán had brought me. The Purple Island. Had that book once belonged to an English household?

I waited until McSherry left, and then fetched it upstairs for a look. There was no inscription in the front pages, and I let go a sigh of relief. But what of the back pages? Inside the back cover, in the top right corner, in faded script: W. Smith.

My belly turned. Quickly as if it singed my fingers, I stashed the book in the rafters above my bed, and promised myself late at night when no one would see I'd bury it deep in the ground. Why would Faolán do it? How could he dare such a thing? Why risk his life to steal from the English, and then bring the soldiers down upon all of us? And then my own voice answered me back, why wouldn't he do it? Why wouldn't a man who'd abducted a woman from her bed and married her in a desperate rush now steal from another man to keep her fed and clothed? And who is more desperate than a man whose beloved wife is soon to birth a child?

It was possible the customer he'd spoken of had the book for some reason and had given it to him. It was possible everything Faolán had told us was true and this was just a strange coincidence. But the back of my neck burned, and my hands began to tremble. He'd done it, and he'd put us all at risk in his selfishness, and me with the most incriminating evidence. Worst of it all, he'd lied to me and hadn't trusted me enough to tell me what he was doing.

Always I'd been the first included in his plans. Always I was at his side. And granted, in this particular venture, I'd not have wanted to participate. But I had not been told. I'd been shut out. Now I was not only worried the soldiers would come, but that I had lost the good faith of my only friend.

The very next morning, the English soldiers rode in.

Chapter Twenty-Eight

Soldiers Riding West

The loss I have sustained by this wicked nation
is too grievous to remember, if hope of
revenge did not breed me comfort.

~ Sir George Carew

A man's piercing shout for the proprietor awakened me, and then my father called for me. Who was there? And the book, it was still lodged in the rafters. Why, oh why, had I not buried that thing in the night? I yanked on my clothes and ran down in bare feet.

In front of the inn, four English soldiers awaited in their thigh-length leather jerkins and boots that cuffed at their knees, each armed with wheel-lock muskets. And they were smiling. McSherry had been right; this was recreation.

The soldiers dismounted, all but one who eyed me sternly. "Ale for my men," he demanded, for which I knew we would not be paid. When I returned with it, the standing soldiers joked and laughed, and then the mounted soldier, their leader, addressed me.

"This is your inn, sir?"

"It is my father's," I said. "He is ailing from a back injury."

"Hmm. How sad," he said flatly. "What do you know of the house raids and cattle raids in these parts?"

"Nothing here, sir. Those troubles have only occurred well east of our parish."

"Nothing, you say." He glared at me and looked down at his men, who smiled in amusement. Then he returned his full attention to me.

"You have not seen a band of rebels ride through here, and yet your establishment is right next to a bridge they would cross?" His voice was stronger now, crisp and cold.

"I have seen no rebels, sir."

"We have a witness who saw three men on horseback traveling the road from Leap, and they seem to have disappeared near Skebreen."

"They may have turned south toward the coast, sir."

"Or they may have sought beds at your inn. Will you produce them, or shall I look?"

"We had no boarders last night sir, but look if you wish." I know not how, but I kept my voice steady. My scalp tightened and felt cold with sweat. He nodded to one of his men, who leapt from his horse and ran into the inn. In his heavy boots he clomped into the byre, through the ale-house, and up the wooden stairs. My father cursed at him as he thundered through every room. The miracle was that our feeble stairs did not break as he clambered down them and burst into the storeroom where he lingered for a few moments, and then returned. By this time my stomach had knotted to the size of a walnut.

"Nothing, sir," the soldier said, wiping his chin with his fist.

The leader scoffed and glared at me, eyes sharp with contempt. "You know something. The proprietor of the local alehouse always knows everything because people, and in particular the Irish, cannot help themselves but to talk, and talk, and talk."

I tried to deny it but he held up his hand to silence me.

"See? There you go. Keep your silence now. We will continue our search for these outlaws. While we are gone, think about what you will tell me when we return. I will expect useful information, and I'll not be as accommodating then. So *think*." He turned his horse and rode off, the others close behind him, but he did not cross the bridge as I expected. He rode west, toward Lord Condon's house.

I ran inside and up the stairs to check on Da. He was angry and grumbling, but otherwise unharmed. "Help me downstairs, Aengus."

"I will, Da. Just allow me a moment to check the other rooms." I ran straight to my own bedroom. The book was not visible from the door. I had to climb on the bed to find it, but it had not been disturbed. If I tried to bury it now, for sure I would be seen. But I had to talk to Faolán. To warn him, and to ask him why.

I settled Da by the fire with his breakfast and waited, watching the road. He grumbled continuously, angry at the early disturbance and questioning why the soldiers needed to harass quiet people so far to the west. "Have we not had enough pecking from the vulturous Algerians on the coast, wi'out the soldiers pickin' our bones here on the mainland?" he said.

"Aye, Da. 'Tis beyond reason."

I did my morning chores with an eye toward the window until at last came what I had been waiting for, a lad driving a hay wagon heading north toward the bridge.

"Da," I asked, "can you get along without me all right for a few hours now?"

"I'm fine; I don' need ye hoverin' over me. What is it now?"

"I would speak to Faolán about the soldiers."

Da glared at me. "An' if it's him they're seekin'?"

"It could not be so, Da," I said without hesitation. "He would have told me."

Da searched my face for a moment. I had no liar's face, never could get away with a stitch under his piercing gaze, but if he saw anything amiss, he let it go. "Be not long," he said, "in case they come back fer their supper."

Chapter Twenty-Nine

A Warning to Thieves

*Big fires flare up in a wind, but little ones are blown out
unless they are carried in under cover.*

~ *St. Francis de Sales*

I begged a ride on the back of the hay wagon to avoid being seen if anyone was watching. The last thing I wanted to do was lead the soldiers right to Faolán, but I had to talk to him. When the wagon neared the path to his house, I leapt off, shouted my thanks and ran up the hill toward Faolán's door. I found him in the garden, digging out rocks with an old wooden hoe and tossing them to the side.

"Good day Aengus, my friend." He smiled broadly. "An' what is it brings ye here this day? Is your Da well?"

"It isn't Da, Faolán. He is fine; I left him sitting by the hearth. But I wanted to tell you we had visitors this morning. English soldiers."

Faolán stiffened and turned to me. "What did they want?"

"Said they were after three men seen riding from Leap, wanted for raiding."

He said nothing, but turned his face away and continued digging.

"They searched every room of the inn."

"Rude bastards. How many were there?"

"Four on horseback. Said they'd be returning this evening to ask more questions."

"This evening. They'll be wanting you to feed 'em. And you came here just to tell me that. Are you thinking I know something?"

"I don't know, Faolán. I came to warn you if you do."

"I see."

"And there's something else. Mister McSherry come by the day before, told us a fella's house was raided over near Drinagh. An Englishman named William Smith."

"Oh. Aye."

"Faolán, the man's name is written in the back of the book you gave me."

He looked up at me then, shock in his eyes. "You must be joking."

"Faolán..."

"And now you're thinking it was me out raiding and carousing and stealing from other folk? Do you really think I'd bother to steal a book?"

"You brought us all those gifts, and I..."

"Aengus. You mustn't think such a thing. You mustn't believe it."

"What should I believe?"

"By God, believe I do what is right and what is best for my wife and child coming. How can you not know that?"

It was me looking into the dirt now, a little ashamed for not trusting him as I should, but still uncertain. "What should I tell them?"

"Aengus, tell them anything you want. Tell them there are no men in these parts engaged in such business. Tell them they're on the wrong track. And for God's sake, feed them well."

"And the book?"

"I don't know how the name came to be there. I came by it as I say, but I'm sorry I gave it to you now. Burn it if you like, or whatever you think is best."

Vivienne came out of the house then and hugged my neck. "Come in for a bite of stew and something to drink." She looked content with Faolán back at home, but her energy had not waned, and she did not stop to eat with us. She kept about her business, scrubbing and arranging things in the kitchen, then rearranging them. When we finished eating, I went outside with Faolán to help him remove an old fallen tree from a corner of the garden.

"If it's not rotted through, I can find a use for some of the wood and clear the way for a bit of corn." Faolán brought Dunerayl to the field and tied the rope to his harness. Dunerayl seemed miffed at being applied to field labor, always looking over his shoulder and puffing his lips. It took more time than I expected to pull the log free, but we managed it, and then I realized I'd been gone from the inn longer than I'd intended. Faolán took me as far as the bridge on Dunerayl, and I started the rest of the way on foot for I could not wait on another hay wagon. I had to get back home to check on Da and get the cook pot going.

I was a quarter of the way across the river when a sharp crack like lightning broke the quiet, and then a quick roll of thunder. Smoke seeped from the eaves of the inn and up like a twisted rope to the heavens. The roof was on fire. I burst forward, running as fast as I could, but the old straw and timbers caught faster than a well-fueled torch. The blazes were running along the eaves near the storeroom, and when I got to the front, an upstairs window burst. Bright orange flames licked out and touched the outer walls. Down the road the soldiers were mounting their horses.

"Stop! Help!" I shouted at them.

"Think about your answers!" One of them shouted back, "*Let this be a warning to all who harbor thieves.*" They left at a gallop and quickly disappeared around the bend.

"Da!" I called. Horse hooves pounded across the bridge, and in seconds Faolán was beside me. We kicked in the door to the alehouse, but Da was not by the hearth. The room had filled with smoke, and the timbers above us smoldered and creaked, threatening collapse.

"Upstairs!" Faolán shouted.

"No, he couldn't go up by himself." I dashed through heavy smoke to the storeroom, gray streams seeping around the edges of the door. We kicked it open and the scorching heat pushed us back. Flames engulfed the jugs and hogsheads, swirling and leaping about, sucking air from the opened roof and shooting to furious heights with the new source of air from the doorway. Amid the flames, a blue light glowed and shimmered, growing taller, a woman's figure in sweeping white robes billowing in the smoke, her long hair rising with the wind, her mouth a painful grimace, her sad eyes focused on mine, sad for me. It was my mother, a *bean sidhe*, the banshee, keening to warn me of a terrible loss, and then she disappeared and Da was before me on the floor, fallen or struck down, a smoldering beam across his back.

"Da!" I fell to my belly and crawled in to grab his legs and pull him free, but he did not answer, he did not move. I crawled farther in but the flames singed my hair and sparks settled into my shirt and burned my skin. I pulled and jerked harder until his shoe came off in my hand and yet he did not move. The hairs on my arms fizzled away. I tried to breathe and the heat seared in my throat.

A horrid scream shattered the air and then came the urgent shouts, a fierce crackle and deafening roar, a massive crack and a powerful jerk from behind as something fell and hit my head.

The next I remember is the curve of Vivienne's jaw as she leaned over me, white as milk. Then the sound of Sheelagh, wailing high and anguished and crying out for Da. I had to get to him; I had to bring him out. I tried to sit up, but Vivienne pressed me down, and then I realized I was outside away from the flames, and Sheelagh was on her knees beside me. Next to her lay Da. His ears, his hair, and part of his face were burned, his shirt in charred tatters about his reddened and bloody arms. His eyes were closed. He did not move. He did not cough or groan or lift a hand to her face. He did not breathe.

"It was…one of the timbers hit him on the head. We thought we might have lost you, too," Vivienne said. "Faolán pulled you both from the fire."

"His head?" I could not comprehend. I could not understand what had happened. "He is…"

"I am so sorry Aengus." Vivienne's tears spilled forth and she squeezed my hand. I looked to Da, and then toward the ruined storeroom and ale-house. Still it all burned and howled, the black and gray smoke swirling up to a dark cloud. Across the yard, Faolán lay on his side coughing, his skin and clothes blackened by smoke and char.

"Faolán brought us out?"

"He did. He is all right; he is not burned. Your father must have hid in the storeroom when the soldiers came. They must have thought no one was inside. Surely they would not have meant to kill your poor father. The roof collapsed before he could get out."

Yes, the roof. The ridge of the thatch that I had not yet repaired. A gaping hole inviting fire in, and a trap to deliver a killing blow upon my own father.

The English soldiers. The filthy, stinking, careless, sadistic, diabolical, monstrous English soldiers. How I hated them. I turned my head and spat, coughed, and spat again. And as much as I hated them, I knew I was worse than all of them, leaving Da alone though I knew the soldiers would return, not being there to protect him, letting him die a frightful death and our business and our livelihood burn to the ground. Depriving my dear sister of her father, depriving myself. I did not deserve to live. I wished right then I could stab myself through the heart and die. For a moment I hated Faolán, too, for saving me. I hated him for bringing the soldiers down on us, whether or not he had. I hated him for already having lost his father, and not knowing as I did now the fresh, agonizing pain of horrific loss. I did not wish to see the sky, nor even to breathe. I neither wished nor deserved the sensation of dirt beneath my back or the soft rain that had just begun to fall. Everything, *everything*, was nothing.

"Faolán, Aengus is returned to us," Vivienne called out to him. He sat up, wiping his mouth on the back of his sooty hand. His face contorted. Our eyes met, and his were reddened and clouded with some emotion, sorrow perhaps and grief. Could he see the condemnation and self-hatred in mine? I dropped my head back and allowed myself to weep, for I could not stop it.

"Will you take water, Aengus?" Vivienne asked.

"No."

Chapter Thirty

Prince of a Hundred Stories

Ar dheis De go raibh a anam
May his soul be at the right of God

~ Ancient Irish saying

It rained through the night while I lay awake on the floor of Sheelagh's house. What was I doing there? She would not look at me nor speak to me, which was well because I wanted naught to do with her wailing and blaming. Our father's body was covered in a hastily made shroud. We did not even have a coffin for him. Her son, Tadhg, and daughter, Radha, were as frightened of me as they were of his corpse, and I could not blame them.

At the first light of dawn, I walked back to the ruins of the inn. The rain had extinguished the last of the embers, leaving a sodden, sludgy black spot on the earth where once had been my world. The chimney remained, reaching up to the sky like a black hand pointing to oblivion, and behind it a vestige of the byre, just a segment of wall crowded by charred and tumbled stones.

I picked up a blackened piece of wood, burnt and warped, possibly a table leg or part of a bed frame but now unrecognizable. I swung left and right as I might swing an ax to crack the heads of those soldiers. How I wished I could kill them one by one with just such a blunt instrument to make them suffer, and make the others watch until it was their turn to die. I roared out my anger from the depths of my gut and hurled the wasted stick toward the river with all my might. I was useless.

Near the fireplace, the flagstone remained where the door had been. I walked over it and through the wet soot and knee-deep debris where the tables and benches had been. So much of my life had happened there. So many jokes and friendly conversations with customers swirled around me and quivered in the air like spirits. I touched the burned corner of the stool where Mister McSherry had been sitting when he'd warned us of troubles ahead.

I could not walk into the storeroom, not yet. The walls were all gone, but the outline of it remained, filled in with tumbled stone, burnt wood, tangled metal, and blackened, shattered pottery. Near the place where the door had been, something among the wet ashes caught my eye. Charred but not completely burned, the spine from the binding of the book Faolán had given me. So it was gone with everything else, the only possible evidence connecting us to any raids. I threw it down as the useless trash it was. Nothing meant anything now.

But there was a voice, a child's voice, pleading in my head. It couldn't be that; it couldn't be nothing. What had Da said to me? *I need ta know it's you a-carryin' on wi' things. Otherwise what have I been livin' fer? What's the bother been all these years?* I was going to have to start over. For him. But how, with nothing to sell and no way to make the money needed to rebuild the place? I cast my gaze around the ruins for anything salvageable. The flagstone, the chimney, the land itself, and everything he had taught me.

"I don't know how to bring it all back, Da, or what it will take to turn this wreck into a working establishment again. But I know I cannot let you down," I whispered to the ashes. "I won't. I'll find a way."

I sat on the old wooden bench in the yard and closed my eyes. The damp earth at my feet still smelled rich, while the leaves of the yew tree bristled above my head. At least the rain had come before the tree was burned, and before the fire could jump to the other businesses and houses. Along the riverbank below me, the Ilen carried on, its waters lapping and trilling along as it had for centuries. There cannot be a world without my father any more than a world without the river. His death was an impossibility, a mistake, a nightmare. It was unthinkable, and yet I could think of nothing else. What is death? How can a person sit before me one moment, and be gone from his body the next? Why would he not be standing in the door to the byre like always when I opened my eyes? But when I looked up, there was no doorway, and there was no Da. There was Faolán, looking worse than ever I had seen him, his face gray, his eyes red, his mouth sagging. And there was Dunerayl, pulling a dray of timbers.

I walked toward him, the ruins of the inn between us. "What is this?"

Tears welled in his eyes. "Only a start, *Teaghrán*. When you are ready. When we have laid him to rest. I am beside you, as always you have been for me. Cork is behind this, I'm sure of it, but we will not let them destroy this. We will start again."

My throat closed. Once again he had known my thoughts. It was a moment before I could speak. "Those are timbers for Glencurragh."

"They were, friend. I cannot build Glencurragh while O'Daly's lays in ruins. I know you grieve the loss of your father sorely right now. I join you in it. But I'll not sleep or eat or rest if you are not my brother."

How could he have known my hateful feelings, my blame cast upon him, when all the while it belonged only to me? How could he have felt the breach between us that was of my own creation, and now need it healed? I was the wrong one. I was the dishonorable brother, ready to cast him aside on account of my own imaginings and resentfulness. I looked down at the wet, black ash. Was there room in my heart to harbor mistrust when I'd lost everything? When I needed him more than ever? I did not long have to ask myself. I crossed toward him and he toward me. We clasped arms and embraced, renewing the treasured bond. How could I question his deeds when I knew his heart?

"Mister O'Daly," came a man's voice from the road, the high-pitched nasal sound of Constable Shipwith, an Englishman from Kinsale assigned to the post of Skebreen and Baltimore, and a regular customer at the alehouse.

"Constable." I shook his hand, as did Faolán. Over his shoulder I saw Sheelagh running toward us, her shawl pulled tightly over her head.

"Dear lad, I came as soon as I was alerted. I am sorry for your loss. A kitchen fire, was it? A terrible, terrible waste it is."

"Aye sir, it is a waste. But it was no kitchen fire, and no accident. 'Twas set by the soldiers through here last. It was a murder, sir."

He gaped at me. Sheelagh arrived in time to hear my words and stepped in front of me, weeping and clasping her shawl beneath her chin. "It is true, Constable. They torched the roof. They murdered him without a care. You must go after them."

"How do you know this?" Shipwith asked.

"I saw them," I said. "They were riding away. They said it was a warning."

"I saw them as well, sir," Faolán confirmed.

I stepped closer, making sure he heard me clearly. "They said they were sending a message to any who would harbor thieves."

"Thieves?"

"Cattle raiders, sir, though I'd told them already we had none in these parts."

"It's true. They had no call to do this, Constable. We have no raiders here. Please, you must do something," Sheelagh said.

"Please, sir," I said. "They can't just do this and ride away laughing."

"Certainly the soldiers were not laughing."

"Laughing, all four of them, Constable."

"They must be hanged," Sheelagh said, her face enflamed with fury.

The constable took a step backward and looked down the road to his left and his right, scratched the sparse gray hair on his scalp and looked toward the burnt rubble. He shook his head. "There be few soldiers in these parts. I've no command of them anaways. Must have been sent from Youghal to look into the troubles at Drinagh. Mayhap the earl sent them to have a look about."

"Cork?"

"Aye. His cousin is bishop of Cork, Coyne, and Ross. Lord Cork might be concerned for his relative's safety."

I looked at Faolán, and touched his sleeve to forestall the anger I knew would be building. My own was simmering just below the surface, but we could reveal nothing to the constable or to Sheelagh without making matters worse.

"What can be done, Constable?" I asked with all the patience I could muster.

"I must make inquiries."

"Inquiries."

"Yes, of course. Due process and all that. I will let you know what we discover."

As the constable was leaving us a dull heaviness grew within my chest. My head began to ache from the struggle to withhold a fierce desire to lash out. Nothing would be done, no letter written, no inquiries made, no consequence at all to the soldiers who had killed my father, and no protection or justice to any of us who lived in Cork's jurisdiction. The old saying "Beyond Leap, beyond the law" now had a very different meaning to me. I had known the protection of obscurity, and now I knew its injury.

Soon the people of the village arrived. The cabinetmaker quickly fashioned a wooden coffin for Da, and we set it outside of Sheelagh's house, where Tadhg and Radha had swept the dooryard, where people would come to pay their respects. They brought food and drink from their own kitchens, coins from their pockets, blankets, clothing, whatever they could spare. Some could spare nothing and brought instead the stories of things my father had said to them, experiences they'd had with him. They talked of his grumble and the way he laughed. Mister FitzGibbon and Mister McSherry brought stools upon which to sit, and placed them under the thatched eaves. They spent the entire day by Da's side. At night we lit lanterns in the yard, and there I read an ancient poem I had altered to honor his memory.

> *Stand aside, maidens, and behold the homeland of*
> *Fintan O'Daly.*
>
> *Now that flames consume the court of Skebreen,*
> *Alas for those still young, who long for their brothers.*
>
> *With heavy heart, I wrap the white flesh in a black shroud,*
> *Fintan O'Daly, prince of a hundred stories.*
>
> *The hall of O'Daly is dark tonight, without fire, without bed;*
> *I will weep awhile, then I will be silent.*
>
> *The hall of O'Daly is dark tonight, without fire, without light;*
> *Except for God, who will ease my cares.*
>
> *Sad it is to see O'Daly's hall*
> *Without a roof, without a fire.*
> *My lord is dead, and yet I live on.*

Chapter Thirty-One

Talons of a Crow

Idleness is a very national disgrace of this island...

~ Richard Boyle, Earl of Cork

We buried Da in the churchyard on the second day, and the following morning all the men of the village converged on the site of O'Daly's. Together we mucked out the tar, charcoal, and ash, and dumped it in the ditch behind. We dug and scraped and scratched the earth to banish the remnants of the fire and expose the bare dirt of the foundation. Faolán worked harder than anyone except for me. What I lacked in muscle power, I made up for in driving energy. I worked until my shoulders ached and my legs trembled, but I welcomed physical pain to dispel the sadness, and with each bit of the tragedy cleared away, we made way for Da's wishes to be honored.

The women brought scrub brushes and washed the soot from the hearth, then checked to make sure the stones were sound. They built a fire there, restoring to life what had been the very heart of the inn. It was good and true, the brightest confirmation that O'Daly's would return.

It was not for me that they worked so hard, and perhaps not entirely for my da either, but for the restoration of what had always been, for the return to normalcy. Everyone wanted the alehouse back, the comfort of the drink, the confidence of a familiar place. They needed to replace the blighted spot on the earth with the landmark that anchored our tiny village in the world. They wanted what Da's inn had always given them: the pleasure of the company of friends, and the occasional news and entertainment of a bard or a traveler. How long had it been since we'd heard music? I must remember to put it high on the list when the new establishment was running, to thank these fine folk with music and song.

In the weeks following, I worked on the restoration from early morning until well past dark, and at night fell exhausted onto my pallet on Sheelagh's floor, beneath the loft where her children slept warm beneath her well-crafted quilts. In the morning I rose before anyone, quick to escape before having to face Sheelagh's scorn. Some mornings I would find things left by the flagstone at the inn—cut stones, boards, nails, or hinges—things Faolán had scavenged on his travels. At once I was gratified and sorrowful. Glencurragh had been my dream as well as his. I longed to see that castle rise, and to be a part of the excitement and opportunity that would have come from it. But the castle construction would be a long time coming now.

For O'Daly's, even with the help I was receiving, I wouldn't be able to recreate the building that had been. The new site would be a single floor, with a small room for me to sleep where the stairway once had been, and a shed for the brewing and storage. In better times I would make more of it and restore the rooms above, but for now my focus had to be on reopening the alehouse as soon as possible. Without it I had no income.

"Why don't the English understand they make rebels of us all when they take away our livelihoods? What do they expect?" Faolán plucked angrily at his saddlebags one day in mid-June. He delivered a gift from himself and Vivienne. Wrapped in a ragged scrap of cloth was a pair of wooden door handles Faolán had fashioned from the old log we'd pulled from the field the day the inn burned down, the day Da was killed. They were sturdy and solid, comfortable in the hand, and Vivienne had smoothed and polished them to a satin shine.

"It is fine craftsmanship my friend," I thanked him. "Far better than what we had before, and something good to come from a terrible day. Where is Vivienne?"

"She has been unwell, but I will bring her next week for the bonfire of St. John. Tell me, Aengus, for I do not understand. Shouldn't she grow heavier? Her face should be aglow and her appetite robust with the babe growing inside her. Instead she seems anxious, her face thin and pale. Her belly grows and her ankles swell, but the rest of her does not. In fact, she is tired much of the time, and I think her more frail."

"I have heard of women having such troubles. She's likely nervous about the birth. She needs medicine to balance her humors. When you come I'll give her some chalybeate mineral water. There's a well along the way to the coast road where I can collect a goodly supply. Some say it cures the colic, the melancholy, and the vapors, makes the lean fat and the fat lean. It can surely restore her. And I'll make a hawthorn poultice for her ankles. She might have a chat with Sheelagh, too. She's already had two brawny babes. Then if things don't improve, ye could send for Mistress Barry."

"It's a fine idea, Aengus. I'll see to it. I'm off to Lord Condon's today, so I think I'll ride on to Mistress Barry's house after, to see can she pay us a visit sometime next week."

"You're to see Lord Condon?"

"Aye, Aengus, I've come up with a plan."

"Ah! And none too soon. What is it?"

"I've made something for him, as well. It's a wooden stand for his writing instruments. It is the finest work I've done, as fine as I could make it. I must convince him I am honorable, that I'm the man he knows and not the man Cork says I am. He must help me and write that petition for Vivienne's money. If only Vivienne was herself, I'm quite certain she could charm him into it. But he's a kind man. I think I can get him to come 'round. If yet he refuses, I'll find a way to gain the favor of Clanricarde and Wentworth, and from there convince the gentlemen of every manor house in Munster that I am honorable and reliable. I have to build from the bottom now that Lord Cork has brought me so low."

"It is no small plan, is it, *Lámha mór*."

"It is monstrous, but there is no other way, and I will not give up. I'm sure that's what Cork wants me to do, and he will never win. Never."

"Would that I could go with you, but I have my responsibilities now."

"So you do. Times have changed for us, no?" He grinned, and for an instant the troubled lines on his face melted away—he was my old boyhood friend again.

"The third part of the plan is dealing with Cork himself. I doubt I could ever bring the man around to actually favor me, but he wields great power over men. I must gain some leverage in our affairs, or at the least weaken his by exposing some of his unsavory dealings."

"Have a care for yourself, Faolán. He's tried to have you killed, he's ruined your business, and he's stolen Vivienne's inheritance. He has a finger in every pie, and you'll not be able to know who is friend or foe."

"Aye, I'll not know his friends, Aengus, but I do know my own. I will find Cork's weakness, and that is where I will strike."

We clasped hands in farewell. His eyes were bright with newfound hope, but when he rode away, my shoulders seized as if pinched by a crow's talons, a warning that troubles descended from sources unseen.

June 23, the Eve of St. John, preceded the ancient feast of midsummer and the birth of John the Baptist. The moon rose early, a half-moon tilted on its side, portending rain. I welcomed the sight, for the days had been drier than usual, tending toward drought, and the village was sorely in need of a good harvest. Everyone in the village gathered in late afternoon, for the bonfire had to be lit by sundown and tended until midnight. Each family brought something to fuel it, mostly fallen twigs and corn trash, but a few larger pieces gave the fire enough bulk to keep it burning.

When Faolán arrived with Vivienne, I expected to see him in better spirits. After all, Lord Condon had agreed to write the petition as requested, even risking Cork's disfavor. But Faolán offered no smile, and Vivienne's appearance startled me. She had dark crescents beneath her eyes, and her cheeks were pale and sunken. Her normally lustrous hair fell dull and limp to her waist. She hadn't bothered to bind it beneath a cap as most of the women did.

I stood next to her and took her hand as the fire was lit and the flames flickered from pure blue to bright orange. Her fingers were cold. I warmed them in my grasp. She smiled weakly.

"What is wrong, Vivienne?" I asked her softly. "You are not yourself."

She squeezed my hand. "I am...well, Aengus, tired, I suppose. Sorry. You are sad, and I am making you more so."

"Nonsense. What have you eaten today?"

"Little. I'm afraid I can't keep much down. I must take great care of what I eat."

The blazes grew taller, and Mister FitzGibbon said the prayers for God's blessings on our crops. Then the children were free to dance and play around the fire. I was keenly aware Da was not among those to say that prayer nor to give out drams to his friends, but the joyful sounds of the children were comforting. On another day I might have expected Vivienne to dance with them. Instead, she leaned against me, raising my concern.

"Aengus."

"Yes, Vivienne."

"I hate to ask, but...I think my nerves trouble me. I wonder, could you find me a bit of that whisky to calm them?"

I looked at her as if she was a stranger. The Vivienne I knew would hardly have asked so meekly, but would instead have demanded, or marched right away and found some for herself.

"It's just that Faolán...thinks I should not have it. But I need it, Aengus. Can you see? Can you please?"

I had nothing left from the stores that had been in the brew house, nor supplies to make anything myself. Opposite me by the fire Mister McSherry held a jug of poitín. I did not hesitate.

"A wee taste o' that, sir?" I asked.

"Aye, Aengus, lad. Take it if ye dare, but bring it back, will ye?"

I borrowed his jug and took a swig from it myself so he could believe it was for me. The taste was bitter, but we hardly had a choice. I carried it to Vivienne. Faolán was talking with some of the other lads and did not notice when she took a long swallow.

"Thank you, Aengus," she said. "I have just been a little...I don't..."

She dropped the jug and I caught her just before she hit the ground. Faolán ran to her side.

"Vivienne!" He lifted her as if she weighed nothing at all and carried her to Sheelagh's house, me running beside him. He laid her on a bed, and Sheelagh wiped her face with a cool, wet cloth.

"What is it, dear? Are ye hurting?" Sheelagh asked. Vivienne looked at her but shook her head.

"I cannot get her to eat," Faolán said. "She'll allow herself a bite of bread and cheese, and sometimes not even that. She'll drink only a swallow of milk. I fear she is wasting away before my eyes."

"Faolán, I am sorry. She asked me for a dram of whisky to calm her nerves," I said.

He flipped his hand to brush the thought aside. "I care not if she drinks, as long as she eats."

"Aengus, bring a cup of the broth from my cook pot, will you?" Sheelagh said.

"She's had no fever," Faolán continued. "No cough, nothing to show any sickness. I tell myself it will pass, it's just the child growin', but she's not slipped away like this before."

"The blood left her head, Faolán. It's the excitement, but she'll be all right. See? She's already getting her color back. Let her stay wi' me a day or so. We'll get her right again." Sheelagh smoothed Vivienne's brow. "Aengus, you go with Faolán. We'll need your bed."

Faolán kissed Vivienne goodnight and we walked past the bonfire, burning much lower now, a few stragglers determined to watch the flames until midnight. We crossed the bridge to Glencurragh on foot, towing Dunerayl behind us.

"Aengus," Faolán's voice was higher than normal and full of alarm. "Of all the terrible things that have happened to us since we first rode to Bandon, this is by far the worst. I fear for her life more than I have ever feared for my own, and yet I am helpless. Anything I try to do seems only to make her feel worse. She wants to make me happy, and she cannot. I tell her I am happy, and she will not believe me. I bring her flowers, and she will not water them and arrange them. I bring her meat for her stew, and she will not touch it. I kiss her hand, and she weeps. It's as if...as if the moment Cork robbed her of her inheritance, he pulled a plug on her and her life seeps out like wine from a cask. My fear for her is greater than any I've faced with my sword or my pistol. I pray God for a battle I can *fight*."

What answers did I have? I could not help her, nor him, and I was failing miserably at helping myself. But then the thought suddenly occurred to me. "Do you know, Faolán," I said, "I've heard tell of a fine apothecary in Ballydehob. A Frenchman, but word is he has very modern thinking."

"I'll go to him. I'll go tomorrow, I will, after I see her in the morning. Then I'll ride up to Bantry to see the O'Sullivans, what's left of them. They'll despise Cork and his conjured lies, and might give me work. Thanks be to God for Dunerayl to carry me there or I'd have no hope at all."

Chapter Thirty-Two

Like Rivers of Blood

*Let the Patient endeavor to divert and make his Mind cheerful
by Exercise, and the Conversation of his Friends. For this Disease
does almost always proceed from sadness, and anxious cares.*

~ Richard Morton

The moon's omen delivered on its promise with soft rain that sprinkled our shoulders just as Faolán left for Ballydehob the following morning. I busied myself with work at the inn, but the rain grew heavier. Instead of washing things clean, it revived the remnant odors of smoke and ash. I was idle and angry. It was time to do as Faolán had; it was time to take action.

There was no sense waiting and hoping for a magical solution to raise the walls of O'Daly's. I needed money. Da had always warned me against taking on debt, but I could think of no workable alternative. I slapped on my cap and walked up the hill to Lord Condon. What he wanted in return for his loan was not the money, but some of the French wine being imported at Dingle Bay. I could order it easily once my trade started flowing again. We shook hands, and I knew I was back in business.

The first thing to purchase, even before building materials, was the brewing supplies. I didn't need walls for that, only my shed. I still had to wait for the hops, but all would be ready when they arrived. In the meantime, a good jar of ale for my customers was sure to attract both money and help.

When Faolán returned, Vivienne relaxed visibly, though he begged forgiveness for a few hours' tardiness and held her for a few moments. I didn't envy the troubles they were facing, but their embrace awakened that empty place inside me that they filled for each other. I shrugged the feeling away.

"You were right, Aengus. The French apothecary in Ballydehob is a bright fellow. I described your symptoms to him, Vivienne, and he said he had seen the affliction before. He called it an 'atrophy of the nerves.' It's like consumption, but not caused by fever or cough. And it is curable, *avourneen,* my darling.

"It's caused by three things. First, by breathing unwholesome air. It can't be that, for you cannot find sweeter air than we have at Glencurragh. Second is the intemperate drinking of spirituous liquors. This would be a concern if we had any, but of late our cupboards have been mostly bare, so we can't blame that. The third cause is violent passions of the mind, my dear. Violent passions of the mind. Here is my poor bride, soon to bring forth her first child, and all the struggles we've had with Lord Cork. Of course this is why you suffer so."

Faolán was nearly breathless, as if he'd just discovered one of life's greatest secrets that could change everything for the better. And who was to say he had not?

"I have a list of things we must do, Viv. You must go on a milk diet, that's the first. I think goat's milk three times a day. Then we must be sure you drink the chalybeate water Aengus brought. Both of those are restorative. Then, every day for the next thirty days, you drink ale with seven drops of balm of Gilead, and seven drops of conserve of red roses. The apothecary prepares the tinctures himself. He assures me they will calm your nerves so you can eat normally. And lastly, you and I will take long walks by the Ilen and breathe in the fresh air. I'll tell you how I'll fix all of our troubles so you'll no more have to worry. What do you say, love? Can you do these things?"

She nodded slowly. "I will do my best, Faolán. It sounds like I may need to visit the privy a lot with all of that drinking."

He hugged her fiercely, and we all laughed. It was a wondrous laugh and a healing laugh, imbued with the hope we would all find our way into happy life again.

"What of the O'Sullivans?" I asked.

Faolán's brow furrowed. "This was the cause of my delay. It is a hard life there, and more English and French folk than Irish, or so it seems, but the O'Sullivans remain tied heart and soul to the land. Times are harsh and no work to be had, not even in the mines. I offered services to Donal as his personal envoy. He said there may be letters going west, but there'd be none going east.

"There's full-on hatred smoldering. The only industry is English -owned, with a poor wage for Irish workers. The clan never recovered from the rebellion and the massacre at Dursey. Carew and his merciless soldiers. Men still speak of the three-hundred-mile march of the clan to the north. Those who remain stand idle in the village, spitting on the dirt, their children in rags. There is only one employment if I seek it, where every spare coin is funneled. You know of what I speak."

"A new rebellion."

Faolán nodded. "It will not die, *Teaghrán*. Though the fighting lads are all slaughtered, the hatred burns the hotter, and new ones rise up. There are camps farther west, beyond Kenmare. They know no defeat."

"Will you?"

"Join them?" He shook his head. "I cannot, not now. Mine is the path of renewal, not more destruction. And besides all that, I must feed my wife and child. There is no higher priority."

"What of the petition to the Lord Deputy?"

"Silence so far, but it was only sent a short while ago. I suppose there is hope yet, but I cannot buy our supper with that."

"Clanricarde, then."

"My thought as well. I could go to him and pledge my service, as my father did. He turned me away once, but I'll lie if I have to, just to get inside and force him to hear me out. I'll call on his duty as a clansman. I'll pledge myself body and soul if I must. He's my last hope. If he spurns me, we'll soon be eating a soup made from stones."

Vivienne sat up straight in her bed, her color rising to meet the determination in her set jaw and sparkling eyes. She grasped Faolán's arm as if she'd just remembered something urgent. "Faolán, you must go. *Go to him.* The time is right, before Parliament meets again. He will sit at the right hand of Lord Deputy Wentworth. He can convince him of our suit."

"Viv, I will go, but how can I until I see you getting better? It is a great distance to the earl's home in Portumna."

She pushed herself higher. "War is coming. I know not when, but all forces converge to it, and all of Ireland will suffer. I dreamt of it. Thousands will perish. Even the women and children will be cut down as they run naked through the hedges. The lanes and ditches will run like rivers of blood. I beg you, secure our protection under his coat of arms. With that we have hope of a future; otherwise, we will be lost."

"You have had a vision," I whispered.

She did not break her gaze from Faolán's eyes, but answered me softly, "I have seen horrors."

"I'll borrow a horse and ride with you, Faolán. You cannot travel such distance alone."

"I'm obliged, Aengus. I know the sacrifice you make. We'll go at first light, and raise the walls of O'Daly's as soon as we return. It is my promise."

Chapter Thirty-Three

Portumna

The name signifies "The Bank of the Oak."

~ *C.L. Adams*

Had I truly considered the distance before us, I might not have joined Faolán on this last venture to Clanricarde. It was the last, because he promised Vivienne when we returned, he would leave her no more until after the baby was born. And last, because Sheelagh so berated us for leaving her for so long to administer Vivienne's treatments. We would be seven days and seven nights on the road each way because Clanricarde was at his family seat, Portumna Castle, on the north end of one of Ireland's largest lakes, Lough Derg.

Our journey was hindered further by the need to hide from English soldiers encountered along the way. We couldn't afford to be stopped for questioning, or be assumed rebels and killed for sport. We hid as well from the Irish, never sure of their intentions. In these troubled times we could be robbed of our horses and even our clothes. When the way was clear, we were swift as the falcon that dives for a kill. But when we arrived at Portumna, we were more like the prey on the ground.

Portumna was a new castle compared to most in Ireland, constructed less than two decades before. Built to reflect all the power and prestige of the de Burgo clan and the earl who ruled it, its grounds were surrounded by an imposing wall of thick black stone. The arch at the gate was far more threatening than welcoming, and the door shut against us was ironclad. Faolán stepped right to it and pounded it with the hilt of his sword. A guard peered down at us from the parapet.

"Who disturbs the peace of the great Portumna Castle?" the guard challenged us. He refused to allow entry until he had secured permission from his captain. He returned to us with a single question. "Do you have something to deliver to our lord Clanricarde?"

"I do!" Faolán shouted confidently. I looked at him as if he was mad, and he shrugged. "I do, Aengus. I have an offer."

Our permission was granted. For this, and as the great door was wheeled open, I gave no thanks, for the fortified manor house before us did nothing to alleviate my anxieties.

"You feel too much, friend. Shrug it off. Remember our purpose, and let's to our business." Faolán marched forward toward the building as if he owned it.

Twenty-two windows glared down on us with the small square panes exactly as those of Carrick on Suir, but no light penetrated. With each step along the formal carriageway, I grew smaller and smaller. And where the entry at Carrick was open and welcoming, here it was imposing, with twelve stone steps leading to the door, each one steeper and blacker than the one before. The whitewashed outer walls gleamed as if impenetrable. I chided myself. There was nothing to fear. We knew Lord Clanricarde and he knew us, and if indeed any war was coming, we stood on the same side. Still, the ants marched in my belly.

We stepped into a great hall of marble floor, paneled walls, chandeliers, and large portraits of the Clanricarde lineage. Tall wooden doors at the end of the hall led in opposite directions. We were directed to the left door, which opened to a large gallery overlooking sculpted gardens and the gently rolling hills of the castle park.

There was no waiting this time. Clanricarde was seated at a desk conversing with his secretary over a stack of papers and a large map. He waved us over. Where once he may have been content to banter with Faolán as he did with the Earl of Ormonde in February, on this day he was ill-disposed, brusque, and impatient.

"You have brought my payment, Burke?" He held out a hand to be filled. His secretary eyed us curiously.

"I have not, sir, to my sorrow. Lord Cork has effectively ruined my income and stolen Vivienne's. We have petitioned the Lord Deputy to restore her inheritance, but we have had no response."

He nodded. "It is of no surprise to me, but no longer my affair. If you've brought no money, then why have you come? You know our terms. I shall have you imprisoned for such false entry." He raised a hand to his secretary.

"Vivienne is with child, sir," Faolán quickly blurted.

Clanricarde stopped. He looked to the farthest window from where we stood, his cheeks coloring, his jaw twitching. He exhaled in a huff and then glared at Faolán. "You know nothing of the world, *boy*. There are things afoot much larger than your little problems. You've failed to secure your wife's inheritance, and now a child comes. I care not. You sought to gain wealth by taking from another, and God punishes you just as he will punish the Lord Deputy for what he now seeks to do."

Faolán cleared his throat, his courage slipping. "What is that, sir?"

"You waste my time, but I'll tell you and perhaps it will expand your thinking. Our Lord Deputy has set his sights on all of Connacht. My land, my father's land, properties that have belonged to our clan for hundreds of years. He salivates for it under the guise of claiming it for the king, and yet we all know it is he who will ride over it, who will slaughter the game in our hunt park, trample the fine gardens with his heavy riding boots and cast out our tenants as if they were yesterday's rubbish. All to his own glory, to build a new plantation with English undertakers of his choosing who will pay him money and money and money.

"He is of the worst sort, our great, magnanimous Lord Deputy Wentworth, and would that he'd return to his family home. He is pure, personal greed flying unchecked beneath the king's ermine cloak. With every word and stroke of his pen, he distresses my father and brings him closer to the grave. And now I must search for deeds that are surely lost if ever they existed, just to prove our land is our land, when it is as clear and as plain as the sun in the sky. And so, no, if you bring me no money, be off with you."

His astonished secretary stepped back from the desk and the cloud of fury surrounding Sir Ulick, but Faolán stepped closer.

"I come to offer my services, sir. Like my father Sir William, I pledge my loyalty and my skills as emissary and warrior to the de Burgo clan and all its causes."

Clanricarde stared, nearly apoplectic, and then he released a long sigh and smirked at Faolán and me. "With your gallant sword, are you prepared to take on a troop of Wentworth's lawyers?"

The secretary grinned, but Faolán did not hesitate. "Lord Clanricarde, I am prepared to take on demons from hell if you so desire it."

"Admirable, Burke. But I have no work for you, and you try my patience. The demons walk the earth in their various disguises. You have already seen that some of the most devastating battles are not on the battlefield and shed no blood. We cannot just kill our enemies anymore. We must outsmart them."

Faolán released his stiffened shoulders and leaned forward. "My lord, you know me. I am not easily intimidated. I do not give up. So tell me, what do you need?"

Clanricarde looked thoughtful for a few long seconds, and then pulled at his long gray beard. "Information. I need to know what Wentworth is doing before he even knows he's doing it. I need to know how he charges his 'Commission for Defective Titles,' where he sends them, what he says, and what he thinks."

"You need a spy."

"Yes, a spy and a phantom that can float through walls and hear a man's thoughts."

"I am your man, sir, your most loyal servant."

Clanricarde's laugh was sardonic. "Mayhap you are, Burke, but I think we are speaking of a world you've not yet experienced. My father is well-connected by blood or marriage to every nobleman in the king's good favor, and still we face this foolishness. By my word, the Lord Deputy is the author of his own death warrant. But I must know, whom else does he terrorize? These are my allies. What are his deepest desires? These will be my weapons. Bring me the information to seal his fate, and I will pay you most generously. That is what I need, and soon. I would not see my father die believing his estate is in ruins."

"It is now my mission, sir." Faolán bowed to him with a wave of his cap.

"We will see the proof of it in time. And what of you, Mister O'Daly?" Clanricarde asked. "Do you pledge your services as well?"

"I come only to accompany my friend, my lord," I said. "The English soldiers set fire to my father's inn, killing him and destroying all that we had. I wish only to restore what was ours in his name."

Clanricarde's gaze dropped to his desktop. "Yes," he said, "this will be our common refrain, I fear. Our descent into lawlessness grows deeper, and those who cause it are blind to it. I warn you sir, if the Lord Deputy continues his course, greater troubles lie ahead, and true restoration may be a long time in coming. I am sorry for your loss. May God be with you.

"Burke," he said in a calmer voice, "I am enraged and impatient, but I am not a monster. Have a care for yourself. Be quick, be smart, and when you come to me again, you'd better have something I need. Fare well with your wife and child." He nodded to his secretary. "Give them a small purse to see them off."

And with that he returned his attentions to the map on his desk and we were dismissed. We followed the secretary into the hall. He brought us a small leather pouch full of coins. It was no great sum, but it confirmed Faolán as a worthy man in Clanricarde's employ, and restored some of his self respect without forcing him to beg.

"Faolán," I asked as we went for our horses, my initial anxiety now turned to cold trepidation, "how on earth do you intend to become a spy?"

He smiled. "It is no different than what I have always done, Aengus. People love to talk, especially if they think they have a juicy morsel. It gives them importance. I simply offer them the opportunity. My only challenge is to find the right people in the right places."

"You promised Vivienne you would not travel after this."

"Aye. It is not a promise I wish to break, but survival demands it. I will need to go to Dublin. I am hoping Vivienne will see the circumstance and release me from that vow. We all must adapt to the world we have before us."

The flies fluttering in my belly settled down as we ate our fill from the food vendors along the castle walls, and then rode southward with haste. When we reached the crossroads at Mallow, we found an inn near the carriage road that served spirits and beer. We ordered supper and sipped slowly with our ears open and eyes downcast. After a while Faolán walked about, making jovial conversation with this group of fellows and that one. When he returned to his stool, he wore a satisfied grin.

"Aengus, it is a splendid thing, is it not, the way the lads love their fellowship and their drink."

"You have learned something already for Lord Clanricarde?"

"Not for Clanricarde, but something that may be of great interest to Donal O'Sullivan. It seems the young Earl of Kildare, who happens to be a FitzGerald and son-in-law to our Lord Cork, is on a progress through Munster this very minute in search of entertainment. In particular, he seeks games of chance. At the same time, a rumor circulates that Cork gave Kildare £350 to pay the workers who are renovating his castle at Maynooth. The workers have yet to see their money. O'Sullivan may be interested in a high-stakes game with this young man."

I smirked. "I believe that falls under part three of your plan."

"So it does, my friend. As Lord Barry told us, Cork is exceedingly generous with the ones who deliver the noble bloodline to his family. It may cost him more than he knows. And there is something else. I heard that Cork sometimes has his letters delivered to Dublin Castle when he is there for the Lord Deputy's privy council. What if his letters should by mistake be delivered directly to the Lord Deputy Wentworth? They say Wentworth always opens and reads suspicious letters, no matter to whom they be addressed, the better to intercept any subterfuge."

"You could arrange this?"

"It may take a little while, working among my fellow runners and messengers, but I am sure it can be done."

"You are becoming even more wily than I thought, Faolán. I have heard something as well. There have been more cattle raids; one along the River Lee and another near Enniskean."

"And what is said of this?"

"The raids are more frequent, and it's not always the English who are targeted. Sometimes it's the Irish landholders as well. The hungry are desperate and do what they must. In any case, the raids draw the soldiers, and the O'Dalys are not alone in having suffered their cruel attentions. They venture much farther west than they are welcome."

"It is a fearsome world, Aengus, where raiders of the sort who killed my father are attracting the soldiers who killed yours."

Chapter Thirty-Four

Passions of the Mind

*Only her Appetite was diminished, and her Digestion uneasy,
with Fainting-Fitts, which frequently did return upon her.*

~ Richard Morton

We crossed the timber bridge over the River Sullane into Macroom. At the
market there, I bought the supplies needed to rebuild O'Daly's using the
money Lord Condon had loaned me. For the things we could not carry ourselves, like posts and studs, we paid a driver to bring on his southbound
hay wagon. And with our last few coins from Clanricarde, we bought meat
pies to bring home to Vivienne, Sheelagh and her family.

In late afternoon we arrived at Sheelagh's house. Vivienne was in the
kitchen garden picking greens. She ran to Faolán, and he swung her into
his arms. They kissed again and again until Sheelagh stood in her doorway,
Tadhg and Radha tugging on her skirts.

"You look beautiful, Vivienne," Faolán said. And it was true. Her hair
shone, her cheeks glowed, and the swell of her belly was more noticeable.
Her eyes glistened with tears of joy, when the last time we saw her she was
ashen gray and shedding tears of sorrow.

"Aye, she has rallied from her troubles," Sheelagh said, "for I've stood
over her to make sure she drank every drop of what I gave her."

Vivienne laughed. "She doesn't joke. Aengus, I didn't expect your sister
to be quite so forceful.

"She's a terror is what she is." Sheelagh cast me a sharp look and a
frown, then hugged my neck.

"She'll be longing for her own kitchen and bed now, Faolán," Sheelagh said. "Ye've been away long enough."

"'Tis so." He handed her the sack of meat pies. "I am grateful to you."

They left for Glencurragh to be home before dark. After settling my uncle's horse, I walked back to the site of the alehouse. It was still an offensive sight, but with less of a sting than it had before, now that I knew it would be rebuilt. I sat on the ground at its center and imagined the walls, the floor planks, the new doors, the serving table with its taps and tankards, and the new windows. The fire glowed, and the dark heads bobbed with laughter in the yellow light; stories were told while good-natured arguments erupted over the music and song. Everything would come back as before, almost everything, except for the routine and expectation of working beside my da. If only I had realized the value of it while I still had him. Nothing could be quite the same anymore, because he would always be absent.

At dawn, Faolán rode hard and fast to Donal O'Sullivan to deliver his information, and returned home at dusk. The next day the last of my supplies arrived and we could begin.

The original footings were still sound, and upon them we placed new sills for the upright posts, ready for framing the walls and the rooms. A few local lads helped place the beams, and then the rafters to support the thatch. The bays were at sixteen feet, and within them we set the studs. When it was time to place the wattle, the interwoven branches set into the notched studs, everyone in the village came around to help. Faolán did all the floor planks, while I worked on the daub. In a week's time we had a building, all except for the roof. I had to hire thatchers to get a weave that wouldn't leak.

The roof and interior details would take the longest, but I had already set my brew to ferment in my shed. In less than two weeks' time I would be serving ale, roof or no.

On the first of August, beneath the light of a full golden moon, we officially reopened O'Daly's as we celebrated Lughnasa, the beginning of the harvest. The moon's color was a favorable omen, a sign of wealth, of rich harvest, of plenty. The new windows sparkled, and the floors gleamed; the tables and benches might have wobbled a bit, but they were sturdy and smelled of good wood. My ale was among the best I'd ever brewed, and I had purchased good whisky for the occasion. I walked the entire village, personally inviting everyone to come and celebrate the new establishment, and in remembrance of my father I had sketched his likeness, framed it myself, and placed it on the new mantel we'd made for the hearth.

Sheelagh was there with her husband, Brian, and their two children, beaming as if she'd built the place herself. Mister McSherry and Mister Fitz-Gibbon moved their stools to the doorway as if they were the proprietors greeting all customers as they arrived. Faolán and Vivienne brought baskets of fresh bread and plump bilberries. Soon the alehouse filled to overflowing, my jar filled with coins, the fire crackled merrily in the hearth, and laughter, the lovely, hearty, breathful sound of laughter, filled every empty crevice. One fellow brought out a little wooden flute, another lad produced a small bodhrán drum, and at last we had music at O'Daly's.

But August passed too quickly with so much work to be done. The nights turned cooler before September arrived, and I knew we could expect a cold winter. By late September I ordered enough wine to repay half of what I owed Lord Condon. The first heavy rains of the season reminded me I would have to do a better job on the roofing of my shed or get used to being cold and wet.

October brought the rains. The river swelled her banks, reaching nearly to my back doorstep, and threatened to wash over our little bridge. As I worked, damp, cold, and alone in my shed, a figure moved across the bridge beneath the hood of Mairead's gray cloak. I ran to Vivienne and brought her quickly into the alehouse before the rain and the river swept her away. I warmed a mug of ale for her and sweetened it with a drop of honey.

"Vivienne, what has happened? Where is Faolán?"

She shook her head. "He had to go, Aengus. His vow to Lord Clanricarde. He was to be home the night before last, and still he has not come. I am afraid for him, and I could not stay alone in the house any longer."

With the cloak removed, I could see the growth of her belly, but it seemed as if the baby grew inside her at the expense of her arms, her legs, and all the rest of her, as a sprout eats away at its seed.

"Have you not eaten and had the milk and the medicines you must take?"

"Oh, Aengus, I have tried. Truly, I have. I just cannot maintain it. I feel as if there's a voice in my head on the one side that says 'you must,' and another on the other side that says 'you mustn't.' I cannot bear it anymore. I am so tired."

"How can Faolán leave you this way?"

"It is not his fault. When he is with me, he watches me as if I'm a sick child, but I've worked very hard to conceal this from him."

"Conceal what?"

"He must feel free to go, to do what he can to restore our fortune, especially for the baby. She will need him."

"Vivienne, he needs you. You must take care of your health."

"Might I have some of your whisky, Aengus?"

"Are you sure that…" I stopped myself. It was not my place to admonish her for wanting drink. I thought I should give her anything she wanted if it would comfort her.

"Sheelagh could come and…"

"No, please. Just let me stay here with you until Faolán comes home."

And so I quieted, built up the fire to warm her, and sat beside her. I tried to understand. There must be a reason why Faolán did not come home when he promised. But at the same time I was angry. How could he not have seen the condition she was in? How could he have left her? She emptied her cup and then refilled it, drinking half in a swallow.

"They all think I am cursed; I know they do."

"Who, Vivienne?"

"You know. Everyone in the village believes it. Either that I am cursed, a bearer of bad luck, or that I am a witch myself. They say I have brought Faolán to ruin and caused the fire that killed your father. That now I am set on killing my own baby."

"You are wrong. I've never heard such talk."

"They would not say it in front of you. They know you would defend me, and I thank you for that. But I see the fear in their eyes, and the mistrust. People used to bring us food and things for the house, or they would stop in when on their way to market. No one stops now. Not one lady from the village has come to visit me, not even Sheelagh. They are afraid."

"Viv, you mustn't believe it," I said, having stopped myself from calling it nonsense, though that is what I thought. "They are busy, that's all. From harvesttime to preparing for winter, there are demands on all of us."

"But it isn't that, Aengus. You know it."

I had to think about it. Had I seen any odd behavior toward her, or anyone whispering rumors in the shadows? I had been so involved with my own business and with Faolán's, I had not stopped to notice. There was enough plausibility, for people of the village did love to gossip, and suspicion was everywhere in difficult times. If one did not know Vivienne, I suppose he could wonder if she was responsible for all the misfortunes.

Worse, if I did not know Vivienne, I myself could be guilty of such fantasy. My gut churned even for the idea of it.

"Vivienne, you must stop. This kind of thinking only makes you sicker. It is the passions of the mind, remember? You must think only about the good things."

She refilled her cup and drained it. "I don't know if I can, Aengus. What are they?"

At that moment I was hard-pressed to name them, and were I to list the positives for her, I was sure she could offer three negatives for each one. But the spirits had worked on her empty stomach and she was falling asleep. I put her in my bed and fixed my own pallet on the floor by the hearth.

The next morning Faolán burst through the alehouse door, his face a crimson fright. I said nothing but pointed to my own bed, tucked into the hallway where the stairs had been before the fire, and where Vivienne still slept. He ran to her.

My frustration with Faolán melted away, because he had not returned alone. In the doorway stood a very concerned Mistress Barry, her kindly round face ruddy with cold. She hurried inside, breathing heavily, her skirts rustling. Under her arm she carried a bundle of instruments and medicines. When she saw Vivienne peering over Faolán's shoulder, she quickly knew her mission and took charge of the situation.

"Out with you, gentlemen. Both of you. Let me have a good look at our wee mother-to-be."

We waited by my shed behind the alehouse, the rain coming in a light but steady drizzle. Our heads were sheltered, but the air was cold and damp, enough to chill me to the bone.

"For a second or two I thought I'd lost her, Aengus. But then I knew she would go to you. If she had not been here I'd have..."

"She was with me all evening, but I'm afraid she is not at all well, *Lámha Mór*."

He nodded. "I do not know what has come over her. She is strict about eating tiny portions she carefully measures. If I try to get her to eat more, she refuses, or gives in just to satisfy me and then spits it out when she thinks I am not looking. It is not that she won't feed the child. She wants to have a healthy baby. But she can't seem to stop herself. If we try to talk about it, we only argue, making both of us feel worse."

"I am starting to see it is not just the eating, Faolán. It goes much deeper than that."

"What do you mean?"

Mistress Barry came outside then, pulling her thick blue shawl over her hair. "Gentlemen," she said, "I believe the baby is fine; I detect a strong heartbeat. But the poor lass is weak, as you said, Faolán. She can barely lift her arms, dear girl. Something's got ahold of her I can hardly fathom. I can stay for a few days to help her back to her feet."

"The apothecary recommended a milk diet," Faolán offered.

"From now on, it must be goat's milk. Chicken's eggs. And meat. She must have good fresh meat for strength, and the marrow from the bones. I will walk her about, try to find a bit of sunshine to restore her energy and circulate the blood. Beyond that there is little any of us can do if she willna take nourishment. Ye must pray for her. We must all pray for her."

Chapter Thirty-Five

Of Unicorn and Bezoar

Remember not the sins of my youth, nor my transgressions.

Psalms 25:7

In mid-October, against all of Vivienne's protests, I stayed for a few nights at Glencurragh while Faolán was away. We supped on thin soup and I filled my belly with her camp bread. She sipped the ale I'd brought her and stared vacantly at the fire, with one hand resting upon her swollen belly.

"Why does he leave so much, Aengus?"

This surprised me. Faolán did not hide things from her but discussed his doings openly. "You know why. He's trying to earn a living. He needs to get Clanricarde what he's requested."

"He is gone when he travels, yes, but he is gone other times as well."

"What do you mean, other times?"

"When he goes out at night and he doesn't come back until dawn or later in the day. He tells me he goes to other farms to exchange labor for food. He comes back tired and dirty, but he carries meat and corn. Other things sometimes. We have plenty, and more than we need in the larder when others have less. What farmer would keep him working all night?"

I looked at the floor, at the kitchen table, at the hearth, and then up at the rafters.

"I thought you knew," she said.

I said nothing. What could I say? My mind searched for explanations, reached for unexplored possibilities, sorted through local farmers who might have such needs, but I could identify nothing useful. It scared me to think of what Faolán might be doing, and frustrated me to think he could not or would not confide in me.

"It doesn't matter." She shrugged off her shawl and sighed in a huff. "He wants to care for me and the baby, and he does it well. I'm satisfied she will have everything she needs. Foremost she will have a good father, and that's what matters, isn't it so? She will be a princess, Aengus. She will not be like me, unloved and shuffled here and there among foster homes until she is old enough to sell into a profitable marriage. She will never have to marry if she doesn't wish it. She will already own a grand castle and will be adored by everyone who lives around it. She'll be strong and smart, accountable to no one's whim, making all her own decisions."

"You are quite certain it is a she?"

"Quite. I can see her, truly. Not her face, exactly, but her small bare feet running up the stairs in the castle. She will blaze with energy, and she will always speak her mind."

"I cannot wait to meet her."

"Yes, you will love her, and be her beloved Uncle Aengus."

Faolán returned the midday following. He had traveled as far as Kilkenny with hopes of obtaining information about Lord Deputy Wentworth's intentions. He did not gather the kinds of evidence Clanricarde needed, but had heard a great deal of useful gossip.

"Some you will not like, *Teaghrán*. Our friend Lord Ormonde has made some enemies. The talk was that he has aligned himself with the Lord Deputy, helping him acquire properties for some of his plantation schemes, even at the protestation of his own family. And he has evicted Irish Catholics who were long-term tenants of his family in favor of new English Protestants who will pay a higher rent. He has debt to pay, but is making his money in harsh ways."

A great weight pressed upon my chest. Faolán was right; it caused me pain to learn this. I could not speak at first. Surely this could not be true. If it were, it would be as if Ormonde had betrayed me personally. I admired him so highly, and believed him a true statesman and a champion for fairness. My stomach cramped so that I might vomit, as if this news was like a storm disrupting my calm sea, rocking my ship with turbulence. But then I righted myself. No matter what he'd heard, it could not change the fact that Ormonde helped us when we needed it. I'd be saddened if the stories were confirmed in days to come, but I would not change my opinion of him.

"Mayhap it is only gossip," I said.

Faolán's frustration continued to grow as long as he had nothing to deliver that would generate money, and yet he'd returned to Skebreen with apothecary powders of unicorn horn and bezoar stone.

"Where did you get these?" I asked him as he stirred pinches of each powder into a cup of Vivienne's milk.

"I happened upon this fellow at an establishment just north of Clonmel. He promises a swift cure."

"Unicorn horn," I said, watching him curiously. As superstitious as I was, I did not believe in unicorns, for no one I knew had ever truly seen one. They had seen spirits. They had seen the fairies in the wood and beneath the faerie thorn trees. They had seen the puca in his yellow-eyed, dark-horse guise. And I myself had seen the banshee, the spirit of my mother, the night my father died. But unicorns, I believed, were a thing of the imagination to entertain children, and I was sure in his heart Faolán did not believe in them either. He was growing more desperate to find something to restore Vivienne. She had started to refuse the tinctured ale, and would drink only a small portion of her milk.

Her belly had now grown to a size that made it easy to imagine a little baby moving inside, and she had developed a slight sway in her walk. I hoped her legs were stronger than her arms appeared to be, that she would be able to carry the weight as it continued to grow. Faolán's face showed worry lines as he watched her move, his brow continuously furrowed. I knew he tried to hide his greatest fear, for it was my fear as well, that he could lose both the wife and the infant at childbirth.

He swept her into his arms, and we walked along the well-worn path to the river. At last the day was crisp, with cool air and bright sun, instead of damp and gray. We walked beyond the bridge until we came to the place where the river widened and two tiny islands pressed against each other as the river rushed around them to the sea. The birch trees grew taller, their trunks bright in the sunlight and their leaves turning saffron with the season. At their roots, the clinging vines had gone brown, and thin tendrils shivered and bobbed in the amber flow.

Vivienne crouched by the stream, cupped her hands and filled them with the cold water. "Do you think God punishes us?"

Faolán and I looked at each other. I suppose I had thought about God's ways after Da was killed, but I did not imagine it a punishment. We knew who was responsible, and I hoped God would punish them. Why God allowed it to happen at all I found impossible to justify. I could only console myself that Da's death was part of a larger puzzle of the world, the intricacies of which I could not know. Still, her question caused us both to consider our part in the situations where we found ourselves.

"Vivienne, we've only done what we had to under the circumstances we were given. I do not think God would punish us for that," Faolán said.

"But we have done bad things, don't you think?" She did not look at us but held her gaze on the water.

"Are you talking about Eames? We had no choice in that, as we have all agreed."

"Not just Eames. Things. Thoughts. I can speak only for myself, but I have hated. Eames, Lord Cork, my mother. Can you be punished for bad feelings and bad thoughts? Some say the thought is as bad as the deed and you must beg forgiveness for it. I have wanted to go to Lord Cork and stab him until he died at my feet. And I have wondered whether, giving nothing of help to us, my mother should receive the same treatment. But I do not ask forgiveness. I only rethink these things day after day. Because of Cork and my mother, I have not brought what you needed to fulfill your dream. It forces you to work in ways you would never have wanted. Glencurragh goes unbuilt, your livelihood is destroyed, and yet I grow, and the baby will come, and your burden becomes heavier and greater."

"Vivienne, if God came to earth this instant and offered me a different life, do you think I would choose it? I would not leave you for one hundred different lives."

She dried her hands with her skirt and looked up. "You will love our daughter, won't you?"

"I will love any child that comes from our love."

"She'll be a queen of her domain, Faolán. Listen to this verse I made up. *Come faerie, come banshee, come soldier with sword, she holds her head high, and rules with her word.* It is for her. Nothing can stop her."

"It is wonderful. Like you, Vivienne. She will be like you."

"Not like me, husband. She will be a warrior, like you." At that, Vivienne smiled in a way I had not seen her do in some time, a smile of true, radiant happiness. As quickly as it came, though, it then faded.

Chapter Thirty-Six

Samhain

Season of mists and mellow fruitfulness,
Close bosom-friend of the maturing sun.

~ John Keats

The approach of Samhain meant the end of the harvest and the beginning of winter, the darkest part of the year. From ancient times, it was always intended as a celebration, a time when the veil between the living and the dead is lifted, and those who have passed on can move to a new life. It reminds the living that, though the darkness comes, the light will return. It is the cycle of all life.

"Remember," Mister FitzGibbon would say every year, "Samhain is not just a time to look back. It is also a time for looking forward."

It is also when the souls of the dead may revisit. A tingling began in my belly, my father being so recently in his grave. I was frightened by the spirit world, but it was not fear that troubled me where my father was concerned. He would not harm me nor any of our family. Of this I was certain. But if I looked upon his face again, I would have to release it to the next world a second time. I dreaded the pain of this most.

The village bonfire recalled the *tine chnámh*, the bone fire of the Celts that symbolized the release of spirits to the next world through the rising smoke. Some farmers brought animal bones to toss into the flames, but most just brought turf or scrap wood to keep the fire going. The longer it burned, the more ale I'd be likely to sell. I hoped the night would bring enough coin that I could pay off more of my debt to Lord Condon. When I ordered his wine, I would also buy some for Vivienne.

My thoughts lingered on her words when I'd stayed with her at Glencurragh. What farmer would keep Faolán working all night? And why had he not told me about it? Was he doing something that could return the soldiers to Skebreen? The idea that O'Daly's might be burned again turned my insides to cold, hard stone. The next time they came, they could burn other homes and businesses, or even the entire village and more of us would be killed. What care had they? And with Vivienne's birthing time approaching, he should not be courting danger.

I resolved to confront him on the matter. When the fire was set, the flames dancing as if they were themselves the spirits, Sheelagh's Tadgh and Radha chased each other in circles around it. Several other children joined the game, and their high-pitched laughter mingled with the crackling sounds of the fire. The smell of the smoke was unsettling, so I stood away from its rise. Faolán brought stools from the alehouse and placed them where Vivienne could sit and talk with Sheelagh.

We stood together, feeding our collection of sticks and turf to the fire. None of the others stood near enough to hear us. It was my best opportunity.

"Faolán, Vivienne has told me of your outings at night, when you do not return until dawn. That you work for farmers. For whatever reason you've not confided in me, I do not blame you, but I fear for you. With this talk of cattle raids, I..."

Faolán turned and gave me a sharp look, his eyes as yellow in the firelight as the wolf at Mallow Castle. He turned away and said nothing.

"Sometimes I have seen Sean and Thomas passing. They don't stop at O'Daly's. They are my friends, but they pass right by."

"I do not ride in raids," he said simply.

"Faolán, we are brothers and friends. I hope you do not lie to me."

He turned so swiftly I flinched, expecting the slam of his fist in my face, but he did not strike.

"Aengus." He spoke softly that others would not be alerted, but the sharp edge in his voice and the bristling of his body forced me back. "I do not lie, but I protect you from things you should not know. I do what I must for my family. The less you know of what I do, the safer you are. The safer we all are. Do not ask of this and do not speak of it. Please, never mention it again."

He returned to tending the fire, and I looked away from him, smarting and sick in the belly. He was right, of course. Whatever he was doing I was better off not knowing, but it angered me all the same because of the danger it posed. And yes, I had to admit I despised being excluded from that part of his life. It put a distance between us that had not been there before.

I wondered if I was becoming like my father, after all my efforts to be accepting and accommodating rather than judgmental and bitter. Would I begin to shuffle about the alehouse grumbling to myself about the way others chose to live their lives? About their decisions and how I knew so much better? Would I carry on each day about all that was wrong with the world and people in it?

Sard it. I would be what I would be. But Samhain was a night for spirits to move about among the living, and secrets to be revealed. I did not wish to be ignorant of what was going on about me or what dangers my friend risked. I needed to know. So, if he would not speak of it, I would be like a haunting spirit that moved through the night to satisfy the questions in my mind.

When Faolán left the gathering to carry Vivienne home, I went to find a horse. My uncle's was rented out, but his neighbor had a mare available, and so I took her. She was small and not as fast as Dunerayl, but strong enough and agreeable. She would keep up to suit me, for I planned to stay well behind when Faolán ventured out for wherever he would go.

I hid the mare in a thicket just west of the bridge until all the celebrating villagers went home to their beds. It took considerable yawning and complaining to send FitzGibbon and McSherry on their way, but as soon as I could close one door behind them, I opened another and slipped into the darkness.

I found my mare and waited with her just out of sight until, sure as the river flows to the sea, came Faolán, walking Dunerayl slowly across the bridge to maintain the quiet, then picking up speed when his hooves met softer ground. I had my skean close at hand and a good fighting stick tucked behind my saddle, to be prepared for wherever he led me. I clicked my tongue, and the mare and I set off after them.

He took the coast road heading east. I stayed well behind, sure he would meet either the Barry brothers or some other companions by the time we could hear the surf, but he never even slowed his pace. He stayed on the main path, never meeting another traveler to cause concern. And on we went for nearly two hours until he came to a cut between two hills that led into a wooded valley.

I knew this place. I looked about as the realization dawned slowly, spreading from my belly and surging across my shoulders and up the back of my neck. With just a bit more light, I'd have been able to see Ross Castle in the distance. We were on properties belonging to the Bishop of Ross. The vast acreage and elevated position as Bishop Richard Boyle had been secured for him by none other than his cousin of the same name, Sir Richard Boyle, the Earl of Cork.

A rush of blood warmed my shoulders and cheeks. *He was true*. He did not lie to me. There was no raiding party gathered, and no other outlaws to draw the soldiers. There was only Faolán, collecting on a debt he felt he was owed. Whatever he was about to do here, I am sure he felt justified and probably enjoyed a bit of revenge. I would rush to help him if I could, but I dared not reveal myself and my shameful lack of trust. I wanted to turn my mare around and run back home, but I could not risk that he might overtake me. I found a place to hide and waited while he did his deed.

The moon had waned five days, but yet I had light enough to see the tops of his shoulders as he moved across the valley. He stopped at a stone wall where an old tree had fallen, but a large oak stood beside it, tall and majestic. He left Dunerayl beneath the oak and proceeded on foot toward the castle carrying a small bucket. I lost sight of him when he reached the valley's far end and copse thick with underbrush. What could he be doing? And what if he were discovered? He might be killed if he were caught. But soon he reappeared from the copse, a bundle held firmly in his arms as he ran back to the wall and Dunerayl.

He wasted no time. He mounted, and Dunerayl leapt over the wall. Across Faolán's lap lay the bundle, and when he drew closer I recognized the hooves of a lamb protruding from one side. I gathered he had used the bucket with some feed in it to attract and capture a hungry wanderer. The horse and rider vanished into the screen of woods and darkness from which we'd come.

They were not discovered, for no other movement stirred between my vantage point and the castle. I exhaled fully. He was safe this night, but I feared for him nonetheless, for the bishop employed warriors and enjoyed the earl's protection. I could not doubt the missing lamb would be discovered by morning. There was justice in the taking of it, and I could not fault him for it, but in the end thieving is still thieving. Would the sin come back to harm Faolán someday?

By mid-morning I was working at the alehouse, trying to ignore the numb-mindedness from lack of sleep. Faolán arrived in a burst of energy. How could he manage it?

"Mistress Barry came to us this morning," he said. "She studied Vivienne carefully, her eyes, her hands, her ankles, the shape of her belly, all the while mumbling away. She sent me out of the house, and when she called me back she sat me down in the kitchen. Vivienne is weak, as anyone can clearly see. If she won't eat there is little to do to force her. She said Viv must be confined now and receive constant attention until the baby comes."

"Where is the birthing to be done? At Sheelagh's?"

"No, she wants to be at Glencurragh. But she needs comforting and coaxing to get her to take the food and keep it down. She must walk about several times a day. She should not be alone. Left to herself she will slip deeper into the hands of this demon-thing that grips her. Mistress Barry said she'd stay for a few days to help bring her strength back. I've packed a saddlebag, Aengus. One last time I ask a great favor. Can you leave O'Daly's in Sheelagh's hands and ride with me to Lismore?"

"You must be joking. Mistress Barry just said Vivienne needs constant attention, and besides, do you truly want to try Lord Cork again?"

"No, brother, but I'm no good in close quarters. In my worry for her, I only frustrate her and make her feel worse. She needs a woman's tender hand. She needs her mother. She protests and claims to hate her, but I think she hides her true feelings. At such a time, what woman does not want her mother? I will fetch her here, but I need your help."

"What can I do that you cannot?"

"Watch my back, *Teaghrán*, just as you did on the way to Portumna. There will be soldiers between Cork and Lismore, and we must ride fast. There is no time to hide as we did before. I don't know what I might come up against in Cork's home territory, but there is more safety in two."

I did not hesitate. The truth is, I wanted to go. Now that I knew his heart again, I wanted to help him, and selfishly I hoped my adventurous days were not completely over because of my new responsibilities. But most of all, it restored me as Faolán's closest friend, included again in his plans.

"I'm not sure that reasoning will be good enough for Sheelagh."

Faolán smirked. "We are a team, you and I. Help me to bring Deirdre back for Vivienne. We must hurry. Her birthing time draws near."

Three days later we crossed the arched bridge over the Black-water, the castle towering above us. The dark clouds rose like brawny shoulders just behind it. At the gate, a surly guard said Cork was not in residence.

"We have come to see Lady Deirdre. Might you at least inform her that we are here? We have come concerning her daughter," Faolán said.

The guard shrugged and disappeared, so we knew not whether he honored our request or ignored it. We waited at the gates trying to determine what to do next.

"Wait for me here, Aengus. I will ride along the castle walls to find another entrance, or a low place where the wall might easily be scaled."

"You will not, Faolán, please. Such an idea is dangerous when you know how Lord Cork hates you. It would surely invite your capture and be an excuse for Cork to hang you as an intruder."

"I've no time to waste here. We must do something quickly,"

A rustling movement came from our left as if a wild animal approached. It was Deirdre's exotic companion, scampering low through the high grasses. The strangely marked boy dropped to his knees where the grasses met the cleared dirt carriageway. He bowed his head and then eyed us curiously. "Mistress sends me to fetch you. Please come."

"What is your name, lad?" Faolán asked.

"I am Saturiwa, name for great chief."

We followed him along the west wall of the castle, tied our horses to a wych elm where they would not be visible from the gate, and continued toward the river. The brush was heavy with ferns, vines, heartsease and goat willow. Clinging ivy on the wall disguised a low and narrow garden gate, unguarded by Cork's soldiers. The boy pushed his shoulder against the door until it gave a low-pitched screech as it parted, and he peeked through. Deirdre pulled the handle from the other side and opened the gate wide.

"Is something wrong?" she said quickly. "Is she not well?" Her face looked strained, her eyes alight with concern. The boy ran behind her and clutched her skirt. She waved us inward to a dark alcove obscured by overgrown vines, and closed the gate behind us.

Faolán removed his cap. "My lady, Vivienne is with child. Her time will be within the month."

"But she is well."

"No, my lady, I'm afraid she is not. She wastes away with each day. The apothecary calls it atrophy of the nerves, but none of his medicines have relieved her of it. The midwife is with her now trying to restore her strength, but it is an affliction of the passions. I thought mayhap you could...I realize it is much to ask...but I thought, as her mother you might know how to heal her heart, or whatever it is that eats away at her, that she might be herself again and a healthy mother to our child."

Deirdre's eyes filled with tears as she looked from Faolán to me and back to Faolán. "I knew something was wrong. I must go to her straight-away. You were right to come. Saturiwa, we must pack," she said. "Do you gentlemen have a carriage?"

We glanced at each other, and Faolán frowned. "No, my lady, we have only our two horses. We can carry a satchel or two, but we'll be doubled up on horseback unless you have a horse of your own."

She pondered for a moment. "I couldn't take one of the earl's carriages, but I might secure a horse and wagon. Let me see..."

And as she thought, the crunch of gravel and a rustle of fabric told us someone approached. We peered around the heavy veil of vines to see Lord Cork himself, fuming in his long brown robe with its foxtail collar. Sparse hair fluttered around his ears. He clutched his robe at the chest and glared at us with a terrible fury. Faolán stepped forward in protection of the rest of us.

"My Lord Cork." He bowed. "We've come to speak to Deirdre. Vivienne is ill and with child. She..."

"You have no business here, in my home, in my garden. Our business was concluded long ago. Deirdre, take your companion and go inside."

"My Lord, I..." Deirdre tried to speak, but he waved her off.

"Go inside; do not speak. *Go now,*" he said, and jutted his chin toward the sky. "Guardsmen!" he hollered in a voice to be heard as far as Cork City. Two men in livery appeared almost immediately and ran toward us. Men shouted from other parts of the castle. And then Cork glared with his dark, tufted brows arching skyward, his voice lowered to a snake's hiss. "You have made a mistake this day. You have trespassed on my private property, and it will be the death of you."

Faolán grabbed my arm and we bolted for the garden door and ran for our horses, still tethered, to the tree.

"Run, fools! Run like the criminals you are," Cork shouted after us. "And never come again or I will hang you from my tower!"

Chapter Thirty-Seven

The Silver Coins

*'Tis just like a summer birdcage in a garden; the birds that are
without despair to get in, and the birds that are within
despair, and are in a consumption, for fear
they shall never get out.*

~ *John Webster*

We galloped from the castle and through the village, and kept going for a mile or so until Faolán spied a dense patch of woods where we could conceal our horses and rest. He dismounted and collapsed against a tree beneath Dunerayl's breathy muzzle. He cradled his forehead, elbows against his knees. I sank down beside him.

"Faolán, do not give up. We will find a way to her."

He did not look up but shook his head. "Our time runs out, Aengus. We cannot wait. I am so afraid Vivienne might die."

I kept my peace until he could compose himself. He clenched his jaw, bracing back the tears.

"What else is it, *Lámha Mór*?"

He smiled weakly at the old nickname, and wiped his face on his sleeve. "It is just...how could everything have gone so wrong, Aengus? It was simple, and it was good. I love her, she loves me, we are good together, but now I..."

"Now what?"

He released a deep sigh. "What has happened to her? Why can't I help her? And why does Cork treat us so? The path was clear at first, and now I can't see the way. I am helpless to change our situation or to bring her back from this strange disease. This was my last hope, to bring her mother and shake her free of whatever it is that grips her. But it is all beyond my understanding. Just as Cork shut the door to the castle, the door has closed on me."

I cast around in my mind for something uplifting to say, but what could it be? That she would get better? The baby would be fine? Lord Cork would free her inheritance and send an army of craftsmen to build Glencurragh, and we would all live happily ever after? I was a fool. I said nothing. The best I could do was sit beside him as his friend, and let him be. Finally my stomach spoke for me, growling noisily. He looked up at me and scoffed.

"I guess life must go on despite our troubles. Come then, *Teaghrán*. Let's find an innkeeper and beg a bowl of coddle."

We rode onto the carriageway again and had traveled just a few minutes when the beat of hooves sounded behind us. We had no cover where we were. Faolán pulled his pistol and I my skean, certain it was Cork's guards chasing after us. Soon a rider came into view, and Faolán slowly lowered his pistol. "It's Saturiwa, on a fast pony.

He rode right up to us, kicking up dirt as he reined the pony to a halt. He leapt from his mount and fell to a knee before us.

"My lords," he said.

"What is it, Saturiwa? We are not lords, and you may speak freely," Faolán said.

"Sirs, my mistress weep, and Lord Cork shout. She cannot come with you today. She send gift for your lady." He untied a wicker casket from the back of the pony, bowed, and handed it to Faolán.

He lifted the lid to reveal several gowns made for an infant, of white linen and embroidered with tiny white flowers, acorns, and leaves. Beneath them a linen handkerchief was rolled into a cylinder. He unrolled it to find a stack of gleaming silver coins.

"Saturiwa, you are sure this is from your mistress?"

"Yes, sir. I help pack it. She wish for you to have it, for the lady. She say, she will come when she can. You go now."

Faolán glanced at me, a little uncertain. He looked down the road to see if the boy had been followed, but there were no other riders in either direction.

"This is most generous, Saturiwa. Are you safe to return to the castle now?"

"I am neither slave nor captive. I am for my mistress only, come and go as she commands without guards."

"All right then; please thank her for this gift. I would not accept it but for Vivienne. She needs medicines and help I can't otherwise give her. Tell Lady Deirdre we are most grateful and hope to see her before the winter solstice."

"I tell her, sirs."

The lad bowed again, mounted his pony in a single leap, and galloped off in the direction of Lismore.

In Cork City we stopped at an apothecary's shop to purchase tinctures and some sweets and wine for Vivienne. For the baby we found a small, rocking crib painted dark green, with tiny white flowers on the headboard. Faolán secured it to the back of his saddle.

We traveled as fast as our horses would carry us, and arrived home again as dusk settled over Glencurragh. Vivienne was alone. Her face lit with excitement at Faolán's return, but it brought little color to her cheeks. She remained thin and frail except for her belly. She seemed more tired, her walk more labored.

"I am well," Vivienne insisted. "Mistress Barry was collected two days ago to tend another woman's labor. I am glad she's gone, for she's worse than Sheelagh. My goodness, such a fuss over me, when what is really important is what is going on in here." She rubbed a hand across the top of her belly. "She is moving quite a bit now, Faolán. See?" She placed his hand where she had rubbed, and his eyes sparkled with pleasure.

"She moves all about, trying to kick her way out already. Aengus, look here." Faolán stepped back to allow me to touch Vivienne's belly, but I was hesitant. She smiled and grabbed my hand.

"It is fine, Aengus, when it is something as special as this," she said.

Her belly was warm and firm where I touched her, the fabric of her gown barely disguising the startling movement within. The shape of the dome shifted, and then a true kick struck my index finger. I jerked my hand away at the surprise of it. Vivienne laughed and pulled my hand back. The shape of her belly shifted again, and I imagined the tiny infant yawning and turning on her side for another nap. A warmth spread from my core down into my stomach and across my shoulders, then up into my face. My cheeks burned. A baby, alive and growing, just a thin membrane away from the air and the space around us. Just a short time away from becoming a new person in the world. Suddenly I longed to hold her in my arms and see her face.

"Vivienne, I believe our Aengus is blushing."

"He has become quite misty-eyed," she said. "It is good, Aengus. You *should* be moved by it. The birth of any child is a wondrous thing, and you will be a fine uncle."

An uncle. I was an uncle already to Sheelagh's children, but I had never bonded to them as I did to this child. I had been a part of her creation in all but the physical act, hadn't I? A part of the plan, a part of bringing Faolán and Vivienne together and of the wedding, a part of the process as the baby developed. And I would, I swore to God and to myself, be the best uncle ever there was for this child. If Sheelagh complained about my favorites, well, so be it. I was already in love.

Faolán untied the crib from Dunerayl's back. Vivienne loved it immediately, her thin fingers tracing the tiny white flowers. I noticed the brittle, broken nails that had once been finely shaped. Faolán then handed her the gift casket. At first she became angry about a gift from her mother and did not want to accept it, but he opened it, and she saw the fine linen gowns. She would not deprive the baby of them.

"I will write my thanks to her, Faolán, but that will be an end to it." She lifted one of the gowns and held it up to the sunlight. "It is expertly woven. So soft." Then she dropped her arms to her sides, as if it was a strain to hold them up. She looked up at Faolán, her face turning ashen. She seemed to sway and then her legs collapsed beneath her.

Faolán caught her, swept her into his arms, and ran into the house. He placed her on the bed.

"Aengus, the tinctures and the wine."

"I have them right here." I poured a cup of sweet wine and added the tinctures Faolán had bought, of black cherry and peony water. With this we also gave her a pill made with powder of licorice. She accepted a few sips of the wine and then pushed it away, her hand trembling, a sheen of perspiration appearing on her forehead.

"Aengus," Faolán whispered, "I cannot leave her now. Please fetch Mistress Barry back."

I forgot how tired I was and how far we had traveled. I leapt upon Dunerayl, and he moved as if he understood the urgency. We nearly flew across the bridge and southward toward Rathmore, veering off to the west toward her house. Her yard was empty and the cottage seemed deserted until Thomas stepped out, drying his hands on a towel.

"She's gone to Mistress Foley's since this morning. She has my uncle's horse, or I could mount up and take you there. It's three miles northwest."

I rode on as if a great tempest pushed at my back. I followed the packhorse road until the house appeared, with the horse tethered. It was nearly dusk, and Mistress Barry was just outside the door.

"Is it Vivienne?" she called to me even before I had reined Dunerayl to a stop.

"She has collapsed."

"Mistress Foley's newborn is well. I can go now. I'll follow you."

Her horse was not as fleet as Dunerayl, so I stayed with her, my anxiety rising with the fear that something terrible could happen while we still traveled. It was full dark when we reached Glencurragh, but Faolán had placed a torch to light our way. Without even a greeting, Mistress Barry dismounted and hurried into the house, closing the door behind her.

We waited. Faolán paced and grumbled, talking to himself in scurrilous terms. I watered Dunerayl and gave Faolán the brush to work the horse's hide, a task I thought might ease and quiet the both of them. After half an hour, Mistress Barry opened the door.

"The babe is not coming, not tonight, and not for another week or so, methinks. But Vivienne's pulse is slow. She is weak and confused. I dunno what has happened in the mere two days since I left her, but leave her be for tonight. You lads can camp out here, and I will stay with her. In the morn we must see to a physician. He may be able to revive her more than I, but if he tries to bleed her, I will clap him on the head with a shovel and send him to the Devil."

She slammed the door behind her, and we were left outside to spend a sleepless and worrisome night. I could not go to the alehouse and leave Faolán alone and tormented, and he could not leave home in fear that something might go wrong. So we lay on blankets side by side, staring at the stars and waiting.

Chapter Thirty-Eight

Grace of God

My mind is troubled, like a fountain stirred;
And I myself see not the bottom of it.

~ William Shakespeare

For a while we just rested, no words between us. Then I found the bread and cheese pressed to an indistinguishable mass in my saddlebag and we devoured it. There was wine as well, and though we had purchased it for Vivienne, I promised Faolán I would order more and we drank it in hopes of getting some sleep. We rested, but sleep came only in light doses and brief intervals. In the darkest part of the night, Faolán lay on his back, his hands laced behind his head. I could see only the line of his profile against the shadowy contours of the yard surrounding us.

"What does God want, Aengus?" he asked.

I leaned on my elbow to look at him. How could I know what God might want? "God?" I said. "What has it to do with God? This plan has always been about what *you* wanted, about Glencurragh. Isn't it still?"

"It is, but…" He hesitated, swiped his hand down his face, and heaved an exasperated sigh. "Aengus, I am thwarted at every turn."

We were silent a moment. I waited for him to continue, knowing he would.

"I worked every day with that plan in mind, to build Glencurragh just as my father dreamed it. But every path led nowhere, and then scavengers picked it to ruins. I ought to have been a famous knight as he was, but…"

"I know," I said. "Times have changed. Even Clanricarde wants only information from you, or money, not battle skills."

"If I married Vivienne, I thought...Yes, I abducted her in hope of greater wealth, but from the moment I saw her, I loved her and treated her like the highborn lady she is. Now there are things that afflict her. We've lost the money. We've lost your father. Nothing I do seems to keep us from tumbling deeper into misery. If something happens to Vivienne and we lose this baby, I'll wonder if there is a God at all. Has he shown me grace? Sent help when I needed it or guided me in any way? I have not seen it, Aengus. Have you?"

I thought for a long moment, not wanting to confirm his despair, rolling onto my back to peer at the stars for answers.

"You were saved from the wolf," I offered.

"I fought for my life, and you helped me."

"Yes, well. You were saved from drowning in the river."

"I was caught on a tree limb, and then you helped me again."

"True, but might not God have placed me there? And then, what about Eames? You didn't die in the cave. He did."

"But why was he ever allowed to take Vivienne? And in the end, it was almost you who died."

I was silenced, the memory of that painful time all too recent. I had barely recovered from it when I lost Da.

"So what does God want me to do? I'd strike a mighty bargain with him if only I knew. If he takes my wife and child, then what is life for? Why should I be here at all? What a futile waste of time it all is."

The sky turned the faintest shade lighter, and in the east a slate blue spread slowly from a center point, finely underlining the clouds. The sun was coming, even if the day would be overcast. It would color the hills and make its relentless climb. Dear God, Vivienne *must* survive. I sat up.

"Faolán. Things change constantly. I could never know the mind of God, but I do believe you would not be brought all this way and through all these difficulties for nothing. Just wait, and we will see in time what it is all about."

"After all the loss you have known, you can still say that?"

"Look there, above the hills. That light strip of sky. It is blue, like clean water. That's an omen of new beginnings. It must mean things will be all right."

"Because everything always turns out right in the end, Aengus?"

"Because omens do not lie."

"*You* do not lie, Aengus. Omens change their meaning all the time."

We fell silent, each lost in our own search for answers, until the heavens were fully lit. The sun had not yet crested the horizon when Mistress Barry opened the door. She looked tired and haggard, but not concerned. "You lads may come in now, I'll warm some ale, and ye can set there by the fire. Vivienne is awake. She is still weak, but she can speak to you now, Faolán. I don't know how, in her condition, but she still carries a healthy babe within her, as feisty as a barn cat."

I warmed my hands on the cup of ale from Mistress Barry while Faolán sat at the bedside. He held Vivienne's hand and kissed her gently. She smiled at him.

"Do you know, Faolán? I have been thinking of things." She cradled the mound of her belly.

"That's good, Vivi. You're a clever girl. Tell me, what have you come up with?"

"When she is old enough, I want you to teach our daughter to read."

"Would you not want to teach her yourself?"

"You're a far better teacher, and she should learn from her father. I want her to read everything you've read, to know what your tutors taught you. Don't let her learn how to spin or to sew. That's for another girl, not for her."

"But you sew, love."

"She'll be a princess, and then a queen. She'll not have time to sew."

"You have very big plans for her. What about our horses?"

"She must learn to ride well. Pick for her the best-quality mount you can find."

"Without question, *cushla ma chree*, pulse of my heart. But you have the better eye for horseflesh."

"You picked Dunerayl. She should have a horse like he is, smart and quick. And promise me she'll never have to marry if she doesn't choose to."

Faolán's back stiffened. "Vivi, are you telling me you are unhappy with our marriage?"

"No, of course not. But I do not want her ever to find herself at the mercy of someone like Lord Cork. I want her marriage to be a match of her choosing."

"All right then, my love. I promise."

"And I'd like to name her Ailbhe. It means white and pure, and that is how I see her. New and clean. No one's handprint upon her. She'll be a fresh beginning, won't she?"

"She will if you say it, Vivi, for who could refuse you? For me, she'll have a mane of gorgeous red hair just like yours. Now will you rest? I will stay right here beside you."

The ale and the warm fire started to work their magic on me, and I dozed off. I jerked awake, startled by some sound, and thought of crossing the bridge and going back home. I would likely find it a mess, and supplies for the alehouse running dangerously low.

Mistress Barry had been in the front yard and pushed the door open. She came toward me, her eyes wide and her mouth open, and then she turned to Faolán, her cheeks flushed scarlet. She beckoned him toward the hearth.

"Faolán," she whispered, "there are English soldiers in the yard, asking for you."

Faolán went for the door, with Mistress Barry and me behind him. There were three soldiers on horseback, one of them pulling a small wooden cart.

"Faolán Burke?" the first soldier asked.

"Aye, I am he," Faolán responded.

"You are arrested for robbery and murder. Sheffield, tie his hands and secure him in the cart."

Faolán glanced quickly at me, his eyes fierce, and I knew he was thinking God meant to destroy him. "Aengus," he said as the soldier grabbed his wrist, "do not tell Vivienne. Make something up. Watch over her and the little one for me. *Please, Teaghrán.*"

I squeezed Mistress Barry's trembling shoulder. She shrieked when they pushed him into the cart. Without a word to us, they turned the horses to leave. I ran after them. "Wait! Where are you taking him?"

"Lismore," the first soldier responded.

"But who was murdered?" I shouted. The first soldier stopped, and the others behind him. Faolán shook his head at me as if to say my questions were not wise.

"Who are you, sir?" the soldier asked.

"I'm his brother. I have been with him. He has committed no crimes."

The soldier smirked. "Tell that to the Earl of Cork, then. They're *his* charges, and Burke must stand for the assize to be judged. Come along. Mayhap the earl will find charges for you as well."

One of the men laughed. Then they rode on, and I ran back to Mistress Barry. "Mistress, I must go after them. They will kill him if someone is not there to speak for him."

"Yes, I know."

"My sister, Sheelagh. She can look after Vivienne until we come home."

"Aye, I will fetch her," she nodded, wiping her cheeks. "Now get on your horse and go, lad."

I ran straight for Dunerayl. If I thought fetching Mistress Barry for Vivienne was an emergency, this one had by far overtaken it. I gave thanks he'd had a night's rest, more than I could say for Faolán or myself. Dear God, what was Faolán thinking now? Omens don't lie, I'd said. The blue light of the horizon. What was it telling me that I could not see? Did it mean a new beginning as I'd said, or did it portend the darkest of days? I stuffed saddlebags with food and water, oats for the horse, and whatever I thought I'd need for travel and rest, and then I set out alone. But I was not alone. I had Dunerayl who was the closest thing to Faolán save the man himself, and Faolán's presence as well, pressing me. *Move quickly, Teaghrán.*

"I will bring you home, brother," I said out loud as if he were next to me. Dunerayl huffed and dipped his head in agreement.

Chapter Thirty-Nine

The Charges

The best apology against false accusers is silence and sufferance,
and honest deeds set against dishonest words.

~ John Milton

Having just traveled the same ground, the way seemed much swifter, and I recognized the landmarks, the places we had stopped to eat, the places we slept. I pushed Dunerayl as hard as I dared, fearing Cork might take action against Faolán before I could stop it.

As earl of the territory, he had great autonomy for handling criminals, but I banked on the belief that Cork was a man of ceremony and would want the proceedings recorded if ever there were questions. He also was accustomed to being in charge of things, and the complete reverence and obedience of his underlings. With Faolán in his custody, he would demand a hearing that would require at least a day to organize. By then I could be present to testify.

I arrived early in the morning on November 10, a Friday with a crescent moon still visible in the western sky. I banged on the gate just as Faolán had before, vexed that his massive fist had made a stronger sound. The guard came slowly and I wondered, had he been sleeping in the shadows.

"Who calls?" he shouted.

"I am Aengus O'Daly of Skebreen, come to give testimony in the trial of Faolán Burke."

"I know of no trial. Be gone with you."

"It is just being arranged. Lord Cork has the man in his custody."

"Then come back tomorrow."

"Sir, I must speak with Lord Cork today. It is imperative. A life depends on it. Will you ask?"

The man grumbled and disappeared, and my anxiety grew. If I could not even gain access to the castle, what then? Two men on horseback arrived behind me, and then these two men called out their names. Another guard peered out, and the gate slowly opened. I rode in behind them as if I was of their party, and then slipped off to the stables to store Duneraryl. I entered the castle through the garden door at the back, avoiding the steward, who might try to stop me. If I could find Deirdre or Saturiwa, they would help me find Faolán and the place where a hearing would be.

There was no one in the hall. I wasn't sure which way to turn, and grew uneasy knowing I had no time to waste. If I could find the chamber where we'd met with Cork months before, if my instinct served, he'd be there again. When I found the rooms, my hunch proved correct.

Cork sat at his desk with four gentlemen seated in a row of chairs to his right. Along the wall behind them were Cork's three lawyers. Faolán was in a chair at Cork's left, facing the four men, his hands still bound, his face bloodied and swollen, his clothes disheveled and filthy. He must have attempted escape and suffered for it. He glanced at me quickly, relief in his eyes, and then fear, and then a hopeless sadness. He shook his head almost imperceptibly and then looked away.

"Mister O'Daly, what business have you here? You were not summoned," Lord Cork said.

"My lord." I bowed my head. "I have come to testify on behalf of Mister Burke. He is charged unjustly, and I am witness to the fact."

"We need no testimony in this proceeding. You have wasted your time. Steward!" he shouted toward the door. I took one of the chairs from where the lawyers sat, and placed it between the four gentlemen and Faolán, facing Cork.

"Surely you would not try a man without hearing all sides, Lord Cork, when a life is at stake?"

One of the gentlemen nearest to Cork's desk spoke up. "It is wise to hear testimony. I am sure it can do no harm, my lord." Cork shot him a searing look, and the man's face went pale.

The steward arrived in the doorway. "Yes, my lord?"

"The guards are ineffective. A *guest* has arrived unannounced."

"Shall we remove him, sir?"

"No, or I should say, not yet. But the guards should be alerted...and chastised for their incompetence."

"Immediately, sir."

"And remind them an assignment has been given. I expect it to be done posthaste."

"My lord." The steward backed out of the room and closed the door.

"Now then, gentlemen," Cork said, flipping a hand toward one of the lawyers, "to the task at hand. Let us begin."

One of the lawyers stepped forward with several sheets of long, stiff paper. He put on his spectacles to read. "The charges against Mister Faolán MacWilliam Burke are as follows."

My throat burned with words. "My Lord Cork," I said loudly. "Your expediency in this matter is to be admired, sir, and please forgive my interruption, but I am compelled to ask. Would not these proceedings more reasonably be conducted in public before Mister Burke's peers? Is that not most common and proper?"

Cork's face reddened and he started to rise from his chair but his lawyer touched his elbow and he settled back down.

"Mister O'Daly, the Earl of Cork has complete autonomy under the King of England in his administration of law and order throughout this region. His methods are unquestionably reasonable and wise. I would ask your silence as the charges are read." He cleared his throat. "Let me now continue. Number one. Mister Faolán MacWilliam Burke is hereby charged with the most ruthless and brutal murder of one Mister Geoffrey Eames, a servant of Lord Cork, on or about February 13, near Mitchelstown. The murder is confirmed; the act is not disputed."

"My lords, your pardon," I said, my anxiety for Faolán piqued. "May I ask please, how this fellow expired?"

The lawyer issued an exasperated huff and glared at me as Lord Cork stared impatiently toward the window. "Of a cracked skull, sir, a most heinous crime."

"Is there proof of this crime? I was with Mister Burke on that date, returning to Skebreen from a meeting in Cashel. He was never out of my sight and there was no murder. There is an abundance of caves, boulders and rocks around Mitchelstown. Is it not more likely that he had fallen? That his death was accidental?"

"Mister O'Daly, you meddle in matters you know not of," the lawyer said. "Lord Cork himself has..."

"Proceed," Cork said harshly. The four gentlemen looked back and forth between the lawyer, Lord Cork, and me and then shared questioning looks among themselves, but they did not speak.

"Number two. Theft," the lawyer continued. "One pearl earring, which had been in possession of the deceased, Mister Eames, when he was last seen at Lismore, was found in possession of a person of Fermoy, who had been given it in payment by strangers."

"May I ask, sir," I said, "as this is most interesting, how we know it was stolen? Could Eames have given it in payment? I wonder if we might see this pearl earring. In whose possession is it now?" Faolán shot a glance at me, clearly questioning my sanity, and quickly returned his gaze to the floor.

Lord Cork turned his hawk eyes on me and then waved his hand impatiently at the lawyer. "Dispense with that. Move on, *move on*."

"Number three. Robbery. Mister Burke is charged with robbing from our Lord Cork's treasury approximately one week ago when he had obtained unauthorized entry to the castle through the garden gate. One stack of silver coins was subsequently discovered missing, valued at £20."

"Ten," a woman's voice said from behind me.

Lord Cork's head jerked around. "Deirdre, you should not be here," he said sternly.

"My Lord Cork, forgive me, please. You were *not* robbed, at least not by Mister Burke. I took the coins myself and sent them to him. The money was for my daughter, Vivienne, who is ill and with child."

Lord Cork motioned to the lawyers in the chairs at the side of the room, and they went to Deirdre and took her by the arms.

"You have allowed these men to upset you, Deirdre. You've become confused. You must go to your room to rest."

"My Lord," Deirdre cried, "I beg you. You *know* what I say is true. You must not harm him."

The two men ushered her from the room and returned, though I could still hear her crying outside the door, and then she ran down the hall calling for Saturiwa.

"We must not allow any more disruptions of these proceedings. There has been too much delay already. Gentlemen, please continue," Cork said.

The lawyer appeared shaken. Faolán's face had purpled with his rage, but he kept his eyes down and his tongue still.

"Gentlemen," the lawyer said, his voice shaky, "you understand your responsibilities in this proceeding." The men nodded.

"You understand your function as a service to the Earl of Cork." The men nodded again, their eyes downcast.

"Well then, we begin judgment, as is your duty. To Charge One, murder. How say you?"

"Guilty," all four men replied in unison.

"And to the second charge, theft."

"Guilty," they replied.

"And the third charge, robbery from the earl's treasury."

"Guilty," they said.

I stared at them, my mouth open. Of the four men, none would raise his eyes to me, Faolán, or Lord Cork. The man closest to me had closed his eyes, his hands shaking on his knees. The second man had turned pale as a bedsheet, and the third a shade of green, as if he would soon vomit. The fourth man sat still as a stone, his eyes focused only on the lawyer.

"Thank you, gentlemen," the lawyer said. He straightened his papers and laid them on the desk for Cork to sign.

"Well-done, gentlemen," Cork added. He turned toward Faolán.

"And now," he said, "for all of your crimes I sentence you to death by hanging. Our scaffold is not yet assembled or I would carry out your sentence immediately. As it is, you will be imprisoned in my tower for two days. With the eighth bell on Monday, you will be brought to the scaffold and hanged until you are dead. May God have mercy on your wicked soul. Steward!" he shouted.

"My lord," the man replied, having been just outside the door.

"Have the guards take Mister Burke to the tower. And please escort Mister O'Daly to the castle gate."

The steward marched me out before the guards had come for Faolán. I feigned an injury to my ankle and crouched in the hallway as if to tend it, the steward standing by until they came, one on each side, with their hands like iron bands around Faolán's arms, guiding him past me. Our eyes met for an instant and he blinked both eyes at me, then he was gone. I knew this signal. It was a secret only between him and me, unknown even to the Barry brothers. We'd agreed on it years ago when we were just boys. We had the owl call, meant to bring us all together. But the blink meant just the opposite: *Save yourself. Run while you still can.*

And run I did. Even as the guardsmen pounded the nails to erect the scaffold, I ran from the castle steps to the stable to retrieve Dunerayl. The steward saw the gates of the castle close behind me. From there, on

Dunerayl's swift legs, we ran for hours to reach Carrick on Suir.

I had only one hope now, that the Earl of Ormonde's power exceeded Cork's; that his centuries-old noble bloodline was enough to intimidate Cork, who had manipulated and paid his way to an earldom, though he came from common stock.

Please God, let Ormonde be at home, and let him be of such kind and generous mind, that he would help.

Chapter Forty

An Act of Mercy

*From the cellar we mounted the Roundlets of Honor and
Preferment until we came into the Council, though
your station was the antechamber to Majesty.*

~ Walter Butler, eleventh Earl of Ormonde, to Sir William Usher

"You cannot expect me to overrule him or question his judgment, Mister O'Daly. He is an earl, and I am an earl. It is not for me to meddle in his business," Ormonde said.

I had arrived just after his suppertime to find him still at table, his red velvet doublet open to a fine shirt and lace collar. He was kind enough to see me even as he dabbed away the gravy from his cleanly shaved chin. He had dined alone, his wife away visiting relatives, and perhaps welcomed the diversion. But once he realized what it was, I'm sure it was not one he would have chosen.

"I would not ask you, sir," I told him, "but that you are the only man in all of Ireland Lord Cork is likely to respect. He has profited from Sir Walter Raleigh's downfall. He has collected properties lost by the failed Desmond rebellions. He is shrewd and opportunistic, but the one thing he cannot purchase is noble blood. He envies you and your family heritage, and would want you as a friend."

Ormonde frowned. "Yes, I know this. I also know he is the wealthiest earl in Ireland and can purchase the loyalty of every judge in the land, as apparently he has done."

"But you have great influence with the Lord Deputy, where he does not. And you have demonstrated your advocacy for fairness and the common good, which could someday serve his needs just as I am now hoping it will serve ours. I ask a great favor of you, Lord Ormonde, and call on your sense of mercy, but not for myself. It is to preserve a good man's life, the father of an innocent baby. Vivienne is sick. Cork has taken away her money. Without Faolán they will not survive."

Ormonde toyed with a gold ring on his index finger. "The lady has not been well treated in all of this. Were she my sister or my daughter, I would be quite perturbed by it. Cork has daughters of his own, whom he treats like royalty. He spends lavishly on them. And yet this treatment of Deirdre and Vivienne. I find it troubling. The FitzGeralds brought a storm of destruction down upon the Munster province, and yet the bloodline enjoys a proud history and remains well regarded throughout Ireland. I wonder does Cork resent them for it. He sees himself the region's benefactor and wants the respect, or rather the admiration, he feels he deserves."

He looked at me as if I might have an answer, but of course I didn't. I simply nodded in agreement.

He stared into the fire grate for a few moments, ruminating while the flames licked away at the birch logs. I waited in silence, not wanting even the sound of my breathing to disturb his thoughts. I prayed his conscience, rather than his politics, would rule his head. At last he returned his attention to me.

"Mister O'Daly, you are a man of good character and loyalty. I admire you for it. I will do this for you. We'll ride at first light. I cannot promise I will be able to change the outcome. If he is set on this course, I may not be able to sway him, and if I must make an enemy of him to do it, I cannot. But I will go with you. And I will try."

Relief washed over me. "May God bless you, my lord."

In Skebreen there was little enforcement of the religion law, and Faolán and I were usually able to avoid attending church services. At Carrick on Suir, with the earl in residence, there was no escaping it. To my good fortune, the earl had his own chapel, which allowed him to call an earlier service on Sunday so that we could travel to Lismore in good time. With his steward, his secretary, and one guard in attendance, we rode for several hours, arriving at the Lismore gate after dark.

Lord Cork was surprised and a little shaken to find the Earl of

Ormonde at his gate after his supper. He came to the courtyard to greet him. "Had you sent word, my lord, we would have prepared a fine banquet for your arrival," Cork said.

"None needed, Lord Cork. I'll thank you for the hospitality of a bed and a brandy. How is that, sir?"

"It is my privilege," Cork replied. "Come to my library to warm yourself while we prepare your room." Then he surveyed the number in Ormonde's party, and frowned upon seeing me there.

"Mister O'Daly, I thought you were returned to Skebreen."

"No, my lord." I offered no more explanation. Rather, let him wonder. Let him be both perplexed and annoyed.

Lord Cork led Ormonde into the castle, and I was led to the servants' quarters by a side door through the kitchen. It did not matter to me the difference. I was glad for a roof over my head, to know I was near Faolán so that I could help him, and I was certain Lord Ormonde would be able to halt the execution.

I slept fitfully and was awakened by light footsteps on the floor and a hand on my shoulder.

"Sir." It was the boy's voice, Saturiwa.

"Yes, what is it?"

"Mistress say they do not wait."

"What? What do you mean?"

"They finish scaffold; they not wait for the eight hour. They hang Mister Burke first light."

I jumped up. It was still full dark outside but I didn't know how soon the dawn would come and could waste no time. "He is a cruel devil. Can you take me to the chamber where Lord Ormonde is sleeping?"

"Yes sir. We go now."

I followed him down corridors that turned sharply left and then right, then up two flights on a narrow back stairway. A door opened to a long, dark hallway with a polished wood floor and a single candle sconce. At the far end of the hall I could see a faint light flickering at the bottom of a closed door, but the boy stopped me where we were and pointed to the door just beside me, the handle adorned with a fringed satin scarf. How would I wake the Earl of Ormonde without alerting the Earl of Cork?

I tapped on the door lightly but heard no response. We would have to cast off propriety and make apologies later. I pulled on the satin scarf, and the latch clicked. I pushed it open wide enough for Saturiwa.

"Go through. Wake him as you did me. Tell him I am waiting in the stairway."

The boy crept in. *Please God*, let the guard be sleeping elsewhere and not on a pallet in the earl's bedchamber. A voice grumbled and then came whisperings, a rustling, and some movements. I backed toward the servants' stairway, fearful Cork might come out of his room and see me there. I waited. And waited. What if he did not come? What if he dragged the boy down to Cork's room and complained of being awakened? What if he ignored the call and returned to his slumber? The time passing seemed interminable, and I plucked at my ears. What was happening to Faolán? Then came soft padding footsteps and Saturiwa through the door alone.

"He come, sir. He say he meet you at tower quick."

"You are sure?" Good God, I did not mean to question him but my fear was running high and if Ormonde did not show up, I would have no recourse.

Saturiwa took my hand the way I'd seen him take Deirdre's. "He come," the boy said. "I take you to tower. Mistress there."

The scaffold was hastily assembled against the north-facing wall of the east wing tower. Such a structure was vulgar for daily castle life, and so it was stored in pieces until needed, and then the guards had to put it back together like a puzzle for the next of Cork's victims. It was a simple raised platform with wooden steps leading up, a sturdy post and arm for the hangman's noose, and a trapdoor through which the body would fall. The sight of it sent my stomach reeling. I wanted to vomit, but if I had, I would have choked to death for I could not open my throat or breathe. Saturiwa squeezed my hand, breaking the fearful spell cast over me.

In the courtyard the guards stopped working while the earl's steward inspected the construction by torchlight. There was still no sign of dawn, but the blackbird's call told me first light was just minutes away. I stayed in the shadows with Saturiwa, and soon Deirdre found us.

"Lord Cork is dressed and in the drawing room. He is coming. He will call for Faolán as soon as it is light enough to see. I think he will make quick work of it," she said.

"Where is Faolán being kept? In this tower?" I asked.

"On the top floor; only one narrow stair leading in and out. There is no escape from there, and the guards would not let me see him. If only we could get him near the gate, we could help him escape, I am sure of it."

A pair of lanterns appeared at the castle door. Some figures moved about in the shadows, and one I believed was Lord Cork. The lanterns preceded him down the castle steps, and the group of people moved toward the scaffold. As they drew near, I recognized the lawyers who attended him, and Cork himself dressed in long ceremonial robes, dark and voluminous.

"Is the prisoner prepared for execution?" he shouted.

"Yes, my lord," a guard on the scaffold replied.

"Bring him forth."

The guard shouted to his men, "Bring forth the prisoner!"

In the darkness we had not realized Faolán was held in the tower doorway just a few steps away from us. His shoulders were hunched, his head down, his hands tied before him. He was led to the scaffold stairs. Cork stepped forward, followed by his recording lawyers.

"Mister Burke," Cork said, "you have been convicted of murder, robbery, and theft. For your crimes you will be hanged this day until you are dead. Have you anything to say?"

Faolán straightened his back, made his shoulders broad, and held his head high. He glared into Cork's eyes, his presence a fierce and formidable sight. But where in God's name was Lord Ormonde? We stepped into the torchlight, Deirdre, Saturiwa and I, so Faolán could see us there for him, and Lord Cork could see there were witnesses to what he was about to do.

"To you, Lord Cork, and to all those present," Faolán said, his voice strong and clear, "I say I am innocent of the crimes for which I am accused, and this execution today is a far worse crime than any of those. For your humiliation in the presence of Lord Deputy Wentworth, you have ruined my family, and now you will leave a sick and pregnant wife widowed and destitute. Is this honorable, sir, and does it make you feel a bigger man? I pray God strike you down for it."

"Enough," Cork said.

"Nay, not enough. For a young girl entrusted to your care by the king, you did nothing and stole her inheritance so that now, more humiliated even than you, she withers away like a dying flower. And you have placed all of this on the consciences of your judges, whom you have paid and then threatened so they dare not make any decision but to approve your terrible crimes, which you now try to validate by donning your silken robes. We see through you, all who stand here, and you will have to execute all of us for the truth not to escape these walls."

"Silence!" Lord Cork gestured for the guards to take Faolán up on the scaffold. Still there was no sign of Ormonde, and my stomach had formed into a sharp-edged rock that was now twisting into my gut.

When Faolán reached the top he turned and looked down over all of us, his face lit by the thin gray light of the coming dawn, his eyes bright with emotion. He looked down at me. "I do not wish to leave you, *Teaghrán*, and I fear for my poor Vivienne."

Deirdre cried out. "Stop this, *please*, my Lord Cork, I beg you for my daughter's sake."

Voices and commotion came from behind us. *At last.* Lord Ormonde arrived on horseback, his secretary and steward walking beside him. He was an astonishing sight, a silver specter, his loose golden hair raised by the wind. He dismounted effortlessly and stood before Cork.

"What goes on here, my lord?" he asked.

"It is nothing of your concern, my lord Ormonde. My sincere apologies if we have disturbed your rest. A criminal must be executed, a most sorrowful act that is among our responsibilities, who are made earls of their territories." He made a slight, dismissive bow toward Ormonde, who stepped closer.

"My lord, I know this man from our meeting at Cashel. He has wed your ward, Vivienne FitzGerald. Is it not wise to keep their union intact? I understand she is with child."

"It is too late; he is convicted of his crimes and he must die. The evidence was..."

"There was no evidence," Deirdre cried and ran toward Lord Cork. "No evidence was given at his trial, only charges. I told you there was no robbery. I took the money myself for my poor daughter and her babe."

"My lord Cork," Ormonde said, "if you execute this man, you will face great difficulty in finding an appropriate suitor for Vivienne. If the king learns she is not well cared for and established, he will be most disappointed. You enjoy the king's favor now. Would you not be better served to maintain that as ever you can?"

"My lord, there was a murder."

I stepped forward. "Begging your pardons, my lords, but there was no murder. I can attest. I am a witness but was not allowed to speak my full testimony."

Lord Cork trembled with fury. "You were not summoned. Your testimony is of no value to this proceeding."

"Never would I wish to interfere in your affairs, my lord," Ormonde said, "but I do wonder if you might purchase greater favor for yourself in the king's eyes by dispensing with this business that could potentially damage your reputation. There are more eyes on this situation than you know. I see tremendous change coming as the Lord Deputy moves forward his propositions. He will call a parliament in Dublin in just a few months. You may wish to preserve your avenue to the king's ear in the purest light."

Lord Cork seemed to stop breathing for a moment as he pondered this. How shrewd of Ormonde to tap into Cork's self-interest. Faolán stood stiff and still in the pale light, and the courtyard fell silent. The guard released his hold on Faolán's arm, and the hangman stepped back. My heart fluttered as a bird in a cage, and I prayed their actions foretold the result.

"And sweeter still could I make it if I were to speak on your behalf with the Lord Deputy Wentworth as he prepares his policy-making agenda. Your misuse of the tithe monies he mentioned in Cashel might well be forgiven if the items for parliament were quite focused on some of Lord Wentworth's particular goals."

Cork then seemed to deflate, but his hands curled into fists. "My lord Ormonde, your counsel is wise for a man of such youth. You are well to warn me. This man is of little consequence if it might disturb the king, and we have larger conditions to address. I will release him..."

A cry came from Deirdre's lips and from my own, but Faolán did not yet move.

"...though with some reluctance. And I shall never forget or forgive his criminal ways. My constable will keep watch over him, and the next time he comes before me for any crime, he will face immediate execution. As for today, for the time and trouble he has cost me and my counselors, he is fined £20, with one month to pay or I will rearrest him." He gestured to the guard, who unbound Faolán's hands and led him back down the steps of the scaffold.

"My Lord Cork, you are a merciful and scrupulous governor," Ormonde said, and bowed his head to him.

"You must break your fast with me, Lord Ormonde. I have received a package of some very fine sausages from Dungarvan."

"You are a most gracious host, Lord Cork," Ormonde replied, "but just a quick taste, for I must be off to my business, and prefer to travel in the cool of the morning."

I waited for the men to turn toward the house, Ormonde's secretary leading his horse behind them, and then ran to Faolán, who was suddenly looking unsteady. Deirdre and I held him and sat with him on the steps of the scaffold. The guards and hangman left us there and went into the castle kitchen for their own repast.

"Thanks be to God," I said, holding Faolán's arm.

"Thanks be to God," Deirdre repeated.

Faolán looked up. "Thank you, the both of you, for not giving up. We must go quickly now, before Ormonde leaves and Lord Cork changes his mind. Deirdre, will you come with us?"

She smiled weakly. "I cannot, not yet. But I will come and very soon, I promise."

Faolán remained a bit shaky as we helped him to his feet, but quickly recovered as we hurried toward the stables to collect Dunerayl. We walked away from the gates of Lismore in minutes, and though I had not been able to thank Lord Ormonde, I was sure he understood, and I would write to him when we returned to Skebreen.

I patted Dunerayl's mane. "Take him home safely, lad."

"Mount up, Aengus. We ride together."

"No, Faolán. Not this time. You go. You can travel much faster alone, and Dunerayl has suffered enough punishment than to carry two grown men for such a distance. Your wife could be birthing a child any day now. You must run to her. I will find my way; do not concern yourself."

"Aengus, it is not safe to travel alone, and I..."

"Go to Vivienne, quickly. I am close behind you."

I was resolute. He grinned at me, my treasured friend. "You're a fine man, *Teaghrán*. Once again you have saved my life, and I am forever indebted to you. Have a care for yourself and hurry home. We'll be waiting for you."

I watched him ride away, not at all afraid for myself. Sunlight had just stretched across the hills and through the treetops, and my joy spread with the warmth of it, that something I had done had saved his life, had halted a catastrophe, and had created hope of a future for all of us. I walked as if the ground was a pillow, as if the fingers of the breeze that touched my face belonged to benevolent faeries. I was weightless and carefree, and before me were beautiful rolling hills and soft trickling waters to guide my way peacefully home. I soon begged a ride on the back of a slow-moving hay wagon, and there curled up for a long and bumpy sleep.

Joyfulness stayed with me nearly the entire journey home, for I was alone and completely free of responsibility or concern, at least for that short while. I walked the last distance from Leap, and it reminded me of the legend of O'Donovan, leaping across that very ravine on horseback to escape the English soldiers. I prayed Cork would keep his word and send no more soldiers to trouble us in Skebreen.

And then shame found me, that I'd neglected O'Daly's for so long and should not leave it again for a good while. But when I arrived in Skebreen, I walked right past my sister's house and then right past O'Daly's. I had first to see that Faolán was indeed safely home, and that Vivienne and the baby were well.

What I found at Glencurragh turned my belly to mush and my aching feet to stone.

Chapter Forty-One

Water and Rye

With hoarse rebuff the swelling sea rebounds.

~ Jonathan Smith

There being no response to my knock, I pushed open the heavy door. The fire burned low and prickly over thin twigs and damp moss, sucking at the fetid air. Faolán lay in the middle of the floor, an arm draped across his eyes, his feet bare. The window was covered to shut out the afternoon light, and no candle burned. I could just see the outline of Vivienne sleeping in the bed, her frame as small as a child's.

Faolán stirred when I touched his shoulder. He welcomed me with a hearty embrace. "You are home at last. There is a jug of clean water and some rye bread on the table. Have some and come sit with me."

I did so. I felt his exhaustion before I could see his face. As he stoked the fire, the flames revealed more clearly the sagging expression and drooping eyes.

"Vivienne has been confined to her bed since we left for Lismore, Aengus. She's weak with misery; she refuses nourishment excepting small crumbs, barely enough to sustain a sparrow. And yet somehow the babe keeps growing. I've begged her until I can beg no more. I wish I could see this snake that has hold of her, and I would cut it to pieces."

"My God, Faolán. Where is Mistress Barry?"

"She will come when the pains begin. She can't do more for her now. The physician examined her and then treated her with chalybeate syrup and white wine with wake-robin, all of which she drank in his presence. It helped for a time. She has a few hours of relief, but soon descends again."

I got up and pulled the blanket away from the window. The light poured over the bed, and I could see her, skin and bones only, her arms encircling her round belly. I knelt beside her to look at her face. She opened her eyes to me and offered a thin smile. Around her eyes was a blackness, not purpled like a bruise but black and spotty, as if someone had smudged them with coarse coal dust. Her cheekbones had no softness and her hair no lustre.

"You must come back to us, Vivienne," I said, a hard knot pressing against my throat.

She nodded. "I am trying, Aengus. I have forced myself in every way possible. I have fought and cried and prayed and cried even more. It is just the babe coming, and I must trust I will be stronger in time."

"Eat something."

"Oh, why must everyone keep saying that? I do eat. It sickens me, Aengus. It repels me. I eat what I can eat."

"If you could have anything in the world, *anything*, tell me, and I will get it for you."

She glanced at Faolán. "I have tried that one, Aengus," Faolán said. "I have tried every plan and scheme I could conjure."

Vivienne said, "When I am empty and clean, the voices grow quiet, and I am at peace. The baby needs peace.

"The *voices*?" I asked.

She looked away. I glanced at Faolán. He just shook his head, helpless. A fear settled into my bones then, unlike any I had known. Something unseen, a spirit, a demon, a strange force far beyond our reckoning, now held the reins tugging each of our lives.

I mixed a concoction of herbs for her and warmed it over Faolán's fire while he held her hand and they whispered softly to each other. I tested the temperature so it was not too hot. We helped her sit up in bed and she slowly drank the potion. She seemed to revive a bit, her eyes shining with the light from the window. We helped her from the bed that she might walk, at least to the kitchen and back, but her ankles were badly swollen and she tired quickly. Faolán stood by her several times a day, insisting she take cool water in small swallows and eat a portion of bread. She could not always keep it down.

By late November, I was busy at the alehouse, still taking the ribbing from my regular folk who did not appreciate my absence when the door of O'Daly's was closed. I promised to make it up to them with an extra-potent brew before the winter solstice. I was in my shed working on it when a carriage came into the village, drawing interest from all who saw it. Bearing the Earl of Cork's coat of arms, it was smaller and less elaborate than the carriage we had seen in Cashel, but it sufficed to raise the hairs on my arms and the back of my neck. What did the man want now?

When the driver opened the door, Saturiwa hopped out and ran toward the alehouse door, and then came Deirdre. I toweled my hands and went inside to greet them.

"Mister O'Daly," Deirdre said, "I am so grateful to see you. I fear we are lost. I have come to find my daughter and Mister Burke. Can you direct me?"

"You are quite close, just a few minutes more once you cross the bridge. I am happy to show you."

She seemed relieved. "Thank you. If we might rest here just a while. Lord Cork's carriage is comfortable, but the ride has been quite bumpy."

"Aye, the way is meant for horses, hay wagons, and sheep."

"I would've walked if I had to. The only reason the earl let me use the carriage was to visit one of his ailing relatives. I will have to conceal my diversion. The man still fumes about his £20 and has no intention of forgiving Faolán's debt. I don't know how poor Faolán will manage it. I wish I'd never given him the coins before, because it has caused more harm than help."

"Faolán will find a way, Deirdre. One thing you must know about him: he always has a plan, and then another after it just in case the first one fails."

I rode with them in the carriage across the bridge and up the winding road to Faolán's cottage. Though it was midmorning there was no activity around the cottage, as if it and all living things around it remained deep in slumber. Saturiwa leapt from the carriage and ran around the yard investigating things. Deirdre and I knocked on the door.

Faolán jerked it open quickly, surprising us. His eyes were red-rimmed and his hair a wild riot, spiking this way and that. "Och, I'm sorry; I thought you were the midwife, but by God, it's glad I am to see you. Please, come in."

The house was warm, the fire bright, and Vivienne sat up in the bed, bracing her arms on each side of her.

"She is having spasms of some sort. We think the baby comes."

"Oh my. Let me help," Deirdre said.

"What are *you* doing here?" Vivienne said.

"I asked her to come, Vivienne. Be angry with me if you must, but we need help from wherever we may find it."

"Not from her."

"Are you in pain, Vivienne?" Deirdre asked.

"Not terribly, but there is twisting and tightening, and I am afraid something is happening. Not that it matters to you."

"I know you don't believe it, but I love you today as I have always loved you. I know I've made mistakes, and I've been badly misguided. I'm sorry for it, truly, Vivienne. Like it or not, I am here, and you are preparing to give birth. Would you not rather have someone who has been through it to help you along?"

The three of us stood over Vivienne's bed, all full of concern for her.

She scowled. "Well, I can't fight all of you in this state."

"Good. Do you have milk, Faolán? I brought some chamomile to calm her." Deirdre opened the door and called out, "Saturiwa, bring my things in, please? Aengus, if you can suggest lodgings for our driver, we'll keep him near at least for a few days."

I cursed myself that I did not have the upper floor of the inn we'd had before, to offer the fellow a bed. He would have to lodge with one of the villagers. Deirdre prepared Vivienne's chamomile while the boy sat in the corner and watched. "Saturiwa gathered some sea holly for me along the way here. We'll make a plaster for your ankles, dear, to help relieve the swelling."

She sat on the edge of the bed while Vivienne sipped the milk and eyed her mother suspiciously.

"Daughter, you will not likely give birth today. The cramping you are having is false until the flood comes. When you feel your waters, then you will know your time is near." She turned to us. "Gentlemen, you may stay if you like, but these are female issues, and you might prefer the outside. Or go down to the alehouse for a while and get our driver settled. There is time yet."

Vivienne looked to Faolán with both fear and resignation. "Please, Faolán, don't be gone too long."

He kissed her goodbye and we rode in Lord Cork's carriage back to O'Daly's.

"Wouldn't Cork be having fits if he could see us?" I said.

"Aye," Faolan smirked, "and it does take some of the sting out of the bill he just sent me."

"What will you do?"

"First, I'll welcome my child into the world, for I can think of nothing else until the babe is born and Vivienne is well. After that there'll be time for a solution."

Chapter Forty-Two

The Hour before Dawn

Long is the way and hard, that out of Hell leads up to light.

~ John Milton

I awakened to what sounded like an explosion at the bridge, and ran outside to find Faolán on Dunerayl thundering across it. He reined up near me. "It is time, Aengus. I'm off to fetch Mistress Barry."

"Take the carriage!" I said.

"It is too slow. Get Sheelagh and the others, will you?" He urged the horse on and galloped off to the southwest.

I ran at once toward Sheelagh's house. Those who saw me would understand and spread the word. The birth of a child was a village event, bringing a gathering of both women and men. It was a social time and a dangerous time. Vivienne would have several around her who'd had successful births of their own, both to celebrate the birth as it happened and to help her should troubles arise. In the alehouse I'd heard too many stories of women bleeding to death after the birth, or of infants dying because they'd been pulled too soon from the womb. I silently begged God for Vivienne's safety. As weak as she was, she would need the strength of many others to see her through the efforts to come.

In two hours' time, Faolán arrived with Mistress Barry riding beside him. O'Daly's would be closed for the day so I could wait out the birth at Faolán's side. We would throw the door wide for all to celebrate once the event was concluded. In the meantime, in case the father needed as much care as the mother-to-be, I brought a small flask.

As was her style, Mistress Barry shooed all the menfolk from the house while the women did the work of women. She'd already assigned each a task to keep them occupied for what could be a long wait. Faolán and I built a pit fire for the men, to ward off the chill of the December wind that swept in from the seacoast. I should have brought a much larger flask, for the contents of my small one lasted only until dusk. Then came the first scream.

High-pitched and anguished, Vivienne's cry heralded a pain none of us could truly know and yet could hardly withstand. I had to stop Faolán from bursting through the door to her.

"What can you do?" I asked him. "You can't save her or lighten her burden. Her only relief will be to birth the baby. She must get through it as best she can. You must trust Mistress Barry."

"I do, of course. Yes. I just…She's in there like this because of me."

"Faolán, we're all here because of you. It is the ultimate act of love to deliver a baby, and she will do it like the lady she is, for the love of you. If she can bear it, we can."

But her labor was to last through the night, with her screams coming in a long succession until she was hoarse and we were alight with anxiety, our skin prickling with every sound. We dozed off several times, only to be awakened by a shout or another terrifying cry. And then in the hour before dawn a brief quiet settled, and then a baby's wail.

"It is done!" Faolán shouted. He jumped up and shook my shoulders. "The baby *lives*." He ran to the door and pushed in, but Mistress Barry was ready for him and the other women shoved him out again.

"Tell him the baby and mother live, but he must wait while we finish our tasks. We'll bring the baby out to him when she's ready," she called.

"She!" Faolán shouted. "Vivienne was right all along. It is now a *she*! Ailbhe is born, Vivienne. *Ailbhe*, my love!" he shouted to her.

No two people were in more need of such joy, and I shared it with them. It was not just a baby born, but also a family born, a future born, while the half moon hung in the sky like a vessel to hold all the wonders and prosperity the world could bring her. The beautiful heiress and the strapping young warrior had produced a daughter, a princess to the Castle Glencurragh.

We waited anxiously to see her. And we waited. It may have been only minutes, but the anticipation made it seem like an hour until at last the door opened and Sheelagh came out with the carefully swaddled infant. Faolán's face lit up as she placed the babe in his arms.

"Careful now; she is small and very fragile," Sheelagh said.

"She is magnificent," Faolán said, touching a finger to Ailbhe's cheek. "Look at her, Aengus. She is perfection. Light as a feather, but full of spirit, those pink cheeks coursing with new life."

"Aye, she's already been throwing punches as we swaddled her. Had she hands as big as yours, we'd all be knocked out," Sheelagh said.

I hugged her shoulders. "Good work, sister. She is fine and healthy."

Sheelagh's face darkened. "Ye must know, Vivienne had a hard time of it. Mistress Barry is taking good care of her to try and get her settled again. She'll need a good bit of rest, Faolán."

He frowned and handed the baby to me. I held her close and high on my chest. She'd been washed clean and smelled of soap and something else I'd never known before, something earthy and yet pristine, sweet like a ripened pear. Her eyes were closed, but she pursed her tiny lips and then spread them into a wondrous smile and gurgled.

Before Sheelagh could say more, Mistress Barry appeared in the doorway and came to Faolán. "Congratulations, Faolán, she is strong and healthy. A little underweight but we can fix that in time. Vivienne did her job well, though she lost a bit of blood. We've stopped it, but the labor taxed her body, and she is very weak."

"I must go to her."

"Hear me, Faolán: Vivienne fought hard, harder than any mother I have seen. She was disadvantaged from the beginning, as thin and frail as she'd become. She needs only your love and kindness. D'ye ken?"

"Aye," he said, calming himself.

"All right. Her mother is with her, but you may go in." Mistress Barry stepped aside.

The village women who had stayed to help quietly left the house, and Faolán rushed past them. I wished to see Vivienne as well but did not want to intrude in that moment. The morning's first light spread through high limbs of the trees. Sheelagh took the baby back inside, and I turned to Mistress Barry.

"Mistress, can you tell me about Vivienne? Will she be all right?"

"She was not right when we started, Aengus. It'll be up to her now. There's damage done. Her heart races, and her waters are not right. Between her mother and me, we'll see what can be done. The one thing I'm certain of is I'll be helping Faolán to hire a wet nurse. Vivienne cannot produce enough milk to keep Ailbhe fed."

I walked back to the village with the others and stayed away for three days to give them time to care for mother and baby, for Faolán and Vivienne to accustom themselves to the new family life, and for all to regain their strength. When I saw Mistress Barry heading for home, I assumed it was appropriate to return, eager as I was to see how the little one was growing and what she looked like after the newborn swell and redness had passed.

I crossed the bridge after my midday meal. My latest batch of ale still needed a week to ferment, so I plucked some sprigs of holly along the river as my gift for the house. Gray mists rose from the river's surface. The sky was dull but for the occasional break when the sun would remind me of its presence. I arrived at the cottage to find Faolán on the ground just outside the door, resting his head on crossed arms.

"*Lámha Mór*," I said, "have you made such a nuisance of yourself to get booted from the home already?"

He looked up, and I swear to the spirits and the marrow of my bones, had I seen the face before the body, I'd not have recognized the man. His eyes were swollen and red, his cheeks wet-whiskered, and behind the whiskers a pallor the gray of stone. His mouth stretched in a grimace more terrible than the old gray wolf in the throes of death, the spittle at the corners erupting from a bitterness too vile to swallow.

I dropped to my knees before him, the holly scattering uselessly upon the dirt. "Faolán, what is it? The babe?"

He shook his head. "Vivienne." He choked and swallowed with difficulty, his Adam's apple pressing from his throat. "She is dying."

My spine seized. "How do you know?"

"I know. We all know. Mistress Barry said there was a chance, after the birth, that she might have lived, but now she has crossed a threshold that allows no return. Her heart, you see. It is fading, and with it my fine, radiant love, and all I've ever dreamed."

"There must be something we can do while she still lives. Something that..."

"Aengus, we can only beg God to let us keep her a while longer. Beyond that we have no syrup, no medicines, and no words that can hold her. Not even the sweet breath of our newborn baby girl." He wept, his shoulders trembling. He rocked back and forth as if stabbed with a blade and tortured with pain. Slowly the spasms ceased, and he slowed his rocking, exhausted. "She is leaving me, Aengus. I have no plan. No thought of one.

What can I do?"

The words came to me as if a spirit whispered them in my ear, and I knew they were right and true. "You can give her peace, Faolán. Give her peace and let her go in love."

He exhaled slowly, and then inhaled one long, deep breath. His trembling stopped. His weeping stopped. He seemed to call on the inner strength he had always possessed, the strength that stood for me when my father died, the strength that made him press on day after day with the hope of a better life, when so many others gave up trying. He pushed himself up and rose to his feet.

"All right, then. Come, Aengus. I do not know how much longer we'll have her. She'll want to tell you good-bye."

The door creaked as we opened it, and a burst of cold air caused the candle on the kitchen table to flicker violently, but it regained its steadiness and burned on. Ailbhe's cradle was next to the table, with Vivienne's green shawl draped across it. I knelt beside it and rocked it gently. Ailbhe gurgled. I presented a finger and she grasped it, her tiny fingers pink and translucent but her grip impossibly strong.

I steeled myself and looked across to the bed where Vivienne lay. Deirdre lay beside her, cradling her, cooling her brow with a damp cloth. Faolán took Vivienne's hands in his and kissed them.

"Look, Vivi. *Teaghrán* has come to see you."

She turned her head to look at me. Her body was nearly skeletal and her skin pale as a morning fog, her hair in dark strings like hanging moss, and yet her beauty still evident. I looked into her eyes. The color was gone, and in its place a black hollowness that raised my shoulders and stopped my breath. I knew then what Faolán meant and why everyone knew she was dying, for her person had left those eyes, as if they were now a dark tunnel through which her spirit still spoke, but her soul already had separated, dissipating in a fine white vapor beyond the black veil of physical life. There was no place to touch her, no thread to grab and hold, no way to tug and pull her back.

Deirdre left the bed to check on Ailbhe, and Faolán climbed into her place to rest Vivienne's head on his chest. She nodded, and I moved closer. Her breath was shallow. I knelt on the floor, my ear near her lips.

"Aengus, my sweet friend. Be good to my baby, won't you? She will love you as I do, as Faolán does."

"I'll be the lucky one if she does."

Vivienne sighed softly. "We share the knowledge, Aengus. I want you especially to know what I have seen, so you will never be afraid. Many people say Paradise is white. It is brilliant, but it is not white. Everything is *golden*, it is vast, and there is vibrant color everywhere. It is as St. Brendan told us. It smells of exotic flowers, and the ground beneath your feet is made of sparkling gems in every hue. It is magnificent, Aengus. It is *splendor*."

A chill traveled up my spine. She still lay in this world, and yet she could see the other. Her body was weak, but how strong her spirit. She turned to face Faolán and pressed her fingers gently to his cheek.

"Take me out, Faolán, to the castle. To Glencurragh. I want to see it."

Faolán looked to me, and I helped him wrap her in the bedclothes just as we'd done once before, until she was like a swaddled infant. She was so light he did not need my help to lift her, but together we carried her to the broken stones of the castle wall and lay her down. She clasped Faolán's hand to her breast, and with the other he cradled her head.

"It is beautiful here, Faolán. The clouds part above us and the sun shines down upon it. Tell me about our castle."

Faolán stroked the hair from her face. His lips trembled. "It will be finer than any built, love. It will rise four stories to the sky, with more gables even than Rathmore, with grand windows overlooking the river and the lovely meadows from all sides. Towers in each corner will have wondrous rooms, each with their own hearth, for our family and our guests.

"The ground floor will bustle constantly with merry people who cook and brew and do all manner of things for the household. And just above, our great room will open wide its doors to welcome visitors from all corners of the world with a roaring fire and a warmed cup of mead. But our room, love, will be the most beautiful of all, and you will climb the alabaster stairs, sunlit by day and candlelit at night, and every morning the sun will warm our bed. From our balcony you'll see the grazing sheep in the far meadow and the frolicking horses in the near one, and every morning we will kiss on that balcony and delight in our great bounty."

"I can see it. I can. It is beautiful, and you are king of it all."

"And you are my queen, *avourneen*." Faolán grimaced; his voice faltered trying to choke back the tears. "I have failed you, Vivi."

"No, Faolán. You have loved me. You gave me hope. Are there any greater gifts?"

"I could not..."

"Our perfect, splendid dreams. Only Ailbhe matters now. Make her strong, like you."

"She is already so. You've seen her make a fist, no?"

"And make her smart."

"Like you. She'll be a schemer."

"And Glencurragh, Faolán. It was yours before me, and now it is ours. Fight for it. And when you do I'll be beside you always. Trust me, Faolán. I will."

His eyes filled. He gave her no reply, only a trembling smile, for his throat was surely as closed as mine. He kissed the palm of her hand, pressed his face to her neck and breathed in deeply of her. At last he released a heavy sigh.

"Go there to that place, *cushla*, if you are ready. I know you are tired. You should have beauty and splendor all around you, to comfort you. All will be well; I'll make sure of it for you, and so will Aengus. Go there in peace, my love."

They gazed into each other's eyes for a long moment, until a single silver tear slipped from his eye and traveled down his cheek. She touched it, and brought her finger to her lips. Then her hand trembled and slipped to her breast. She took a soft breath. When she released it, she was gone.

Chapter Forty-Three

Deep-Red the Bracken

Trí na haoiseanna, thar am, mo ghrá
Throughout the ages, beyond time, my love.

~ Gaelic saying

Faolán rocked her body against his and wept. I wept as well, but moved away toward the wall to give him whatever privacy he needed. His pain was unimaginable to me, for my own was unbearable, a wound so deep as if someone had shoved a pistol against my gut and fired the shot, leaving me alive but gaping and bloody.

After a time Deirdre came out of the house. When she saw Faolán and her lifeless daughter, she came close and dropped to her knees.

"My baby is gone," she said. "Poor, poor baby." Tears streamed down her cheeks as she reached out to touch Vivienne's hair.

"I would not exchange a moment of my life with her," Faolán said. "But I should never have taken her. I brought her to this."

"It is not your fault. She struggled with an affliction most of her life, long before you knew her. Lord Cork's cruelty just made everything worse."

"Shall we take her into the house now, Faolán?" I asked gently.

"Yes. She is cold."

I helped him carry her as Deirdre followed. We placed her on the bed, and Faolán lay beside her, holding her close.

I left him in his grief and turned toward the cradle. I had forgotten about Saturiwa, who crouched beside it beneath the kitchen table. He had been watching, and crawled out. He went to Vivienne's body, touched her face, and then her hand. Then he went to Deirdre, weeping silently by the fire. He knelt beside her, but turned to me. He placed his palm over his heart, and I returned the gesture. He nodded, turning his attention then to Deirdre. What wisdom did this strange child possess?

In her cradle, Ailbhe slept contentedly. A terrible sorrow washed over me. She would never know her beautiful mother, would never understand her humor or her special insight, never know her inner torments. She would never feel Vivienne's arms around her or know the nurturing words and touch that only a mother can give. Already, I missed her immensely. But the poor babe would never know what she missed in her ma.

Faolán succumbed to his exhaustion and fell asleep holding Vivienne's body. He stayed with her for hours until Deirdre and Sheelagh pulled him away so they could wash and dress Vivienne's body.

The following day, we brought her body to O'Daly's using Lord Cork's carriage. We placed her in a wooden coffin for the wake. Everyone in the village came, including the old folks and the children. We were small in number in Skebreen, but looked after one another as best we could. Each household brought a little something to share, be it bread, fruit, cheese, meat, or sweets.

If we truly find peace in passing, Vivienne had done so, for no more peaceful face had I seen. The women who prepared her body had washed away the darkness of her disease. She lay without tension or furrow, her lips not smiling but smooth and perfectly formed. Her hair was silk, and her hands like the cool white marble of a Grecian statue. My face began to heat and my eyes to fill. I walked away so that Faolán wouldn't see. He might assume I wept for Vivienne or for his loss of her, but the truth of it was I wept the most selfish tears of all, and the more painful for having to hide them. Vivienne and I had shared a secret bond like I'd never shared before with anyone else. I wept for myself that I would never again have someone who understood me as she had, who believed things I believed, whose tenderness exceeded anything I'd known. She was not mine and never would have been, but I loved her truly.

In death she looked more beautiful than I thought possible, but the wake was somber. Many of the villagers scarcely knew her in the short time she'd been in Skebreen, but if any believed she brought ill fortune, they concealed it well. They all showed great compassion for Faolán. He sat in a chair near the fire where my father used to sit, not for the warmth but to be near the door. There were many times he could take no more sympathy and went outside to my shed for solitude.

Between those times, he was happy to show off his infant daughter, who quickly gained popularity for the fuzz of ginger hair and her playful, impish face. The mothers hovered over her and kept her fed on goat's milk and drops of honeyed wine.

"She'll be a scrapper, that one," Mister FitzGibbon said.

"Aye, so she is, sir, a little sprite," Faolán said.

"She looks to me like a mischievous little faerie. A little elf, as they say on the continent."

"Elf, is it? I like the word." Faolán rubbed his chin. "Ailbhe is much too formal for such a face. I'll call her Elvy."

And so, being a cheerful and lovable thing in the midst of such sadness, the name tossed about like a leaf in the wind until everyone in the alehouse called her Elvy.

Whilst the crowd milled about and the menfolk quieted, focusing on their drink, MacTiege climbed atop a table in the center of the alehouse a few short feet from Vivienne's coffin. All in the room took notice, including Faolán. MacTiege was a large man and well respected, but rare to speak unless a powerful force inspired him.

"This day, my fine folk of Skebreen, we bid farewell to the beautiful Vivienne, who leaves us too soon. Her face was like the sunrise, her hair colored warm like the sunset, and now like the summer she is gone. And so I bring you this ancient poem." He recited:

> *My tidings for you: the stag bells,*
> *Winter snows, summer is gone.*
> *Wind high and cold, low the sun,*
> *Short his course, sea running high.*
>
> *Deep-red the bracken, its shape all gone—*
> *The wild goose has raised his wonted cry.*
> *Cold has caught the wings of birds;*
> *Season of ice—these are my tidings.*

If an entire room of people can weep at once, so it happened. And in the quiet moments following, some headed for the comfort of their own cottages and their own soft beds. As the crowd thinned, Faolán sat next to Vivienne's coffin, his arm across the rough-hewn edge, staring solemnly at her still, quiet visage.

Deirdre placed her hand gently on Faolán's shoulder and sat beside him. She folded her hands in her lap and faced him sadly. "Faolán, I must ask you something of difficulty."

Young Saturiwa, who had stayed near Elvy's cradle most of the evening, came to wait beside me.

"What is it, Deirdre?" Faolán asked, his voice strained.

"Despite what Lord Cork and his lawyers have claimed, you know, I know, and Vivienne knew she was a FitzGerald, of noble blood."

"She was unmatched."

"It is so. We must not let him, or anyone else, succeed with the notion she was anything less."

"We must not," Faolán agreed. "She was, and is, extraordinary."

"What are your plans for her tomb?"

Faolán looked up sharply. "Her tomb? She is to be buried here, at Glencurragh, where Elvy and I will see her and speak to her every day."

Deirdre looked down at her shoes. "Faolán, for a beloved woman of high birth, she must have an appropriate tomb, in a churchyard, with her family. Anything less only confirms Lord Cork's cruel deed."

Faolán looked away, his face losing color. "What are you suggesting, Deirdre?"

"Let me take her back with me, dear. I promise you, I will see to it she has a well-made tomb befitting her station and bloodline, and that Lord Cork pays for it."

It seemed for a moment that Faolán would vomit, for I was likely to do so myself. His face turned a pale green and his eyes filled with tears. He placed his hand over Vivienne's folded fingers.

"It is to lose her twice."

Deirdre waited silently for a moment, and then placed her hand over Faolán's. "I know it is a painful thing that I ask, but it is a good and right thing. What he did to her, if it did not kill her, did hasten her death. Let us show him, and everyone, who she truly was. She belongs where the name FitzGerald is chiseled deeply in stone, where it will last forever."

"Why would he do it, Deirdre? The hateful man that he is? Why would he spend a single coin for her remembrance?"

"To atone. He grows old, Faolán. He does good deeds to make up for his greed and his unsavory dealings. He will see it as a way to acknowledge the FitzGerald legacy without actually sanctioning it."

Faolán's breathing was labored, but he brought it under control and then sat up straight, his back tall, his hands on his knees before him. "Deirdre, it pains me more than you can know. I had not given it much thought, had not wanted to. She deserves better than what little I can give her here. I do want to see her buried properly. I do want her to be remembered. If you are quite certain you can accomplish that, you may take her body, but there are conditions."

"Of course, Faolán." She nodded.

"Promise me it will be the most beautiful tomb in the churchyard, and very expensive."

"It is my exact intent."

"And let her monument be inscribed, *Lady of Castle Glencurragh, Mother of Ailbhe*. She deserves at least that."

"It will be my honor, Faolán, and my mission. I will insist on it."

"And if for any reason he will not do it, you must return her to me."

Again she nodded, and her tears slipped down her cheeks.

They remained there for a few moments, just watching Vivienne and lost in their own thoughts. Saturiwa grew impatient and tugged on the hem of my doublet.

"Saturiwa, you must be sleepy. Would you like to rest on my bed?" I asked. But he shook his head and seemed to want to tell me something. I pulled him to the space behind my serving table where we would not be overheard. "What is it, lad?"

He looked at me most seriously. "War coming, Mister Aengus."

He was just playing a make-believe game. *Wasn't he?* But his face remained serious. I went to my knees so that he and I were face-to-face, and I looked at him carefully. "You have a vision?"

"War start in little ways, one day grow big. People fight, but a great brown army will come."

The back of my neck stiffened. "What have you seen, Saturiwa? You can tell me. I have seen things as well."

"Soldiers bring guns and fire, kill people, burn everything. Send the people away."

"The people? Send the Irish away?"

He shrugged and shook his head. What difference did he know

between English, Irish, Old English, Catholic, or Protestant? He saw soldiers and death, and that was what mattered. I did not know if he meant the army would send them away, or if we should send people away before the army came.

"Mistress say, when time come, she will have place for the baby, and help you and Mister Burke get away."

Something cold and solid shifted within me then, and I knew if war came I would never leave Ireland. Come what may, even if it meant the end of me, I would not leave my home. I hadn't lived long enough to see the land ravaged the way it had been in the Desmond wars, but I had seen battles, and I had seen killing. I would survive or I would not, but I was firmly rooted to the earth where I was born.

"Thank you, Saturiwa. I will not forget. Go with Deirdre now."

Before I would think any more about his vision and his warnings, a bitter day lay ahead.

Chapter Forty-Four

Elvy

The world's chase has turned against me.

~ Seán Ó Coileáin

On the morning after the wake, we sealed Vivienne's coffin and loaded it into the carriage to be taken back to Lismore. I loathed, as Faolán did, to let her be in the hands of Lord Cork again, but there was justice in it. Vivienne would be laid to rest across the bridge from Lismore Castle, at the church of Tallow, which the earl had restored only a few years earlier. It would take some doing to get Cork to erect the monument Vivienne deserved, but Deirdre swore it would be done. We stood beside the carriage, both of us clenching our jaws against the tears, as Deirdre waved good-bye.

Thomas Barry arrived on his uncle's horse, and Faolán gave him the fine gray cloak to return to Mairead in Clonakilty. The cloak was unharmed, as Mairead had asked so many months gone, but the wearer could no longer use it.

The next day, Mistress Barry brought the news of a wet nurse in Glandore who was willing to take Elvy. Faolán would have to leave her in the woman's care for several months, and pay the woman for the service. "She's given birth to her own child, and can feed yours as well," Mistress Barry said. "She's promised to treat the babe as part of her family. Ye pay a fee for her maintenance, of course, but truly it is best for the child."

So beaten down and lost in his grief for Vivienne, Faolán seemed resigned to losing everything else as well, but the idea she presented made my stomach turn. When Mistress Barry left, I confronted him.

"You cannot be serious about this, Faolán. Elvy's but a few days old. You can't just leave her with a stranger and walk away." We'd made a small box for her to sleep in when she came to the alehouse, and placed it near the hearth to warm her, but not too close. Faolán looked poorly, his body thin, his clothes loose and rumpled. For the look in his eyes, he might have been shipwrecked alone on a barren island.

"I haven't exactly the parts needed to feed her properly, Aengus. I'm afraid she'll die if I don't take her."

"Are we not a fine village here? Do we not take care of each other? Look at her, Faolán. Isn't she well? Does she not look healthy?"

"She does, Aengus, but I..."

"Faolán, please," I said, my voice rising, "please don't take her from us. She needs you and she needs me, and we promised Vivienne we would look after her. No one will love her and care for her the way we will."

He looked at me, the pain clear on his face. The warrior had lost his fight, so I delivered my killing blow. "If you do this, Faolán, you are doing the same thing to Elvy that was done to Vivienne when she was a babe. Do you think Vivi would wish that?"

Surprise filled his eyes, and then resolve. "You are right, Aengus. *Right.* Of course she would hate it. I must do everything in my power to raise Elvy as if her mother were here. To raise her to be the queen of Glencurragh, just as we'd planned. That's what she's destined to be, not some orphan toss-about."

"She belongs here. And do not fear, Faolán, she will be well nourished. Sheelagh will help us. She knows everything about caring for young ones."

Sheelagh was of mixed minds when I told her what we'd decided. While she welcomed the recognition for her considerable expertise as a mother, the responsibility it entailed was quite different.

"Aengus, I have two of my own that nearly overwhelm me; what am I to do with another? How could you obligate me without asking?"

"It's your advice we'll be needing, Sheelagh, not your full attention. She has Faolán, and she has me to look after her."

"Oh, aye, two irresponsible lads whose only experience with raisin' a baby is stepping outside when the diaper is changed."

"I'll grant you we've much to learn, but Sheelagh, truly, could you have sent either of your babes to a stranger for months on end?"

She frowned. "No, I could not ha' done it. I will help where I can, particularly with the feeding until we've seen what works best for Elvy in place of mother's milk. But ye've got to watch her constantly, Aengus, to make sure she thrives, to keep her from hurtin' herself, and to teach her how to behave."

"We can do it, Sheelagh. We must."

She scoffed, but then she smiled. "You lads barely know how ta behave yourselves. Don't make me laugh."

That night both Faolán and Elvy stayed with Sheelagh's family, that Faolán might learn Elvy's proper care. At dawn when I awoke, Faolán rode alone on Dunerayl past the windows of O'Daly's, heading west. Where was he going? He'd mentioned nothing to me the night before.

Hours later he returned on foot, looking as if he'd been beaten, perhaps assaulted by a woodkern encountered on the way, but there was no blood or other sign of injury. I walked out to meet him.

"Faolán? What is it? Where have you been?"

"I've been to MacTiege. I have sold him Dunerayl."

My stomach dropped to my gut, and my chest ached as if I'd been slammed with a mighty club. "You what? How could you do that? You need Dunerayl. You love Dunerayl. He *belongs* with you."

Faolán gripped my shoulders and looked into my eyes. His complexion was ashen but his eyes were bright and resolute, and seared with pain. "Aengus. I have known no greater ache than losing Vivienne. After that, all else is of little consequence. I love Dunerayl, but I had no money to feed him, no business from which to earn, and even if I had I can no longer do it, because I must be at home to care for little Elvy. I needed money to feed and clothe my poor daughter. There was no other choice. MacTiege has paid me well."

"But we could have done something, we could have sold something else, there might have been a way..."

"Aengus, hear me. I have sold all the fine clothes we were given at Mallow. I have sold tools and anything I could spare from the house. I've sold my pistol and my saddle. Truly, I have nothing left but a baby to care for and a heavy debt to pay. Without Vivienne I can't..."

His words caught in his throat, and the enormity of it all seemed to strike him down. The resolve left his face as if he was splashed with cold water. He reached for me but stumbled and then collapsed at my feet.

I dragged him into the alehouse as quickly as I could manage and laid him by the hearth. I gave him ale and bread to restore him until slowly he revived enough to sit up.

He took a deep breath and looked at me through the most weary eyes. "Aengus, support me in this, I beg you."

I stared at him. My friend with all the strategies and plans, so greatly reduced. But I was now the resolved one. "Faolán," I said, "here is what we will do. Every night, Elvy will be with you while I am serving customers here. And each day, she stays with me, while you find work. Whatever it is you need to do, do it. And if you need to work at night, so be it; she'll stay here with me at O'Daly's. Everyone loves her anaways. Between us we will make sure Elvy is always with someone who loves her. We will pay off the debt to Lord Cork, and we will buy back Dunerayl. *We will.* You will not be beaten by this, Faolán, nor will I."

His eyes filled again, but I had one more point in my quiver. "Faolán, remember your father. All we have done this past year has been in his memory. What would Sir William have you do now?"

He closed his eyes, forcing the tears to stream from the sides, and he quickly wiped them away. He held his breath for a moment, and when he looked up, a familiar light gleamed there.

"He would stand me up, Aengus." He ran his hand through his hair and stopped at the back of his neck, then looked me square in the eyes. "I still have my body. And I still have my sword."

Chapter Forty-Five

March 1635, Skebreen

There must be a beginning of any great matter, but the continuing unto the end until it be thoroughly finished yields the true glory.

~ Sir Francis Drake

Goat's milk with honey worked quite well for Elvy in her first few months, but then she grew to hate it, refusing even a taste. We switched to cow's milk, but it was harder to come by and Faolán had to pay more for it. He did whatever was called for without complaint: farm labor or construction when he could find it, and running messages on foot as he'd done before he had Dunerayl. Because of Lord Cork's long reach, he still had difficulty finding higher-wage jobs, but he never gave up.

Every morning before he brought her to me, he held Elvy in his arms and walked her around the castle foundation he and Vivienne had marked out for Glencurragh. Though she couldn't yet understand it, he told her the story of Sir William's dream, what the castle and grounds would look like, and how she would reign over all of it. He sang songs to her and told her about her ma.

I awaited her arrivals eagerly. Her eyes followed every move of my face when I fed her, and my heart thudded within my chest whenever she gripped my fingers with her tiny pink hands. I carried her with me through all my daily tasks and waited impatiently for her to wake from her naps. I grew envious as the dusk settled, when I knew Faolán would come for her, and I never minded when he said he would be gone for the night.

"There is farmwork, but it is far from here," he said, not meeting my eyes. "I might not return until dawn."

I did not protest. Why would I? I knew what I knew of his forays into the darkness. My trust in him was complete. As for infant care, it was difficult, but I was surprised to find that I loved it. I didn't seem destined to be anyone's husband, but fatherhood, or at least unclehood, suited me perfectly. Knowing this helpless being needed me and depended on me to protect her lifted me above the mountains and into the clouds. I had usefulness and purpose. There was power in it, a great deal of responsibility, some pride, and a depth of love that was entirely new. In treasured moments my body expanded with elation. It was the closest I would come to being a god.

When she slept I watched her breathing, and marveled at the soft pinkness of her skin. Constantly I wanted to touch her, to stroke her fine hair, to cuddle her, but I had to discipline myself lest I wake her and spoil her. Most of my customers were fathers, too. Happy to escape their own noisy households for the relative calm of the alehouse, they didn't mind a cry or two from Elvy, and often claimed her as their own for a go around the room.

I believed this arrangement with Faolán was perfect for all three of us, but when Sean and Thomas rode through toward the bridge, my fears for Faolán revived. Those two were not fond of labor, always seeking a more lucrative adventure. They were good friends who loved Faolán, but there was sure to be more scheming than working if they were about.

Local gossip about cattle raids continued, and reports of missing sheep, missing wares from barns and sheds, and a few burnings but thankfully not near Skebreen. The stories were becoming commonplace. Most folks shrugged the rumors away unless it was their sheep, their barn, or something belonging to any of their kin. In spite of the reports, the constable hadn't come around for weeks. I only hoped if there were to be a visit from some authority, it would be the constable and not the torchbearing soldiers.

I never mentioned these rumors to Faolán, nor questioned him on his comings and goings since the night of Samhain. But one morning when he came to collect Elvy, his head and neck were bloodied, his lip split, and his hands bruised and scraped. My protective instinct rose up, and I held Elvy away from him.

"Faolán, what has happened? Where did you go last night?" I looked over his wounds—ugly but nothing lethal.

"I took a fall, Aengus. Do not become a nagging wife."

This was a stab that caused my bubble of patience to burst forth. "How do you call me that when all I do is look out for Elvy and for you? I saw the Barry brothers, Faolán, and this was no fall, so don't treat me as a fool. What are you about, getting yourself killed? Bringing an entire troop of the English soldiers upon us? Am I supposed to stay silent when I fear for Elvy, and for the whole village?"

"I told you before, it is better if you don't know what I do. Know this: I do what I must to support my daughter. And know as well, there is more going on than you can see, and there's reason and purpose to it." His voice softened. "Trust me, *Teaghrán*. What I do is for all of us."

I released a sigh and set Elvy on the floor on her belly. She flailed her arms and legs with giggles, gurgles, and drooling. I kept a wary eye that she would not tire and bump her head. "Faolán, it was well for a while for me to pretend the world had gone quiet and we were safe and had nothing to fear, but I don't wish to be ignorant. If there is reason and purpose, I would know it. The specifics of your outings I've no need to learn."

Faolán leaned toward me, forearms on his knees. The stony hardness in his face shifted, and a new light brightened his eyes. His brow softened with the burden of secrecy lifted. I saw the warrior again, his jaw firm and noble, the blood on his face only enhancing the aura of strength dawning from somewhere within.

"Aengus, there are men *in* this land who think of we Irish as vermin. We are to be eradicated, the island wiped clean of us. Remember that poet, Spenser, who lived here among us? He could have sipped ale in this very place when your father was alive. And others, his contemporaries, who've suggested Irish woodkerns should be hunted and killed just like the wolf.

"Aengus, they wrote of these things *in books*, as if so assured of their rightness they hadn't a fear of publishing them. Well, sard it, *no man*, not even an outlaw, should be hunted and exterminated like a wild animal.

"I'll tell you this. In my darkest moments, and I've had many in these past months, I'd begun to believe them, that Ireland no longer belonged to the Irish. I thought our time as a race was done, we couldn't survive, and we would all fall away. I felt badly, bringing poor Elvy into this world only to suffer and die.

"But I have since learned. Did you know, Aengus, there are many others like us? I'm talking about men *of* this land, who say no, we are not vermin. We are a *nation*. Isn't that a most astonishing idea? And even more astonishing, that we've held on to our clans so tightly, and to our old traditions, that we hadn't comprehended it before?"

"What do you mean, a nation? We are Ireland."

"Aye, but we've meant it as a place, not a nation. A nation is sovereign. It protects its people and its boundaries. And its ideals. The citizens of a nation should unite against a common enemy, just as England united against Spain. As long as we feud amongst ourselves, we are easy for the English to pick apart, and the taking of our land to enlarge theirs is just a natural progression."

"True, the English use old quarrels between clans. They promise riches to one clan if they'll help ruin another, but the riches never come."

"Exactly. You see it, Aengus! Then, do you also see that our moment is coming?"

"I see possibilities." I didn't tell him what Saturiwa had said. Not because I didn't want him to know. He knew what was coming of his own volition, and Vivienne had predicted it as well. But I didn't want to give voice to the boy's vision and thereby validate it, not even to myself. Whether it was two years away or ten, I loathed the coming of war, and even the idea of it. "What if you are successful in uniting people to such strength that you can expel the English? Will Skebreen, and for that matter Glencurragh, be swallowed up by the nation?"

"No, Aengus. The opposite. It means we'll be recognized as citizens in our own country. Much like things used to be under Brehon law. We'll own our property and build on it without fear of it being taken, and Elvy will have her castle. It will be as always it should have been, but better and stronger."

"I wonder," I said. "Someone always takes the spoils of victory. Is it better to stand up and fight, or dig in and find a way to survive what comes?"

"Aengus, we can't just hide beneath a rock and hope it all goes around us. Fighting *is* survival. Not fighting is dying. Now comes the opportunity we didn't even know we've been waiting for."

"What opportunity do you mean? Why now?"

"Because now there are Irish men of power, like Clanricarde and Ormonde, but also O'Neill in the north, and a fellow named O'Moore in Dublin. These men have tried to play by English rules, giving over bits and pieces to appease and maintain what they could of their lands. Now it's come clear that compromise with the English doesn't work. The English are corrupt and greedy. They lie and manipulate the very laws they've established to eliminate us and take the land.

"Irishmen are uniting, Aengus. It's only a matter of time for their powers to connect with enough strength that we can take it all back. Ireland the island will become Ireland the nation, but first, these men of cruelty and greed have to go. When England shows its weakness, we'll strike."

"Another bloody war, then," I said, seeing no way around it. "How will we have the numbers to meet theirs? And the weapons?"

Faolán nodded. "The minds are coming together, and from that will follow the bodies and the means." The belief was printed all across his face, lifting his cheeks, sparking his eyes.

I scratched the back of my neck. I'd been through enough with Faolán to know that belief didn't guarantee success. Both armies in a war believe God is on their side. The scars of the Desmond wars were still fresh across the land, and in my mind so was the image of Sir William's body, his legs sprawled, his head tilted oddly. A shiver seized my shoulders and neck, but I shrugged it off. Without belief, without passion, nothing lasting could be accomplished.

"What is it, Aengus? Did you see something?"

"No, I just fear for your safety."

"There will be fighting one day, I can't deny it. When it comes, I'll be prepared for it, and I won't be alone. I trust Vivienne's word. She'll be beside me, helping and protecting me, and at last we will have what is ours."

Faolán reached down and lifted Elvy to his lap. She smiled and pressed her fat palm to his chin. "Elvy won't have to live in fear as we have. She'll not scrape a living from the dirt because she's the wrong clan, the wrong blood, or the wrong faith. She'll live free. That's our mission, Aengus. Yours and mine. We might go about it in different ways, but we share the same purpose: a good future for Elvy."

She lay on his thighs with her tiny feet on his belly, happily waving her pink arms about. He cupped her head in his big, firm hand. "Elvy the princess," he said to her. "*Come faerie, come banshee, come soldier with sword, she holds her head high, and rules with her word.*"

I helped him clean his wounds and gather Elvy's things, and the two of them headed to Glencurragh for the day. For many hours Faolán's words returned to me, about an island of fiefdoms versus a nation. The sound of the word *nation* appealed to me, suggesting a proud ship in full sail on the high seas, or an Athena-like woman with flowing hair and a bright sword in her hand. I imagined the fierce beauty of Ireland: the iron mountains, the sheer cliffs, the great stone coastlines to protect us, and the rich pastures, soft rolling hills and immense blue skies to sustain us. The world was changing, and even Faolán's dream of a castle would change, as the structure his father envisioned was no longer viable in a world where cannons could pound them to dust. But a new dream, and a nation of our own. Now that would be a grand and wondrous thing.

When they returned at dusk, Elvy was on Faolán's shoulder looking lovely in a white linen gown with silk embroidery, one that Deirdre had sent to her months ago.

"I thought you had sold everything, Faolán." I took her from him and hugged her close, smelling the sweet spice of her hair.

"I kept just this one. She looks very well in a finely made gown."

"So she does." She looked at me, and for an instant I saw the same peculiar smile I'd seen from Vivienne long ago, as if she knew a perfect little secret that would make everything all right. "*Alanna dhas,*" I whispered, "my pretty child."

He sat with us by the hearth until the Barry brothers came for him. Then he buttoned up his doublet, grabbed his saddlebag, and kissed Elvy gently on her forehead. She smiled and kicked.

He headed for the door, but turned before leaving. "Aengus, I may have a way to get Dunerayl back after all. I'll need your help. I'll tell you more once I've worked it all out, but I'm going to need him. It's clear I must go to Dublin, and soon. That's where the decisions are being made, and where I'll find information to satisfy Clanricarde. Something he said once keeps returning to me, about the Lord Deputy being the author of his own death warrant. It could be a key for Ireland, and I must understand it. It's where my destiny lies, I'm sure of it."

He tipped his cap and flashed me a wink and a grin. My friend had returned from his mournful wasteland. Oh, he would still mourn, but now he turned that force into action. The blood roared into my ears and caused my fingertips to tingle. It meant life was returning to us. It meant hope. The back of my neck warmed with pleasure and the excitement of what might come next.

May God be praised, Faolán had a plan.

Author's Note

This book is a work of fiction, built within the structure of a real and specific time and place. Though it stands alone, it was written as a prequel to my first novel, **Sharavogue**, featuring Elvy Burke as protagonist. The main characters, including Aengus, Faolán and Vivienne, as well as supporting characters such as Deirdre, Mistress Barry and the Barry brothers, Pol-Liam, Geoffrey Eames, the Massys, and any family members, are all fictional.

The earls of Barrymore, Clanricarde, Cork and Ormonde, and the Lord Deputy Thomas Wentworth, did exist in the time and place, but the accounts of interactions with the main characters are fictionalized. Their personalities and tendencies are based on what I learned about their beliefs and activities from their own personal writings or biographies, but are by necessity imagined. Thanks to the work done before me by other researchers and authors, I was able to weave in rich details, such as Wentworth's gift of a beaver hat to Lord Cork after he'd lost his own to a gambling debt. My apologies to the descendants of these men for any characterization I may have used in building the story to which they might take exception.

Most of the locations did exist. Historical maps indicate a property of 176 acres at Rathmore, just to the north of Baltimore in County Cork. On a property of this size there very likely was a manor house or one or more country houses, but I have found no clear record, and only a small remnant of a castle along the river, now the site of a boat yard. Lord Barrymore's Rathmore House described in this book is fictional.

On the other hand, Ormonde's Carrick on Suir, the ruins of Mallow Castle and the Rock of Cashel are very real. You can host your wedding reception at Lismore Castle, and tour the Mitchelstown caves.

There is a bridge at Skibbereen (in this book I've used the older spelling, Skebreen), although not the same bridge described in the chapters. A bridge most likely existed to support commerce between three castles. According to Cork historian, Gerald O' Brien, there were three castles in Skibbereen— Gortnacloughy, Lettertinlish and Curraghmacteige. The latter once covered the area where the fictional castle Glencurragh is sited. The castle name Glencurragh is taken from a subdivision that exists there today. When translated,

Curraghmacteige means "the castle of the son of Tadhg." He would have been the grandson of the King of Cork who once lived in Blarney Castle. (Thank you, Eddie.)

The hero's name, Faolán, was chosen for its Gaelic meaning, "wolf," and was first used in my novel Sharavogue, where the character is introduced as the warrior father of the protagonist Elvy Burke. There are several spellings of this name, and the one I found most frequently included an accented á in the second syllable, although it is frequently without accent. The proper pronunciation of this name is "FWAIL-on" or in the Anglicized version, Phellan. I have recommended "Făl-awn" (Fallon) in the pronunciations list, to make it easier for American readers, to ensure the name was not a stumbling point to hinder reader enjoyment.

An interesting note is that anorexia, the disease that killed Vivienne, was found in both women and men in the 17th century and probably earlier. "Phthisiologia: or, a Treatise of Consumptions" by Richard Morton in 1720, describes "nervous distempers" and "violent passions of the mind." He details a disease that causes a loss of appetite leading to consumption of the body. "At first it flatters and deceives the patient," he writes, "for which reason it happens for the most part that the physician is consulted too late." Anorexia is a disease of control, so that when the patient Vivienne loses control of the last cornerstone of her life, her inheritance, she exerts a sad and damaging control where she can, and considers it right and normal.

About the quotations

Collected by the author from various sources, the quotations at the beginning of each chapter come from the 16th and 17th century speakers and writers, with few exceptions. The first quotation in Chapter One is from *The Eve of St. Agnes*, a poem by John Keats published in the 18th century. The poem quite beautifully addresses a legend that existed much earlier. St. Agnes is the patron saint of chastity and purity who died very young in 304 AD. She is often represented with a lamb, the symbol of innocence.

Thank you for reading this book. It has been quite a journey, and I hope you have enjoyed it.

The Prince of Glencurragh

Book Club Questions

1. The Prince of Glencurragh takes place in the 17th century, during a time of great change for Ireland, when old systems, traditions and ways of life are being replaced. The shift from Brehon law to imposed English law is one example. How does this affect the characters? What other changes did you see?

2. How did you experience the book? Were you engaged immediately, or did it take you a while to get into it? How did you feel reading it—immersed, detached, disturbed, confused, or something else?

3. Consider the main characters—personality traits, motivations, inner qualities:
   - Why do characters do what they do?
   - Are their actions justified?
   - Describe the dynamics between characters (in a marriage, family, or friendship).
   - How has the past shaped their lives?
   - Do you admire or disapprove of them?
   - Do they remind you of people you know?

4. Faolán and Aengus have been best friends from childhood. What do you think of the dynamics of that relationship? Has it changed at the end of the book? In what ways? Did they learn something about themselves and the way the world works? What about Vivienne? What does she represent to the story?

5. What main ideas—themes—does the story explore? Are there any symbols used to reinforce the main ideas?

6. What passages struck you as insightful, even profound? Perhaps a bit of dialog that was funny or poignant or that encapsulates a character? Was there a particular comment that states the book's thematic concerns?

7. Is the ending satisfying? If so, why? If not, why not...and how would you change it?

8. If you could ask the author a question, what would you ask? Have you read other books by the same author? If so how does this book compare? If not, does this book inspire you to read others?

9. Has this novel changed you—broadened your perspective? Have you learned something new or been exposed to different ideas about people or a certain part of the world?

(Questions adapted from LitLovers.com)

Selected Sources

Adams, C.L. Castles of Ireland: Some Fortress Histories and Legends. Elliot Stock, London, 1904.

Bakay, Louis, M.D., F.A.C.S. The Treatment of Head Injuries in the Thirty Years' War (1618-1648), Johannis Scultetus and His Age. Thomas Books, Springfield, Illinois, 1971.

Barnard, Toby. The Abduction of a Limerick Heiress, Social and Political Relations in Mid-Eighteenth Century Ireland. Irish Academic Press, Dublin, 1998.

Berleth, Richard. The Twilight Lords, An Irish Chronicle. Barnes & Noble Books, New York, 1994.

Brereton, William. Travels of Sir William Brereton in Ireland, 1635 (extracted from the *Travels in Holland, the United Provinces, England, Scotland and Ireland, 1634–1635)*. Corpus of Electronic Texts: a project of University College, Cork College Road, Cork, Ireland, 2007, 2010.

Carleton, William. Traits and Stories of the Irish Peasantry, Vol. II. Colin Smythe Limited, Gerrards Cross, Buckinhamshire, Great Britain, 1990.

Carte, Thomas. An History of the Life of James Duke of Ormonde, from his Birth in 1610, to his Death in 1688. London, 1736.

Daly, E., Healy, A., Leahy, P., Bourke, E., Byrne, J., O'Brien, G.,...Downey, L. Journal, Vol. 7, 2011. Skibbereen and District Historical Society. Inspire Design and Print, Skibbereen, Co. Cork, Ireland, 2011.

Feheney, John M. Biographical Dictionary of Lower Connello: Brief biographies of people of distinction associated with the parishes of Askeaton, Rathkeale, Croagh, Cappagh, Co. Limerick, Ireland. Mardyke House, Cork, Ireland, 2012.

Hardiman, James, Esq. The History of the Town and County of Galway, from the Earliest Period to the Present Time. W. Folds and Sons, 38 Strand Street, Dublin, Ireland, 1820.

Heritage Unit of Cork County Council 2013. Heritage Bridges of County Cork. Carraig Print, Inc., Carrigtwohill, Co. Cork, Ireland, 2013.

Morton, Richard, M.D. Phthisiologia: or, a Treatise of Consumptions. Printed for W. and J. Innys at the Prince's Arms and West end of St. Paul's Church Yard, London, 1720.

Ohlmeyer, Jane. Making Ireland English: The Irish Aristocracy in the Seventeenth Century. Yale University Press, 2012.

Nunan, Joe. The Planting of Munster, 1580 – 1640, Public Outreach Series. Blackwater-Archaeology Research, 2012.

The Edinburgh Medical and Surgical Journal, Vol. 63, 1845. Longman, Brown, Green and Longmans, London; John Cumming, and Hodges and Smith, Dublin, 1845.

The Natural History of the County and City of Cork, Journal of the Cork Archeological and Historical Society, Vol. III. Guy and Co., Ltd., Cork, Ireland, 1894.

Townshend, Dorothea Baker. The Life and Letters of the Great Earl of Cork. Ulan Press, London, 1923.

Wedgwood, C.V. Thomas Wentworth, First Earl of Strafford, A Revaluation. Phoenix Press, London, 1961.

Wilde, Lady. Ancient Cures, Charms and Usages of Ireland: Contributions to Irish Lore. Ward and Downey, London, 1890.

Wood, Juliette. The Celtic Book of Living and Dying: And Illustrated Guide to Celtic Wisdom. Chronicle Books, San Francisco, 2000.

About the Author

Nancy Blanton's passion for Ireland's history comes from her father, who treasured his Irish heritage and loved everything about the people, the land, the pubs, the stories, the songs, and most especially the horses.

Her first novel, **Sharavogue**, about 17th century Ireland and the West Indies, won Florida's Royal Palm Literary Award for historical fiction. Her non-fiction book, **Brand Yourself Royally in 8 Simple Steps**, is a guide for authors, artists, and business consultants who need to be memorable to potential customers. The book has become a basis for hands-on personal branding workshops.

She wrote and illustrated a children's book, **The Curious Adventure of Roodle Jones**; co-authored the award-winning book **Heaven on the Half Shell: the Story of the Northwest's Love Affair with the Oyster**; and spearheaded production of **Rising Tides and Tailwinds**, a corporate history book for the Port of Seattle centennial.

Her blog, *My Lady's Closet*, focuses on writing, books, history, personal branding, historical fiction, research, and travel.

Nancy has worked as a journalist, magazine editor, corporate communications leader and author. She has a bachelor's degree in journalism, a master's degree in mass communications, and has won numerous awards for her products and professional leadership. She lives in Florida.

Connect with Nancy:

Blog: nancyblanton.com
Facebook: Nancy Blanton.Author
Twitter: @nancy_blanton
Pinterest: blantonn

CPSIA information can be obtained
at www.ICGtesting.com
Printed in the USA
LVOW13s1501090518
576567LV00012B/163/P